THE ACCIDENTAL EDUCATION OF JEROME LUPIEN

Also by Yves Beauchemin

THE ACCIDENTAL EDUCATION OF JEROME LUPIEN

YVES BEAUCHEMIN

TRANSLATED BY WAYNE GRADY

ARACHNIDE

Published in English in Canada in 2018 by House of Anansi Press Inc.
www.houseofanansi.com

House of Anansi Press is committed to protecting our natural environment.
As part of our efforts, the interior of this book is printed on paper that contains
100% post-consumer recycled fibres, is acid-free, and is processed chlorine-free.

22 21 20 19 18   1 2 3 4 5

Library and Archives Canada Cataloguing in Publication

Beauchemin, Yves, 1941–
[Empocheurs. English]
The accidental education of Jerome Lupien / Yves
Beauchemin ; translated by Wayne Grady.

Translation of: Les empocheurs.
Issued in print and electronic formats.
ISBN 978-1-4870-0280-0 (softcover).—ISBN 978-1-4870-0281-7
(EPUB).—ISBN 978-1-4870-0282-4 (Kindle)

I. Grady, Wayne, translator II. Title.
III.Title: Empocheurs. English

PS8553.E172E4813 2018   C843'.54   C2018-900677-3
                    C2018-900678-1

Book design: Alysia Shewchuk

Canada Council   Conseil des Arts   ONTARIO ARTS COUNCIL
for the Arts   du Canada   CONSEIL DES ARTS DE L'ONTARIO
                                        an Ontario government agency
                                        un organisme du gouvernement de l'Ontario

*We acknowledge for their financial support of our publishing program
the Canada Council for the Arts, the Ontario Arts Council, and the Government of Canada.*

Printed and bound in Canada

MIX
Paper from
responsible sources
FSC
www.fsc.org   FSC® C016245

To my sons, Alexis and Renaud

As much as real life may have inspired them,
the characters and events described in this novel
are fictional.

When he stepped off the straight and narrow path of
his peculiar honesty, it was with an inward assertion of
unflinching resolve to fall back again into the monotonous
but safe stride of virtue as soon as his little excursion into
the wayside quagmires had produced the desired effect.

—Joseph Conrad, *An Outcast of the Islands*

MANIWAKI

ONE OCTOBER NIGHT in the early 2000s, a few minutes after sunset, an orange moon rose into a turbulent sky from which an icy rain was falling. The moon's bizarre colour, as if it had been dipped in blood, gave its features so sinister an expression that pedestrians passing beneath it stopped to look up and stare at it with their mouths opened in wonder. The night hours passed dismally, lugubriously. Gradually the moonlit sky, dotted with trembling points of light, spread over the land and crept into a hotel room in Maniwaki, where it illuminated in the darkness the face of a sleeping man whose lips emitted deep sighs signalling a troubled sleep. Clearly the dormant youth had not enjoyed the previous day, and neither was he looking forward to the one ahead.

And in fact, when the man woke around six in the morning, the first thing he did was to cast a disgruntled gaze about the room, furnished with consummate banality.

"Son of a bitch," he sighed, sliding his legs out of bed. "I feel like someone's been beating me all night with a two-by-four."

He dragged himself to the bathroom, took a shower, dressed, and, still yawning, stepped out into the hall, his eyes glazed with sleep.

A heavy-set young woman with an inviting demeanour, though she was not particularly attractive, stood behind the reception desk in the lobby.

"Good morning, Mr. Lupien," she said, with more friendliness in her tone than professional courtesy warranted. "I hope you had a good night?"

The previous evening, from her very first glimpse of him, she'd found the unfamiliar client from Montreal easy to like: he was tall, had a confident manner and a shock of gorgeous red hair that gave him the appearance of a mischievous little angel fallen from heaven.

"Not really," he replied, rubbing his brow and stifling another yawn.

"Did someone disturb you?" she asked, sounding disappointed. "Was it the paint fumes? We just repainted, maybe the floor wasn't properly ventilated...?"

"No, no, it wasn't that," said Jerome, waving his hand in order to convey the matter was personal.

He forced himself to smile. Then, clearly wanting to change the subject, he turned towards the open window to the left of the counter.

"Looks like it's going to be a nice day," he said.

Quickly he added, "Is the dining room open?"

"It will be soon, Mr. Lupien, in about fifteen minutes. But the papers have just arrived, you can go in now and read them. Oh, and I almost forgot—Christ, what was I thinking?—your friend left you a message."

She reached into a drawer, took out an envelope, and handed it to him.

"Mr. Pimparé?" said a startled Jerome Lupien.

"Yes. He checked out a couple of hours ago, at least. You weren't aware? He told me he'd let you know."

"So how am I supposed to get back to Montreal?" said Jerome, crestfallen. "I came up with him in his minivan!"

Angrily, he tore open the envelope. As he removed the note inside it, a couple of twenty-dollar bills fell out and floated to his feet.

"What the hell?" he grunted, bending down to pick them up.

He crumpled the bills in the palm of his hand and read Pimparé's message scribbled in large, haphazard handwriting on the back of a page torn from a desk calendar:

Hi, Jerome,
Just got a phone call (it's 2 in the morning). My sister Rosalie
(I only have the one) is in the hospital on her death bed. Have
to get back to Montreal right away to see her one last time.
Sorry to mess you around, I didn't want to wake you. I've
left you $40 for the bus. If that's too much, keep the change.
See you later, maybe. Again, sorry about this,
*   Donat*

Jerome, arms by his sides and his mouth agape, was speechless. His air of astonishment made him look like an innocent and vulnerable child, arousing in the receptionist's heart a burning desire frantically searching for a way to express itself.

"My God," she murmured, evidently touched. "What are you going to do, Mr. Lupien? Is there any way I can help?"

Her words touched him like a mild jolt of electricity.

"Thanks," he said coolly, "but there's nothing to be done.

Not a thing. Did you say the newspapers have arrived?" Suddenly he was impatient to be rid of this plump, well-intentioned woman who was getting on his nerves.

He sat down at a table in the dining room and began flipping through the *Journal de Montréal*, so upset that if ten minutes later someone had asked him what he'd been reading he wouldn't have been able to tell them.

A group of guests entered and headed to the back of the room. It was soon filled with the sounds of raucous conversation.

"Like I was saying," said a man with a goatee and the deep, resonating voice of a Russian tenor, "Rosaire told me when we were in the *dépanneur* last night. We saw it again yesterday! Really! There was no mistaking it! A rack of antlers that'd have a hard time getting through the door." And then, pointing at the entrance to the dining room, "As big as that! I'm sure it was him, there can't be two moose with a rack like that in the whole world."

"Well, if you're right," demurred one of the others — thoughtfully and a little skeptically — "then the Monster of Maniwaki is back. Which is odd. I was sure he'd died of natural causes, no one's heard a peep out of him in three years... you're sure of what you're saying, Raymond? Me, I wouldn't put money on it."

"It's also been three years since you told us your family was as big as it was going to get," replied the tenor. "And now your wife's pregnant again."

A ripple of laughter greeted the man's perspicacious observation.

A young waitress with indigenous traits, her eyes dark and penetrating, appeared at the kitchen door with a carafe of coffee and moved towards Jerome's table.

"Two eggs over easy, ham, toast, and a glass of orange juice," said Jerome. Suddenly he'd been overcome by a feeling of deep shame and could speak only softly as he watched the stream of coffee being poured into his ceramic cup.

It was a shame that continued to grow in him. There was no getting around it. The day before, he'd been hoodwinked by that dry old buzzard, Donat Pimparé — the man with the easy, hail-fellow-well-met manner but also a curiously duplicitous look, as if lurking behind the benevolent twinkle of his eye there was another, more sinister person secretly laughing at him.

AFTER TAKING A stab at political science and then psychology, Jerome Lupien finally found his true calling as a man of letters; he enrolled in French Literature at the Université de Montréal, and earned a B.A. that let him imagine a career in teaching, journalism, publishing, or some other related field. Upon graduating, he decided to reward himself for the remarkable feat of his having combined university studies with part-time work as a waiter in an Old Montreal café by taking a year off — the first several weeks of which he spent sleeping, living the good life, and windsurfing. He planned to top off his sabbatical year with a long hitchhiking trip through South America.

Then, towards midsummer, his uncle Raoul, who had become a partial invalid, gave Jerome his hunting equipment. As an adolescent, Jerome had gone on dozens of hunting trips with his uncle, so he was fairly familiar with guns — which, to his father, were an abomination. Jerome's memories of those trips were filled with marvels that passing time had embellished. So, one afternoon, handling the rifles and carbines his uncle had sent him and seeing how assiduously oiled and polished they were, he was so moved that tears came to his eyes. A hunger for the hunt took hold of him and held on unrelentingly; come the night, he dreamed of going on safaris in shadowy forests in which he came face to face with herds of deer, moose, or caribou, which he would slaughter in a terrifying burst of gunfire, half blinded by the clouds of acrid smoke that made him cough and laugh at the same time.

He dedicated a weekend to courses — "Arms Management" and "An Introduction to Hunting" — in order to get his permit, which he received a month later. Yet, even with it, he felt he needed to have someone experienced with him on his first adult foray into the woods. And so, in early October, he'd surfed the Internet to look for a hunting guide, came up with Donat Pimparé, and the business was settled in no time.

It was Pimparé who suggested they get themselves to Maniwaki.

"I know it's a bit far," Pimparé had said, "and sure, there'll be some expenses, but in the past five or six years I've found no better place for big game. I've never led a hunting party up there that hasn't come back without an animal. If you don't wanna come home empty-handed, pal, then Maniwaki's the place to go."

Fifty-eight-year-old Pimparé lived in Sorel and had accumulated a lot of experience as a guide. And since Jerome, two months earlier, had totalled his beloved Mazda in an accident from which he, fortunately, had escaped unharmed — other than three demerit points off his driver's licence — Pimparé offered to drive them both up to Maniwaki in his minivan.

"If we get a moose that's too big for the van," he joked, "you can come back by bus."

Which was what he would have to do, apparently. But without the moose.

PIMPARÉ HAD PICKED him up two days earlier, arriving at Jerome's apartment on avenue Decelles around noon. Since they weren't planning to hunt until daybreak the following morning, they took their time driving north, stopping here and there for coffee, which the guide followed each time by smoking two or three cigarettes once they were outside, cursing the law that banned smoking in public places. Jerome asked him, diplomatically, not to smoke in the car either, and the guide consented with good humour. "You're the client, see," he said, "and the client's the boss." Pimparé turned out to be an agreeable and even entertaining companion who made Jerome laugh time and again with his stories of an adventurous and colourful life in which absurd episodes rubbed shoulders with dramatic and even, at times, tragic events.

"Jack of all trades, that's me. I've lived through ten thousand heartaches, and I could write you a book as big as a tractor about women and what they're like, because I've known all kinds of them, all races, every age, from hot young babes to an old Grey Nun, and every colour you can imagine. Ah, women! They've taken me up to heaven, down to hell, and everywhere in between, but if anyone tries to tell me we can live without them, I'd call him a professional liar and bury my boot up his ass. What's more, I can tell just by looking at you that you know what I'm talking about, am I right?

"A little bit," Jerome replied, flattered.

After that the guide talked about his family, which included a few oddballs of both sexes, if he did say so himself, though also some very good people. He had an older brother who was a real pistol and an architect, too, no less. Yes, sir! Worked in Rome doing building maintenance for the Pope. Not to mention a niece who played the violin in the Montreal Symphony; she was a real firecracker herself, that one.

He had, however, never said a word about having a dying sister.

Night was falling by the time they arrived in Maniwaki, tired and hungry. The town wasn't much to look at. Like most northern towns and villages, it seemed cobbled together from bits of this and pieces of that—whatever had come to hand—and, in its inchoate miscellany, the garish coloured signs of American chain stores seemed in their natural setting. Despite the lateness of the hour, huge tractor-trailers loaded with their cargo of stripped logs roared up and down the streets at regular intervals. Pimparé had reserved two rooms at the Hotel Maniwaki, an enormous building on Main Street clad in white aluminum siding tarnished by the sun. The smell of fried meat and onions floating down the hall made their mouths water, but the receptionist informed them that the kitchen had just closed. They settled for poutine and bad coffee in a snack bar down the street from the hotel, where they ordered sandwiches and fruit juice that Pimparé packed into a cooler for them to take into the bush the next day.

"Right, then, Jerome," said Pimparé, getting up from the table with a loud belch. (The trip seemed to have rendered him markedly at ease with his client.) "Tomorrow, we rise and shine at four in the morning. Don't forget to tell the hotel to wake you up. I'll be in the lobby at 4:30."

They returned to the hotel and went to their rooms. Pimparé had suggested separate rooms out of consideration for his companion, because, he said, he snored like a lawn-mower. Which was fine with Jerome; in fact, he preferred it that way.

The next morning they met in the lobby at the specified hour, Jerome's brain still fuzzy despite the complimentary coffee he'd brewed for himself after the hotel's wake-up call got him out of bed. But he forced himself to emulate the perpetual high spirits that seemed to be his guide's professional personality trait.

"Sleep well, my friend?" asked Pimparé with a big, yellow-toothed grin.

"Like a log."

"Yeah, well, me, I slept like a whole cord of logs! I'm so full of piss and vinegar in the mornings it's almost scary."

He turned to the overweight young man who, standing half asleep behind the reception counter, was yawning incessantly into the palm of his hand.

"Not you, eh pal? Spent the night in the saddle, did you?"

"Not easy to do behind a counter," said the young man, amused.

And then he yawned again.

"Oh no? Well, I've done as much a few times, I can tell you."

Pimparé left the hotel with Jerome in his wake, raising his arms and sucking the fresh night air deep into his lungs as he made his way down the sidewalk.

"Wow...you can smell the forest right here in town, ain't that so?"

Jerome nodded. His companion's energy did away with his sleepiness and reawakened his lust for the hunt that had subsided during the night.

"Okay, let's get going," said Pimparé, striding towards

the van parked nearby. "We still got a long road ahead. The ZEC Pontiac* is a good hour from here. And when we get there we need time to choose a proper spot for a lookout."

They drove through the little town, slumbering under a dark canopy of clouds presaging autumn rain.

Events had begun to unfurl with the relentless rapidity of a melodrama.

After driving a hundred kilometres or so, Pimparé turned off the highway and onto a dirt road that dipped and twisted through the pines, before suddenly bringing the minivan to a halt. His face took on the dour, intent expression of some priest of an earlier age watching a victim burn at the stake.

"We go on foot from here," said Pimparé, making as little noise as possible as he prepared to leave the vehicle. "Moose don't like *heavy metal*."

Jerome emitted a small, knowing chuckle, as if to convey this wasn't his first time in the woods.

They got out of the van, each with his rifle — the guide's was a spare in case Jerome's jammed — and made their way along the road. Pimparé was also carrying a backpack containing ammunition, food, some blankets, and sundry supplies. The road quickly degenerated into a trail that grew rougher and rougher. Rising and falling, the path was strewn with fallen trees, swampy sink holes, and slippery patches of granite. The progress of the hunters, creeping between moss-covered rocks, was difficult. Soon the trail was no more than a vague track through the bush only a practised eye could detect. The light of early morning was diffuse, and the two hunters were enveloped in the deep fragrance

---

*   The Québécois designation of "ZEC," a Zone d'Exploitation Contrôlée or "controlled harvest zone," is a region in which hunting and other activities on public lands — here in the region of Pontiac — are regulated.

of the forest, which pressed in on them as if it might swallow them whole.

Pimparé suddenly stopped and looked around, pensively.

"We should go a bit back towards the van," said Pimparé. "We'll never be able to carry out an animal this far."

Then he set out back the way they'd come, followed by his relieved companion. After a few minutes their walking was easier, and he stopped again. Something in the vague light of a small clearing to his right had caught his attention. Leaving the trail, he slipped silently into the cover of the trees and signalled for Jerome to join him. A slight depression in the ground behind a birch tree, carpeted with dry pine needles, gave them a hidden view of the clearing.

"We'll set up here," whispered Pimparé in the gravelly voice Jerome found amusing. "The wind's blowing this way, and now it's just a matter of luck and patience."

They knelt down, rifles at the ready, and the waiting began.

At first, his eyes glued to the clearing, Jerome jumped at the slightest sound. From time to time he cast a sidelong glance at his impassive guide. Slowly his concentration lapsed, a mild numbness spread through his arms and legs, and his thoughts drifted off with the sounds of the trees. Time collapsed, and he relived a childhood fantasy that brought a smile to his lips. He was lost in the sky and piloting a small airplane with a paper-thin body, light as a glider. His plane danced on the wind, did barrel rolls, pirouettes, and dives, then broke through the clouds to emerge in full sunlight surrounded by birds flocking and singing around him. Far below, the tiny Earth was an insignificant dot. Gone were parents, teachers, laughter, duties, assignments, defences, punishments, food he had to eat and foods that were forbidden, times when he needed to sleep, times when he had to get up. He was king of the universe without a care in the world, and simply by pressing a red button he could transform his glider into a bomber. His eyes crinkled with joy and, realizing the inanity of such daydreaming, he smiled ruefully.

A sudden jab in the ribs brought him back to the present. Pimparé, stone-faced, was staring at something in front of him. Jerome looked in the direction of Pimparé's gaze and saw, advancing slowly into the clearing, a moose with gigantic antlers, swinging its head from left to right and suspiciously sniffing the air.

Discreetly, the guide pointed to Jerome's rifle, signalling him to bring it to his shoulder.

Jerome's shot rang out. The moose leapt frantically and disappeared into the woods.

"Missed," said Jerome.

"Maybe not," replied Pimparé as he jumped to his feet. "Stay here. I'll go see."

When he saw the young man was about to follow him, Pimparé repeated, "Stay here! A wounded moose can be dangerous, my friend."

Pimparé crossed the clearing slowly, rifle in hand. When he reached the far end, he looked closely at the ground. Then he disappeared into the forest. Jerome's heart raced. He stood up and leaned on his rifle, muzzle up — which was extremely dangerous. "I've never seen a moose with antlers like that," he said to himself. He'd only ever actually seen a moose in photographs, his uncle having taken him hunting just for small game.

Pimparé reappeared at the edge of the clearing and slowly walked towards Jerome, his shoulders slumped.

Jerome waited until Pimparé was close and then said, pitifully, "I missed him, didn't I?"

The guide nodded. He'd planted himself right next to Jerome. "It was the Monster," he said.

"The *what?*"

"The Monster of Maniwaki. You don't know about him? A moose with a set of antlers like nobody has ever seen: sixty-two points! He completely vanished for three years. Everyone thought he was dead—well, he wasn't . . . we'll get him next time."

"You should have taken a shot!" exclaimed Jerome, redfaced with shame and anger.

Pimparé shook his head. "I'm not the hunter, pal. I don't have a permit. I'm just the guide."

Pimparé knelt down on the ground again, his rifle across his knees, but his gaze was jumping left and right and he couldn't keep from frowning. It was clear that his heart was no longer in it. Jerome knelt beside him and forced himself to focus on the clearing, cursing quietly because of his clumsiness.

"We're wasting our time," declared Pimparé, suddenly. He stood up. "When that shot was fired, every animal for miles around was alerted. We could stay here all day without seeing so much as a grouse. We have to set up somewhere else."

They walked slowly back to the minivan. The guide's good humour, which Jerome considered as much a part of his personality as the colour of his hair or way of walking, had disappeared along with the moose. Pimparé seemed perturbed, even anxious, and was replying to Jerome's questions in monosyllables. And then all of a sudden, as if he'd compelled himself to do so, he was heaping encouragement upon Jerome, assuring him this was just a temporary set-back and that the next day, or the next, they'd get their trophy because they were in one of the best hunting districts in Quebec. In fifteen years, he'd never come back from Maniwaki empty-handed.

"Trust me, Jerome, you're going to fill your freezer to the top with thick, beautiful, juicy moose steaks. Your girl-friend will love you — nothing like moose meat to put lead in a man's pencil!" he added with peal of ribald laughter that ultimately sounded forced.

Just as they reached the minivan, the sky, darkening since dawn, cracked with loud thunder. The men took refuge in the vehicle, unable to leave because of the lashing water that rendered the road impassable.

Jerome turned to his guide with a discouraged look. "We have to admit it," he said. "Our hunting trip has been a complete bust."

"Not at all!" replied Pimparé. "Rain this hard never lasts long. As soon as it settles down, we'll find us another good spot, don't you worry. I'd even say it doesn't bother me at all that it's raining cats and dogs."

Pimparé went on to explain that, in the bush, the sound of rain masked other sounds and gave animals confidence to come out and show themselves: hunting would be easier than ever.

The storm ended around 10 a.m. and gave way to a rain that was light but steady and felt as if it would last forever. They moved the minivan. Pimparé had decided to move closer to Indian Lake, some twenty kilometres away. A couple of years earlier, he said, he'd led three or four different hunting groups in the area, each time with great success.

Forty minutes later, they arrived at the lake. Pimparé

easily found a rudimentary shelter that previous hunters had built in an old cedar tree, about five or six metres off the ground. They climbed up to it on large nails that had been hammered into the trunk to make a ladder. They installed themselves inside and out of the rain, and the waiting resumed. At sunset, it was still raining. The roof of the hide, apparently constructed only for fair weather, kept some of the water out; the rest fell on their shoulders and ran down their backs. Jerome, soaked to the skin, dead tired, starving and sullen, could think only of getting back to the hotel, but Pimparé, every bit as uncomfortable as Jerome, insisted they stay on a while longer.

Finally, with darkness setting in, they broke camp. Jerome almost tripped over an exposed root as they returned to the minivan in silence. The greenhorn hunter thought despairingly of all the money he'd just tossed to the wind — or water. There was another day ahead, of course, but, without being able to explain it, he knew it would be no more successful than the first.

Pimparé yawned behind the wheel, doing his best to avoid the potholes and washouts the storm had carved into the dirt road.

As they arrived at the hotel, Jerome noticed a bizarrely orange moon rising out of the parting clouds. It seemed to be looking down on the Earth with a mocking smile. He wanted to point it out to his guide, but Pimparé was already inside.

They ate swiftly, then went up to their rooms.

"Better luck tomorrow," said Pimparé, smiling broadly and giving his client a hearty clap on the shoulder.

Jerome, drunk with fatigue, fell into bed without even taking the trouble to wash.

The rain stopped.

"MONSIEUR LUPIEN," RISKED the receptionist, blushing as she spoke. "I know it's none of my business, but . . . well, you don't really look very well. Is there anything I can do?"

Jerome had left the dining room and was standing in the middle of the foyer, hands in his pockets, staring out at the street with a distraught look.

He didn't seem to have heard her. The receptionist, scarlet now, repeated the question.

"Thanks, but no," replied Jerome, startled. "It's very kind of you, but—"

He went back to his staring, though not untouched by the receptionist's gaze, brimming with kindness.

"But what?" she asked, smiling.

"Nothing. I had an idea, but it's not important." He adopted a more blasé tone. "This bus terminal, is it far from here?"

"No, not at all. It's on Main Street, near the Co-op."

At which point a grey-haired woman, out of breath and holding two young boys by the hand, appeared in the hotel entrance and advanced towards the reception desk—or rather, was dragged there by her two charges, who seemed to find it irresistibly attractive.

"No, hold on, hold on," the woman protested, feigning anger. "Stop pulling me like this! I'm not a wagon!"

"Yes, you are, Grandma, you're a wagon!" cried one of the boys, and he broke out in giggles.

An animated discussion ensued between the grandmother and receptionist concerning a man who should have been on the premises but apparently couldn't be found anywhere.

Jerome decided to go back to his room and pack. His single desire was to get out of town. Gathering his toiletries in the bathroom, he was startled by the reflection looking back at him from the mirror.

"Don't you look like a dumb-ass jerk!" he apostrophized aloud. "A born fuck-up. What a dickhead!"

He threw his things pell-mell into his travel bag, then checked the room to make sure he hadn't forgotten anything.

His anger grew and grew. He gave a great kick to the wastepaper basket he saw beside the table, sending it bouncing against the heater with an enormous clatter.

Then, ashamed of his violent gesture, he calmly made his way to the ground floor.

"I've prepared your bill," said the receptionist, as if sharing good news. "And you're also paying for Mr. Pimparé's room, is that correct?"

"Yes," he replied, frowning as he looked down at the counter.

She handed him his receipt, smiling for no discernable reason.

"I'm told you saw the Monster yesterday, you and your guide?"

"Yeah," said Jerome. "News travels fast, I see."

"That's all anybody's been talking about around here since last night. Too bad you missed him, it would have been an amazing prize. And your picture would have been in all the papers. A big shot would have paid six figures to have had your luck!"

The more she talked, the more she saw the tension in Jerome's face but, carried away by a surfeit of shyness that was rendering her idiotic, she rattled off sentence after sentence in the hope of extricating herself from the quagmire into which she was, in fact, sinking deeper and deeper.

"I'm sorry," she sputtered as he began moving towards the door. "I talk too much."

She sounded so downcast Jerome was touched. He went back to the desk and smiled at her, his annoyance having subsided.

"Don't worry, mademoiselle. It's not you who should be apologizing."

The emphasis on the "you" in his sentence sounded like an accusation against someone else, and suddenly a light went on in Jerome's head. He set his bag down, gripped by an idea.

"Where can I rent a car here?"

"You want to drive back to Montreal?" asked the receptionist, surprised. "It'll cost you an arm and a leg! You should take the bus, really. There's one leaving in half an hour," she added, looking at her watch.

"It's not for driving back to Montreal... I want to do a bit of a sightseeing before I go... It won't take more than an hour or so, I wouldn't think."

She stared at him in a sort of rapture, holding her breath. The man's masculinity reminded her of Roy Dupuis righting all the wrongs in one of his detective roles. A tidal wave of love started to surge within her.

Speaking like a sleepwalker, she said, "If it's only for an hour or two, you can take my car. It's parked behind the hotel."

Never before had she behaved like this with a perfect stranger (which was what this man was, after all). She felt sweat running down her back.

"You'll lend me your car?" exclaimed Jerome, with an air of astonishment and gratitude that broke down the last of her defences. She handed him her keys.

"You promise you'll be careful with it, won't you? It's almost brand new. My first car. It'll take me five years to pay it off."

Jerome thanked her warmly and, despite his impatience to get away, chatted with her for a while. He knew how to be polite, after all. Her name was Clairette Milhomme, she'd been born in Chicoutimi, studied hotel management in the south but, when she ran out of money, had needed to interrupt her studies and take a ten-month job here in Maniwaki — she lived alone, she was careful to point out, in a tiny one-bedroom apartment, which would do fine until something better came along.

"And you?" she said, with an engaging smile.

He gave her a quick, five-sentence summary of his life and then, increasingly frenetic, excused himself for having to cut their conversation short: urgent business was calling him away. If she wasn't too busy, he said, he would greatly enjoy talking with her when he got back. Thanking her again for the car, he left the hotel, his underarms wet and head pounding.

An hour and a half later, he turned onto the dirt road that he had been taken down the day before in Pimparé's minivan. It was nearly ten in the morning. Wide-eyed, jaws clenched, he drove with infinite caution, racked with fear that he'd not be able to find the clearing where the fabled moose had walked and thus not be able to answer the questions torturing him since he'd got up. The task proved difficult: during the night, the preceding day's cover of heavy grey clouds had dissipated, and bright, joyous light radiated now from a clear blue sky. The forest had undergone a metamorphosis. The landmarks of which he had only vague memories seemed to have disappeared.

But then an exclamation escaped his lips. He stopped the car, got out, and knelt down to examine the road. The storm had washed away almost all of the tire tracks from the previous day—even the road itself in places—but under an immense maple that had protected a section of the road were grooves in the softened dirt that indicated a vehicle's coming and going. Had someone been there after the storm, during the night, or earlier that morning and then left again? Had it been Pimparé? The tire tracks seemed identical, but for an amateur such as he was comparing mud with mud wasn't easy. Perplexed, he scratched his forehead.

Jerome returned to the car and continued along the road, but soon came to a halt again. The road was now a path no longer passable by car. He saw no more fresh tire prints and got out of the car to look on foot, panting slightly, hoping for a landmark, a clue, a footprint—anything, no matter how small, that might lead him to the spot where they'd been on the lookout the day before. He walked this way for a quarter of an hour, more and more discouraged, and was about to turn back when he stopped abruptly and let out a happy whistle. A large rock covered with moss and resembling an immense, partially deflated balloon appeared on his right; he remembered having noticed it when he and his guide had taken to their hiding place. Returning to his position of the day before, he saw to his left, filtering through the trees, the light that had attracted Pimparé's attention: it was the clearing.

Noisily he rushed towards it, crashing through the woods to the sound of breaking branches and scuffled leaves, oblivious to the scratching, nearly falling twice, before bursting into the open and running across the clearing. The palm of one hand was bleeding. He stopped, out of breath, and looked around.

Immediately, he found what he'd been looking for.

In front of him, a little to the right, was an opening in

the vegetation—a rough passage obviously blazed by a large animal.

He strode towards it and stopped to listen.

A motor was coughing in the distance, no doubt a chainsaw. He looked down at his feet and, on a bed of crushed ferns, noticed a long streak of congealed blood.

He pushed his way farther along the passage. After a few metres, it changed direction, and he could see more patches of blood. Hardly able to breathe, he followed the meandering path to its end, then stood still and gave a muffled cry.

In front of him, slumped against the trunk of a moss-covered tree, was the Monster of Maniwaki. Its mouth was stretched open, a rictus of atrocious suffering, displaying a set of enormous yellow teeth.

The top of its mangled head, covered in a bloody mush, was missing its rack of antlers.

Jerome studied the cadaver for a little while, then quickly retraced his steps. Shaken and nauseous, he climbed back into the car and returned to the hotel.

"I *did* kill it," he muttered again and again. "And he knew it . . . the bastard!"

"Worth six figures," the receptionist had gauged was the value of the antlers.

How much were they worth? A hundred thousand dollars? A hundred and fifty? More? The antlers belonged to him, and he wouldn't stop until he got them back.

JEROME WAS BORN in Montreal in 1982. His father, Claude-Oscar Lupien, was a native of Quebec City but had been living in Montreal for many years. As a young man, he'd dreamed of becoming a dentist but, in the end, he'd had to settle on making dentures, a craft he practised at home. "It's a bracing profession," he'd say, always getting a laugh from new patients, "I only wish it paid a bit more." Claude-Oscar was naturally happy and sociable, and a bit of a fantasist, and despite his grumbling he made a good living.

His wife, Marie-Rose Brunelle, a small, self-effacing woman with a patient demeanour and a practical nature, was a piano teacher. Getting to know them, one might well have expected the pair to have swapped trades. Claude-Oscar was more of an artist, and his wife better suited to technical work, but who says the course of life follows paths of reason?

Claude-Oscar came from a big family and had no desire to relive as a parent what he had suffered as a child. In truth, he wouldn't have minded at all if the family lineage had stopped with him. His wife, on the other hand, would have had a dozen children had she been able — girls, especially. As it turned out, the couple had two boys: Jerome, the eldest, and the long-awaited Marcel, who had just celebrated his eleventh birthday.

These twists of fate had been disappointments to each for different reasons, but that hadn't stopped either from being attached to their male offspring. Bad luck often makes good hearts, and the couple eventually came to believe that boys were what they had always wanted, and definitely no more than two.

But, upon Jerome's return to Montreal, it was not to his parents that he recounted his misadventure, but to his friend Charlie Plamondon, whom he'd known since high school and who was now his confidant — at least to the extent that men ever really do have confidants.

Charlie worked as a technician at Micro-Boutique, an electronics store on Park Avenue. He was a gifted young man with phenomenal powers of concentration when bent over his work table, though with equally phenomenal powers of lassitude when it came to anything else. He was of medium build, a little on the chubby side, and his skin pockmarked with acne, which meant that when it came to attracting the opposite sex he had little to rely on but his charm and gift of the gab. He tried to divert attention from his natural faults by sporting a cocky hairdo. His full head of black hair was thickened with gel and raised along the middle of his skull to form a long ridge in the punk style, vaguely reminiscent of a shark's fin. Wherever he went, he was noticed. He'd grown as well a short but also very full beard that, its contours carefully trimmed, covered the lower half of his face in a shadow that hid his acne-related defects.

On the night of October 9, Jerome invited Charlie out for a beer at a bar on Côte-des-Neiges and told him about his problem.

"Six figures?" said Charlie, astonished. "For moose antlers? Are you kidding me?"

"Check it out online if you don't believe me. You didn't see the thing. It was so scary, you can't imagine. There are old guys with deep pockets who would give their left nut plus HST to be able to hang a sixty-two-point set of moose antlers on their living-room wall."

"Well, all I can say is that you never really know how much something like that is worth until someone pays for it. Until then it's a lot of hot air."

"I read an article from the January issue of *Hunting and Fishing* magazine on the Internet about an American from Boston who paid a hundred and forty thousand smackers for a set of antlers with only sixty points. Mine had two more than that!"

"You hear a lot of things..."

"Sure, I can see you weren't born yesterday," replied Jerome, his smile withering.

Jerome took a long slug of beer and, with a loud sigh, set his stein back on the table. Then he sat back in his chair and stared at the wall above his friend's head.

"Listen, old man," said Charlie, changing his approach, "you've had a bit of bad luck. You ran into a real con artist and he pulled the wool right over your eyes."

They were silent for a moment.

"I'd like to know what you'd have done in my place," said Jerome at last.

"I don't know, I probably wouldn't have done any different from you," confessed Charlie, sensing it was time to lighten things up a little. "I don't know anything about hunting, and even if I did—well, at any rate, you can't predict everything, especially when you're honest types like you and me.

"But," he said, raising his finger like a pontifex, "if you'd had your own car then you wouldn't have been saddled with a guide and those antlers would now be hanging in your own living room."

"Thanks for consoling me, Charlie. Whatever would I do without a friend like you?"

Charlie started to laugh but wanted to make amends.

"What could you do? You could find yourself good company instead of having to listen to a goof like me talking nonsense."

And, raising his hand, Charlie ordered two more beers.

THE CONVERSATION WITH Charlie had reinforced Jerome's determination to settle the score with the guide who had so perfidiously taken him in. It had also convinced him he needed a new car as soon as possible, though it would have to be a used one as his finances were hardly in the best of shape. These two resolutions were to have consequences that would turn his life upside down and profoundly alter his world view.

Jerome was impatient to exact his revenge, and since finding the right car might take several days, if not weeks, he went to his parents' house on rue Fleury and asked to borrow his father's Chev — which of course meant he had to recount the story of his misadventures, something he would have preferred not to have done until his honour was restored. (A son doesn't like to be seen as a patsy in the eyes of his progenitors, thereby exposing himself to a series of lectures about the values of prudence and wisdom and so on.)

His visit promptly earned him an invitation to dinner the very same day. He arrived at six o'clock. It was a Friday night. In the dining room, amid the lustrous gleam of the Sunday silver, a bottle of Salice Salentino softly shone at the centre of the table, which was covered with a linen tablecloth brought out only on special occasions. For a year now — and especially since his breakup with Dorothy, who had been treated like a member of the family — the increasingly infrequent visits of the elder son were considered major events.

"Expecting company?" asked Jerome, when he saw the set-up, tongue in cheek.

"Yes," replied his father in the same tone. "You."

Marie-Rose, who had greeted her son at the door, was gently massaging his neck and shoulders.

Clamours of protest floated in from the kitchen.

"Oh, no, not sweetbreads again!" came his brother Marcel's voice amid a flapping of unlaced tennis shoes.

"Mom, you make sweetbreads every time he comes here."

Marcel appeared at the dining-room door, flushed with indignation.

"Stop raising such a ruckus," Marie-Rose told him calmly. "I made some spaghetti for you."

Jerome gave Marcel an affectionate poke in the ribs.

"So, little bro', still as whiny as ever?" He handed his brother a bag filled with comic books. "I brought you some *Red Ketchups* and an *Astérix* I picked up at a garage sale the other day."

"Hey, cool!" Marcel said as he grabbed the bag, wide-eyed with pleasure. "Thanks a lot, Jerome!"

He took himself to a corner of the room and switched universes.

"Let's eat!" ordered Claude-Oscar, tempted by the smells coming from the kitchen. "Let's eat! I had to fit fourteen sets of dentures this afternoon and now I can't wait to put the one Jesus gave me to good use."

Marcel looked up at his father.

"You don't have dentures, Pop," he said. "Those are your teeth."

Claude-Oscar winked at him teasingly. "You know, son, I've always admired your powers of observation."

The meal was jovial until the moment when Claude-Oscar said, a little carelessly:

"So, I gather the hunting trip didn't go so well, eh, Jerome? Otherwise you'd have brought us a bunch of sirloin and filet mignon."

Jerome's expression was suddenly stern.

"You hit the nail right on the head, Pop."

And he launched into an account of his hunting trip with the incomparable Pimparé. He exaggerated the finesse of his intuitions out of all proportion, telling them how he discovered—too late, alas—the scam of which he became the victim. At least he'd avoided the dishonour of being another of the simpletons who went on smiling without ever being aware they'd been duped until they heard the giggles of the pitiless crowd. Consternation froze the faces of his parents and even that of his kid brother, who listened with his jaw hanging open and mouth half full of spaghetti.

"A hundred and fifty thousand bucks!" cried Marcel, almost choking as he tried to swallow.

"Good Lord!" sighed Marie-Rose. "Good Lord! How horrible! How beastly some people can be! My poor boy! And you say you *paid* him!"

Claude-Oscar dropped his knife and fork, the sweetbreads on his plate suddenly tasteless. "You must take this to the police, Jerome," he said gravely.

"I'd rather he took it to a lawyer," said Marie-Rose. "The police will just drag their feet, they already have their hands full..."

Her son looked at her with a determined expression.

"Mom, I've decided to settle this myself."

"Yay!" said Marcel, clapping his hands. "I hope you're going to punch him in the nose, Jerome! He's a crook!"

"Can we all just calm down?" scolded Claude-Oscar.

His parents' efforts to dissuade him from taking justice into his own hands served only to convince him that, in their old age, they had become cowards, and complacent ones at that.

They stopped before they became angry. After quietly praying, Claude-Oscar, tired of the struggle, finally gave in and lent Jerome his car so that he could drive to Sorel. But he made his son promise he would take a friend with him when he confronted Pimparé. Back in his apartment, Jerome called Charlie, but a prior engagement meant he could not join him. He called two other friends but neither could get away on such short notice. And so he felt liberated from his promise.

AROUND FIVE THE next morning Jerome was driving towards Sorel, having drunk three strong coffees, both to wake himself up and to bolster his courage, since there was really little of the fighter in him and, though not admitting as much, in truth he was in some doubt as to the wisdom of this expedition. But soon righteous indignation was bubbling up in him, and in his heart pounded the drum song of the righter of wrongs. By taking revenge for the hurt he'd suffered, he'd be making the world a little more just. A bittersweet smile tugged at his lips. Suddenly, the road seemed very long. He drove faster. He wanted to deal with the sonofabitch the moment he woke. The effect of surprising him, the confusion that slows the mind of anyone suddenly awakened from sleep, as well as the strange solemnity that suffuses encounters at sunrise—he'd not spent three years studying novels without their influencing his imagination— all of this, he figured, would work in his favour. He needed to stack the deck, because Pimparé would be a tough adversary.

Donat Pimparé lived in Old Sorel, on a peaceful street overlooking Place Royal, one of the most charming spots in the city. The one-storey house in front of which Jerome parked was clad in cedar shingles and not in good repair. Its foundations were beginning to turn black and the front door opened onto an open deck that spanned the entire façade.

All of a sudden Jerome was aware that his visit might well go very badly, for a thousand and one reasons.

"So much the better," he muttered to himself as he hopped up the two steps to the porch in a single bound.

He rang the bell. A carillon of weak, trembling chimes sounded from within. A moment passed. Jerome coughed, then looked down at his shoes: one of his laces had come undone. He rang the bell again, wiped his sweaty palm on his pants, then turned at the sound of an old truck slowly pulling away, backfiring and emitting the sound of rattling sheet metal as it did so.

"Shit," he muttered. "He's not home — or else he's playing possum, the bastard."

He retreated a step and wondered whether he should park his car farther away and out of sight and then walk back and, hiding somewhere, wait for his prey to show his face. He heard footsteps. The door opened and Donat Pimparé appeared in the doorway looking greasy, his features subdued, hair ruffled, and wearing a set of flannel pyjamas far too big for him that had little ducks on them wading in a pond. He looked grotesque.

"Well, well," he exclaimed, the voice hoarse. "Look who's come to visit! What are you doing here this morning, Jerome?"

He was trying to sound pleasantly surprised, but his discomfort was evident.

"I hope I'm not disturbing you too much," said Jerome, disingenuously.

"Uh, er — no, no, not too much. It's just that I was asleep, eh? An old habit of mine. What time is it, anyway?"

"It's 7:20."

The truck, backfiring, jolted along the street again. Pimparé, standing bleary-eyed at the door, was manifestly trying to assess the situation, surely testing one hypothesis after another in his attempt to explain Jerome's impromptu visit. Then he realized that his lack of hospitality might undo him.

"Come in, my boy! It's not my habit to receive people on the doorstep. My mother brought me up better than that, you know."

"I'd prefer to stay out here," said Jerome, coolly.

"All right then, so what can I do for you this morning?" he sighed, his diffidence mixed with impatience.

Jerome looked him straight in the eye and, amazed, sensed no fear there.

"Give me back my antlers."

"Your — what was that?" babbled the guide, suddenly flustered.

"You heard me. The antlers you stole from me. I'm the one who killed that moose, and the antlers belong to me. Where are they?"

There was a moment of silence. Pimparé's face turned purple. His lips began to tremble.

"You're nuts, pal. I don't know what you've been smoking this morning, but it's done something to your head. There ain't no moose antlers here ... *and I'm not a thief!*"

Pimparé had raised his voice as he delivered that last phrase, his tone menacing. Jerome was seized by a horrible doubt. What if the guy was telling the truth? What if someone else — someone they hadn't seen at the time, maybe a hunter who'd come along after they'd left — had taken the precious bounty? Nevertheless he was able to maintain appearances and continued in the same unflappable tone.

"I'm not crazy, and you know it as well as I do. So unless you want me to file a complaint with the police, give me back my antlers. And be quick about it."

Pimparé's mouth hung half-open, and he glared at Jerome with protruding eyes. He seemed to be having to make an incredible effort simply to draw air into his lungs, his constricted throat refusing to allow it. The swollen veins at his temples were bulging. He looked as though he were about to die of indignation.

"Okay, my lad, okay! Umm, nobody's asking you to leave," Pimparé finally managed to stammer, wheezing and short of breath. "But I've never seen anything like this in my life! Never! You drive a hundred kilometres to wake up and insult an honest man first thing in the morning! Do I deserve this kind of treatment—*me*, a man my age, who has always done his level best to do the right thing?"

He extended his arm over Jerome's head to point to something across the street.

"The proof, my boy, that I've done nothing to be ashamed of is right there, behind you. Just turn around and look, you little piece of shit!"

Jerome turned to see what Pimparé was on about, and received a kick in the seat of his pants of such force that he was propelled right off the porch and almost landed flat on his face on the sidewalk.

"Let that be a lesson to you!" Pimparé screamed, his voice an unprecedented falsetto. "You go around insulting honest people, you get your ass kicked!"

And Pimparé slammed the door. Jerome—stunned, filled with rage—raced back up onto the porch and started hammering on the door with his fists, hurling insults. After a moment, he had to stop: his hands were bleeding.

THINGS WERE NOT going to rest there. That disgusting buffoon would pay for his crimes. Jerome would talk to a lawyer, even if it meant going into debt. The outrage of it, never mind the humiliation!

Only one name came to his mind and it was that of François Asselin, Esq., a lawyer who'd been writing a legal column in *La Presse* for a number of years. His headshot inspired confidence. A man in his sixties, with a thin face, a piercing gaze, and a smile filled with assurance; his was the very image of a seeker of justice—and one who took pleasure in his vocation. Without breathing a word to anyone, Jerome telephoned Asselin as soon as he got back to Montreal. He got him on the line right away. A meeting was arranged in the lawyer's office at 4703 rue Saint-Denis for two o'clock the following afternoon.

At the appointed hour, Maître Asselin, hands folded under his chin, bestowed upon his client a look that seemed to want to draw out of him any facts that might help, no matter how slight.

"I'm listening, Monsieur Lupien."

Jerome's first impression was that Maître Asselin was very likely born and raised in France. He articulated every syllable clearly and with an almost military precision, expressing himself in short, clipped sentences. (Later, Jerome learned he'd grown up in a working-class district in southwest Montreal.) He started to tell the lawyer his woes. From time to time the lawyer would interrupt him with a brief question and then, with a slight movement of his head, indicate that he should continue.

"A hundred and fifty thousand dollars, you say? That's a lot of money. Who would pay that much?"

Jerome, a little irritated, blushed.

"A collector, obviously."

"A collector with a lot of money."

"They exist."

"Do you know any?"

"Not personally, no. But everyone knows they're out there."

"That's been documented?"

"Yes. In a recent issue of *Hunting and Fishing* magazine I read an article about an American who paid $140,000 for a set of antlers with sixty points. Mine had sixty-two."

"We'll have to verify that. It's the basis for your claim. You're a student?"

"I just got a B.A. in literature from the Université de Montréal."

"You have a job?"

"Not yet."

"How much money do you have at your disposal?"

Jerome felt as though he were being interrogated, as if he were the criminal, and found Maître Asselin less agreeable as the conversation went on. His annoyance must have shown, because the lawyer quickly softened his tone.

"I ask these questions, Monsieur Lupien, so that you don't spend your money uselessly. There are two pitfalls to this case, as I see it. One is a dearth of evidence for the claim you are making—the missing antlers may be worth a lot less than you think—and secondly, if you'll permit my little play on words, a dearth of funds that cannot sustain the pursuit of your quarry to the point that justice has been served. In which case, everything you will have spent will have been wasted. Do you see?"

Jerome's face brightened a little.

"I don't have much money, you're right to say so, but I tell you I'm prepared to go into debt just to teach this jerk a lesson! As for the value of the antlers, I'm certain that what I said is true."

"Hmm, I see, I see," murmured Maître Asselin, nodding. "Nonetheless, I'm going to ask you to do some research into the subject. The bottom line is there has been a theft—you had a hunting licence, I presume?"

"I did. But he didn't."

The lawyer made a tent of his fingers, his elbows resting on the desk.

"Good. So listen, Monsieur Lupien, if these antlers are worth what you say they are, we must proceed with some dispatch, assuming it isn't already too late. Certainly this guide of yours didn't steal the antlers in order to hang them on his own living room wall, did he?"

Jerome laughed derisively.

"If he hasn't rid himself of them yet," the lawyer continued, "he's trying to. We have two paths before us—to have him watched by a private detective, which is very expensive, or report him to a wildlife conservation officer."

Jerome was silent.

"I advise the latter. You could, of course, report this man Pimparé yourself. But if the report comes from our office, there's a better chance of it being taken seriously—and of more rapid action."

"Go ahead and report him."

"Good. I would ask you first for a retainer of $1,000."

Jerome jumped a little in his seat.

"Can I pay with a cheque?"

"A certified cheque, yes—or cash, whichever you prefer."

IT SOMETIMES HAPPENS that Fate—that blind assassin who turns on the unsuspecting without even knowing them— suddenly appears like a witch straight out of *Macbeth* and, selecting some unfortunate soul from the human multitudes, derives undue pleasure in overwhelming his victim with cruel attentions.

A week or so after his morning encounter with Donat Pimparé, Jerome remembered something Charlie had said in the bar on Côte-des-Neiges, when he'd told his friend about his troubles. If he'd still had his car, Charlie had said, he'd not have had to bother with a guide who would totally rip him off, and he might have come back with the famous antlers himself, or, at the very least, choice steaks that would have fed himself and his friends for the whole winter.

The time had come for him to buy a second-hand car — one that would provide him freedom, guarantee his independence, and allot him decent status.

After a quick Internet search he found a site on which several car ads caught his eye. One was for a 1996 Toyota, "for-door [sic], colour black, only 38,000 clicks and in exellent [sic] condition" — unlike, he could only hope, the vendor's spelling. The car belonged to a certain Sylvain Losier, and he was asking $1,500 for it. When Jerome checked with Charlie — his friend had worked for a time as a mechanic's helper in his father's garage — he said it sounded like a steal.

"But," Charlie added quickly, "as you know, what ads describe and what they're actually selling are often two very different things. You've made arrangements to see it tonight? If you want, I'll come along with you. I've got nothing else on."

Losier lived on rue Florian, near rue Ontario, in the Hochelaga-Maisonneuve district, a part of Montreal known for the vigour with which it initiates its residents into the vicissitudes of life.

At seven that evening, Jerome rang the bell of an apartment in a building with a brick façade and an exterior staircase in the Montreal style that had for years been waging a losing battle against rust and rot. A woman in her early forties opened the door, cigarette in hand, babies squalling behind her. There was still a pertness to her face that, at one time, must have been extremely pretty.

"You came about the car?" she said hoarsely. She was scrutinizing them closely (Charlie's shark-fin Mohawk seemed to impress her). "You've come at a bad time. My husband is out making a delivery, he won't be back for an hour."

"But we made an appointment with him," Jerome replied, annoyed. Charlie grunted.

"Okay, no problem, I got the keys to the car. Here," she said, holding them out to Jerome. "Take it, you guys look all right. You see that black Tercel down there, near the corner? Okay, that's it. Look at it as much as you like, but don't forget to bring me back the keys when you're done. I'm trusting you, okay?" she said. Then she turned to shout into the apartment: "*Roland!* Leave your little sister alone. Don't make me come in there!"

At first glance, the Tercel looked to be in remarkable condition. They started it, listened to the engine, pumped the accelerator, looked under the hood, felt the tread on the tires, checked for signs of rust, and found almost nothing wrong with the car.

The woman watched them from her balcony.

"Drive it around the block if you like!" she called down to them. "Don't be shy!"

"It's like it just came off the assembly line, Charlie," Jerome exclaimed after they'd turned a couple of corners. He was ecstatic.

"Looks good, but if you plan on buying it you should totally take it to a mechanic and have him look it over. And don't make the mistake of taking it to this guy's garage, they could be in cahoots. Take it to your own garage. Just saying."

"What do you take me for, Charlie?" Jerome laughed. "I stopped shitting my diapers a long time ago."

"Yeah? But what about pissing?"

"Call my husband anywhere, any time," said the woman sweetly when they returned her keys. "He has a mobile." She said the word as though a cell phone was an outrageously luxurious commodity.

Jerome called Losier right away. They agreed that Losier would take the Tercel to Armand Valiquette Auto, where Jerome had been a client for three years. They would meet there the next afternoon.

The Tercel passed its inspection with flying colours, and Losier confided that he had to sell the car for financial reasons. Until recently he'd been working in the warehouse of a distribution centre, but a wave of layoffs had put him on the street. The car actually belonged to his wife, who was a hairdresser.

"With five kids we've no choice but to sell it. You know what it's like . . . Gotta feed the kids, and now winter's coming and heating the apartment will cost a packet. Anyway, I still got an old jalopy that'll get us through until things turn around."

Losier was of medium build, neither fat nor thin, and drooped a bit in the shoulders. His face was unassuming and his skin grey and pitted. He was the epitome of the nice guy worn down by forty years of a mediocre, uneventful life. The only indication of any resistance to the general levelling of the life that was his penniless, proletarian existence was a large, luxurious, brown moustache masking his upper lip and imbuing his smile with a certain irony.

When the inspection was over, the mechanic wiped his hands with an old rag and gave Jerome a discreet nod: at that price, he should jump at the chance.

Jerome asked, "When can your wife get down to the registration office, Monsieur Losier?"

The man shuffled, looked down at the floor, and coughed a few times—as though he wasn't sure how to pose a humiliating question.

"It's just that, ah...I have a small favour to ask you, Jerome."

Far from putting him off, Losier's use of his first name brought a smile to Jerome's lips; he saw it as a naive attempt to establish a sense of their being equals that would make his asking a favour easier.

"A favour? What kind of a favour?"

"Would it...would you mind if the wife and me hung onto the Tercel for another two or three days, long enough for me to change the shocks on my old jalopy? They're completely shot, and Lucie needs a car to get to work. I'll bring it over on Wednesday at the latest, I promise. Cross my heart."

Jerome, puzzled, pursed his lips, annoyed at the hitch. But if he refused, he worried, would he not risk losing the golden opportunity altogether?

"Sure," he said at last. "If you guarantee I'll have the car on Wednesday."

"That'll sure make things easier for me," replied Losier, looking relieved. But then—his eyes downcast, his feet shuffling pitifully—he started coughing again.

"There's something else, too," he said.

Losier seemed so mortified that Jerome, in an act of compassion, forgetting the difference in their ages, placed a protective hand on his shoulder.

"What is it? What do you want to ask me?"

"I don't really know how to say it, but...well, it's like this—"

His breath came in short gasps, as if he were on the point of sneezing. The garage mechanic discreetly stepped aside and started giving orders to a younger assistant.

"It's like this," Losier began again, looking towards the rear of the garage as he spoke, as if the sight of Jerome was causing him unbearable embarrassment. "I need a—well, like a down payment. On account of a little problem I'm having trouble taking care of..."

"How much do you want?"

The man finally found the courage to look his interlocutor in the eye and swallowed with difficulty. He smiled feebly at Jerome and, his voice cracking, said, "Is—eight hundred—is eight hundred too much?"

He opened his hands in front of him and stared at the tips of his fingers as if he'd never seen them before.

A few minutes later they parked the Tercel in front of a Co-op and Jerome came out with a plump envelope. During their short trip, Losier, sweating and stammering, had tried to raise the amount to twelve hundred and in the end Jerome had agreed to give him a thousand.

"Huge, huge thanks, Jerome," said Losier, his face beaming. "Okay, here's your receipt, and I'll get you the registration right away—well, a photocopy of it, but that's just as good as the original. All that matters is the information on it."

"I know, I know," said Jerome, with a somewhat condescending smile.

Losier, moved almost to tears, persisted in thanking him and promised he would show up with his wife at the registration office to transfer the ownership to Jerome on the following Wednesday. Jerome gave him his telephone number.

"Phew!" he sighed when the poor devil dropped him off in front of his apartment on Decelles after telling him for the hundredth time just how grateful he was. Playing the Good Samaritan, mused Jerome, takes patience!

But he smiled when he thought of the extraordinary return he was getting for his little act of charity.

DESPITE THE SATISFACTION his good deed had provided, Jerome told no one about it. Why not? He couldn't say, exactly. Be that as it may, his mind would drift off in another direction—and for good reason. The first name Lucie, which Losier had used a few times when talking about his wife, reminded him headily of another Lucy, a young woman from Toronto who had moved to Montreal to learn French—but also, it was pretty clear, to spend quality time with a few "French guys." He'd had a brief assignation with her six months earlier and, what with his sex life now being as barren as the rock at Percé, he'd decided to call her again. Things had gone well, and nights in his apartment had become so torrid that his neighbour had taken to pounding on the wall with his fists.

The Wednesday came, then the Thursday. He heard nothing from Sylvain Losier and decided to ring him.

"Ah! Good to talk, Jerome," said Losier. "I was just about to call you. I've had a hell of a time, would you believe, finding the shock absorbers I need at the scrap yards, but I should be able to sort it by tomorrow at the latest. I hope that doesn't inconvenience you too much?"

"Umm...Okay, okay," said Jerome, disappointed but

resigned to keeping up his part as the Good Samaritan. "But I'm really going to need my car on Saturday. I've got a trip planned."

"No worries. You'll have it by then for sure, Jerome. You can count on me."

And after thanking him profusely, Losier hung up.

Saturday arrived. By noon, Losier still hadn't shown any sign of life. Jerome called him and he picked up right away. That was the advantage of cell phones, Jerome assured himself, you could pin anyone down anywhere at any time — the miracles of technology!

"Ah, Jerome! I'm really sorry. I found — finally — those goddamn Ford shocks. Even used, they're costing me a packet, for Christ's sake. They're delivering them here tomorrow afternoon and they'll take a couple of hours to install, so you'll have your car first thing Monday morning. Sorry about this, old man, I feel really awful about this. I never thought it would take so long!"

"Well then, so much for my trip. I'll be waiting here Monday morning," said Jerome laconically. Then he hung up.

He was feeling less and less like talking to anyone about the delay.

"I get the feeling he's put both feet in the same boot, poor fella," he muttered to himself. "A week to find shocks for a Ford! You'd think he was looking for Napoleon's *pissoir!*"

A call from Lucy, whose deliciously veiled suggestions prompted a significant bulge in the front of his pants, soon made him forget this new development with the car.

The next day, a Monday, Jerome lounged in bed until the middle of the afternoon. He had a formidable hangover and an amorous Lucy pressed against him. She, miraculously, seemed to have escaped the effects of a well-lubricated night at a discothèque.

The phone rang. After several clumsy attempts, he succeeded in grabbing the receiver as Lucy covered his back and buttocks with playful kisses.

"Jerome?" asked a now-familiar voice. "It's me. Sylvain. Glad I caught you, man."

"What's up?"

As he spoke the words, he caught a whiff of his own bad breath and winced with distaste.

"I'm in Sainte-Agathe."

"Sainte-Agathe? What're you doing in Sainte-Agathe, Sylvain?"

"It's a terrible story, Jerome!" said Losier, tearfully. "I won't go into it over the phone. You wouldn't believe me anyway! Long story short, I ran out of gas right in the middle of the highway!"

"In my car?"

"Uh, yeah. In your car."

"*What's happening?*" Lucy asked in English, sounding worried. "*Problems?*"

He gestured that everything was under control and went back to talking to Losier.

"What the hell were you doing in Sainte-Agathe in my car, Sylvain? I thought your wife was using it to get to work."

"That's just it, Jerome. We're in shit up to our eyeballs, her and me. But I'll get everything sorted, don't worry."

"I don't get it."

"I'll explain, I'll explain. Tomorrow. When I bring you the car. I feel, like, really bad about this, if you only knew. I didn't sleep a wink last night."

"Neither did I. I'm on the verge of never sleeping again,

Sylvain. You're going to bring me the car tomorrow? You promise?"

"I swear."

"What time?"

"Three o'clock. Wherever you like."

"My place, as agreed — and Sylvain?"

"Yeah, Jerome?"

"My patience has its limits, my friend. I've been waiting for my car for a whole week now. That's long enough, don't you think?"

At the other end of the line, his partner in conversation, apparently overcome by emotion, was shaken by a monstrous, interminable fit of coughing. He sounded as though he was choking on a fistful of sawdust. Gradually the coughing subsided. Jerome heard Losier clear his throat, spit, and inhale a deep lungful of air.

"Sorry, Jerome," said Losier, wheezing. "I don't know what else to say, man…It's terrible, what I been through."

"I can hear that. So, good luck. But see you tomorrow at three, got that? Three o'clock?"

"I got it, man."

Jerome hung up and laid his heavy head upon the pillow.

"No, no, Lucy, not now, please," he mumbled. "Could you get me some Tylenol, my sweet? And a big glass of water?"

JEROME COULDN'T TAKE it anymore, not even remotely. The same anguish and humiliation he'd felt after his disastrous hunting trip came rushing back to haunt him: the sense that he'd been taken for a ride; that he'd joined the vast ranks of the unfortunate idiots whose hair grew above an absolute void. Stretched out on his bed, legs spread, he blinked in time to the sadistic hammer pounding inside his head.

Seeing him in his sorry state and getting no response to her anxious questions, Lucy slipped quietly out of the apartment, saying she would call him later that afternoon.

He felt a bit better towards evening. He got up and reheated a spinach pizza. But the thought of Sylvain Losier would not leave him. He needed to talk to someone about what was going down but the very idea of talking to Charlie had him break out in a cold sweat. He knew what Charlie would say. The words *jerk*, *stupid*, *no-no*, and *naive* would make up the bulk of his speech, including the introduction and the conclusion, and he had no heart for any such epithets. He thanked heaven that Charlie hadn't called for a while. He would have to make up a story to save face. But he had no energy to make up such a story.

He decided to call his parents. With parents, there was less risk of being bombarded by criticism. After all, a good part of their reputation was tied up in that of their progeny, the product of their loins, and the education they'd given them. And then, of course, there was love, which ignores faults, plasters over cracks, finds excuses, and detects the tiniest light at the end of the longest tunnel.

And so Jerome phoned his parents. They both picked up at the same time.

Their son's latest misadventure provoked the usual reaction from Claude-Oscar, he of the hypersensitive artist's soul trapped in a denturist's body. His febrile imagination, constrained for years in a boring job with no prospects, shrugged off its straitjacket and he cried out in a frenzied, delirious voice: "I don't believe it! You're joking, right? You're kidding me. Tell me you're kidding me. You're not kidding me? You're telling the truth? You've fallen into a den of thieves, my boy. You'll never see that car. They'll try and squeeze the last penny out of you and are probably working on new ways to screw you as we speak. Have you cancelled your credit card? Put a hold on your bank account? They're going to take you for everything you've got, if they haven't done so already!"

"Dad!" Jerome tried to interrupt. "Dad! Stop your bull, for crying out loud!"

"Claude-Oscar," said Marie-Rose, placatingly, "you're exaggerating—as usual."

"You'll see! You'll see! Was I wrong on our trip to the Gaspésie when everyone was convinced that..."

"Can I get a word in?" interrupted his wife.

"Say what you like, but if this business turns into a catastrophe, don't blame me. I warned you—what am I saying? It's *already* a catastrophe, I'm sure of it!"

"Jerome," said Marie-Rose, "have you reported this to the police?

"Not yet. I'm waiting until..."

"I'd have reported him right off the bat!" cut in Claude-Oscar.

"Do it now, Jerome," continued Marie-Rose, ignoring her husband. "The police can find out if the registration papers he gave you are legitimate."

"They're in his wife's name."

"What were you thinking?" grumbled Claude-Oscar. "Giving a thousand-dollar down payment to a total stranger before you even went to the licensing bureau—"

"Since no one has yet invented the machine to take us back in time," said Marie-Rose—she was beginning to show signs of impatience—"I'd suggest, Claude-Oscar, that with your consent we deal with things as they are now."

"Good, good, okay. I can see what I have to say is

completely useless, as usual, so I'll leave you two to discuss the matter in peace. I'll just go back to my dentures."

Mother and son talked for a while. Jerome, relieved at having confided in someone, was eager now to go into action.

"Try to calm Dad down a bit, will you?" he said before hanging up. "He's going to get ulcers again. Or one of his famous forty-eight-hour migraines."

"That's where he was heading, the poor soul," sighed Marie-Rose. "What can I do? He makes absolutely no effort to keep himself under control. None. You don't think it worries me?"

The cool, detached demeanour she'd employed until then had given way to little rivulets of emotion. She took a deep breath and stopped talking, incapable of going on.

"Don't worry, Mom, I'll get myself out of this, you'll see."

"Let us know how it goes, Jerome, and do be careful!"

HANDS IN HIS pockets, Jerome strode about the kitchen, glancing now and then at the cell phone he'd left on the table. Was Losier an arsehole or simply someone to be pitied — or was he both? Jerome decided he would give him one last chance — but also crank up the pressure. He'd be chill but unmovable. *Tough love*, as the English say.

A moment later he had him on the line. Christ, he always had him on the line. Maybe that was part of his strategy, to stay in his victim's good graces. Hard to say. But Losier seemed genuinely terrified by the ultimatum that Jerome delivered — that if he didn't, as promised, deliver the Toyota the following afternoon at three o'clock on the dot, Jerome would immediately lodge a complaint with the police.

"Listen, J-Jerome," stammered Losier, his voice agitated,

"try and understand my situation, my friend, I've been unemployed for six months and with five kids in my care and a wife who works part-time for peanuts. I don't have the money for the goddamn shock absorbers yet—but hang on, wait a minute, I know how to help you get by till tomorrow! I'll call my cousin Bob and get him to lend you his car. It's a '92 Pinto. Burns a bit of oil, but other than that it's in first-class shape."

"Don't bother," said Jerome. "I can wait until tomorrow. Three o'clock. Because at three-oh-five I'll be at the police station, Losier. I'm done with this shit. Have I made myself clear?"

"Yeah, Jerome, I get it."

Losier's tone was humble, it was scared, it was servile and repentant; the tone a man uses, the seat of his pants soiled in a moment of terror, to beg for his life as he bares his chest and that Jerome decided heralded the onset of remorse. But immediately Jerome pushed his empathy aside. If he got the car the next day, it would be a battle hard fought and won. To hell with feeling!

"What a fuck-up," he muttered, hanging up the phone.

The exchange brought him back to his senses. He was still deeply uneasy, of course, enough to keep him vigilant, but the dreadful tension that had tortured him for days was beginning to let up.

He grabbed a beer from the fridge and drank it in front of the TV, sitting on the sagging, emerald-green couch that, throughout his childhood, had bestowed its bourgeois opulence upon the family living room and then been given to him when he'd moved into his apartment. He flipped from one dumb program to another, until he found an American film he'd heard about and tried to follow its thread. But, after just a few minutes, its story of the upper class and their horse-racing travails, full of neighs and whinnying, struck him as a pathetic family drama signifying nothing. The pedestrian French dubbing didn't help much, either. After yawning two or three times, he decided to go to bed. Once there, he started thinking about Lucy. He'd been cavalier with her that afternoon, perhaps even a bit rude. Without a doubt she was offended, which would explain why she'd not called him back. But he knew how to get back in her good graces. He got up and called her. To his great surprise, she responded to him charmingly on the phone. Spend the night together? Great idea, though the weather was so brisk she wasn't sure she wanted to go out. On top of which she'd taken a shower and was lazing about in her pyjamas. But, if the prospect of fifteen minutes on the métro didn't put him off, she'd reserve a spot for him in *her* bed.

The next morning, after lying in till eleven at Lucy's place — she'd had to get up early to attend her "French Canadian Culture and Society" class at McGill U. — Jerome headed back to his apartment. In four hours he would know what was up with Losier — know for sure whether the man was a piece of shit or just a born loser. Worry had gripped him again. In the métro, one of his shoulder blades began to itch, then his left knee, then both calves; he scratched, just as a small, dry cough made him hunch his shoulders, even though he didn't have a cold. A black man with the look of an athlete, sitting across from him, gave him a supercilious look. Jerome realized he must have appeared ridiculous and plunged into reading *Le Devoir* in order to hide his misery from the other passengers. Coming to terms with his situation seemed a tenuous undertaking.

Back in his apartment, he listened to the two messages

on his answering machine. The first was from his father, the other from Charlie. He'd no appetite to speak to either of them and took a shower instead. (His night with Lucy had been particularly active and demanded certain hygienic measures.)

That done, a terrible hunger came over him, despite the copious breakfast he'd eaten at Lucy's. Along with the itching and the dry cough, he knew the hunger to be another symptom of a panic attack. He decided to kill it under a pile of toast and peanut butter. The remedy (a huge portion) was effective: his hunger was replaced by a vague nausea.

Twelve-thirty: another two and a half hours to go. What would he do with all that time? Impossible to read, he couldn't concentrate. Vacuum the apartment? The place could use it, but he'd rather have turned to dust himself and been sucked up by the machine.

A horrible suspicion suddenly crossed his mind. What if he'd fallen into the hands not of a petty criminal who contented himself with defrauding people whenever the chance presented itself, but of a professional crook and his sophisticated schemes, complete with hidden staircases, emergency exits, false identities, and so on and so on?

He went over to his desk, turned on his computer, opened the site on which he'd found the notorious Tercel, and started to browse all the offers of used cars. After a few minutes, he stumbled on a post for a 1999 Saturn, "for-door, colour blue, 35,000 clicks, exellent condition"—for which the seller was asking $1,400.

Son of a bitch! The same spelling mistakes! Ignorance was widespread, but typically people had their own way of showing it, did they not? There was a phone number— different from Losier's, it was true—but even then, what stopped him from having more than one number?

Jerome, needing to be sure, grabbed his cell and tapped in the number, wondering what accent to put on. Haitian? English? Spanish? He settled on Spanish and spoke in a high-pitched tone.

"Hello?" said a familiar voice.

Rounding his syllables as though he had a mouthful of barley sugar candy, Jerome asked if the Saturn advertised on the website had air conditioning. No, at that price, sir, it wouldn't be fully loaded. But on the other hand, if you take into account the fact—

He hung up. Without a doubt, it was him. But who was this *him*? The bastard had surely used a false identity. There had to be a way to find out. Jerome knew his address, at least—or that of the woman serving as his accomplice. He decided to get over to rue Florian at once. What was there to lose? It wasn't as though his Tercel was ever going to show up.

He left the apartment, flagged a taxi, and gave the address.

"Wait for me," he told the driver. "I won't be long."

"Don't hurry on my account, pal," replied the driver, laughing. He was a large, balding man, the crown of his head shiny with perspiration. "Me, I love the sound of a ticking meter. It's relaxing."

Jerome walked down the street, his heels clicking on the sidewalk, his demeanour vengeful. He was just about to climb the staircase to Losier's apartment when a gasp escaped him: there was "his" Tercel, parked right in front of the house.

Imprecations ready, he climbed the stairs four at a time and rang the doorbell, doing his best to see what he could between the grey muslin curtains blocking the view through the window. He heard footsteps and made out the form of a diminutive figure approaching. When the door opened, a tiny girl in blue overalls and pink shirt stained with what looked like caramel was looking up at him.

"What do you want?" she asked gravely.

He heard a woman's voice from somewhere in the apartment and felt the chance of the moment slipping away.

"Is your father home?"

She shook her head and moved to close the door.

"Who is it, Henriette?" called the woman in a piercing voice.

"It's a man, *Maman*," said the child, turning around.

Jerome bent down towards her and put his best smile on.

"What's your father's name?" he asked, gently.

The girl looked surprised, hesitated, and then, as if providing evidence, said, "Sylvain Tardieu, of course."

"Thank you."

He ran down the stairs and had barely thrown himself back into the taxi when the apartment door opened again and a woman in a yellow, short-sleeved cotton dress, arms hugging herself against the cold, came out onto the balcony and peered anxiously after the cab moving off down the street.

An hour later, at the police station, Jerome learned that five complaints involving the sale of automobiles had already been lodged against Sylvain Tardieu, alias Losier, and that he was being investigated. The tone with which Detective-Sergeant Boilard communicated this information — a mixture of hauteur, boredom, and a measure of pity — led Jerome to believe there was little chance he would ever see his money again. But he asked the officer anyway.

"If you like, you can take him to small claims court," the detective-sergeant said wearily. "At least it won't cost you much and you'd easily get a judgement against him. But as for getting your money back, these guys never have a cent to their name, my friend, they spend whatever they have as soon as they get it on drugs, drink, women, trips to Mexico, and God knows what else…"

It was a dejected Jerome who returned to his apartment on the métro. He'd still not called either his father or Charlie back. When he did try his parents, nobody answered. They were probably out shopping. He called Charlie's work number. He would remember Charlie's succinct answer for the rest of his life.

"Go buy *Le Journal de Montréal*, Jerome. There's a headline you'll find interesting."

Charlie sounded a lot like Detective-Sergeant Boilard, though there was no way his friend could have learned about the latest developments in the Toyota case.

Despite Jerome's insistence, Charlie wouldn't tell him what was in the newspaper. Jerome's heart was beating wildly as he hurried to the corner convenience store and bought the paper, rolled up tight in his hand so that he wasn't tempted to read it on the street. He hurried to the Brûlerie Saint-Denis on Côte-des-Neiges and found a quiet corner where he unrolled the paper.

A server approached, smiling.

"Small latte, as usual?" she asked.

Jerome turned his preoccupied face up towards her, nodded, and went back to reading.

On the right of the front page, above the fold, was a photo of a moose with an immense set of antlers; to its left, a headline stretched over three columns.

WHO KILLED THE MONSTER OF MANIWAKI?

On page two, an article recounted the tribulations of a certain Donat Pimparé, a guide with the Society of Outdoor Recreational Establishments of Quebec. Some wildlife conservation officers had met with Pimparé a couple of days prior in relation to the illegal sale of an unusually large rack of moose antlers to a rich American from Princeton, New Jersey. Pimparé affirmed having spotted the animal two weeks earlier while accompanying a novice hunter, although the hunter had failed to kill the animal; his client had then asked to change locations, which they had done. When, the next day, Pimparé returned to the site where the pair had seen the Monster, the guide killed it, despite not having a hunting permit, though he claimed to have the right to dispose of the antlers any way he liked.

His version of the facts, said the article, was being contested.

Jerome jumped as if someone had stuck a pin in his ass, his coffee cup dancing in its saucer.

"Goddamned liar! Those are *my* antlers!" he shouted wildly and to the astonishment of other clients.

A few minutes later, in a quiet corner of a neighbouring bookstore, he called Maître Asselin.

"Have you seen the story in this morning's *Journal de Montréal*, Maître?"

The lawyer gave a long, caustic laugh.

"I may have had something to do with it, Monsieur Lupien."

"Ah, I see! So it was you..."

"As I told you, should the denunciation come from a lawyer, things are likely to proceed with more dispatch. Was I wrong?"

"But you might have warned me! I just found out about it. It hit me like a ton of bricks!"

"Sorry, I completely forgot. I'm buried in work these days, I don't know what I was thinking. So sorry."

"So what do we do now?"

"We wait to see what happens. There's a lot of money involved in this case. The accused, as you can imagine, is going to fight this tooth and nail."

"Sounds like it's going to cost a bundle."

"No doubt."

"I'll have to borrow the money. I'm not working at the moment—not regularly, at any rate."

There was a moment's silence.

"Is there someone who can help you out, Monsieur Lupien? I don't know, maybe your parents?"

"I don't want my folks getting mixed up in this," replied Jerome, stubbornly.

"If they have the means, then you're making a mistake, my friend. We have a very good chance of winning this case. This guide's breach of faith is clear. For example, the note he left you at the hotel, the morning after the hunt, is incontrovertible proof of his lying. Not to mention that— listen, let me have a think—I don't usually do this, but I can see myself working for a percentage on a contingency basis rather than for my hourly rate."

"Really?"

"Maybe. But to be frank with you, I don't like doing it. Let me evaluate the situation carefully—oh, sorry, Monsieur Lupien, I have another call. We'll speak again. Good day."

Jerome paced back and forth, cell phone in hand, in front of a display of books about the Second World War, the Holocaust, and apartheid. He was clenching his teeth.

Despite the hope his lawyer had instilled in him, he felt discouraged, even disgusted. He looked for a place to sit down but the bookstore offered none.

"Life!" he muttered, moving towards the exit. "What a shit show. Assholes. Assholes everywhere!"

That evening he went to a hardware store and bought a litre of paint remover.

"The strongest you have," he said to the owner.

When night fell, he went back to rue Florian. The black Tercel was still there. After making sure no one was looking, he poured the paint remover over the car, bumper to bumper. Then he walked away as briskly as he could, the empty can in a bag that he dumped three blocks away, his mind not exactly at peace, but somewhat more contented.

AFTERWARDS, A STRANGE torpor came over him, the kind you might experience after receiving two hard uppercuts to the jaw. It was completely unlike him. He spent most of his time holed up in his apartment, sitting in front of the television, hunched over a crossword puzzle or buried in a mystery novel. His beard and hair grew, giving him a kind of Robinson Crusoe look, messages accumulated on his answering machine, emails on his laptop, mail in his letter box; he laughed at these the way a castaway laughs at a swimming pool. At first, out of loyalty, his friends were compelled to visit him, then they did so out of pity, then not at all — except for Charlie, who grew more and more intolerant of Jerome's apathy and came close to falling out with him a few times.

"Silly fool, he's depressed and too proud to admit it," thought Charlie. "As if being depressed were anything to be ashamed of! There's no one sicker than the person who refuses to be cured. This story is going to end badly, I can tell!"

Charlie phoned Jerome's parents to try to get them to help pull their son out of the slough of despond into which he was sinking more deeply with each passing day, but they declared themselves as helpless as he was when faced with Jerome's distress.

"My poor Charlie," sighed Marie-Rose, "we've invited him for dinner three times in order to help, and three times he's slammed the door in our faces the minute we broached the subject. He's almost as bad as my husband."

"Which is saying something," sneered Claude-Oscar in the background.

Only Lucy, after considerable effort, was able to pull Jerome out of his depression, though even she was not always up to it. In the end, she gave up and had a little tryst with one of her McGill professors — he taught a course called "The Communal Life of the St. Lawrence River Valley Peasantry, 1850–1950" — and stopped seeing Jerome.

"I think," she told Professor Pettigrew-Dansereau one night, sipping a cognac as she furrowed her brow as if in ponderous thought, "that the poor boy's problems . . . um" — she went on in English — "*have reactivated his old French Canadian roots. In my opinion he suffers from a . . . um . . . renewed outbreak of sociological immobilization*, don't you think?"

"*C'est en effet très Canadian-français, ça,*" agreed the professor with a bright smile — and then, in English: "And it doesn't seem to make for very good fucking, does it, my sweet?"

He ran a comforting hand along her thigh.

Jerome considered his girlfriend's defection as the third in a series of hard knocks, but a betrayal that he, alas, had in some way brought on himself.

One night he woke up with a jolt, as though someone had pulled him awake by the ear. Sitting bolt upright in bed, panting and distraught, he looked around in the darkness. Between the heartbeats pounding in his ears, he heard the distant rumbling of a bus somewhere in the city, and the sound, despite its familiarity, filled him with a sense of terrible dread.

"What the hell am I doing here?" he asked himself.

He didn't mean what was he doing in the place he occupied, at that moment, in his bedroom, nor in the building, the city, nor even the planet but, rather, what was he doing — *in this universe*! It was as if all the banality and routine insignificance that make up our daily life — that allow us to maintain our myopia in those moments in which we examine our existence — had been smashed into a million pieces by an enormous mace wielded by a giant. Who was it who, without offering the slightest reason for it, had decided to make him appear to himself like some infinitesimally tiny particle of dust lost in the vast unknown, to be meaninglessly buffeted this way and that and condemned to live in perpetual turmoil and suffering?

Son of a bitch! He was having a metaphysical panic attack! This had never happened to him before. How was it possible? Vague memories of reading Nietzsche and Schopenhauer for some long-forgotten philosophy course bubbled to the surface of his consciousness, sinister and grimacing phantoms who amused themselves by terrorizing him with their echoes of nothingness, their fear and loathing and sickness unto death. He tried to calm himself by saying that, after all, his condition was shared by eight billion other human beings, all of whom were, like him, trying to get on with living on this planet. But it was no use! He felt that from then on his thoughts were condemned to wander about in a kind of galactic void, glacial, desolate. Pascal's famous dictum came tremblingly back to him: "The eternal silence of these infinite spaces terrifies me."

Ah! Damn books! Damn culture! They were killing him, driving him crazy! O that he could not be as ignorant today as on the day of his birth! Was learning not just the accumulation of ever new ways to be unhappy?

Suddenly his intestines began to churn and a quivering bout of diarrhea sent him scrambling to the bathroom, sobbing as he ran. His damp feet stuck to the floor, he banged his head against a doorframe and swore. Once he'd recovered, he paced about the apartment, turning on all the lights in all the rooms, sweating, panting, bleary-eyed, with no idea what to do about his head. He gave a series of little groans, sat down, stood up, time and again pressing his hand tightly against his chest as if his heart might burst through it.

"Is this what it's going to be like from now on?" he muttered again and again in despair.

He knew full well that his anxiety was feeding itself. He rifled through his medicine cabinet, looking for some kind of medication to break the vicious circle that was torturing him, and found nothing but a bottle of valerian, long past its best-before date. He'd bought the tablets two or three years ago for insomnia. He swallowed some, not expecting much of them, and decided to get dressed and go out.

A cold November wind was blowing down the deserted street, which in the light from the street lamps looked wider and longer than it was. In the distance, cars were climbing Côte-des-Neiges towards downtown. He started to walk, breathing deeply, and soon began to feel better; the sense of unreality and frightful loneliness that had seized him was beginning to recede. He would have liked to talk to someone—to anyone, about anything—but what kind soul would listen to him at three in the morning? He walked as far as boulevard Edouard-Montpetit and heard the rumbling of a bus behind him. But this time, curiously, instead of filling him with despair, its roar comforted him. There would be a driver on the bus, and no doubt a few passengers. Their presence struck him as an unexpected gift. He ran to the next stop, some twenty metres down the road, and waited. The bus came to a halt with the usual grating and huffing, the door sighed open, and on he got. The fifty-something female driver, stocky and full in the flesh, had a lively face with rosy cheeks. She cast him a mechanical look and then, her eyebrows raised, a more appraising one. Jerome slid his card through the reader and found a seat farther on. At the back, spread across two seats with his back propped against the window, his knees raised, a man of indeterminate age with a blond ponytail and a fringed leather cowboy vest was reading a newspaper as comfortably as if he were in his own study. Jerome tried to look through the window, but all he could see was his own face reflected in the dark glass.

"What am I doing here?" he asked himself again (except this time there was nothing philosophical about his question). "Am I going nuts? No," he answered as quickly. "Were I nuts, I wouldn't be asking myself." But in his mind he doubted the logic of his reasoning.

The bus stopped at a red light and the driver turned to steal a quick look at him.

"Damn it," Jerome said to himself. "I must look so weird I'm making her nervous."

He bent over in his seat and hung his head. Decidedly, this nocturnal promenade had not been a good idea. And yet he did feel better. Where would he get off? He had to get off somewhere, buses are not shelters. Repeatedly asking himself these questions, he fell asleep. Nothing woke him: not the bus's abrupt stopping, not its shakings and bumping. When four frozen teenagers passed his seat, pushing each other and laughing boisterously, he didn't hear a thing.

EVENTUALLY HE WAS startled awake by a tap on the shoulder. Standing beside him, the driver was looking down and smiling, though not without apprehension.

"End of the line, sir. You'll have to find somewhere else to sleep."

He jumped to his feet and asked, his dry voice croaking, "What time is it?"

"It's a quarter after five, sir. I'm finished my shift and the bus is going back to the garage. You're on Mont-Royal, near Fullum," she added before he could enquire. "You've made the rounds twice! You were sleeping so soundly I didn't have the heart to wake you, even though it's against regulations for you to do so. But now, sir, you really do have to get off."

"I'm sorry," he said, heading towards the exit.

He stood on the sidewalk rubbing his neck to get some of the stiffness out of it, the result of sleeping for two hours sitting up. As he was thinking about the best way to get home, the bus suddenly appeared to his right in a cloud of exhaust as it made its way back in a wide turn to the garage. Jerome backed up to get away from the stinking fumes. When the bus was gone, a yellow Honda stopped beside him.

The blotchy-cheeked bus driver rolled down her window. "Still here?"

And then, after a moment's hesitation, "Can I drop you off somewhere?"

"Thanks, ma'am, but I'm okay," said Jerome, blushing.

"You sure?"

Obviously, he inspired pity in her.

"Come on, get in," she said, her voice filled with concern. "You look like a little dog lost at the North Pole."

He wasn't crazy about the comparison, but he got in out of weakness, fatigue, and because he couldn't think of a good reason not to.

"Where do you live?" she asked as he sat down beside her.

He gave her his address.

"I'll drop you off at the Mont-Royal métro. From there you'll be home in fifteen minutes. Okay?"

"You're very kind. Thank you so much."

The woman put the car in gear, smiled, coughed, and cast two or three covert looks at her passenger as the Honda headed west. Now she was the one who seemed ill at ease.

"I've never let a stranger in my car before," she felt obliged to tell him. "In my job, you see lots of things... I don't know why I made this exception... I guess you have the kind of face that inspires trust," she said, laughing. "What do you do for a living?"

"I'm a university student," he replied, wanting to keep things simple.

He introduced himself, told her a bit about his studies, and then fell silent. A crushing desire to sleep came over him again and he was having a hard time speaking in coherent sentences.

"My name is Marlène Guibord," said the driver. She coughed again, humming a little ditty to herself. "It looks like things aren't going so well for you."

"They're not, no... But it'll pass. It's almost passed now."

Out of the corner of her eye, she looked his way again

and, pouting skeptically, asked, "Problems at school? Tell me to shut up if I'm being too nosy ..."

"No, no, not at all. In fact, I'm taking a bit of a break from school. A sabbatical, you might say. I want to travel. But I've had a few setbacks."

He stopped talking.

A moment passed.

"You know," she said, "after work I usually get some breakfast at the Première Moisson bakery just over there ahead of you. I have to eat, after all, and I always need to settle my nerves before going to bed. Nights behind the wheel can be stressful, if you know what I mean. Do you feel like joining me? My treat. I've never invited a passenger on the STM to join me, but there's a first time for everything, right?"

He looked at her, surprised, even a little cautious, but the childlike smile won him over.

"You're very kind," he said. "And I am a bit hungry."

"Well, we'll soon fill you up," she said happily.

Moments later, they were entering the bakery. A warmly scented atmosphere enveloped them in an aroma of vanilla, cinnamon, and chocolate. Jerome sighed with relief. To their right, displays of pastries gleamed in brightly lit glass cases; on top of them were assorted treats. To the left, a dozen tables awaited customers wanting to eat in; a couple of old-timers in ball caps, each settled in a different corner, were reading *La Presse* as they ate their brioches. A slender young employee, with long black hair and delicate features, was cleaning a table absent-mindedly. She raised her head and her face lit up at the sight of her quinquagenarian regular.

"How are you doing, Madame Guibord?"

"Same as always, my dear," replied the driver with officially certifiable optimism. "And the little one?"

"I wish I had his energy!"

Marlène Guibord turned to Jerome.

"Have a seat, I'll go order. What do you want? A brioche? A muffin? A Danish? A piece of cake? With coffee, of course. Me, I'm drinking decaf, because in fifteen minutes I'll be hitting the sack."

He hesitated, then said, "A bran muffin, if they have one—"

"They will. I'll bring two, you look hungry."

"And a coffee."

"Au lait? Come on, don't be shy, it's my treat."

"Okay, a café au lait, if you want."

"I want *everything*. But it's your choice. Okay, I'll be back in a minute."

He sat and watched the employee now cleaning another table just across from him. She was pretty, but something about her suggested the suffering and exhaustion that he imagined came to unwed mothers of little means. And he suddenly realized his own troubles had vanished.

The driver came back with their order on a tray; she'd chosen an impressive *pain au chocolat* for herself, still warm from the oven and covered with sliced almonds.

"I should never come here," she said, taking the seat across from him. "I've gained more than ten pounds in two years thanks to these devilish pastries. I'll have to level with myself one of these days."

"Empty words, empty words, you fat old thing," thought Jerome, suddenly seized with malice. "And you're going to gain five more." It took all of Jerome's self-control to suppress a smile. But he knew his musings to be petty and cruel, and decided to redeem himself even if his companion, quite naturally, had no idea what he was thinking. And so, in response to Marlène Guibord's very first question, about his life and interests, he wanted to provide her proof of his trust in her and recounted, at great length, the story of his recent misadventures — even including details of his Toronto girl-friend's infidelity. And the more he told her, the more the anguish and despair that had gripped him earlier played a part in his narrative.

"And so tonight," he concluded with a sigh, "I was feeling so alone — as alone as a shaved dog lost on a highway — that ultimately I found myself on your bus."

She listened attentively, impassively, all the while eat-ing her *pain au chocolat* and taking small sips of her coffee.

They studied each other in silence for a moment.

"Yeah," she sighed, "that's a terrible story — blow by blow — you've had some rotten luck. It's like the devil him-self has taken you under his wing."

She took another bite, washed it down with a mouthful of coffee, chewing slowly with a look of pure delight.

"Eight years ago, the devil adopted me, too, and I thought he'd never let me go, the bastard. Which is why I was on a bus tonight, too."

Jerome raised his eyebrows inquiringly.

"Yeah," she went on quietly, gazing off into the distance, "when your husband has been snorting coke for years and then one fine night he leaves you with three kids to look after, and before going out the door kicks the shit out of you so bad you have to spend the next two months in the hospi-tal, you really start to believe you've become Satan's fiancée. And then, when you do get back home, the bits and pieces of your life more or less put back together, you have to do what you can to put food on the table, right? So after you've cried every last tear in your body, you go out and look for a job, even when you don't know how to do much, and you end up taking courses on how to drive a bus..."

"Really?" was all Jerome could think of to say, her story impressing him.

She looked at him with a gentle smile, holding her coffee cup tightly in her hands, and he thought he could discern a steeliness creep into her gaze, as if she were telling him there were a lot better reasons than a rack of moose antlers, a second-hand car, or an unfaithful girlfriend for someone to pity himself as he was doing.

And suddenly he felt like being mean to this woman who had done nothing but shower him with kindness.

Marlène Guibord took a last gulp of her coffee and slipped the rest of her *pain au chocolat* into a waxed paper bag.

"So, can I drop you off at the métro?"

IN MID-DECEMBER, JEROME went back to his waiter's job at the café in Old Montreal. He'd given up his plans to travel and in truth had no idea of what to do with the rest of his sabbatical year. After numerous discussions and arguments with family and friends, he'd finally been convinced to file a complaint against Sylvain Tardieu in small claims court. Towards the end of January, he received a judgement in his favour—but winning his court case didn't necessarily mean money in his pocket, especially as, two days later, the scumbag in question was thrown into jail for a year. All that accrued to Jerome, in the end, was the private satisfaction of revenge taken on a crook and the more ethereal pleasure of having scored a moral victory.

"But man, if only I could get my antlers back," he sighed.

In the end, Maître Asselin agreed to represent Jerome for a percentage of the take, but warned him the case might go on for months, if not years, before it was settled.

The night of anguish that had ended on the bus and in his meeting the congenial Marlène Guibord had had a strange effect on him—and of which he was not immediately aware. A sort of cauterization seemed to have been performed on his being, as if certain fibres had been destroyed and others created, so that he had grown a sort of carapace. The formerly idealistic young man easily aroused to indignation, who was sensitive to the pain and injustices experienced by his fellow humans—but whose compassion, it has to be said, rarely translated into more than words quickly forgotten—was replaced by an altogether more detached man, one prone to irony and indifference, and who left an impression of cynicism and *froideur*. It wasn't always the case, but was more and more so.

Shortly after his court victory, he suggested to Charlie that they go see the latest Dardenne brothers film at the Quartier Latin. Afterwards, they'd gone to a nearby microbrewery on the rue Saint-Denis, where their conversation, fed by good, strong beer, lasted until just before midnight. Leaving the brewery to take the métro, they noticed an old rubby walking unsteadily towards them with his hand out, obviously a lover of beer himself, if with a more restricted budget for it that he was trying to augment despite the lateness of the hour. The cold was biting, and a pool of water on the sidewalk had turned to ice. The man stepped awkwardly on it and fell down, his back and head hitting the pavement with a sickening thud. For several seconds the man didn't move—just lay with his mouth open and eyes drawn—and then he started kicking his legs trying to get up. Jerome and

Charlie rushed towards him. The man, in all his pain and misery, had managed to struggle to a sitting position and was rubbing his head, which was bleeding. He was short and dumpy — a great round thing, his age hard to know — and his deeply lined face had been more or less melted by alcohol.

"Fer chrissakes, I'm a goner," he grumbled in a tremulous voice. "Help me up, youse," he said to Charlie, who had bent over him. "Pull harder'n that, *tabernac*'! Didn't ask ya to fall on top o' me, me with me ass on the ground — ferget it, lemme be!"

"Come on, Charlie," said Jerome, backing off in disgust. "He can take care of himself."

His friend pointed to the pool of blood forming on the ice. "We can't leave him like this. Come on, help me."

Jerome turned. "Rule number one in cases of accidents, chum: don't move the wounded."

While they were talking, the man, huffing and puffing, got to his knees and, body bent forward, his hands on the sidewalk, tried to stand up.

"We don't have a choice," said Charlie. "Get back here!"

Jerome obeyed, but reluctantly. After several attempts, they succeeded in getting the rubby to his feet and, each taking him by a shoulder, propping him up against the wall of the Théâtre Saint-Denis.

"Not so fast, boys," muttered the wounded man. "Everythin's spinnin' roun' like a son of a bitch."

Jerome, nostrils pinched, turned to his friend and frowned: the man was giving off an abominable stink. Charlie took his cell out of his pocket and said to the rubby, who was tottering, "We have to get you to Emergency, old man. I'm calling an ambulance."

The man, head raised, seemed to be concentrating on a

point in the sky and mumbled a few unintelligible words.

"Well, I've done my good deed for the day," said Jerome. "I'm out of here. See you later."

And with that he strode off towards the métro station. He was about to go down the stairs when a familiar blue-and-red flashing made him turn around; a police car had stopped in front of the Théâtre Saint-Denis, and two officers got out to relieve Charlie of his role as Good Samaritan.

Jerome shrugged and hurried down the station steps.

A FEW DAYS later, the two friends had a fairly lively discussion about the incident. They were having dinner in Charlie's apartment on rue Marie-Anne. They'd ordered a pizza, and Charlie, who fancied himself a connoisseur of wine, wanted Jerome to reap the rewards of a *historic discovery* he'd made the week before: a Château Drobeta-Turnu, a red from southeastern Romania (though a northern section of it) — a Merlot-Grenache aged in American oak casks that, he said, would make a good many reputable Bordeaux producers envious. They'd quickly gone through one bottle, and as the second began to suffer from a pronounced emptiness, masculine frankness took control of the conversation.

"You've changed in the past month or two," Charlie observed a little abruptly.

"Yes, of course I have. I'm a month or two older."

"Don't try to turn it into a joke. I'm serious. I find you changed, Jerome — and not necessarily for the better."

"Oh, well, sorry about that. Do you have any specific details?"

"Among other things, I'm thinking about that old rubby we saw on Saint-Denis. I've seen you be more compassionate, to put it mildly."

"Not everyone has Mother Teresa's blood running in their veins like you, Charlie. Maybe you received a transfusion?"

"No, I've still got my original blood. But I didn't recognize you that night, Jerome, I really didn't."

"What can I say? When a stinking drunk falls down on the sidewalk in front of me and starts hurling insults at anyone who comes to help him, I start thinking maybe there's somewhere else I have to be."

"I understand that, Jerome. He pissed me off, too. But you still can't leave a bleeding man outside in minus-ten-degree weather. Anyway, as I said, that's just one example. Do you want another? Last Thursday, when I told you my father had just been operated on for prostate cancer, it was like I told you the Val-d'Or hockey team was going to finish in last place again this year. It was a serious operation, Jerome; he could have died. If I thought on it more I could come up with plenty other examples but I don't keep a list, it's not my way of doing things. Some of them would make you laugh; no doubt, you'd find them insignificant. But I don't. In fact, chum, it's your attitude in general that I find hard to take. It's like you just don't give a shit about anyone anymore, no matter what happens, good or bad. Like you've cut yourself off from the world. You're polite, you're kind, but inside you're as cold as ice."

"There you go, Charlie, I've made up my mind: I want you to be my confessor. You're perfect for the job. All you have to do is take a few courses in morality and theology and get ordained. You'll still be able to fuck, though, you have my permission for that."

"You see?" said Charlie, refilling their glasses. "You make fun of everything. It's like something inside you has turned to ice."

"And yet this evening is making me feel more and more hot-headed—okay, okay, maybe that wasn't the joke of the century, scratch that. But I must say, in passing, that this wine of yours isn't bad for the price. It won't cause any bankruptcies in Bordeaux, but it's not bad."

"You want to change the subject, Jerome? Are you afraid of what I'm trying to tell you? Does it make you piss your pants?"

Jerome's face went from flushed to fiery red.

"Never mind what I do in my pants, asshole, I'm perfectly capable of taking care of myself. I've had to, lately. And Charlie, what makes you such a moralizer all of a sudden? And frankly, more than a little naive. Life isn't a piece of cake, or haven't you noticed yet? You've got to protect yourself, see it coming, be on your guard, unless you want to end up at the bottom of the heap along with all the other social misfits. Is that what you're reproaching me for? Not wanting that?"

Charlie gave a sarcastic smile, took a drink of wine, and smacked his lips with a satisfied air to let Jerome know that his criticism of the Drobeta-Turnu hadn't affected him at all. But the turn in their conversation had started to worry him. He needed to find a way to change the topic without losing face but couldn't come up with one.

"All this because you weren't able to buy that jalopy," he ended up saying, though without much conviction.

Jerome brought his fist down on the table with such force that Charlie had to grab the wine bottle before it fell over.

"You've got it all wrong, man!" Jerome shouted with a spray of spittle. "You're spinning off the road at three hundred miles an hour! Who said anything about a jalopy? It's not just the bloody car! Those goddamned antlers amount to a $200,000 loss for me, maybe more! It's a disaster...And there's...there's..."

His voice quivered and a sob rose in his throat. With a violent effort of will, he calmed down, emptied his glass in two gulps, took in a deep breath, and, looking towards the ceiling, asked in a resolute voice, "Are we going to open another bottle?"

Although in his opinion they'd already surpassed the limits of reasonable consumption, Charlie got up (necessarily leaning on the table), went over to the counter, and returned with a third bottle of the remarkable Château Drobeta-Turnu. He tried to uncork it but his hands were no longer under his command.

"Here, let me," said Jerome.

The cork came out with a joyous pop. He filled their glasses and brought his to his lips. "I find it gets better by the hour. Curious."

Charlie, relieved that his friend was his old self again, slowly nodded in agreement.

A moment passed.

"And so?" said Jerome.

"And so what?"

"So, you've consigned me to the category of the heartless, is that it?"

"No, of course not," said Charlie, who'd rather stack bricks all night or change fifty babies' diapers than resume that particular conversation. "It's just that—"

Despite the fog filling his skull, he tried to find a frank and diplomatic way to say what he had to say.

"It's just what?" said Jerome, attempting to focus on the vacillating gaze of his friend.

"Look, Jerome," Charlie said, shaking his head like a

horse bothered by a horsefly, "why don't we save this discussion for another time? We're both pissed to the gills, I don't know what the hell I'm saying anymore, neither do you, and we're risking another fight that could last for months. I don't want to lose you as a friend—and I don't think you want to, either, am I right?"

Jerome grimaced spitefully.

"Well," he said, "since you won't grace me with the profundity of your reasoning, I'll give you a piece of my own mind. A little compensation. It disturbs you to see me embrace the old 'every man for himself and to hell with anyone else' line—not terribly appealing, is it?—but wake up, Charlie boy, that's how everybody wants to act but they won't admit it. The only exceptions are a few idiots and one or two saints no one ever runs into anyway—oh, wait, I'm forgetting the classic example of parents when it comes to their children. Not hard to explain: the reproductive impulse is pushing them, more so for species generally. Cows do the same for their calves. But despite that particular instinct, every day the newspapers are full of family dramas so horrible, thank you very much, that Children's Aid doesn't have enough room for all the damaged children. So, if you can't stand that I've decided to adapt myself to real life, that's your problem. But take some advice from a friend, Charlie. Do as I do, you'll feel a lot better about things."

And with a smile he poured more wine into his glass, a satisfied glow spreading across his foggy countenance.

Charlie broke out laughing.

"Well, if I'm a confessor, then you're some kind of preacher, and a hell of an odd one at that."

Ten minutes later, two sets of snores sounded in the apartment—one from the living room, where Jerome was stretched out on the sofa, laboriously sleeping off his wine, and the other from the bedroom, where strange nightmares haunted Charlie.

VARADERO

SEVERAL DAYS WENT by without the two friends seeing or speaking to one another. Was it because of their nocturnal discussion? In truth, the vapours of the Drobeta-Turnu had pretty much addled their brains, so that when they did reunite they made no allusion to that night. It was as if they had forgotten all about it, though perhaps it was the sneaking suspicion that their lives were about to take on a whole new trajectory that prevented them from revisiting their conversation.

The weeks rolled slowly by, with a succession of freezing spells followed by bouts of rain, as sometimes happens when winter and spring meet and lock horns — and which seemed to have been the pattern of the preceding few years. Jerome continued to work at the café on rue de la Commune and began an affair with the owner's daughter. Her mother, a highly principled woman from Rouen, France, seemed to have turned a blind eye to the liaison, flattered that her daughter was dating a university student; she may have entertained vague hopes of having Jerome as a son-in-law, a business partner, as he seemed energetic and resourceful and hardly lacking in gumption.

But, by the beginning of April, Jerome had become profoundly fed up with his job and the grey slush that Montreal had been slipping around in for ten days. He decided to take two weeks off and go to Cuba, and he was never seen at the café again.

By that Tuesday evening, he was in the 31-degree heat of Varadero, in a gigantic five-star hotel built in the shape of a horseshoe, surrounded by a clutter of fake *palapas* that served both recreational and utilitarian purposes. The Internet site on which he'd made his reservation had promised "the full gamut of delights," carefully specifying that the establishment was run by a Spanish chain.

He spent the first days of his vacation sleeping, swimming, stuffing himself at the buffet table in the dining room, and strolling about the hotel grounds, stopping at one of the many open-air bars to order daiquiris in his tourist's Spanish. Despite the drinks being served up with engaging smiles, he had to knock back an incalculable number of them in order to feel even the beginnings of anything like euphoria.

The combination of heat, sun, and *far niente*—the barefooted, bathing-suited walks on the fine sand—stirred a sexual excitement in him that, if not satisfied as quickly as possible, threatened to put a damper on his holiday. The lack of a suitable companion began to weigh on him. The quality of the selection offered at the hotel at this time of year was not, generally speaking, high; its clientele consisted mainly of retirees—elderly couples who'd tired of Florida, sexagenarian spinsters who'd come to Cuba in the hope of finding a soul sister under the coconut palms, survivors of the scalpel who'd decided to give one last thumb to the nose of the Grim Reaper — or else young couples and their offspring desperately trying to combine a second honeymoon with their obligations as parents. Jerome, sorry he hadn't tried a little harder to convince his girlfriend to accompany him, was reduced to having to make love to himself.

He set about finding a pretty woman who'd agree to share his bed or welcome him into hers. In the course of his comings and goings, he'd noticed at least half a dozen potential partners, but all of them were cast in the same mould: women in their forties, no doubt executive assistants, who had a frigid air or looked as if they were fighting off migraines while forcing themselves to appear relaxed. But most of all he was suddenly aware of the paucity of his own talents as a seducer; in this unfamiliar environment (it was his first trip to Cuba) he found himself unusually diffident, hesitant, even a bit tongue-tied, and afraid of being rejected. Which was no doubt why one of the senior secretaries he tried to chat up in the hotel lobby by asking, "Is this your first time in Cuba?" drily replied, "Why, does it look like it is?" before shrugging her shoulders and striding off in the direction of the elevators.

"Thanks a lot, bitch," he muttered under his breath, "you just did me a favour, buzzing off."

He was depressed for the rest of the day, though the next morning seemed to offer him a change of fortune. He'd left the pool after swimming a few lengths when his gaze met that of a tall, blond woman lying on a deck chair, her little girl curled up beside her. The woman threw a smile his way. He smiled back and went over.

"You're a good swimmer," she said.

"Oh, thanks," he said modestly. "I used to be much better, I don't swim much these days."

"Well, you're still pretty good," said the woman. "Don't you think so, Andrée-Anne?"

"He swims better than you do, Mommy."

"Do you mind if I join you?" Jerome said, pulling a beach chair over, his heart beating more quickly.

The woman was in her early thirties and nicely filled out. She had a pretty face and a particular expression that came to Jerome like a deeply comforting balm after a long period of drifting—like the first breath of air of a sponge diver who, on the point of drowning, reaches the surface and fills his lungs with oxygen.

They began talking. The little girl, after wiggling for a moment in the embrace of her mother, became bored and jumped off the chaise longue to run towards the wading pool, where a dozen other children were fighting and yelling and having a good time. She was Eugenie Métivier, a dietitian who worked for the Metro grocery store chain; she lived in Montreal and was returning the next day, delighted with her week in Cuba, although she'd found it too short.

"I really needed this," she sighed, without elaborating.

Jerome introduced himself without going into too many details. As he spoke, his brain made several fevered calculations. He found the woman very attractive, and she obviously felt the same about him. They had barely twenty-four hours to get to know each other better—not much time, but better than nothing. But the presence of the child might complicate things. It was a matter of not wasting time and getting straight to the point, but elegantly.

"This afternoon we're going to visit a sugar plantation," Eugenie announced. "Are you going?"

"No," he said, barely concealing his disappointment. "You have to sign up for it, I guess?"

"Yes. By now all the spots are probably taken, but you never know. They'll be able to tell you at reception. Would you like to come?"

Group excursions horrified him, but he couldn't let it show.

"Why not? I'll go check it out."

He hurried to the hotel. Spending a few hours together would be very useful, a touristic prelude to the night of fucking he so desperately craved.

"It's full," he said dolefully, when he returned to the pool a few minutes later.

"I suspected it would be."

And then, having nothing to lose, he went all in.

"What time do you get back?"

She gave him a strange smile, a mixture of shyness and devil-may-care.

"Around five or six, I would imagine."

"I'd like to see you again. I'd *really* like to see you again. Would it be possible tonight?" he added quickly, looking her straight in the eye and blushing to his ears.

She started to laugh.

"Sure, I'd like that. After all, we're on vacation, aren't we?"

He was about to put his hand on her arm when a loud shriek came from the wading pool. Andrée-Anne had slipped on a puddle of water getting out of it and banged her head on the tile floor. Her mother was beside her in an instant. The child was hysterical, and bleeding profusely. A small crowd gathered, an employee ran over, and it was decided to take her to the infirmary. Jerome wanted to accompany mother and daughter, but thought it would be awkward and, after giving Eugenie a sign of encouragement (which she didn't seem to notice), he went back to his room to change.

He didn't see her again until two hours later, in the lobby, after lunch, as they were getting into a car for the visit to the plantation. Andrée-Anne had a large bandage on her forehead and gave him a timid wave. Her mother smiled, it seemed to him a little distractedly, perhaps even coolly.

An insufferable feeling of frustration came over him, like an unscratchable itch that filled him with discontent and prevented him from concentrating on anything. He was burning up with desire and, at the same time, felt like a windsock tossed back and forth by contrary winds. The sensation made a mockery of his vacation, turning it into a kind of punishment.

HE DECIDED TO walk to Varadero, five or six kilometres from the hotel. The exercise would do him good and help pass the time until evening. He set out at a brisk pace but, after a while, a strange feeling came over him: during the past few days, he'd become used to the fact that a hotel meant constant neighbours, but now he found himself completely alone. Every once in a long while a vehicle would pass him, some vintage American car with faded paint or a pathetically old rusted-out truck held together by spit and chewing gum and pouring out black smoke as it laboured to prolong its hazardous longevity. He wiped his forehead with the back of his hand, the sun beating down on him. Jerome felt as though someone were amusing themselves by holding a hot iron to his head and bringing his brains to a boil. It was like a mini-sauna under his T-shirt; he could feel the sweat running in rivulets down his back and thighs. But, in spite of everything, a euphoric feeling of freedom possessed him; he'd escaped the slushy, morose spring that was gripping Montreal and, wherever he looked, he saw joyously exuberant colour. With every inhalation, rich, deep, spicy aromas filled his nostrils. He slowed his pace, dizzied by the heat and the onslaught of new sensations, and sought out a shady spot. Varadero was still far away. Then, ten metres away, he saw a fenced enclosure of old grey boards that offered a bit of shade. Squatting on his heels, he was able to rest for a moment.

A 1950s-vintage Mercury, bright lemony yellow and looking as if it had just come from the paint shop, appeared on the road. The car slowed down alongside him, and a burst of laughter rang out from inside it.

"*Pobre crio,*" came a mocking female voice.

Then the car picked up speed again and was gone.

Had she been laughing at him? The hell she was! She must have been one of those tarts who'd do anything for a tenner from a tourist.

He went over to the fence and inspected the ground at the foot of the palisade. It was covered with short, dry, brown grass — were there tarantulas, scorpions, or other such dangers in Cuba, he wondered — and then, satisfied, stooped down and crawled into its shadow. Compared to the open air, the temperature in its shade was delicious. He closed his eyes and began to drift into a heavy torpor. After ten, fifteen, maybe twenty minutes, he couldn't tell, he suddenly heard a small grating sound and a thin voice drew him from his siesta.

"*¡Hola! ¡Señor! ¿A donde va? ¿Quiere subir?*" — Where are you going, would you like to get on board?

An old peasant sitting on a cart pulled by a donkey was waving in Jerome's direction.

Jerome guessed what the old man's offer was about. Everyone on the island seemed to be finding ingenious ways to supplement their incomes thanks to the tourists. In such circumstances, Jerome must have struck the peasant as an unexpected opportunity.

He jumped to his feet, ran up to the cart, and threw a leg over the side. The man gave him a wide grin, revealing a mouthful of large, solid, yellow teeth.

"*¿Varadero?*" the cart driver asked, pointing down the road as the donkey—one ear flopping, the other standing straight up—turned a suspicious eye to his new passenger.

"*¡Si, si!*" replied Jerome as he slipped his hand into his pocket to take out his wallet.

After several polite refusals, the man accepted the single dollar Jerome offered him, and the cart rattled on. Its driver, diminutive, quick, and nervous, might have been in his sixties. His wrinkled skin was a dull brown, vaguely reminiscent of the colour of the grass at the foot of the palisade.

"The man makes the country, the country makes the man," Jerome told himself and, without particularly knowing why, he was proud of the thought. Who was it who'd first said it? Hugo? Péguy? Hemingway? Miron? Well, this time it was *Jerome Lupien*.

Twenty minutes went by. The sun was sadistic. Jerome felt as though a red-hot helmet had been placed on his head and that his shoulders were baking; more and more, he was tormented by thirst. Each kilometre made him happier to have made the acquaintance of the cart driver, their exchanges reduced to not much more than smiles and occasional big gestures punctuated by onomatopoeias or what sounded like them.

After several minutes, the fields that, on either side of the road, had been divided by hedgerows and outcrops of trees gave way to huts, dilapidated agricultural buildings, and hovels around which packs of children and a few adults mingled; they were nearing the town. The cart stopped abruptly at a crossroad at which a small, bumpy, dirt track branched off. The peasant driver turned to Jerome and, gesturing histrionically and repeating the name Varadero several times, indicated that he wasn't heading into the town but that Jerome would find it quite easily.

Jerome thanked him with an exaggerated bow, hopped down from the cart, and resumed his journey by foot, waving again to the carter who, hands cupping his mouth, appeared to be shouting good wishes to him.

Very quickly, he reached Varadero. The town seemed fairly wretched—its streets paved but without sidewalks and lined by greying shacks in front of which children played among chickens. He was desperate for a cold beer to be enjoyed in shelter from the sun. He picked up his pace and kept an eye out for any establishment—a bar, café, or restaurant, it didn't matter, as long as he was able to relieve his thirst. Soon he saw a building with large windows that appeared to be a grocery store and went in. Rows of poorly stocked shelving ran the length of the store, impeccably maintained but giving the impression of irremediable poverty. Along one aisle, he was taken aback: three containers of Irresistible brand dishwashing liquid—the same line sold by the Metro supermarket chain in Quebec—were arranged front and centre on the otherwise almost empty shelf. By what weird combination of circumstances did they find themselves in Cuba?

"*No cerveza, señor,*" said the short, half-bald man behind the counter, his tone placating. Hands behind his back, he'd been observing Jerome for several minutes.

"*¿Agua mineral?*" Jerome asked.

"*No agua mineral,*" replied the man, lifting his shoulders as if in apology.

But motioning for Jerome to wait, he left the counter and returned, smiling, with a bottle of lemonade.

Jerome paid him, left the store, and drank the lemonade in three long gulps. It was so sweet it only increased his thirst. He walked on. Others cast surreptitious glances his way, some with a hint of a smile. Most were dressed very modestly, though their clothing was clean and in good repair. He passed the half-open doorway of a small house with a lime green–painted stucco front ravaged by time. An old woman hurried out of it with an armful of flowers and tried to sell him a bouquet. But he didn't need flowers, he needed a beer.

"*Cerveza,*" he implored her.

"*¿Cerveza?*" she said, pointing towards the end of the street. "*¡Alli! ¡Alli!*"

He bowed for the second time that day — "*¡Muchas gracias, señora!*" — and continued on his way.

A few minutes later a shriek of joy escaped his lips. Across the street was a low gabled building with a few metal tables and chairs in front of it, set back a little from the road. Above the door a sign stretched across the entire façade:

EL SOMBRERO

A LOS TRES PICOS

Manifestly this was a place where he'd be able to get something to drink. Jerome crossed the street, practically running.

"*Cerveza, cerveza,*" he cried with the fervour of a ship-wrecked sailor who sees a lifeboat.

A clamminess that could have been cut with a knife permeated the joint, but the beer it served was excellent and almost cold. He sat down and drank two, one after the other, and began to feel a little tipsy. A rancid smell of fried food hung about the room, Jerome the only customer. The diminutive, lean woman who'd welcomed him with an affecting smile had asked, "*¿Canada?*"

"*No*," Jerome corrected her. "*Québec.*"

"*¡Ah, francés! Un francés,*" she'd concluded, nodding her head up and down several times as if he'd brought her particularly good news.

After that she'd said nothing more to him, busying herself with two small boys who, yelling wildly, ran in and out through a door opening onto a small courtyard. He ordered a third beer. "*Lento*, Jerome, *lento*," he told himself. "You don't want to be crawling back to the hotel on your hands and knees."

Legs stretched out, he sipped the beer as a pleasant torpor got the better of him. How would his evening end? Ah! *Don't even think about it.* Let the chips fall where they may! Live for the moment! Strategizing puts you into a corner.

All the liquid he'd drunk suddenly demanded attention. He looked about the room.

"*¿Los servicios?*" the woman asked, guessing his thoughts. She pointed to a door half-hidden by a stack of plastic chairs. In the cramped bathroom stalls, the smell of Javex battled heroically with the reek of old urine, and the sink, cracked and inadequately repaired, leaked water onto the tiled floor. He wrinkled his nose, held his breath, and peed as quickly as he could. Above his head a small window let in a bit of air. Through it he could see the end of an alley and, next to a wall, two men talking animatedly. One, in his early twenties, looked like a tourist.

He returned to his table. Hardly had he sat down when the owner, somewhat flustered, approached with her two children and gestured that she had to leave because of them but that he could finish his beer at one of the tables on the terrace. All smiles and excuses, she pushed her two boys ahead of her to the door, opened a parasol above one of the outside tables, and pulled out a chair and invited him to sit. Then she locked the door to the cantina and bustled off with her children, suddenly grave and silent.

He took a few more sips of his beer, but it was lukewarm and he was no longer thirsty. Looking around, he was wondering which direction he should take when he heard someone cry out from the direction of the alley. The scream was not one of joy or anger, but of fear.

He jumped up, knocking the table so hard his half-filled beer glass fell off and smashed on the pavement. The scream was followed by the furious swearing, in Spanish, of someone hoping for something really bad to happen.

Not really sure of what he was doing, Jerome found himself in the alley a few steps away from the two strangers. One of them, a man in his forties, was deeply tanned and short, but with a bulldog's chest and the physiognomy to match. He was holding the young tourist by the collar of his shirt and, a knife in his other hand, was keeping him from getting away.

"What's going on?" yelled Jerome, hands on his hips.

The accumulated frustrations that had been building up in him for months had come boiling to the surface, making him throw caution to the wind.

"*¡Socorro! ¡Socorro!*" shouted the gringo. "Help! He's trying to kill me!"

Bulldog-man sneered. Still holding on to his victim, he turned towards Jerome and, with a few menacing flourishes of the weapon in his hand, invited him to make like the wind and vanish. Jerome was fixed to the spot. A mortal chill ran through his body and he felt his knees quake; this was fear, the real thing, in all its enormity and shame. But instead of making him run away, the fear made him contemptuous of himself, and his rage rose and burst its bounds. Spotting a rock on the ground near the wall, he threw himself on it and, his hand shaking but his eye steady, heaved it with all his strength at the man, who fell to the ground, stunned.

"Go! Run!" he yelled.

They raced to the street and crossed it.

"My car's just over here," said the stranger, turning to Jerome, crimson-faced. "It's the little Honda down there by the pink wall."

"Stop," said Jerome, taking him by the shoulder. "We've got to walk slowly. We don't want to draw attention to ourselves. We don't want to deal with the police, on top of everything else."

The other man obeyed and immediately slowed his step to match Jerome's. They walked in silence for a while, like two *flâneurs* stupefied by the heat, furtively glancing to their left and right.

"How can I thank you?" murmured the young man in an anemic voice. "I'm pretty sure if you hadn't turned up when you did, that dog would have run me through with his knife. That was pretty cool, what you did."

Jerome waved him off with an insouciant smile. In truth,

he was the first one to have been surprised by his action, and it filled him with pride.

"You'd have done the same thing yourself," he said out of politeness.

"Hmm, I was never much of a fighter."

The stranger looked back to see what was happening behind them: two men were standing in front of the café, talking and gesturing.

"Look straight ahead," Jerome told him. "No one saw anything, nothing happened. We're just walking. Life is good! What's your name, by the way?"

"Felix Sicotte. Yours?"

Jerome told him his name and learned that his companion was staying at the Iberostar—the same hotel as him.

"I'm here with my mother," Sicotte said. "Some vacation, eh?"

Jerome didn't reply. They came up to the Honda.

"This year's model," he said, surprised. "You don't see many new cars around here."

"It's my mother's," said Felix, unlocking the doors.

Felix was making a commendable effort to appear calm, but once behind the wheel he couldn't resist the temptation to look behind them.

"Man, there's a whole army in front of the café," he said, a trifle fearfully.

"Let's get out of here," said Jerome, getting into the car. "I'll take the Iberostar any day, a Cuban prison, not so much."

The Honda peeled away with a slight spinning of the tires.

"Hey, take it easy, man!" said Jerome. "What are you trying to do, get us arrested?"

"Sorry," said Felix, contrite.

They were soon back on the road that Jerome had travelled in the cart, keeping to the left. Felix drove slowly, even forcing himself to whistle, with dubious results. Jerome glanced at him from time to time: his type—handsome, blond, with a candid and lively demeanour—was easy to like, but there was also something childish about him. He seemed a touch naive, something of a spoiled baby. Was he in the presence of one of those rich kids who'd been raised on soft, satin cushions and never known any hardship in his life?

Until then, Jerome felt that everything had transpired as it should, that events could not have been otherwise. Not until the car passed through the gates of the Iberostar did the full implications of his act of blind courage strike him— and all this for a stranger! He was still proud of what he'd done but, at the same time, the impetuousness he'd displayed astonished him. It also prompted a vague sense of uneasiness, since it didn't seem at all in character. Was his dumb action the symptom of some sort of inner crisis?

"Am I falling into another little depression?" he wondered.

He was drawn out of his reflections by a tap on his shoulder.

"Come on, I'll buy you a drink," said Felix with a big smile. "You've earned it."

FELIX BROUGHT THE car to a stop in the hotel parking lot, and they made their way to the bar, which at that hour was almost empty. Potted palms were randomly placed in the shadows. A wooden arch shaped like a donkey's back disgorged a steady stream of water into a fake river that meandered through the room. They sat at a rattan table near the bar, behind which a man with a dozy expression was wiping glasses.

"What'll you have?" asked Felix. He seemed full of self-confidence now that he was back in his element.

Jerome thought for a moment, his arms tight against his sides; the air conditioning had jolted them from the dog days of Cuba to the chill of a Quebec autumn.

"Rum," he said. "No ice."

"Good idea. I'll have the same."

Felix turned to the waiter and said a few words in Spanish. Abandoning his languor, the waiter bowed and smiled; the next instant, the drinks arrived at the table. The two men clinked glasses.

"You speak Spanish?" Jerome asked Felix.

"Yeah . . . I come to Cuba fairly often. My parents own shares in this hotel."

"Ah, I see."

"This time," said Felix ironically, "I have the pleasure of my dear mama's company, but usually I come down with a girlfriend or a few friends, it all depends."

Jerome sipped his rum and listened, distracted by the jaunty sounds of a mariachi band coming over the speakers. His picture of Felix Sicotte was becoming clearer.

"Do you mind my asking why that bandit was holding a knife to your throat?" he asked, setting his glass on the table. He looked over at the barman, who was smoothing his hair with a comb.

"You can ask me anything you want," said Felix, laughing. "You saved my life!"

Then he turned serious.

"I was conned. I fell for his tricks like an imbecile. Yesterday, I met that dog in a pickup joint not far from the café you were in. I was looking for some good hash. He promised me some primo stuff at a good price, but the delivery had to be made *piano-piano*, if you catch my drift, because that kind of thing is really frowned upon here by the Cuban authorities. You can be made to disappear fast. And me, idiot that I am, I agreed to meet him in that alley. He wanted me to show up at ten at night, but I figured something was up so I insisted we do the deal in broad daylight. As you saw, it was lucky I did—but I learned my lesson."

He stretched his arm across the table and held Jerome's wrist.

"Keep this between us, okay? If my mother hears about it, she'll kill me. She should be showing up any time now. It's her cocktail hour. Another round?" he said, raising his already empty glass. "It'll settle our nerves a bit."

"As you wish," replied Jerome.

As their drinks arrived, Felix looked up and waved at a middle-aged woman, thickening a bit about the middle, who'd just come into the bar.

"There she is," Felix murmured between his teeth. "The general has entered the room! Take care."

He took a mouthful of rum, and then—

"Mama," he said, rising as she approached their table—a polite but surprising gesture. "Allow me to introduce Jerome Lupien, a new friend I just made in Varadero. Jerome, this is my mother, Francine Desjarlais. Watch yourself," he added jokingly, "nothing gets past her."

She shrugged.

"A fine thing to say about your mother," she said, shaking Jerome's hand. "Felix, you'll have your new friend running for the door."

But her laugh was genuine. She was a woman of average

height, and fairly plain, but with a keen and intelligent eye and an abundance of auburn hair, with blond highlights, that fell to her shoulders. She wore a silk dress patterned with palm trees under a full moon, and its neckline plunged farther down than Jerome dared look. Francine took a seat and gave Jerome a quick look of appraisal that made him realize Felix was right: he'd just been submitted to a rapid preliminary examination. Then she raised her hand in the direction of the bar without saying a word, and immediately the bartender started grabbing bottles; the sound of crushed ice followed.

"What happened to your shirt?" she asked her son all of a sudden. "One of the top buttons is missing. Have you been in a fight?"

Felix, caught short, looked embarrassed. He turned to Jerome. "See? I told you."

"*What* did you tell him?"

"That you run the household with military precision: left, right, left, right, stand at attention, present yourself for inspection!"

"Okay, okay, I get it. The gentleman would like to change the subject. Sorry, no go. Tell me, what kind of scrape did you get yourself into this time, Felix?"

"I didn't want to tell you, because I knew you'd throw a fit. But I'll tell you now — not that I have much choice. So here goes: I made an unfortunate acquaintance in Varadero this afternoon, and if Jerome hadn't happened to be there completely by chance, I'd no doubt be in a hospital at his moment — maybe even a morgue."

And, to Jerome's stupefaction, he told his mother about the incident in great detail, though omitting the part about his arranging to meet the man in the alley and instead making the whole thing look like a simple attempted robbery.

Francine turned to Jerome. "You knocked him cold with a rock?"

"Er...yes, ma'am. It just sort of happened. He would have come after me, too."

"My word, aren't you the brave one! *You'd* never do anything like that, would you, Felix?" she teased her son.

"I was done for, Mother!" said an irritated Felix in his defence. "He had me by the collar with one hand and was about to plunge his knife into my gut with the other! I'm not Superman!"

His mother shrugged and, bringing to her lips the straw in the great ball of a glass that had been placed in front of her, sipped her cocktail, eyes half-shut with pleasure.

"Okay, dearies," she said, raising her head after a moment, "I strongly advise you to lie low here at the hotel for the remainder of your holidays. You've not exactly made friends in the neighbourhood, to say the least. But what yarn did that man spin to get you into that alley, Felix? Was he going to give you an address, maybe? Or..."

"Now, Mother," interrupted Felix with an offhandedness that amazed Jerome, "in case you've forgotten, I'm an adult and have had all my shots. There's no call for you to go poking your nose into my private life."

She forced a laugh and dropped the subject. Jerome listened to this curious exchange between mother and son, trying to hide his astonishment. It was the mother who surprised him most. He'd never met a woman like her. Her air, her mannerisms, and her comportment all gave the impression that nothing could either surprise or dismay her; that the rules, regulations, and opinions of ordinary mortals were not only a matter of indifference to her, but trifles she'd never given a thought to in her life. And all this without ostentation or bravado: this was who she was, period. It was like being born with two arms and two legs: she'd taken note of them a long time ago but given them no further thought since.

Her cocktail done, Francine ordered a second. Then, turning towards Felix and Jerome, she said, "Same again, my angels?"

Jerome, who had just finished his drink, shook his head and stood up to take his leave. He wanted to stay sober in anticipation of the evening and — who knew? — the night he hoped to spend with his new acquaintance of the afternoon. After all, it never hurt to dream.

"You're going back to your girlfriend, I suppose?" asked Francine Desjarlais coyly.

"No, ma'am, I'm travelling alone. For the moment."

"Oh really? Too bad. Such a handsome young man." And then she added with a beguiling smile, "The Cuban sun always provides such inspiration — or so I'm told."

Jerome laughed. "I'm not short of inspiration, it's just the way things are."

"Well then, if you have nothing better to do, have dinner with us. You've saved my scoundrel son's life, and you should be suitably rewarded. Suite 1402, seven o'clock. We'll be expecting you."

Jerome hesitated.

"Yes, Jerome, do come," insisted Felix, no doubt wanting to avoid a one-on-one dinner date with his mother.

"We eat very well here, as you'll see. The kitchen always prepares something special for us, none of the dining room buffet fare — which isn't all that bad, if you'll permit me a little self-promotion. And they're not stingy with the booze, either."

Increasingly, Jerome found her vulgar, but it was a pleasant kind of vulgarity. He agreed to come and regretted that he'd done so immediately: it complicated his plans for the evening. Effectively, there was nothing to do but leave early if he was not to muck up his date with Eugenie Métivier. A bit rude, yes, but civility did not seem to be a quality Madame Desjarlais held in any esteem. She seemed, in her own way, as off the wall as her "angel" son.

He went to his room, took a shower, brushed his teeth and hair, changed, and then stepped out onto the balcony and leaned against the railing. It was almost five o'clock. From the seventh floor, the view of the sea and the surrounding countryside was commanding. As he watched, little pinpoints of light appeared and then disappeared on the foamy crests of the ocean. The deep, heavy, rhythmic sound of the waves said to him, "I'm always here. No need to hurry." Jerome sighed, relaxed his shoulders, and stretched out on the chaise longue the hotel had provided for its aficionados of indolence and the tropical heat.

He started to strategize in a detached and slightly ironical way. Presenting himself too early *chez la belle Eugenie* would make him seem like a starved puppy. But showing up late might be interpreted as indifference. Oh, why the hell had he accepted that dinner invitation? He was chasing two hares at once, as usual. That said, sometimes it was possible to catch both, and it was an extremely pleasant turn of events when one did. But in this case, which was the hare of choice — Felix or Eugenie? In fact, he'd buggered things up, no getting around it: he had to settle on a single target, and quickly.

He stood up and leaned on the railing again. For a time, he watched a band of unruly children chasing one another around the swimming pool as a tall, lean man in blue jogging gear waved his arms and tried to settle them down. Then, about three or four hundred metres farther out, at the end of a long *allée* of palm trees, the hotel's iron entrance gates opened to let in a yellow car he recognized as the one assigned to the group that had travelled to the sugar plantation. Suddenly he opted for a new approach and decided he would telephone Eugenie and inform her he'd had to accept an invitation to dinner—but that he'd be free mid-evening. In this way, he'd show himself to be both interested and independent, which seemed to him to be about right.

He let a quarter hour go by to give mother and daughter time to get to their room and then, his palms sweating a little, picked up the phone. Within seconds, he had the woman on the line.

"Oh, Monsieur Lupien," she said. "I was just about to call you."

Her "Monsieur Lupien" ran down his spine like a fistful of ice cubes.

"Is something the matter?" he asked, trying to keep his voice light.

"I'm afraid so," she said. "It's Andrée-Anne. I don't know if it was the sandwich she ate for lunch or the fall she had at the swimming pool, but the poor thing started vomiting just before we got back into the car. She has a bit of a fever now, and is complaining of a headache. I'm going to have to take her to the hotel doctor..."

She took a deep breath. "Unfortunately, I don't think we can get together this evening. I'm so sorry."

"Okay," said Jerome.

But something caved within him. Deep disappointment drained him of all his energy. What was going on? He'd never reacted this way to a cancelled date in all his long history of hooking up.

"It's a real shame," she said. "And we're leaving tomorrow morning, so—"

"Oh, well," he said, cutting her off. "Maybe another time."

"I'm...I'm very sorry, believe me. I..."

She faltered, stuck for a way to finish the sentence. Jerome waited and said nothing, searching in vain for the word that would let him hang up.

"Look," she said suddenly and with purpose, "if you'd like, Monsieur Lupien, perhaps we could get together in Montreal?"

"Really?" he said happily. "Well, that would be great."

"Let me give you my phone number, and...you're staying in Cuba until when, exactly?"

"I'm leaving in five days. And, Eugenie, while we're on it, maybe you could drop the 'Monsieur Lupien' and just call me Jerome."

She laughed. "I'm a bit shy, I guess, please excuse me. Do you have a pen and paper handy, *Jerome*?"

"I have everything I need."

He wrote down her number, said he hoped her daughter would improve, and wished them both a safe flight home, trying to hide his elation but also trepidation, and hung up. "Okay, Jerome, well done," he said with a sardonic smile. "Are you about to lose your head? Must be the effect of all this sun—and self-restraint!"

In the end, things hadn't turned out too badly. Instead of cashing in on his efforts right away, he'd staked a claim that would come to him soon enough, although, unfortunately, having to wait left him in a state of frustration more acute than ever.

"Having kids sure puts a damper on your sex life," he grumbled, going back out onto the balcony. "What the hell, though, it's not the first time I've had a dry spell... Meanwhile, I'll just have to take myself in hand, put this damn thing to rest. She's a plucky little thing, though, this young mother, and very attractive. Well worth the wait, I think."

"Oh yeah?" said a mocking voice in his head. "Do you really believe what you just said?"

He lay down on the chaise longue and fell asleep. An amazing game of golf (he'd never played golf in his life) began to make him groan; his hands clenched, his legs began to tremble. Then the sudden, deafening cry of a gull woke him up with a start; the bird seemed to have brushed his head in passing. With a beating heart he watched it fly off into the distance, then quickly glanced at his watch.

"Holy shit! I'm going to be late."

He dashed into his room, brushed his hair at the mirror, then hurried up to the suite occupied by Madame Desjarlais, a partner in the hotel and a jocular parvenue, and her son Felix — a serious contender, from all appearances, for the title of hothead.

"BEWARE, MY FRIEND," murmured Felix as he opened the door. "Mother's on the rampage."

Jerome wanted to know more, but Felix put a finger to his lips.

"She's waiting for us in the living room," he said, leading Jerome towards a pair of large frosted-glass doors. He opened one and stepped aside to allow Jerome to enter.

Madame Desjarlais was stretched out on a sofa, her feet up on a hassock, a newspaper spread on her lap. She held a martini glass in one hand and a cigarette in the other.

"So, you're punctual," she said, sarcastically, "that's something in your favour."

Since she was silhouetted against the light of the large bay window looking out over a terrace, Jerome couldn't make out her facial features, making her sharp tongue seem sharper.

He bowed his head and sputtered, "I hope nothing terrible has happened...I'd feel awful if..."

"If what? What has Felix told you?"

"Nothing, Mother, I've not said a thing to him. I thought I'd leave that pleasure to you."

"Some pleasure! Go on, sit down," she said, gesturing towards a sofa. "What'll you have to drink? Beer? Wine? A martini? Rum?"

She softened her tone.

"I've got a Barbancourt Grande Réserve I can safely say is pretty good."

"Thank you, I'll have some of that, then."

Felix went to a small cart laden with bottles, poured rum into a couple of glasses, then went to sit next to Jerome on the sofa and handed him one of the drinks.

"So, guess what, my dear Jerome," Madame Desjarlais began. "My son's foolishness and your subsequent heroics this afternoon just cost me $1,800 U.S."

Jerome sensed that her anger, though genuine enough, was part of a carefully laid-out scenario.

"What happened, ma'am?" he asked *sotto voce* and not meeting her gaze.

"You can call me Francine, Jerome. No more of this 'ma'am' stuff, it makes me feel like an old harpy."

Jerome smiled. "Of course."

"Anyway," she continued, "an hour or so after we saw you in the bar, a police officer came and knocked at my door. Someone, it turns out, jotted down the licence number of Felix's car and reported it to the police. The captain wanted to question my adorable little boy here, but luckily he was in the shower at the time. We discussed the matter for a good half-hour—I couldn't get rid of him and was in a total sweat, I tell you!—and finally I managed to slip him all the cash I had on me at the time, and he left after giving me a smart salute."

Felix, after giving Jerome a sheepish look, winced and knocked back a large swig of rum.

"What about the guy I—well, knocked out?" asked Jerome antsily. "How is he?"

"Not good. He's in the hospital. Intensive care."

"Will he be all right?"

"I certainly, certainly hope so, my dear. It's also possible the policeman was exaggerating the whole thing in order to squeeze more money out of me, but I wasn't about to ask any more questions, you understand."

She took a long drag of her cigarette, then studied the smoke as it floated and swirled in the air before slowly disappearing, as if what they'd been discussing was inconsequential. "My husband hates cigarettes," she said. "He's not here, so I smoke as much as I like."

"If he'd seen how much you've been smoking these past few days, Mother," said Felix, grinning, "he'd probably divorce you."

She stared at him for a few seconds, as if preparing to reply, then apparently thought better of it.

"Well," she said, getting to her feet, "Carla must have our dinner ready by now—let's eat. Are you hungry, my little lambs?"

She strode towards the doors opening onto the terrace, slid them open, and, the two young men in her wake, led them to a pergola almost buried by the luxurious growth of plants climbing from several clay pots arranged around it. A table had been set for three in the shade of its arbour, and on it was an enormous platter of seafood and crudités basking in the glow of two tall candles, their flames fluttering in the warm and humid air.

"Mother's going whole hog this evening," Felix murmured into his companion's ear. "You've really caught her eye, if you don't mind my saying."

A young Cuban woman, her skin very black, appeared at the door, with her hands behind her back and a smile on her lips. She was dressed in the hotel uniform and the lace-bordered apron of a dining-room maid, but was wearing a pair of elegant high-heeled shoes that seemed to set her in a class apart; Jerome was quite taken by her natural beauty. After a brief exchange in Spanish with Madame Desjarlais, she bowed, went inside, and returned with a bottle of Champagne in an ice bucket.

"Tonight, we celebrate with Champagne," said Madame Desjarlais, indicating where she wanted Jerome to sit and then addressing Felix. "It's important," she said, "to know how to thank someone who has rendered the kind of service this young man did you, Felix. I wonder, you little rascal, how I manage to put up with your shenanigans."

"Well then, thank you, kind sir," said Felix, giving a clownishly exaggerated bow to Jerome, who didn't quite know how to respond.

The meal started with a toast, which Jerome accepted with appropriate modesty. If he'd worried the night would be tedious, he needn't have done. Madame Desjarlais drank freely, talked openly, and seemed to know how to live well. Jerome was struck by the contrast between her behaviour during dinner and the cutting remarks she'd made to her son earlier. She proved to be a remarkable raconteur with an inexhaustible repertoire of comic and sometimes quite improper stories that she delivered with the polish of a professional salesman. Many of them were unfamiliar to her son, who laughed at them constantly. That said, Felix held his own. He amused himself by teasing his mother with his own mordant wit, and Jerome realized the son was clearly not the airhead he'd thought. The dinner proceeded gaily, and Carla brought a second bottle of Champagne. From time to time, apropos of nothing, Francine quizzed Jerome about his life, his tastes, the university courses he'd taken, and his plans for the future. She was particularly impressed by his degree in literature.

"What about you?" asked Jerome, a bit tipsy. "You must have a profession or do something, no?"

"My husband is in business," she replied. "I help him out when I can."

"As a general helps his soldiers," laughed Felix. "Boom! Boom! She beats the drum."

"Say what you like," said Francine, who then turned to Jerome. "My husband, Severin, is a financial consultant specializing in public relations, things of that nature. This hotel in Cuba is my own little folly. He hardly ever comes here, poor man, he's been twice in eight years. What can you do? He's a workaholic who doesn't know how to enjoy life. When he does finally learn—poof! It'll be too late."

"Maybe he enjoys life when you're not there, Mother," observed Felix wickedly.

She stared at her son for a second, frowned, and then pointed to the nearly empty Champagne bottle and signalled for him to order a third.

"And you, Jerome," she asked, "are you enjoying your Cuban vacation?"

"I'm trying to," he said, with a sigh, "but luck hasn't been with me, I'm afraid." He rubbed his hands nervously, sighed again, and, the Champagne opening doors in him that normally he would have kept closed, he elaborated. "Tonight, for example, I'd arranged a rendezvous with a really lovely woman — and when I say *really lovely*, believe me, I know. But unfortunately she has her little daughter with her, and just before I came here I discovered that our plans were mucked up because the dear little thing has come down with a fever. And they're leaving in the morning!"

"How frustrating for you, my sweet."

"No kidding! I could chew the edge of this table."

She laughed and placed a hand on his arm: "Some things can be arranged," she said, smiling enigmatically.

She said nothing more, and Jerome, though intrigued, didn't dare ask what she meant.

JEROME LEFT AROUND ten o'clock, his head spinning so much he decided to go for a walk on the beach to help dissipate the effects of the Champagne. On his way out, he stopped at the bar and drank two large glasses of cold water to try to quench his terrible thirst.

At that time of night, the beach was deserted. A tremendous roar issued from the sea, imperceptible in the darkness, drowning out all other sounds and speaking to him of solitude and things everlasting. He took off his shoes and socks and put them in one of the cabanas placed at the edge of the beach for clients needing a bit of shade, then walked along the edge of the waves that crashed at his feet, and sometimes reached up to his calves. Now and then he looked up at the cloudless sky. And the sky, like cloudless skies everywhere, spread its mysterious expanse of silent stars above him, as it had done since the beginning of time.

Then he did what people often do in such circumstances: he began to take stock of his life. He hadn't meant to conduct such an examination, but it came over him forcefully, directing his thoughts, affecting his mood. As he furiously kicked at the gentle waves lapping about his feet, insistent, taunting questions consumed his mind. Where was he heading in life? He had no plans, no attachments, lived day to day, his mind tormented by trifles. What kind of man would he be in twenty years? What would people think of him, himself included? Had not the insignificant ways of the ordinary citizen, the run-of-the-mill consumer, not already planted its seed, transforming him into just another of the faceless individuals one meets every day on the street, on the subway, at the barbershop or the grocery story — everywhere one looked — people who mouthed nothing but platitudes with preposterous sobriety? How could he avoid such a banal existence? Did he even want to avoid it? What would he do when he got back to Montreal? Teaching didn't appeal to him. If he wanted to become a journalist he would need contacts, and he had none. Go back to being a waiter in a café again? The idea sickened him. Should he continue his studies? Send out eighty-seven random resumés? To whom? And to apply for what?

"Enough of this!" he thought. A catatonic listlessness

crept over him. He needed to sleep. He turned on his heels, retrieved his shoes and socks, and headed back to the hotel, staggering with fatigue.

With his heavy head and fumbling fingers, it took him a while to unlock the door to his room. Finally, it opened. The fetid air, what with the air conditioner off, pinched at his nostrils. He went over to the French doors and opened them wide, then decided to take a shower. He felt as though his skin would stick to the sheets if he didn't. He stood for a long time under the warm water. It did him some good. Then he turned it off and lay down on the bed.

He was punching his pillow into a comfortable shape when the phone rang. A flood of sinister thoughts washed over him: the police wanted him for questioning, his father had suffered a heart attack, the hotel was on fire.

"Hello?"

"Oh, you're there, finally," said a woman's voice. "Give me a moment, I'll be right up."

"You'll be — who is this, please?"

"It's a surprise," replied the voice, laughing. "And not one I think you'll regret."

There was a click; whoever it was had hung up.

Sitting on the edge of his bed, he lost himself in conjecture. He hadn't known Eugenie Métivier for long, but he didn't think it had been her voice. The woman on the phone spoke with a faint Spanish accent, one he couldn't place. She was either a Québécoise who'd lived in Cuba for a long time, or a Spanish woman who'd lived in Quebec. Suddenly he realized he was naked, and that someone was coming up to see him. He turned on a bedside lamp and hurried to the closet. He'd barely thrown on a bathrobe when there was a knock on the door.

"Yes?" he called out, trying to imbue his voice with confidence.

"It's me," sang the unknown woman.

He opened the door and was fixed to the spot, stupefied.

A ravishing woman with long, blond hair stood before him, a smile on her lips and made up like a movie star. Her slinky blue satin dress was very short, her patent-leather shoes had spike heels, and her diamond necklace sparkled in a décolletage that descended into a bulging bosom such as he could only fantasize about, a musky perfume emanating from her body. Her flashy elegance fell just short of vulgarity, and the combined effect was clear: "Pleasure for sale for those who can afford it!"

Jerome had never consorted with such a high-class escort and was embarrassed. "I think you must have the wrong room," he said, smiling timidly.

"And me, I don't think I do," she said mischievously. "You're Jerome, right?"

He nodded.

"Well, then, you're the one I've come to see."

She stepped closer.

"Anyway, from the description I was given I'd have recognized you. The handsome young man in room 712, that's you. Mind if I come in?"

She smiled and moved closer still, closing the door behind her.

"I've come to give your holiday a boost," she cooed in a voice as smooth as silk. "And don't worry, dear, it's on the house."

"On the house? I don't understand. You mean—"

"I mean the hotel is taking care of the tab, my pet, and I'm taking care of you."

She placed her left hand between his legs. He stepped back as if he'd been burned with a branding iron. He thought things over for a moment as his face turned red and then, in a spontaneous change of mind, seized the woman by the shoulders and looked at her in wonder.

"Jesus," he said, "you're the most fuckable woman I've ever seen."

"Glad you think so," she said, laughing, "because that's exactly what I'm here to do."

He kissed her neck, her chest, then pressed his hungry mouth to her lips.

"Oh," she countered, stepping back. "I see the knight has raised his lance, and what a nice one it is! ¡Va haber accion! Do you mind if I use your bathroom?"

"Make yourself at home. But first tell me your name."

"Hilda. I'll be all yours in two minutes."

He sat on the bed and looked down at the carpet, then at his rigid, purple-tipped erection. He felt he was in a dream. Francine Desjarlais had certainly found an original way to thank him. Should he take his bathrobe off now? What did it matter? It would come to the same thing in the end. He threw it on the floor, but decided not to stretch out on the bed right away, it would be too corny.

Hilda (surely a nom-de-lit) came out of the bathroom wearing nothing but a slip and a black lace bra. The effect was rapturous, her animal beauty magnified a thousandfold. Jerome, intimidated once again, cleared his throat.

Despite a pain in her neck that had been bothering her all day, the prostitute continued to smile at him with all her coquettish charm. Truth to tell, she would rather have been spending the night at home, but she had to satisfy this young stallion, this was what she was being paid for, and well. He would probably want to go at it two or three times. *C'est la vie.* At least he wasn't repellent, as were certain regulars she'd had to put up with.

They made love rapidly — too rapidly for Jerome's liking — then lay in the darkened room and talked. He asked about her life. That happened to her often, and she had her answers at the ready. In her line of work, she couldn't get around it. But as she liked him, she lied much less than was her habit.

Jerome had been right. She was born in Quebec but had lived in Cuba for a decade. In Montreal, she'd studied at the Conservatory of Dramatic Arts, landing small roles here and there before realizing that life on the stage was not for her. She first came to Cuba as a tourist, but Fate smiled on her almost immediately and she'd been able to create a comfortable niche for herself thanks to some top-level civil servants. All she'd had to do was be careful, and discreet, and things turned out very well.

"Do you have anything to drink?" she asked him, lying back on the bed.

He did not. She adored Champagne. He had a bottle sent up and they drank two glasses before making love again. He felt as though he were in an American movie.

"For you, the bar is always open, my sweet," she said, running her hand over his ass. "Don't be shy. I like making love with you. Could you pour me some more Champagne? When I drink Champagne with a handsome guy like you, I'm in seventh heaven."

He didn't question the sincerity of her flattering remarks. Pleasure overrode everything, and the pleasure was intense. She was an expert in the field, and she was also good company. There was in her the kind of joyful, if uneasy, tension that is often found in beautiful women in their mid-thirties able to appear ten years younger.

By 3:20 in the morning they had made love four times.

"My God," she said playfully, "you're *insatiable*! I don't know about you, but I'm getting a little sleepy."

So was he, to be honest. A rest would do them both good. He nibbled and sucked her breasts one last time, then settled in beside her and fell asleep like an anvil falling into the sea.

At six o'clock he awoke with a start, in bed alone. The French doors were still open, and he could hear the hiss of a pesticide sprayer in the distance. There was no one on the balcony or in the bathroom. Discreetly, she had gone.

JEROME RAN INTO Felix a few times before heading home to Montreal, but saw Francine Desjarlais only once more — the morning after his night with the beauteous Hilda. Although he was unaware of it at the time, the few words they exchanged in the dining room's morning bustle would have huge consequences later in his life.

"So, Jerome? Did you have a good night?" asked Francine, with a smile that made him turn as pink as a virgin.

"Very good, ma'am, thank you for asking," he said, looking down at his feet. "I was just going to phone you to..."

But he stopped, ill at ease and afraid of seeming crass if he went into details, or a jerk if he didn't show at least some acknowledgement of the gift.

"Oh, it's a good thing you didn't call that early," she said, amused by his embarrassment. "Felix is still snoring his head off. It seems he doesn't have your head for Champagne."

"Er, it wasn't Felix I wanted to speak to, it was you. In any case, thank you very much."

"Getting a good night's sleep is so important for good

health," she went on with an ambiguous smile, "even more so for an *intellectual* such as yourself. And sometimes you have to go to great lengths, you understand. Anyway, I like you, you've got spunk, which is not something I see all that often in this world. Here," she said, fishing a card from her bag and handing it to him. "Give me a call if you feel like it when you get back to Montreal. I'd like you to meet my husband. You never know, he might have something to offer."

"I won't let you down, ma'am," he said as a drop of sweat burned its way into his left eye. He watched her walk towards the door with a quick, sharp gait, as if she'd spent the previous night drinking nothing but water.

Judging by Felix's comportment when Jerome ran into him at the swimming pool that afternoon, the young man knew nothing of the singular reward his mother had accorded her son's saviour. He talked about the terrible headache that had tortured him until noon, promising himself he would never drink Champagne again (a wine he'd always found insipid), and then, between dives, he talked about a project he'd been nurturing for several months; all he needed now was his father's endorsement.

"I want to launch a start-up of the future, my friend," he said. *"Electronic cigarettes."*

"Uh, well . . ."

"You don't smoke, do you?"

Jerome shook his head.

"Have you ever?"

"I stopped three years ago, after a bout of bronchitis that lasted half the winter."

"Lightweight. Me, I've been smoking since I was thirteen. But I've cut down a lot in the last four months. Now, I vape."

"Vape?"

"Yeah, vape. I'd give you a demonstration, but I don't have any more cartridges."

He explained how an electronic cigarette worked. Jerome had never heard of such a thing. Unlike an ordinary cigarette, an e-cigarette produced not smoke but a vapour that looked like smoke—hence the origin of the term, to vape. It ran on a lithium battery, and the vapour could contain a certain amount of nicotine, a little or a lot or none at all— but, most importantly, no carcinogenic tar.

"It's perfect if you want to quit smoking without quitting. You can gradually cut down on the amount of nicotine and still enjoy the old smoker's ritual, know what I mean? The cigarette after dinner, the cigarette after sex, the cigarette after a big emotional crisis…I've been researching the subject for months. The market is taking off big time, and there's a ton of money to be made in it. Everyone wants to stop smoking, but most of us never manage. This is a helping hand."

"Hmm. Big plans," said Jerome, irony in his voice. "You sound like Mother Teresa. For someone who smokes hash, you talk a good game."

Felix laughed and punched him on the shoulder.

"Enough with the goofy comments," he said. "This e-cigarette can also help free me from hashish, my friend. All I need is a bit of willpower. There are times, I admit, when I smoke too much of it. It cuts me off from reality, which isn't good. But anyway, when you get back to Montreal, come over to our place and have a look at the different models I've bought. I tell you, Jerome, this is the next big thing!"

Jerome happily accepted the invitation. It provided him with an entrée into a milieu he'd always found intriguing but that had been inaccessible to him until now: the world of the big-time movers and shakers.

MONTREAL

THE DAY AFTER his return to Montreal, Jerome felt he should see his parents. An early warm spell had rid the city of ice, leaving the streets and sidewalks littered with dark splotches that dried as you watched. He showed up the same day as the postcard he'd sent from Cuba a week earlier, and his parents welcomed him with a joy and tenderness that did not quite conceal their growing concern over the bohemian life he'd been leading for a while, now.

He brought a gift for his mother — a CD by Ernesto Lecuona — and for his father, a classic bottle of rum aged in oak. He'd bought a terracotta devil's head for Marcel, but he was still at school and wouldn't see it until later in the afternoon, when Jerome would already be gone.

Marie-Rose wanted Jerome to stay for dinner, but after two weeks away, he had too many things to take care of and explained he couldn't stay that long. He promised he'd come back in a day or two.

"And so," Claude-Oscar risked asking when Jerome was at the door, "what are your plans, my boy?" The same question could be read in the worried eyes of his mother as she stood behind his father.

"Oh, I've got one or two irons in the fire," Jerome replied, looking away. "I'll tell you about them soon enough."

He bid adieu to his parents and walked away from the house quickly. He had laundry to do, a fridge to replenish, an answering machine to empty, dozens of emails to read — and, no doubt, bills to pay. But, first and foremost, he was impatient to tell his friend Charlie about the trip. After all, it wasn't every day you knocked a thief out in an alley and then spent the night with a first-class bombshell who'd have given the statue of Jean de Brébeuf a hard-on. Not to mention the pretty dietitian from the Metro chain who'd like to open her own grocery store for him — and whose heart was no doubt leaping every time her phone rang.

Charlie had to work overtime that night, so he wasn't able to see Jerome. But, given his friend's impatience, he agreed to have a quick bite at a small restaurant near the old Jean-Talon subway station, a few steps from his office. He said he could spare forty-five minutes.

Around six o'clock the two friends were seated at a table in a Pizza Pizza, on rue Jean-Talon. Charlie congratulated Jerome on his Cuban tan and his healthy glow. He'd swapped his gelled shark's fin for an Iroquois cut that made him look a bit fierce, but that hadn't prevented him — the first news he shared with Jerome — from making a conquest of the new receptionist in his office. And their affair was going very well.

"But you," he went on, looking closely at Jerome, "if I'm not mistaken, I'd say you've put on a few pounds."

"Oh? Maybe because of the Champagne. I drank quite a lot of it, I guess."

And then he recounted his adventures in Varadero. Charlie listened, mouth agape, unable to utter a word. It's what Jerome had hoped for; his triumph was now complete.

"Has anyone ever told you," Charlie finally managed to utter, "that you are...completely nuts, my poor friend?"

"That's jealousy speaking," sneered Jerome. "Look at you, you're frothing at the mouth with envy. You wouldn't have minded fucking my little Minute Maid yourself, would you?"

"Who wouldn't? That's not the point. Did you think for a second, for a single second, of the risks you were taking? You committed a *criminal act*, my good man, and for *what*? To save the skin of a suspect stranger who's probably fed up with having you on his conscience, a mama's boy who'll want to square things with you as soon as possible. Never mind the fact that Fidel's prisons aren't exactly five-star hotels. They may be easy to get into, but getting out is another matter. And now, on top of it all, you want to see his slut of a mother—who, if you ask me, is probably a part of the criminal underworld."

Jerome put a hand on his arm. "*Calma, calma,* Charlie. If I get the feeling there's anything risky, I'll back out and that's that."

Charlie shook his head, his expression grave.

"Like it or not, Jerome, you're in it up to your ears. It's like someone has twisted a hook in your back. That Desjarlais woman can drag you anywhere she wants, any time."

"You forget," retorted Jerome, "that her sonny-boy is just as implicated as I am."

"No, he isn't, Jerome. You're the aggressor in the affair, Felix, he was just the victim, a stooge who wanted to buy drugs, though a victim all the same. As far as Felix is concerned, his is just another story of someone scoring some hash—but you, you might have added murder to your fine list of achievements. Have you thought about that?"

"Oh, come on, she would have told me. And fine, let's suppose, if it makes you feel any better, that's what happened. Now the police have her payola in their pockets. And she won't be saying anything, so don't worry."

"Maybe," said Charlie, exasperated. "But you never know, your good lady might get it into her head to turn you in. Why wouldn't she? What do you know of her? Nothing, except that she's okay with hiring prostitutes. At any rate, if I were you I'd stay away from all of them—her, her son, and all the others. Jesus, I would!"

He jabbed his fork into his last piece of pizza assertively, carefully cut off the crust with his knife (he hated crusts), and finished his meal in two bites.

"Gotta go, Jerome," he said as he rose. "I'm swamped at work. Think about what I said and, while you're at it, you could set about finding a job. It'll take your mind off things—especially off insane ideas—and it probably wouldn't do your bank account any harm, either."

Jerome looked annoyed. The day's quota of judicious counsel had been met. They shook hands and Jerome, brooding, watched his friend depart and finished his coffee.

AFTER NINE HOURS of the sleep of the dead, Jerome woke up tense, grumpy, and disoriented. He threw on his dressing gown and walked around his apartment, randomly moving objects about and then returning them to where they'd been. He pressed his tongue to the front of his mouth and ran it across his teeth, grimacing. The night had left a bad taste in his mouth. Was it his conversation with Charlie? A dark battle seemed to be raging within him, but he couldn't put his finger on what it was about.

He finally shuffled into the kitchen, turned on the coffee maker (a Christmas gift from his parents the previous year), made himself a strong espresso, and sipped it as he stood at the window, smirking at his neighbour dismantling his Tempo carport, the plastic sanctuary that protected his 2001 Ford from the rigours of a Montreal winter. Charlie's worries still seemed exaggerated, if not infantile. Poor kid, despite the Mohawk do, his brain was going soft. The way he was headed, he'd soon be afraid to step outside after dark.

Still feeling crotchety, he took a shower and got dressed. His cantankerous mood persisted and was hampering his usual top-of-the-morning good cheer. Opening his wallet to count his cash — Charlie was right, his resources were dwindling — Jerome came across a slip of paper and unfolded it: it was Eugenie Métivier's phone number.

And that's when everything was illuminated.

He'd meant to call her as soon as he got back. But if the interest she'd shown in him hadn't evaporated since her return to Montreal, then naturally she'd want to know about his life, his tastes, his preoccupations, and sooner or later she'd ask him how he got by. "Oh," he'd have to reply, "I'm sort of between things right now, but something will turn up soon."

And he didn't like that answer. It put him in a bad light. He wanted her to think highly of him, which meant he wasn't seeing her as just a one-night stand. And, if that was the case, then he'd have screwed up royally! Alternatively, he might tell her flat-out lies. But why did he want her to have a high opinion of him? What was happening? For it to be so important that he shine in her eyes, then it followed that he must have a bloody high opinion of her. Something like that, anyway. Except that no, it wasn't that, there must be something else going on. You can't have a high opinion of someone you barely know, any more than you can love a book you haven't read. *Love*. Right. He'd said it. The inveterate word: the word that had inspired millions of phrases, caused millions of books to be written, made rivers run, and rivers of tears be shed. Love had brought on fevers, chills, sighs, insomnia, duels, trances, and delirious pleasures—and caused billions and billions of bone-headed gaffes. *Calme toi*, Jerome, *calme toi*. Take one step at a time. Sure, he found her attractive. But no more so than a lot of other women. In truth, even at the Iberostar he'd seen better turned-out women than her, and not all of them struck him as unattainable. And he wasn't counting all the pretty young things he'd come across ever since puberty had started to work on him, some of whom had been so radioactively beautiful they'd haunted him for days and even in bed, given that's what we're actually talking about. So the question remained: What was different this time? Had he swallowed some kind of love potion? Was he living his own version of Tristan and Iseult? Such bedtime stories were utter hogwash, of course. Four or five years earlier he'd read Joseph Bédier's adaptation of the famous legend, and all he remembered of it was being so incredibly bored that his neck had hurt. He recalled the two lovers, gazing into each other's eyes as dazed and confused as if they'd been in a car crash, and, standing behind them, King Mark—who, despite his grand airs, had struck him as a laughable cuckold. Poor Bédier would have been disappointed by Jerome's response to his work, and Wagner, who had written a whole opera about the unfortunate couple, would have sent him packing. But whose fault was that? He found these sorts of romances about as moving as a handful of rusty nails rolling at the bottom of a garbage pail.

In fact, the only love story he'd ever lived through — and unrequited! — had been when he was seventeen, towards the end of high school. The object of his desire — she'd had magnificent blond hair that reached down the middle of her back and bounced around on her beautiful ass — had, after a few furtive kisses and dozens of letters back and forth in their three-week correspondence, laughed in his face in front of everyone when during recess he'd asked her to the prom. Oh, the bitch! He could have strangled her! That said, he'd chosen his moment well: it had been a Friday, and the weekend was about to begin. Sweating in his shame and rage, he'd gone straight home and given himself two extra days off school, pretending to be sick. By the time he went back to class, everything seemed to have been forgotten — and he pretended to have forgotten the matter, too. But the public humiliation she'd inflicted on him had instilled in Jerome's future relationships with women a deliberate, cynical *froideur*. He'd comport himself with the utmost care, nurturing the wariness he felt with subterfuges and manipulations and developing a hunter's instinct for firing only when he was sure of his target. By degrees, this tactic bore fruit. Over time, he'd perfected his techniques, and learned as much from his failures as from his successes; the prophylactic distance he maintained between himself and the women he coveted seemed to work on just about anybody.

There had been dry spells, of course, when nothing seemed to work — when he appeared to have lost his touch — and there were also times when no woman attracted him, as if he'd lost his taste for the chase completely. When that happened, he'd go back to his books, to the Internet, to swimming and bike rides, and spend long nights in bars and cafés talking with friends. But those periods never lasted long, and over the months and years he'd ended up with the reputation of a ladykiller he found not at all displeasing. Truth to tell, from time to time he would thank, *sotto voce*, the little blond-haired pain in the ass for having taught him a valuable lesson in love.

But this morning, where did he find himself? In the situation he hated most: he was the trembling supplicant, alternately drawn and blushing at the thought of a woman among so many others whom he'd met at a hotel in Cuba, a woman he couldn't get out of his mind. What a business! Maybe he was just horny? There'd been a few such cases, and he could take them or leave them, the last woman freeing him from the spell of the one before. But it wasn't that. He had a feeling that even if, at the start, things were only so-so in bed, the important consideration was this: *he needed her in order to go on living*—or, at least, to feel alive. What a dangerous, ridiculous situation. What an appalling dependency. And the cause of it all, it seemed to him, was not anything in her, *but in him*. When, for instance, he left the kitchen and went the bathroom to check himself in the mirror, he could see the problem was still there, looking right back at him! Unless he was very much mistaken, he'd *fallen in love*. And with a woman burdened with a child like a litter of puppies. How well chosen was that word *fallen*! Whoever invented that term had hit the nail on the head. Because it really was a fall. Or, more so, a nosedive. He was tumbling down a steep slope, scraping his elbows, ass and knees on a scree of gravel without the faintest idea of what was waiting for him at the bottom.

Yeah, well, maybe his plan to take a long journey through

South America as the icing on the cake of his sabbatical year hadn't been such a bad idea after all. But he didn't have the money for it now. And even supposing his finances did permit it, there was no guarantee that the vision of his porcelain mother and child would leave him. It was intolerable! A wave of anger commingled with fear swelled up inside him. Sitting at the kitchen table, his espresso cold in front of him, he breathed with difficulty, his face turning red, his hands sweating. He jumped to his feet and, filled with resolve, went into the bedroom. He stripped, laid himself out on the bed, and, brow furrowed in concentration, diligently started to masturbate in an attempt to free himself. Relief came slowly, as he had trouble focusing. After three or four minutes, he sighed and groaned and lay staring up at the ceiling, eyes half-closed, a warm stream dripping down his thigh. The feeling was disagreeable. Still lying on his back, he reached for a box of tissues beside the bed and carefully wiped himself, then closed his eyes. He was almost asleep when some sort of internal commotion abruptly pushed him to his feet.

"You're a fucking idiot," he mumbled with scornful derision. "Letting a passing fancy take over your life...a fucking idiot."

A few minutes later, dressed again, he went back into the kitchen, made himself another espresso, and, after hesitating briefly, called Felix Sicotte.

JUST SEVENTEEN AT the time, Charlie Plamondon had met Jerome on a July Saturday morning after Jerome, riding his bicycle down the middle of rue Ontario, ran over a shard of glass from a broken bottle and crashed spectacularly. Jerome had managed to get up — completely stunned, blood dripping from his elbow — with cars wheeling around him as if nothing had happened. It was one of those days when the register of human solidarity was at an all-time low.

But the low didn't apply to Charlie, who ran towards the fallen cyclist, directed traffic away from him, then helped Jerome drag his bike to the sidewalk.

"Jesus," muttered Jerome, sponging blood from his elbow with a paper towel he'd found in his pocket, "what the hell did I hit?"

Despite his obvious attempt to appear stoic, Jerome couldn't dispel the anguish in his face. The cut on his elbow was three inches long and undoubtedly required stitches.

"Your tire is pretty well shot," observed Charlie, seemingly more interested in the technical side of the accident. "Do you live far from here?"

"Yeah, far enough...31st Avenue, near Beaubien."

Charlie smiled elatedly.

"Well, you're in luck," he said. "My father works in a garage close to here. He's a mechanic. He can fix your tire and you can ride your bike home."

"I don't have much money," said Jerome. "Maybe two bucks. And I should find a pharmacy and buy a bandage for my elbow."

While they talked, large drops of blood spattered on the sidewalk, each splash quickly bordered by a circle of dark red dust.

"Don't worry about that, they've got a first-aid kit at the garage. As for the tire, we'll figure something out."

And grabbing the handlebar, Charlie pushed the bike along the sidewalk with his head high, as self-satisfied as the Good Samaritan taken aback by his own generosity.

Seeing the two teenagers come in, Normand Plamondon

lifted his head from beneath the hood of the Ford he was working on, great puffs of steam rising from it, gave a whistle of surprise, and approached the two of them. He was a small, barrel-chested, and lively man with a brown, prematurely aged face and a curious way of walking with his head thrust forward, as though he were about to pounce on something.

"You okay, friend?" he called in a loud, piercing voice without bothering to look at his son.

The huge bloodstain on Jerome's white T-shirt gave his arrival a dramatic effect.

The salt-and-pepper head of a sixty-year-old man appeared in a door to an office. The man raised his eyebrows, snorted, then disappeared with a grunt that could have meant anything.

Five minutes later, Jerome's elbow was disinfected and bandaged, and the bicycle tire well on its way to being repaired.

"Go across the street and get a coffee, boys," Normand Plamondon told them in a low voice. "Bossman don't like people hanging around the garage. It's a wonder he let me work on the bike."

Charlie was about to say they weren't *hanging around*, but the circumstances didn't lend themselves to prolonged discussion. He led his companion to the small corner coffee shop on the other side of the street.

Which is where things began to liven up. The boys had already introduced themselves, but now they became more fully acquainted. Charlie's family lived in the area, on rue Wolfe. At the time of the accident, he'd been running an errand for his mother, who was a cashier in a nearby Dollarama. The young man, who had an easygoing manner, had confided that his mother didn't like her job but, not having found anything better in the vicinity, had to resign herself to it, since the family's financial situation wasn't good. His father had once owned his own garage but had declared bankruptcy three years earlier and the trustees had squeezed the last penny out of him, as trustees tend to do. Now he worked for a hard-ass who paid him next to nothing.

"And I can tell you he's not exactly a charmer, to put it mildly! If he fucking smiled even once, I swear his face would crack! I'm surprised he didn't come yapping after my papa just now. It was probably your bloodstained T-shirt that shut him up."

Jerome listened and tried to hide his astonishment. It was the first time he'd heard the tribulations of the rank and file described with such brutal candour.

"What about you? What does your old man do?"

"My father?" Jerome corrected. "He's a denturist. He makes dentures, you understand? And my mother teaches piano — classical music."

Many young people who, privileged by birth and whose opinions are based on a handful of received ideas and barely understood experiences, have a sometimes simplistic view of life. That was the case with Jerome. He felt he was in the company of one of a large family of losers, someone condemned to a limited life because he'd never had any prospects, whereas Jerome — there was no other way to put it — was one of those whose natural destiny was to succeed.

"I see," said Charlie with a tinge of sarcasm in his voice. "Aren't you the lucky bastard. Born with a silver spoon in your mouth."

And for a second, they eyed each other like sparring partners.

"No need to exaggerate," said Jerome, opting for modesty. "Our house isn't even paid for yet."

Then he remembered he was the debtor of the two and, wanting to show a more sensitive side, added, "I'm sure things will pick up for your dad. He's just going through a bad patch."

"I don't think so," sighed Charlie. "He's always been dogged by bad luck."

Charlie shook his head as if to rid himself of an unpleasant thought. "Shall we head back?" he said, standing up. "Your tire should be fixed by now."

Jerome tried to pay for the coffee, but Charlie stopped him. In an abrupt, curt tone, he said, "No. Let me. It's my pleasure."

What an odd little squabble, thought Jerome. We don't even know each other.

The bicycle, propped up against a garbage bin, was waiting for them. Charlie's father came over, wiping his hands on an oily rag.

"If it was up to me, my friend, I wouldn't charge you," he whispered. "It didn't take me more than ten minutes, but I'm not the owner here. So I have to charge you five bucks."

Jerome blushed. "I don't have it on me," he said, "but if you can wait a few—"

"I'll lend you the money," interrupted Charlie with a vindicated air.

"No, no," replied Jerome, increasingly annoyed. "You've done enough already. I'll just hop on my bike and bring you the cash in half an hour."

"*Normand!*" called a grouchy voice from the back of the garage. "I need a boiler!"

"I'll let you guys figure it out," said Plamondon *père*. "You have to pay at the counter," he added, looking at Jerome. He pointed to the door where, some twenty minutes earlier, the owner's salt-and-pepper head had appeared, and which, at that very moment, reappeared, looking about the garage like a policeman's flashlight sweeping the scene of a crime.

Charlie hurried towards the man with his five-dollar bill in hand, while Jerome, with a shrug of his shoulders, took his bike and went out to wait on the sidewalk.

He was furious at this stranger smothering him with devotion, but at the same time felt guilty for feeling that way: How could anyone take offence at such kindness? He was being flooded with good deeds; any more and they'd drown him.

Charlie, smiling, came out of the garage exuding an air of satisfaction. Jerome forced himself to return the smile.

"Thanks again, eh. You're cool. I'll go home and get the money and be back with it as soon as I can. Can you wait a bit?"

"Sure, take your time," said Charlie. "I'm not going anywhere."

And then he nodded his head like a serf before his master.

Thirty-nine minutes later, Jerome came to a halt in front of the garage, out of breath. His benefactor, who was sitting on a block of cement pushed up against the wall, folded the *Journal de Montréal* that he'd read through a third time.

"You didn't have to rush," he said. "You look like your heart's going to burst right out of your mouth!"

"Here," said Jerome, panting. "Thanks again." He handed Charlie the money and tried to find something friendly to add, but a fit of anger brushed all his good resolutions aside.

"Actually, if you don't mind my saying so, you went over the top. Are you like that with everybody? You'll do yourself in, believe me."

Charlie stiffened, his face turning purple.

"What? I do too much? Maybe so. Or maybe you, you don't do enough? Ever think of that?"

Jerome stood, slack-jawed. The two eyed each other in tense silence, venom in their eyes, then turned on their heels and walked off in different directions.

FRANKNESS, EVEN WHEN it hurts, makes an excellent foundation for friendship — perhaps the only one. It was no surprise to Jerome when, a month later, he returned to Maisonneuve College for the new term and found himself face to face with his Good Samaritan. He'd had time to reflect on his behaviour towards Charlie and felt badly about it. But since he didn't know where he lived and couldn't quite summon the courage to go to the garage and ask Charlie's father, he'd had to live with his remorse.

His reaction was instantaneous.

"Sorry, Charlie," he said, holding out his hand. "I behaved like an ass that day. I don't know what came over me. It must have been the cut on my elbow, it hurt like a son of a bitch."

"I'm the one who should apologize," answered Charlie, prince that he was. "I reacted like a complete prick."

Their impromptu reconciliation was the start of a friendship that had lasted eight years.

Charlie didn't change much in that time; he was always the kind of guy who wanted to save the planet and its inhabitants. But he'd learned over time to temper his generosity — or, at least, to employ a host of strategies not quite so rash and more suited to circumstances. However, the frivolity with which Jerome seemed to be living his life after his return from Cuba awakened in Charlie the quixotic behaviour of his adolescence. And that morning, perched on a stool in the kitchenette that Micro-Boutique employ-ees retired to for their coffee breaks, ignoring the chatter going on all around him, Charlie was mired in sombre con-sideration of the future his friend was bringing down on his head.

Suzanne, the tempting receptionist Charlie had been sleeping with for some time, came up quietly and, leaning towards his ear, whispered, "What's going on? Did you just find out you have cancer?"

Charlie nearly jumped out of his skin.

"No, no, my health is fine, don't worry."

"But you're the one who looks worried. Are we going to get together tonight, my big wolf?" she asked, keeping her voice low. "My Psycho course is over at nine."

He jumped again. "Your *psycho* course? Did you really say your *psycho* course?" He looked aghast, as if he'd just had a blinding revelation.

"Yeah, my Psycho course... Haven't I told you I'm taking a Psycho course? No? Anyway, from the look of you — and don't be insulted — I think you'd make a great study subject for a psychologist."

Her remark was overheard by Benoit, a technician who'd been a colleague of Charlie's for a few months and was busy working his mouth around an enormous piece of carrot cake. "That's what I've been telling him all along," he said, his voice muffled with cake. "I'm sure he'd advance the science!"

Laughter rang out around the kitchenette. Charlie shrugged, quickly left the room, and went to his cubicle. A second later, he was surfing the Internet.

"Yes, yes — Frémont, Joëlle Frémont," he mumbled with a satisfied air. "She's the one for the job..."

And while Jerome was at home punching in Felix Sicotte's number, Charlie, believing he was doing the right thing (when so often we're doing exactly the opposite), was contacting the aforementioned Frémont.

JEROME HUNG UP and, his head reeling, staggered to the kitchen table and flopped onto a chair, his face livid, his back running with sweat. For a moment, he was unable to think; a riot of contradictory feelings filled his head with frightening chaos. Minutes went by. Then, little by little, he began to focus on the positive aspects of the news he had just received.

His intention had been to call Felix in hopes of being invited to his house and in this way meet his mother again. He wanted to see if the job offer she'd hinted at had any chance of being realized. Because at the moment he desperately needed a job, any job, so long as it would put him in a good light with Eugenie.

It was a woman who answered the phone, the voice tremulous, and she told him Monsieur Felix was not presently at home. When would he be back? Jerome asked. There was a short silence, and then the woman, apparently embarrassed, asked, "May I tell him who's calling?" Jerome gave his name and a second later was talking to Francine Desjarlais.

Which is when the news — good and bad — came his way. Felix had needed to leave Montreal for health reasons, she'd said, but everything would be back to normal soon enough.

"He often spoke to me about you, Jerome," said Francine. "He considers you a friend — and I can understand that, after the service you rendered him!"

But about that service, she went on — lowering her

voice — things hadn't turned out so well in Cuba. She'd found out, the previous night, that her son's assailant had died as a result of his wounds.

"But don't worry, I've got everything in hand," she'd hastened to add. Or rather, she added with a bitter laugh, "I've a hand plunged deep in my own pocket. At any rate, this is the sort of thing that happens when you deal with crooks. So what if one of them dies from time to time, it's no great loss to the planet and between you and me I'd even say it culls the herd, so to speak. And don't forget you were coming to someone's defence, you can always use that as a legitimate excuse, right? As you said, that bastard was getting ready to do serious harm to Felix. In other words, you acted like a hero. That's the way I see it, anyway."

Curiously, she seemed delighted with the whole business.

"Thank you, ma'am," Jerome replied, his voice barely audible. He took the phone to the sink. He had a sudden and powerful need for a glass of water but dared not interrupt the conversation.

"I'm glad you called," she went on in the same cheerful tone, "because I'd like to arrange a meeting with you."

"Oh?" A timid thrill insinuated itself into his dismay.

They arranged to meet at three that afternoon, and Francine Desjarlais ended the call by reassuring him, with a confidence that never seemed to desert her, that he had absolutely nothing to worry about as far as the events in Cuba were concerned.

He had to lean on the kitchen table with both hands in order to stand up. He went over to the sink and ran himself another glass of water, and then another. Far from restoring him, the water increased his anxiety. A feeling of being frozen spread out from his chest: it was the coldness of death, a death that he had inflicted on another in the most brutal, primitive way imaginable.

He sat back down. His hands had left two glistening imprints on the Formica tabletop: the palm prints of an assassin. He now belonged to an infamous coterie that populated the pages of newspapers.

"I'm a murderer," he said out loud. "I killed a man."

A new kind of misery descended on him such as he'd never experienced before. It came not so much from a sense of guilt — all things considered, his act had been involuntary and, more to the point, he had committed it coming to someone else's aid — as it did from a feeling of total, ineluctable solitude. He was now and forever would remain a being apart. How many humans belonged in this category? Not counting soldiers, to whom feelings of apartness came naturally (and whom he'd always held in a measure of contempt, being a pacifist by nature), there were remarkably few — proportionately speaking, of course. If all of them were gathered together in a single place (he imagined a tightly knit, silent crowd in a field bathed in diffuse light), each one of them would still be alone — as alone as if they each lived on a deserted planet. All this, because he'd taken from a fellow human being the most precious thing anyone could ever possess, the only thing that counted. Man, when it came right down to it, could do no more than perform one of two absolute acts: give life, or take it away.

No doubt this suffocating feeling would diminish over time; eventually he would share his secret with someone, and that would alleviate it. But, in his own eyes, he had been fundamentally changed, and a part of him would always remain a stranger to the rest of him.

Suddenly, he thought about Eugenie Métivier. How could he dare arrange a meeting with her now? Not only was he unemployed, he was also a murderer!

He pondered that idea, staring at nothing, biting his cheeks, and then without warning brought his fist down on the table with a loud bang, as if it had a will of its own. His water glass jumped into the air, fell onto the floor, and rolled to the middle of the kitchen.

"That's enough!" he shouted as he got up, his face scarlet and twisted with anger. "Is my life going to come to a halt because I helped that little idiot?"

He looked at his watch. If his upstairs neighbour hadn't gone to work, she must think he'd lost his mind or was on a bender.

This couldn't go on. He needed to calm himself down before his three o'clock appointment and before any meeting with—good Lord, yes! He said he'd see Eugenie!

The idea of hitting the bottle was an inspiration. He went to the pantry, knelt before the lower cupboard in which he kept a few bottles of wine and spirits, and took out the cognac, a Christmas gift from his father. Then he picked up the water glass from the floor and half-filled it. Four minutes and a few grimaces later, he'd emptied the glass. Claude-Oscar would have been speechless if he'd seen his son guzzling cognac as if it were medicine, the effect of which did not take long. His cheeks puffed out, his vision blurred, Jerome stumbled his uncertain way towards the bedroom and fell flat on his stomach on the bed. Twenty seconds later, he was asleep.

It was the ringing of the telephone that woke him. He reached his hand towards the bedside table, picked up the receiver, and, with relief, realized before he'd said a word that his mini-binge hadn't inflicted the usual hangover; he'd be refreshed and ready for his meeting, then.

"Hello?" he uttered, his voice scratchy.

"Holy shit, did I wake you up!" said an astonished Charlie. "Are you sick?"

Jerome had had time to clear his throat and, amused, said, "Not at all. It's just that I haven't spoken to anyone since I got up. I was reading."

Glancing at his watch, he was relieved to see that it was only 12:45.

"What are you reading?"

"Nothing that would interest you. It's only for cultured readers."

"Go to hell... If I showed you just how cultured I am, you'd be bursting with envy. Listen, I've got to go back to work in a minute, so I'll cut to the chase: we've got to get together tonight."

"Not sure I can."

"No?"

Charlie's disappointment was obvious.

"But tomorrow's good, if you like — why do you want to see me?"

Charlie hesitated for a moment.

"There's someone I want you to meet."

"So you're concerned about my love life now? That's very good of you but I'm doing pretty well on my own. But thanks anyway."

"That's not it at all. We'll talk about it later, I've got to go. See you tomorrow, then."

And he hung up.

Sitting on the edge of his bed, Jerome ran his fingers through his hair, yawned, made a few faces to stretch his

cheek muscles, and then let out a deep sigh. His short conversation with Charlie had done him good, as if during the
few minutes it had lasted he'd returned to being the person he was before learning about—*the Incident*. From now
on he needed to keep himself very busy if he was going
to keep the overwhelming distress at bay. Wasn't that the
remedy Charles Dickens, one of his favourite authors, had
used to fight off the chronic anxiety he feared would drag
him into madness? Coping in this way had allowed him
to write masterfully and full of temper, inspired as he was
by his courageous combat against injustice. Humanity had
profited much more from the situation than if Dickens had
simply been prescribed anti-anxiety pills.

He took a long shower and finished it off with thirty
seconds under ice-cold water, a stimulation that put him
back on his toes. Then he ate a chicken sandwich and drank
a glass of vegetable juice before rifling through his wardrobe
and deciding to go out and buy a few shirts. The ones he had
seemed to have lost their freshness, and on this day it was
necessary to be impeccably turned out. Not enough cash?
He had his credit card. That's what they were invented for.

He took the métro to Ailes de la Mode, on rue Sainte-
Catherine, and left the store with two superb shirts, one in
silk and the other in linen—and $198.12 further in debt. He'd
slipped the second one into his briefcase while trying on the
first in the fitting room (always wise to carry a briefcase, it
made you look more serious) and when you spend that much
on a single shirt, you have to economize.

Sicotte and Desjarlais lived at 27 Caledonia Road, in the
Town of Mount Royal, or "TMR," a part of the city famous
for the fence that unequivocally establishes the difference
between the neighbourhood's social standing and that of

the less fortunate surrounding districts. To Jerome, as to most middle-class *Montréalais*, Mont Royal was as unfamiliar as the South Pole. Even the métro neatly avoided it, as if out of respect—though no doubt also for practical reasons, as the families of the cosseted district owned at least three cars each.

His watch said 2:15. He needed to find the cheapest and quickest way to his destination—and still keep up appearances. Hands sweating, he took out his cell phone and, a stroke of good fortune, connected with the transit authority's information service almost immediately. An agent with a somewhat bored voice told him the nearest station to the location of his meeting was L'Acadie. He had just enough time to get to it. From there he could take a taxi.

It was 2:55 when, his throat so tight he could barely breathe, he rang the doorbell of an imposing two-storey brick townhouse that, vaguely Loyalist in style, stood at the corner of Portland Avenue and Caledonia Road. Promptly, the door was opened by a slender, petite young woman with olive skin and facial features so taut they seemed to be stretched. She bowed and, with an enigmatic smile, said, "Monsieur Lupien?"

Her accent was slightly Spanish. "You are expected. If you would follow me?"

Despite his nervousness, Jerome could not help noticing with amusement the bizarre contrast between so frail a woman and the massive door she was closing behind him.

She led him into a rectangular hall with parquet flooring covered by a thick, antique-rose carpet and lit by a crystal chandelier that gave the room an air of great splendour, despite there being no one else in it apart from the two of them; the chandelier seemed to Jerome out of proportion to the space in which it hung. "Questionable taste, our madam," he said to himself. "She likes the sizzle more than the steak."

His self-confidence had returned.

They moved on to a sumptuous salon with a monumental fireplace and a grand piano that appeared never to have been played. He expected to be received here, but to his surprise, the young woman approached the other end of the salon and pushed open a door that led to a corridor and a part of the house that, invisible from the road, had its own entrance. The next instant he was in a quite ordinary room, a good part of which was occupied by metal filing cabinets and lit by tall, barred windows. Sitting behind a desk and staring at a computer was Madame Desjarlais, who looked up when he entered.

"Monsieur Jerome," she exclaimed happily, "right on time, too! My happiness is now complete. Thank you, Alma," she added to the young woman. "I'll call you later."

Alma nodded and fluttered off like a butterfly.

"Sit down, Jerome, sit down," said Francine Desjarlais, indicating a chair. "She's darling, my *protégée*, don't you think?"

Jerome politely agreed. The epithet "darling" would not have come immediately to mind regarding the delicate young woman who seemed to hover at the edge of immateriality.

"And pretty smart, too, believe you me. She arrived here from Colombia with her family five years ago. Political refugees. I mean her father, of course, maybe one of the sons, too. The eldest, I'm not sure. But what can you say, they only tell you what they want you to know."

"Colombia's a hard place," answered Jerome, if only for something to say.

"Everywhere's hard, my dear friend, we mustn't put too much faith in appearances."

She stared at him for a moment with a benevolent smile, then her face took on a more sombre expression and, sighing, she said, "It's my husband I wanted you to meet today but — wouldn't you know it! — he had to hurry off on urgent business, and I have no idea when he'll be back."

Jerome almost offered to come back another time, but worrying that he might appear servile, contented himself with looking disappointed; then, afraid of not seeming sufficiently accommodating, he crossed his legs, uncrossed them, coughed, and fixed his gaze on a wastepaper basket.

"In any case," continued Francine Desjarlais, "it's not as serious as all that. Severin and I work independently on most of our files. After twenty-seven years of marriage, I'm sure you understand."

She leaned forward with her elbows on the desk.

"Let me tell you again, Jerome, how much you impressed me in Cuba. You seem to me to be an energetic young man — forthright, brave and, from what I hear," she added with a complicitous smile, "you know how to enjoy the good things in life."

"When such things are offered to me as generously as they were by you, ma'am," replied Jerome, blushing slightly, "then they are very hard to turn down."

"Oh, I certainly didn't want you to turn them down, my dear," said Desjarlais, laughing. "The bill would have been pretty well the same."

Jerome thought her response vulgar, but he forced himself to laugh heartily.

"Let's get down to business. You didn't come all this way to listen to such pleasantries. I'd have preferred you to meet my husband, but as it is I've spoken to him of you and he knows that my instincts are good. So I feel authorized to give you certain details concerning the proposition we'd like to make. He'll sort out the rest. You see, we need someone who—"

Jerome raised a hand to halt her. "Excuse me, ma'am—"

"Please, call me Francine."

"Excuse me, Francine, but I have to stop you right there. The other day, you told me your husband was a financial consultant. And I have to be frank, numbers aren't my thing. If you're looking for someone to—"

"That's irrelevant. In effect, Severin's more of a lobbyist, to be precise. You know what that is?"

"Of course," said Jerome, eager to appear in the know. "You only have to read the papers or watch television. He's someone who represents the interests of companies to the government."

"That's right. It's a, let's say, *delicate* field. One that demands a great deal of diplomacy, patience—and intuition."

"I've never done anything like that," Jerome said, a little taken aback.

She laughed wrily. "I don't doubt that, a man your age. At any rate, I was telling you about my *husband's* profession. I'll leave it to him to explain what we would expect of you. Still, I can say right now that if you perform the task we'll be giving you well, you won't regret working with us. We've never been stingy here. It's not the house style."

Jerome's trepidation had more or less dissolved. If he'd been asked how he approached life, he would have replied, "With passion!" Thus, despite the dearth of information furnished by Francine, he felt he was being offered the chance of a lifetime. All of a sudden, he imagined the splendid business card he'd be able to present to Eugenie Métivier! An infantile headiness came over him. He wanted to stomp his feet on the floor but, inwardly beaming, managed to retain a calm demeanour.

"I thank you for the confidence you're showing in me, ma'am," said Jerome, trying to control the slight tremor in his voice, "and I hope—"

"Francine. My name's Francine. This 'ma'am' business gives me varicose veins, my dear."

He laughed. He would have kissed her hands, if he could.

"I should hear from my husband in an hour or two," she said, getting up from her desk. "Will you leave me your telephone number? Here, write it on this piece of paper. Severin will call you sometime this evening. Wait here, I'll have Alma show you out."

He stared at her, anxious once more, a silent question in his eyes.

"Is something wrong?" she asked, surprised.

"Umm, that guy—the guy in Varadero—is he really ... dead?"

She shrugged.

"Yes. And I hope the devil sticks a poker up his ass. Can you imagine, the police hounding me about that business all the way up here. They talked about extradition and a whole pile of such nonsense. I had to dip into my wallet yet again, though this time it's taken care of for good, so think no more about it. It's as if it never happened. Promise me?"

He swallowed uncomfortably, but managed to answer in a reassuring tone, "I promise."

She called Alma, her *protégée*, on the intercom, as Jerome stood before her with a worried look on his face. Francine frowned slightly and, with a hint of impatience, asked, "What's the matter now, Jerome?"

"Does Felix know?" he asked.

"Felix is in a detox centre in Portage, my dear, and he'll be there for another few months yet. It was a difficult decision for him to make but, really, he didn't have much choice. So no, he's unaware and, under the circumstances, I don't think it would be a good idea to tell him."

The dejection he sensed in her voice made him regret having asked.

IN THE TAXI on the way home Jerome struggled with a second bout of euphoria, this one of a different origin, and one so powerful he all but lost control of himself. After a moment, the young Haitian taxi driver, intrigued but then annoyed by the stomping of his client's feet behind him, turned and said coolly, "So, what's with you, friend, you work at the Cirque du Soleil or something? You trying to keep in shape?"

"Sorry, sir," said Jerome, embarrassed—and the stomping stopped.

"I'm not the enemy, I assure you. I wouldn't hurt a fly. Know why? Because I believe everyone has the right to live—that's what my mother always taught me, and my grandmother, too. But hey, man," the driver went on, laughing, "you were really doing a number on my floor back there, and this car is definitely not new, she's been through seven winters already. Imagine that! She's an old lady now. Have to go easy on her."

"I'm really sorry," Jerome, increasingly embarrassed, repeated. He decided he'd give the driver a huge tip, which was probably the aim of his little speech in the first place.

Ten minutes before, he'd been engaged in polite conversation with the impossibly frail Alma as they waited for the taxi she'd called. But she'd been summoned by her boss and had to fly off. Alone in the vestibule, he'd looked out at the street, leaning on one leg and then the other as the minutes weighed on him more and more heavily. The surge of anguish that had been rising in him since Francine told him about the tragic nature of the incident in Varadero came over him again, drowning bit by bit the day-to-day landmarks of his life on which he relied: the day, the week, where he was and his reason for being there, all of it faded and disappeared so that he was carried away by a sort of vertigo. He was an assassin, in a house of diabolical mirrors refracting his image back at him in a multitude of angles, fighting his surrender to some horrid version of himself.

"*Never*," he told himself.

He would have to do as Dickens did and throw himself into his work. That was the only way for him to regain his equilibrium. He took out his cell phone and tapped in Eugenie Métivier's number without the slightest idea of what he was going to say.

A courteous, impersonal voice answered—that of a very busy woman nonetheless careful to do things properly.

"Eugenie Métivier, here. Can I help you?"

"Eugenie, it's Jerome Lupien. Sorry to be calling you at work. I won't take up too much of your time. I wanted to see how you are doing and was wondering if we could—"

"Jerome! How are you? I was just thinking about you this morning."

The change in her voice filled him with happiness, the kind of incredulous joy a collector feels in front of a true find, the voracious joy of a hunter on the point of making a big kill. Had theirs been no more than a seaside flirtation that evaporated when the vacation was over? Apparently not. They exchanged just a few words (Eugenie, in effect, overwhelmed) and agreed to meet at her place that evening at seven for a casual dinner.

He'd hung up, absorbed in his thoughts, when Alma reappeared as if from nowhere and pointed towards the street.

"Your taxi's here."

He bowed to her without a word and practically ran from the building, climbed into the cab, and hollered: "5207 avenue Decelles, please," as if announcing a great victory.

And now the driver was ending his short speech with a few favourable observations concerning Quebec and its weather; about Montreal ("A safe city, sir, and I know what I'm talking about: my brother-in-law drives a taxi in Detroit!"); the kindness of most customers ("They're generous, especially the Québécois. I wonder why that is?"); and sundry related topics, all with equal gravity. Jerome answered in polite monosyllables. His euphoria gradually abated, replaced by more tactical thinking. The evening augured well: getting laid seemed a sure thing—assuming, of course, that sweet little Andrée-Anne didn't come down with the flu or fall or hurt herself and agreed to go beddy-byes before eleven o'clock. On the other hand, moving too fast in these matters usually meant they didn't last very long. Sex, at its most ideal, is like snow in sunlight. What line should he take? He needed to come up with three or four different strategies in order to be able to adapt to whatever circumstances presented themselves. Because love, in its early stages, was much like a battle and he had no clear plan, no strategy for retreat. Surprise attacks? Evasive manoeuvres? Nothing came to mind. Like a nitwit, he was already on his knees before this woman. The only need he felt was to press himself on her. He had ants in his pants and, at the same time, tears in his eyes. What a ridiculous situation! It had been ages since anything like this had come over him! The experience was magnificent—and terrifying. And the more he thought about it, the more tangled were his reflections.

The driver, intrigued by his silence, glanced at him in the rear-view mirror. "Things not going so well, my friend? You've got enough cash on you to pay the fare, I hope."

A five-dollar tip took care of his worries.

Entering his apartment, Jerome no longer had any idea what to do. Why, in his case, was joy so often followed by such stupid torments? Why did the prospect of spending an evening with a beautiful woman put him in such a state? Why, for Christ's sake, couldn't he be *like everybody else*?

As luck would have it, a message from Charlie on his answering machine provided a diversion Jerome couldn't ignore. His friend had called from the Micro-Boutique, where he worked, and demonstrated a high degree of eloquence.

"Jerome," he said gravely, almost philosophically, "I'm taking my coffee break half an hour before everyone else so I can be alone in the kitchenette, because I have something important to talk to you about—something that should concern you. Yes, my friend, it's about your life, nothing less. And I even have a proposition to make, a proposition that came to me after *considerable* reflection. Yes, I know, you're probably already groaning like all the other morons of your species. And I'm actually glad to be talking to your answering machine, because it won't interrupt every chance it gets. So, I'll get to the point."

Charlie cleared his throat with a nervous little cough.

"I want to introduce you to someone, Jerome, some-one who'll stop you going south, because you're really and truly losing it. I've already talked about this a few times. Your life is circling the drain, and you know it, and I worry about that, obviously, as a true friend should. The person I want you to meet is a psychologist. I've been to see her three times — I won't go into details at the moment, if you don't mind — and she really has been a great help. Her name is Joëlle Frémont, she's a specialist in *rebirth*, a kind of therapy that was introduced in Montreal — and this is important — by a student of Leonard Orr, who first came up with it. As you probably already know, *rebirth* is one of the greatest successes of the New Age movement. *Rebirth* has saved thousands of people, Jerome — and, if you let it, it will save you, too."

Jerome turned off the machine. Two red spots appeared on his cheeks, and his mouth had thinned and curved down at the corners, announcing, with crashes of thunder and flashes of lightning, a storm on the way.

"What's come over him? He's been smoking super strong hash, or what? He's the one who needs to be *saved*, as he put it."

His anger was so great he knew that Charlie, in his clumsy way, had touched a nerve. If this were a serious con-versation — and if the happy prospects of getting a job and meeting Eugenie had not that very day opened up to him — he'd have agreed that his life had for a long time been going to the dogs. And there was still the possibility — moot now, but who knew what the future held? — of his being impli-cated in a homicide.

He took his cell phone and feverishly entered a number.
"Hello?" said Charlie's voice.

"It's me," said Jerome, coolly.

"Oh, hi. You got my message?"

"I did, all right! Listen to me, Charlie, pal, and listen well. Two things: first, I'm on the point of getting a job that will make you drool with envy. And second, I've got a date tonight with a woman who'll bowl you over. So — and I mean this in the kindest possible way — take your rebirth bullshit and shove it up your ass!"

There was a moment's silence at the other end of the line.

"Your reaction," said Charlie with astonishing calm, "is quite normal. I reacted the same way, the first time."

Jerome was so outraged be broke into a sweat.

"Except that in my case, chum," he spat into the phone, "the first time is the last time. Do me a favour and spare me your idiocy, okay?"

"As you wish," said Charlie, stoically. "But you're the one who's losing out. Take some time to think it over, okay? Sorry, I have to go now. Need to get back to work. We can talk about this later."

Jerome stormed about the kitchen.

"Jesus H. *Christ*," he grumbled, running a hand through his hair. "Has he caught some kind of Jehovah's Witness virus? He should be locked up, the idiot..."

He needed to think about something else. He didn't want anger to ruin a day that had started so memorably.

The techno-pop tones of his cell phone began to chime.

"Severin Sicotte here," said a deep, gravelly voice. "Am I calling at a bad time?"

"No, not at all, Monsieur Sicotte," Jerome said eagerly.

His underarms had turned into little steam baths, and he reminded himself to change his shirt before his date that night.

"You met my wife this afternoon. Would you have some time to see me, too?"

"Yes, of course, sir. Whenever you like."

But, realizing that meeting with Mister Sicotte might screw up his evening with Eugenie, he frowned and two dark stains appeared on his shirt.

"Very good of you," answered the deep voice. "I'm at the Ritz-Carlton at the moment, on Sherbrooke. Do you know it?"

"Yes, of course," replied Jerome. He'd never set foot in the hotel, but remembered that de Gaulle, Churchill, and Céline Dion had stayed there.

"Can you be in room 342 in, let's say, half an hour?"

"Absolutely, sir."

"Not asking too much?"

"Not at all."

"Sorry to make you speed down here like this, but I've got a full slate today — and the day is far from over. See you soon, then."

Jerome closed his cell phone, checked his watch, then looked with dismay at his shirt: he'd need to change. He took it off, went into the bathroom, sprayed his armpits with eau de cologne, put on a clean shirt, and decided to pack another in his briefcase, just in case. All of which took a good eight minutes.

"At least there are plenty of taxis around here," he told himself, dashing down the stairs and onto the street.

SEVERIN SICOTTE CAME into the suite, paced a little, then stopped abruptly and started to sniff, turning his head from side to side and flaring his nostrils. Above the heady vapour of whisky that filled his nasal passages, he'd detected a suspicious and detested odour.

"Olivier, I smell cigarette smoke," he growled, turning towards a small, nervous man with a bald head who, closing the door, had followed him into the room.

Olivier heaved a deep sigh, as though his boss's pique was nothing compared to his own. Quickly, he opened one window, then another, turning on the air conditioning as Sicotte watched with a mixture of annoyance and pleasure at seeing his wishes so promptly satisfied.

A hazing of first-year students in the Faculty of Law at Laval University in 1977 was at the root of his hatred of cigarette smoke or anything else that affected his breathing. That year, the initiation committee for the ninety-two frosh had forced the unfortunate newbies to cram like sardines into a room that was fit, at most, for twenty. Some of them had needed to climb onto their comrades' shoulders in absurdly contorted positions. Then, so graciously supplied by the committee, they were forced to smoke Gitanes while singing "Alouette, Gentille Alouette" in harmony and without a false note until the organizers were completely satisfied. The torture had gone on for thirty-eight minutes. Six students had thrown up. Three passed out. One — on a lark, it turned out — had to be taken to hospital, though he was released later that night. During the entire initiation ceremony, Sicotte had been jammed into a corner beneath a bed under a cloud of pestilential smoke, his left hand crushed by the heel of a fellow initiate and his head pressed against the chest of a comrade fighting off a panic attack. The experience had marked him for life, instilling in him a tendency to claustrophobia.

"I'm accustomed to receiving better service at the Ritz," grumbled Sicotte. "This fellow will be here in five minutes, there's no time to move."

"This is not the first time," observed Olivier, "that I've advised you to book the same room. That's the only way you'll know the air you'll be breathing."

"You're joking, surely: reserve a suite at the Ritz-Carlton for months at a time? It would cost a fortune!"

Olivier said nothing, but the smile playing on his thin, pale lips indicated that in his opinion what constituted a fortune for ordinary mortals was no more than petty cash for others.

Sicotte went over and sat behind a large Empire-style desk, remarkable for its exquisite detail, took several sheets of paper and documents from the briefcase that accompanied him everywhere, and placed them before him. Then he began sniffing again, turning his head from side to side with a dissatisfied air. Before long, coughs shook his shoulders.

"It's going nowhere, that bloody smell," he complained. "Turn up the air conditioning, Olivier."

"It's already at maximum, boss," Olivier called from the next room. "We'll just have to wait a bit." Then, sticking his head through the doorway, he said, "Should I ask room service to send up some coffee?"

Sicotte nodded.

A knocking at the door saw Olivier disappear, and during the interview that followed not a sound gave away his presence in the next room.

Sicotte got up to open the door and, in a voice that did not quite achieve the warmth he was intending, said, "Monsieur Lupien? Thanks for coming so quickly. Again, I apologize for arranging this meeting at the last minute. My schedule is appalling, if you only knew. But I must admit," he added with a smile that was somewhat forced, "that after my wife told me about you I was impatient to make your acquaintance."

"Not a problem, sir, thank you," babbled Jerome, who, from the moment of entering the chic hotel, had felt like a country bumpkin.

"Please, sit down," said Sicotte, escorting him into the room. He pointed towards a sofa chair and sat on the couch facing his visitor. Leaning forward with his elbows on his knees, he concentrated on Jerome with an engaging smile. Jerome, blushing, returned the smile and, not sure how to conduct himself, squirmed uncomfortably on the couch.

Enunciating carefully, his voice grave, Sicotte said, "First of all, I want to thank you for the courage you showed during that sad business in Varadero. If it weren't for you, my poor son might already be six feet under the ground."

Jerome, who'd decided to play the modesty card, made a gesture to indicate that he'd done only what anyone would have.

"In places like that," his host went on, "life is hard, everyone knows that. You've heard stories, I certainly have. And, of course, it goes without saying how sorry I am — how very sorry, believe me — that certain complications have arisen. But all that's taken care of, as my wife has explained. Thank you a thousand times."

Sicotte's face brightened as if a light had been trained on it.

"Can I offer you coffee, some wine, mineral water? Coffee, you say? Good. I've just had some sent up."

Hardly had he finished the sentence than there was a knock on the door.

"And here it is."

Once the coffee had been served, with the famous hotel's usual decorum, things developed rapidly. Within a few minutes, Jerome had presented his curriculum vitae: he'd earned a B.A. from the Université de Montréal, where he'd been interested in a host of disciplines, including applied and political sciences. He was crazy about foreign literature (in translation, of course, except for works in English)—and, if he thought it relevant, had won first prize in the televised Dictée des Amériques competition three years prior.

"You can write, then?" said Sicotte, visibly impressed. "That's good, that's good."

He took a sip of coffee, thinking, his eyes half closed.

"My wife said you don't smoke, is that right?" he asked, placing his cup on the table.

"No, I don't smoke," Jerome replied, taken aback. "Is that important?"

"It is for me. I don't like cigarettes. Smoking kills."

He brought the cup to his lips again, took a mouthful, replaced the cup on the table, and began gently tapping the floor with the tip of his foot.

Sicotte was making a decision, Jerome could sense it. His toes itched and curled in his shoes. He hadn't even asked what kind of job they were talking about. "Oh boy," he told himself, "it's a good thing I brought an extra shirt. I'm sweating like an ox pulling a house."

"You see, Monsieur Lupien," said Sicotte, looking up, "I'm looking for someone who's resourceful, dynamic, able to edit texts—in French, of course, but also some in English. After all, we're in America, are we not? With or without experience, it doesn't matter, as long as he knows how to learn."

"Well, I can assure you I have no experience at all," said Jerome, his voice bittersweet, "but I do learn quickly." And then, the situation appearing more and more absurd, he asked, "What kind of job are we talking about, exactly, Monsieur Sicotte?"

"I'm looking for someone to work in a, shall we say, secretarial capacity. Someone who can, when necessary, also act as liaison, a go-between, if you will. You see, Monsieur Lupien, I am a professional lobbyist by trade, but one thing leads to another, and sometimes I have several irons in the fire."

"You're a lobbyist for whom?"

"I'll explain all that when and if it becomes necessary. It's rather hard to explain."

"So he's hiring me!" Jerome told himself.

He was hard put to contain his excitement. Through an internal free association of ideas that surprised him, his thoughts turned to Eugenie Métivier. His impatience to see her increased tenfold.

"If my offer interests you," continued Sicotte, "I'll try you out. At first, I'll hire you as a sort of . . . textual editor, for my correspondence and things of that nature, is that okay? Because I must admit that, despite being a lawyer, writing has never been my strong point. In fact, it bores me, if you must know. But I have a great deal of respect for those who *do* know how to write."

Quickly, he added, "You work with a computer? Well, of course you do, your generation has been in the information age since you were in diapers. We old fogies, we had to learn it late in life, and that's not always easy! But for young people, it's like flying is to a bird, eh? Now . . ."

He straightened and leaned back against the couch in a languid pose, as if to talk about something totally unimportant.

"So what are your terms, young man?"

Jerome, taken unawares, was speechless.

"How does a starting salary of $50,000 a year sound?"

The gleam that appeared in the young man's eyes brought a subtle smile to Sicotte's lips.

"Your work schedule may vary, though," he continued. "Most of the time you'll be working thirty-five hours a week, but, if something urgent comes up—in special cases—you'll do as I do and won't count your hours."

"That's perfectly fine with me, sir," replied Jerome, doing his best to sound interested though not *too* eager.

Sicotte stood up and extended a hand. "Great. Then it's a deal, my friend. Tomorrow morning, nine o'clock, at my office on Caledonia Road. Now I'm afraid I must see you out, I have a client due to arrive any moment."

Jerome, walking as if on a cloud, was at the door when the lawyer called him back.

"Your briefcase . . . you forgot your briefcase."

"Oh shit, yes! You're right, sir," said Jerome, suddenly turning back the way he'd come and, still in a trance, picking it up where it sat beside his chair as his new boss watched, bemused.

"We can call one another by our first names now, can't we, Jerome? In a team, words like 'sir' go out the window."

"Yes, of course, sir—er, I mean, Severin."

Jerome blushed.

"*Severin*," he repeated. "See you tomorrow, then."

Sicotte waited until the door closed, then placed his eye to the security peephole to make sure Jerome was gone. When he came back, Olivier Fradette had reappeared.

"So, my friend, what do you think?"

"I think you've done well, boss. He doesn't strike me as an idiot, quite the contrary, but he's still fairly naive. That'll help us bring him along nicely—and it'll be that much easier with that Damocles sword hanging over his head . . ."

"It's a sword made of rubber," said Sicotte, laughing, "but he doesn't know that. And if he does find out some day, after the little jobs I'll have given him, it won't matter. It's quite amusing, all of this, don't you find?"

Fradette nodded. He was smiling slightly, flattered that his boss was talking to him on an equal footing. After all, he'd only been in his service for eleven months and one week. Yet that had been long enough to provide eloquent proof of his loyalty.

IT WAS A quarter to six when Jerome was back in the lobby of the Ritz-Carlton; his date with Eugenie Métivier was at seven. But first he needed to change his shirt for the third time that day—had he come down with yellow fever, for Christ's sake? Never, in all his life, had he sweated so much! Then he had to buy a bottle of good wine—he didn't want to appear unaware of social niceties by showing up empty-handed—and get to 159 avenue Querbes, in Outremont. He asked a clerk where the bathroom was, came out wearing a fresh shirt, and then, coming back through the lobby, slipped two dollars (this wasn't the Holiday Inn, after all) into the hand of a fifty-something porter who, dressed like a governor general, hailed a cab with an imperious gesture.

Ten minutes later, time in hand, he got out of the taxi in front of the Complexe les Ailes shopping centre on rue Sainte-Catherine, where there was a provincial liquor store.

"I'll be right back," he said to the driver. "Don't move, okay?"

Another seven minutes and, his purchase in hand, he was back on the road to Outremont. A monstrous traffic jam caused by an accident held them up for twenty-seven minutes more: far ahead, sirens were wailing and lights flashing.

The taxi driver talked about his children's futures—three boys, two girls—and his wife's health problems. (She was a seamstress at Peerless Clothing and taking French courses after work.) Jerome forced himself to stay calm, not least as he didn't have another shirt to change into. They entered the tony district at 7:14. During the delay, he'd phoned Eugenie to tell her he was going to be late. He'd just had a stroke of extraordinary luck, he said, and couldn't wait to tell her about it.

"*Voilà*," said the driver, "we're here." He was looking with satisfaction at his meter. "Not too bad, really, considering the traffic!"

Jerome settled the bill (once more with a generous tip) and stepped out onto the sidewalk, bottle of wine in hand and his heart beating wildly.

Eugenie lived on the second floor of a nice enough brick building set back a little from the road. Like most of the houses on adjacent streets, it was built in a post-Victorian style and adorned with the sort of august features a rising middle class preferred. An old maple tree, already in bud, provided shade to the façade of the building and, one above the other, its two balconies and their ornate railings.

Jerome climbed the stairs that led to the second floor slowly, careful not to work up a sweat. He rang the bell and the sound of a muted trumpet and chords of a piano carried through a large front door and the lace curtain covering its bevelled glass windows. A question came to mind that he was surprised hadn't occurred to him before: Was Eugenie divorced, widowed, or a single mother, which in certain circles was often the case these days?

He didn't have time to pursue the thought at all. The door opened and there she was, smiling and more beautiful than he remembered. Behind her he heard a child's scurrying steps.

"Who is it?" he heard a child's voice say. "Who is it?"

"I've told you who it is, my love, it's Jerome. He's come to visit us, you remember him, don't you?" The young woman leaned down to Andreé-Anne, who was hugging her mother's legs and staring at the visitor with an expression that was both curious and timid.

"Come in, please," she said to Jerome, smiling broadly. "Your visit seems to be a big occasion."

She didn't know how right she was.

The little girl ran back into the apartment, bubbling with laughter.

"Will you give me your coat?" Eugenie asked.

There was a brushing of hands, a tender gaze, and Eugenie's half-closed eyes told Jerome the evening would not be lost. She hung up his coat, and Jerome walked into her spacious living room, furnished in the Scandinavian style now back in vogue.

"Nice place you have," he said, trying to assume an easy, relaxed tone (though all the while wondering what time the daughter would go to bed). "Have you been living here long?"

"I bought the duplex two years ago," Eugenie replied as she caught up with him. "After my divorce. But come, sit down and tell me whatever is this extraordinary thing that just happened to you. Can I get you anything? Beer? Wine? A martini?"

"Is that Miles Davis you have on?" he asked, pointing to a hi-fi standing before them in all its minimalist brushed-steel-and-mahogany glory.

"Yes. You're a fan of jazz?"

"Well, not really, but who doesn't know Miles Davis?"

Oblivious to the non-sequiturs that marred their conversation, they did their best to banter casually, two strangers pretending to have known each other for a long time.

"So," she began again, "what can I get you?"

"I'll have a glass of red wine."

"I found an excellent one the other day—from Spain, a Juan Gil Monastrell, if you like an oaky wine. But," she added, laughing, "don't worry, I'm not going to make you drink some grocery-store plonk, even if I do work at Metro."

"Bring on the Juan Gil," said Jerome, gamely.

Spritely and with grace, she turned on her heels and left the room. He sat himself down in an easy chair, stretched out his legs, took a deep breath, and smiled. The sound of tinkling glass came from the kitchen, accompanied by her humming, and with the humming floated in tantalizing odours that made his stomach growl. In the next room, the little girl chattered as if she had forgotten his presence. Things were going well. *La vita è bella!* He found her more appealing than ever, this Eugenie, with her hair tied back to reveal the delicious oval of her face. She was both simple and refined at the same time—not at all the snobbish Outrement type that popular legend would have had him expect—and, on top of it all, there was something in her manner that suggested calm, a clarity of mind, and self-confidence. No longer was she the shipwrecked person she'd appeared to be by the Iberostar swimming pool. Obviously, they were both in seduction mode this evening. As for the rest, he'd know soon enough. His detachment surprised him. What had gone on inside him? Just a few hours before, he was struggling like a madman, unable to think anything but *I-need-her-if-I'm-to-go-on-living*. Does she like me or not?

We'll see eventually. It was as if the image of the beautiful castaway at the centre of his life had been smashed; now it was a simple matter of the good, satisfying fuck they both felt they needed.

Eugenie reappeared, walking carefully with a tray on which she'd placed the bottle of wine, two balloon glasses, and a plate of hors d'oeuvres.

"Okay," she said, setting the tray on a coffee table, "tell me what happened."

She sat across from him, they clinked glasses, Jerome smacked his lips appreciatively, then launched into his story, and almost got to the end of it.

"Mommy!" screamed Andreé-Anne, as if someone had jabbed her hand with a dagger. "When are we going to eat? I'm hungry!"

"Come into the living room, my pet. There are some nice little snacks in here. We'll sit down to eat in five minutes."

She turned to Jerome and added, in a low voice, "She stuffs herself like an ogre as soon as she gets home from daycare, but really I think the little mademoiselle just wants attention."

Andrée-Anne appeared with a colouring book and stopped to give Jerome a long, disapproving look.

"Can I see your colouring book?" he asked in a friendly tone, believing it the right thing to do.

She shook her head slowly.

"It's private," she said very seriously.

He laughed and his reaction seemed to please the little girl. She smiled, came closer, and reached towards the plate of hors d'oeuvres. "Are these olives spicy, Mommy?"

"No, dear, not a bit. Here, take one of these crackers and some cheese, too."

"Oh, that's too bad," said Jerome. "That's the last one and I wanted to eat it."

"Mommy can make more," said the girl, looking him straight in the eye.

And then she shoved the cracker and cheese and olive in her mouth, turned her back to him, sat on the floor, and started colouring in her book.

"Tell me," said Jerome, "how old are you? Five?"

"I'm going to be five next week," Andrée-Anne announced as if it were an achievement. "There's no more green crayon, Mommy."

"I'll buy you one tomorrow or the next day, my treasure, when I go shopping."

Jerome had the agreeable sensation of being a part of their intimacy. And, his infatuation hurtling forward, he told himself, "This is just the beginning!"

"And so then," said Eugenie, turning towards him again to continue their conversation, "tomorrow morning you begin your career as a lobbyist? That's fun. You're going to meet all sorts of interesting people."

"Well, I won't be a lobbyist tomorrow morning. I have to learn the ropes first and prove myself. Who knows? They might sack me after a week…"

"Well, I have confidence in you," she replied.

There was an aplomb in her voice that let him know her confidence in him extended beyond an assessment of his professional capabilities. Jerome was flattered and, at the same time, uneasy.

But his attention was soon directed elsewhere.

"Can there be such a thing as a blue butterfly?" Andrée-Anne asked him as she put the colouring book on his lap.

In the middle of the left-hand page, a butterfly with blue

wings was fleeing the gaping jaws of a small spaniel as yet uncoloured. He looked at the image for a second, trying to come up with a plausible answer.

"I don't know but, regardless, your butterfly is very pretty."

He was trying to avoid the platitudes of a benevolent uncle playing at being a child. But how was he to do that?

"I coloured it at school this morning," said the little girl, having suddenly become talkative. "Myriam said there can't be a blue butterfly, and that it was ugly, but Myriam is mean to everyone and she's not a good drawer — not at all! — and I think I've seen blue butterflies on television. Real ones, I mean, not just in cartoons."

"What matters, though, is that they're beautiful. And yes, as a matter of fact, I think I saw some on television not so long ago."

"Really? When?"

Eugenie looked at her watch.

"*À table*," she announced, rising to her feet. "Will you bring the wine, Jerome?"

The meal went well. As you find in the houses of the well-to-do, there was a pass-through between the kitchen and the dining room, and Jerome, becoming more and more gallant as the level of the wine in the bottle lowered, offered to take the plates from his hostess and she, increasingly familiar and relaxed, was happy to let him do so. After picking at her food for two or three minutes ("Mommy, you know I don't like duck"), Andrée-Anne left the table to watch a DVD in her room until it came time for dessert, which is when the conversation between Eugenie and her guest took a less guarded turn.

"I think you're adorable," declared Jerome as he passed behind her with a load of dishes. He kissed her neck. "Are you going to let me spend the night?"

She looked up with a coquettish smile.

"I certainly can't let you leave given the state you're in."

Their lips were just touching when his eye fell on Andrée-Anne, immobile at the door and watching them with an accusatory air. Their kiss ended up being shorter than he'd hoped.

"Are we going to have dessert now?" asked the child in an acid little voice.

"We'll have it when you're called, Andrée-Anne," answered her mother, contending with an incipient impatience.

But then, in a softer tone, she said, "Okay, come here, love. I think we're ready for dessert, don't you, Jerome?"

"Absolutely."

Dessert served and eaten, they returned to the living room. Andrée-Anne, after giving Jerome a long and suspicious look, installed herself in a corner with a tablet that soon emitted a series of strange beeps. But before long—and to the young man's great satisfaction—she started to yawn and squint and rub her eyes.

"Time for beddy-byes, my sweet. Come put your pyjamas on and brush your teeth. Will you say goodnight to Jerome?"

"Goodnight," she mumbled without looking at him.

Eugenie turned to her guest and said, "I'll be ten minutes." She led her daughter to the bathroom and, through the half-open door, he heard the sounds of a tap running and the sighs of a child being hastily washed.

"I'm not having my bath tonight?" said Andrée-Anne.

"Not tonight, my sweet. I have company."

"You're rubbing too hard, Mommy!"

"I'm sorry, little darling, I'll be more careful. But how did you get so filthy? Give me your foot."

A minute went by. Protests were followed by sighs. Her foreshortened bedtime ritual was making mademoiselle grumpy and she was whining about everything and nothing: she had soap in her eyes, her pyjamas were old and ugly, her portion of dessert had been smaller than everyone else's.

"You never liked it when Daddy drank wine," she complained all of a sudden, "but you, you've been drinking all night."

"Your father drank *every* night, Andrée-Anne, and he drank *a lot*. We're not..."

The door closed and prevented Jerome from hearing the rest, but the intimate scene had interested him immensely and put him in a good mood. He began humming "Ode to Joy" to the rhythm of a waltz, salacious images whirling in his head.

Suddenly, a spasm in his stomach struck him like a blast of cold air spreading through his body. "Yup," he said to himself, clenching his moist hands, "I'm starting my new job tomorrow. I need to be at my best... really at my best, or else..."

Suddenly he was seized by a great idea.

"All right," he told himself, "good... that'll work... I can figure this out... After all, I'm not just any old... You're not just *anyone*, Jerome, you're *Jerome Lupien*! You're not—"

He heard a door open, the pitter-patter of bare feet, and then another door close: Mommy had put her little sweetheart to bed. *About time!* "Ode to Joy" started running through his head again, more bouncily than ever, and Jerome sank back into the easy chair, tapping his feet and staring up at the ceiling, lost in voluptuous reverie.

Eugenie appeared before him with a smile both radiant and tender.

"Andrée-Anne's in bed," said Eugenie quietly. "She'll be asleep in four or five minutes." Eugenie came over and sat on the arm of the chair he was sitting in. "They have so much energy at that age," she sighed, stretching an arm over the chair's back.

He looked at her with a duplicitous smile.

"I feel I've got a lot of energy tonight, too," he said. "You?"

He caressed her thigh and slipped a hand under her dress. She slid into his lap and they melted into a passionate embrace.

"No, no, not here, Jerome, please," she whispered, pushing him back. "We should wait a bit, I'm sure she won't be asleep yet."

He threw himself back, breathing heavily while Eugenie, standing in front of him with a worried expression, her cheeks flushed with desire, straightened her hair and clothes.

They examined each other for a moment.

Jerome smiled sardonically.

"I'm going to explode any minute."

"And how do you think I feel?"

She took a few steps away from him, tilted her head towards her daughter's bedroom, then returned to Jerome with a finger raised to her lips: "A few more minutes and we'll be fine," she said. "Can I get you anything?"

"Sure, why not," said Jerome. "It'll help pass the time." Then he had another great idea. "How about trying the wine I brought? It's a Montecorna 1998, not at all bad if you like Ripasso—and a good year, too." (From time to time, he liked to show off the knowledge he'd gained as a waiter.)

They went into the kitchen where, instead of opening the wine, he tickled her and the sweet nothings he whispered in her ear made her smile. She responded to his caresses with equal ardour.

"Stop, please," she said suddenly, "you're getting me too excited."

She looked away from him and laughed, a little embarrassed at having let herself go this far with a man she hardly knew at all. He gazed at her tenderly and stroked her hair.

"You're so beautiful, you'd make a monk forget his vows."

She burst out laughing.

"Well, well, that's the first time I've had such a *Catholic* compliment. Come to think of it, maybe you'd have more luck with bishops than with me."

But Jerome, heady with desire, continued feverishly, "And to think that I gave up an afternoon with you and went to Varadero instead... What a disaster that was!"

"Don't speak too soon," she said, wagging her finger. "You might still be disappointed."

There was a trace of worry in her voice.

He shook his head and held her by the shoulders.

"Not possible. When I look at you it makes my knees quake. Let's have a drink!"

With trembling hands, he uncorked the bottle while she retrieved the glasses from the living room, and as they took little sips of their wine they devoured each other with their eyes. After a moment, she went to peek into her daughter's room, and came back on tiptoe, signalling for Jerome to follow. They came into a spacious bedroom in which, massive and dark, a great big Victorian bed stood in contrast with the modern furniture of the rest of the apartment. On a side table, a porcelain vase lamp glowed in the blue-tinged shadows. The air smelled of jasmine. "She planned this, the little vixen," thought Jerome with a certain ecstasy.

Without saying a word, they quickly stripped off their clothes, dropping them in a pile on the floor, and jumped onto the bed like two starving people at a feast. Their frolicking was silent, precise, and vigorous, almost rough, satisfying a hunger that had gripped them for too long. (The earnest lovers of Verona would have been shocked.)

And then, already, it was over. Collapsed into one another, they caught their breath and exchanged astonished looks tempered with pleasure.

"That was good," murmured Eugenie.

"But quick."

"But good."

"You're wonderful . . . Let's do it again."

She laughed. "I have no doubt we will."

They dozed off. Twice Jerome woke up and looked at his watch; he absolutely couldn't be late for work on his first day! But the night had only just begun.

Around 2 a.m. he opened his eyes again, but this time it was love that awakened him. Eugenie, under the exhortation of his caresses, was slowly emerging from sleep and sighing contentedly when the familiar pitter-patter of little feet could be heard on the other side of the door, which opened.

A small, sleepy voice called out in distress, "Mommy, I had a bad dream, I want to sleep with you."

"What is it, my sweet?" asked Eugenie, sitting up in bed, a bit bewildered.

Andrée-Anne stopped and stared at Jerome, who had turned briskly onto his stomach with his face plunged into the pillow as if he were ashamed.

"Who is that?" asked the child in a frightened voice.

"It's Jerome."

"He's sleeping with you?"

There was a touch of aggression in her voice.

"Yes, Andrée-Anne, we decided to sleep together tonight."

A short silence ensued. The child stood still. Sniffled.

"I want to sleep with you."

"You can't, baby, you'd disturb Jerome. Go back to bed, sweetie-pie, your bad dream has gone now and it won't come back."

"No, I want to sleep with you, Mommy. I'll sleep on your side. I won't move, I promise, and I won't talk either, I promise."

The discussion went on a little longer; the child was on the verge of tears and it was Jerome's turn to sit up in bed.

"Come on in, Andrée-Anne," said Jerome in a resigned voice. "You won't disturb me."

And the rest of his night, initiated with such passion, culminated in a long meditation on the place of the father in a family, and that of his valorous companion, the mother.

VERSAILLES

THE NEXT MORNING, the nineteenth of April, Jerome presented himself at 27 Caledonia Road at nine o'clock, dark circles under his eyes, his gait a little wobbly, though fortunately able to draw on the copious reserves of energy nature so generously provides humans under the age of thirty.

It was a little man — half-bald, his wrinkled face creased with smiles — who welcomed him.

"Monsieur Lupien," he said, offering his hand. "I'm Olivier Fradette, Monsieur Sicotte's assistant. Please do come in, sir, I beg you. A little brisk this morning, is it not, for April? I'm expecting my boss to be here any minute. He had a business breakfast that was supposed to be over by 8:30, but things must have dragged on, as is often the case. Which is why he asked me, yesterday, to be here to welcome you should he be detained, as Madame Desjarlais is also out, would you believe — and which is unusual, I must say, this early in the morning."

As he was submitting the stupefied young man to this deluge of comment, Fradette helped him off with his coat, hung it on a hook, and, signalling for Jerome to follow while turning back several times to smile at him, crossed the brightly lit hall that had so impressed Jerome the previous day, and led him down a corridor to Francine Desjarlais's office. They walked beyond it and came to the end of the corridor and three other doors. As they'd passed Francine's office, the door had opened slightly and Jerome thought he'd seen Alma, Francine's evanescent secretary, inside.

While Jerome was responding as best he could to the litany of banalities his companion was putting his way, the task at hand an obligation to be polite, he tried to think. The grotesque opulence of the hall that surrounded him smacked of the parvenu and, what with the salacious reward Francine Desjarlais had proffered him in Cuba and a thousand other small details, produced in him an increasingly disturbed impression. "What the hell have I got myself into?" he asked himself. "What kind of work am I going to be asked to do? This is beginning to seem bizarre. Keep your eyes peeled, kiddo."

"Ah, here we are," said Fradette, proudly. "This is the boss's office."

And with an exaggerated gesture he opened the door and stepped aside to allow Jerome to enter.

The large room was lined with carved oak panelling, daylight streaming through two large windows that looked onto a snow-covered garden slowly emerging from winter. But Jerome's first impression was of the gold and marble detailing that enveloped him in its magnificence. He stood in the doorway, speechless, overwhelmed as he was by the exquisite marquetry, inlaid with tortoiseshell, ivory, and delicately chiselled bronze and gold leaf. Never had he seen the like, except perhaps in period dramas. At the centre of the room was a majestic desk, the corners of which were inset with bronze figurines that gave it a regal appearance. On its flat surface stood an ultramodern, factory-made halogen lamp and a pile of dog-eared file folders that seemed comical in such a context. Behind the desk was a chair of the same ornate style and, facing it at an angle, two smaller ones. To the left was a sofa and a low, marble-topped table. Facing the door, between the two windows, stood a filing cabinet, topped by a filigree of sculptured gold at the centre of which the cabinet-maker had inserted a clock.

"Wow!" finally escaped the stunned Jerome's lips. "I've never seen anything like this before."

Fradette gave a small, satisfied chuckle.

"Not bad, eh?"

"You'd think we were in Versailles!"

"Well, my friend, you have a good eye. In fact, this all came from the workshop of André-Charles Boulle, the famous cabinetmaker to Louis XIV—and Louis XV, too, I think."

"Really?" exclaimed Jerome, walking about the room in amazement.

Suddenly, he remembered the admiration Balzac had for Boulle's pieces—a ruinous passion that, to the benefit of future generations, obliged the author to write like a demon to pacify his creditors.

The irritation that the ostentation of the corridor had produced in him started to fade.

"Oh, when I say this is Boulle," Fradette corrected himself, "I mean to say *copies* of Boulle, of course—but antique copies, just the same. Authentic Boulle work goes for millions today, my dear sir. Even the richest admirer would have to work pretty hard if he decided to furnish his office in real Boulle. But come in, please, Monsieur Sicotte will be here shortly. Here," he said, moving towards the sofa, "have a seat, make yourself comfortable. May I offer you a coffee?"

Seeing the young man's hesitation, he added, "Ha, you'd be ill advised to say no. The boss is also a connoisseur of fine coffee. So, what can I get you? A latte? Cappuccino? Espresso? Single? Double? How about an Americano? A Turkish coffee, perhaps? We have it all here."

"A latte, then, if you don't mind," said Jerome, impressed.

"Monsieur Sicotte has always been crazy for beauty," declared Fradette when he returned a few minutes later with two lattes. (Jerome couldn't help smiling at this stab at popular speech.) "I might even say," he continued, setting the cups on the table, "that he's a *very* fine connoisseur."

He sat down at the far end of the sofa, took a sip, puckered his lips with an air of satisfaction, and looked inquisitively at Jerome.

"Well?"

"Delicious, thank you."

For a few minutes they drank their coffee in silence.

"This office has another advantage for Monsieur Sicotte," Fradette suddenly declared, with a malicious sparkle in his eye. "It's a good distance from Madame's. The boss likes his peace and quiet."

"Ah, I see," said Jerome, hiding his astonishment at Fradette's indiscretion. "Er, I'm afraid I don't know him that well..."

"I see my remark has surprised you," Fradette continued. "You have assigned me to the category of trash-talker, I suppose. Yes, yes, I won't deny it, your reaction is quite normal... But I must tell you one thing: it's Monsieur Sicotte

himself who insists there be total frankness between us—
within limits, of course. It's no good working together, he
often says, if we don't share exactly what we are thinking.
No hypocrisy, no false politeness, that's the order of the day.
I was just putting that philosophy into practice. That way
we all know what we are dealing with in one another. It
cleanses the air amazingly, as you'll see."

A buzz came from the inside pocket of Fradette's jacket.
He quickly took out his cell phone and, turning his back
to Jerome, began responding in monosyllables to someone
who was evidently greatly agitated or angry. Whoever it
was spoke so loudly that Jerome, despite being some distance away, could hear and understand certain phrases of
the monologue the man was shouting into the telephone.
(It was evident he was in the grip of a terrible fury.) So it
was that the young man clearly heard most of a whole sentence: "Jesus fucking *Christ!*" the man spat into the phone.
"I'll teach him to show me some respect, the goddamned..."

The phrase caused Fradette to move farther away from
Jerome. Finally, looking at Jerome and raising his shoulders
in a gesture of apologetic helplessness, he left the room.
Jerome, alone with his coffee, was able to reflect to his heart's
content upon the enormous disparity between the style of
Sicotte's office and the ordinary, even banal, furnishings of
his wife's—a disparity no less evident in their characters.
He asked himself what were the precise tasks fulfilled by
this curious little man, Olivier Fradette, and by the vapor-
ous Alma. And finally he wondered what awaited him in
this strange place that seemed to get stranger with every
passing minute.

He finished his coffee, yawned, and ran his eye again
over the splendour surrounding him. Minutes passed. He

fought off the desire to get up and run his hands over all this magnificence; good manners and caution counselled him to save that pleasure for later.

"Excuse me!" bellowed Fradette, his face red as he burst back into the room. "Good gracious! What a way to welcome you on your first day!"

Jerome smiled.

"Please, no need to apologize for doing your job."

"That was Monsieur Sicotte," the assistant said, returning to the couch. He raised the cup of cold coffee to his lips and quickly set it back down with a grimace.

"Monsieur Sicotte?" repeated Jerome, surprised. He had a hard time relating the filthy swearing he'd heard over the telephone and the masterpieces of André Charles Boulle, cabinetmaker to Louis XIV.

"He's been held up and begs your forgiveness. Something unexpected, not unusual in this business. He won't be able to be here before eleven. Consequently, he's asked me to look after you."

"I can come back later," Jerome offered politely. "You must surely have a great many things to do."

"No, no, no . . . Everything's fine, everything's fine. In fact, I'm to give you a little test. I say a little one, but it's important and Monsieur Sicotte puts a lot of stock in it. I'm certain you'll pass with flying colours — you may even find it amusing. If you don't mind, then, would you be so good as to follow me? We'll head over to the shopping mall on rue Sherbrooke — Place Versailles."

And then, he added with a wink, "We'll still be in the court of the Sun King."

They went out into the corridor.

"Excuse me," said Fradette, "I'll be back in a second."

Jerome watched him scurry down the hall, elbows flapping like a dancing puppet, and disappear through a door. A moment went by. He coughed, rubbed his cheek, and inspected the hall. The walls were café au lait, and plaster moulding in a Corinthian style ran along the top of them. The carpet, also café au lait (the whole seemed an oath of devotion to the cult of coffee), had a pattern of interlacing roses — very Old English, and oak wainscotting carved in an intricate pattern. Nothing to rival the Boulle details, of course, but still, for a simple corridor, great effort had been made to achieve the *ne plus ultra* of conventional chic. Clearly, no leftist plot had ever been hatched on these premises.

Suddenly from the depths of the house came a female voice. Anxious, almost tearful, it seemed to be speaking into a telephone, but the distance made it hard to understand what was being said. Jerome recognized the voice of Francine Desjarlais, and he thought of her son in the detox centre in Portage. Had something bad happened to him? There was no doubt the unfortunate Felix was an ass, though he was a sympathetic one when all was said and done. And moreover, in a certain way, Jerome owed his new job to him — if he ever actually got it.

"Here I am! Here I am!" Fradette called out as he reappeared. "Sorry to have kept you waiting. I couldn't find the books. Shall we go?"

"Books? What books?"

"You'll see, you'll see. I can't say anything more at the moment."

His face had taken on a baiting, mysterious look. He seemed to be enjoying himself, though no more than if he were planning a harmless prank. He took Jerome by the arm, and the two men moved swiftly towards the exit.

When they reached the silent foyer, they put on their coats.

"Brrr! What a cold spring this has been!" muttered Fradette as they left the building. "It must be hard on lovers, don't you think?"

And he gave Jerome another of those mystifying looks Jerome was beginning to find unpleasant.

The sky had completely cleared, and from it came a cold light that illuminated the smallest details with pitiless precision. As they walked towards a shiny Camry that seemed to want to collect in its icy black skin all the ultraviolet rays of the glacial day, Jerome stole a glance at his companion. He thought he read in the man's charmless face — craggy, desiccated, dull as a potato — a mean and preoccupied expression. It seemed, to him, the face of a man easy to despise. *"Hey, you,"* he reprimanded himself. *"Enough of that.* What do you know about him anyway, imbecile?"

And to make up for his somewhat uncharitable thoughts, he put on a big smile and leaned towards Fradette, who had slid behind the wheel and signalled for him to get in. "I've heard good things about these Camrys," he said. "You made a good choice."

"Yes, thanks, it's not a bad car. Which reminds me, Madame Desjarlais tells me you don't have a car. You need to get one."

"I'm in the process of looking for one," said Jerome, blushing.

"Bah! It's not that urgent… And anyway, there's this little test for you to pass. But I'm confident, I'm confident," he said quickly, "no need to worry."

"Where exactly in Place Versailles are we going?" Jerome asked, more and more intrigued.

"I'm not entirely sure. It's up to you."

"Up to me?"

"Yes...to you, and to circumstances, of course...Do you know how certain historians characterized Napoleon? No? They said he was *a man of circumstances*. That was his strength. He never boxed himself in with plans that were too restricting, so he was able to adapt to events and make the best decisions possible. It worked out very well for him, at least for a time. I try to be like him...in my own humble way, of course!"

Fradette, looking straight ahead, laughed as if at some sort of in-joke.

"Jesus," thought Jerome. "Is this guy crazy? What have I got myself into, for Christ's sake?"

He asked no more questions but, increasingly perplexed, diverted himself by contemplating the luxurious houses on either side of the street.

Three-quarters of an hour later, after exchanging at best a few words, they stopped in front of one of the entrances to the mall. Fradette turned to Jerome.

"We chose Place Versailles despite what I said earlier, not for its name but to make the test easier for you. The clientele here, as you know, is mostly francophone. That'll give you an advantage."

"Whatever you say," sighed Jerome. He stepped out of the car to join his companion, who was whistling and swinging his briefcase as he waited.

"These notorious books, am I going see them at last?" asked Jerome, unable to put the brakes on his impatience anymore.

In reply, Fradette opened his briefcase and showed him the books. There were two, brand new and still wrapped in cellophane with their price tags on. The first was called *How to Succeed in Business from Scratch*, by a certain James Sharrett. On the cover of the second, a more stylish volume, was a nymphette in her birthday suit, exhibiting her most intimate charms and holding a banner above her head that read, in flowery characters, *Love in Paris in the Roaring Twenties*.

"Naughty, isn't it?" sniggered Fradette, letting his syrupy gaze dwell on the illustration. "And this is nothing compared to what's inside . . . I have a copy at home. It doesn't quite make one abstemious, if you know what I mean."

Fradette snickered, Jerome laughed. But his laughter was hardly that of a man at ease.

"And what am I supposed to do with these?"

"Come on, we'll grab a coffee and I'll explain everything."

He led Jerome into the mall, and a short while later they were sitting at a table in the Bon Café, where, another latte in front of him, he learned about the test he was imminently to undergo — one that would allow his prospective employer to assess his street sense, self-confidence, and ability to get on with people.

He had, Fradette explained, an hour in which to sell one of the two books or, better, both of them — at a reasonable price (at least $5 for the Sharrett and $15 for the book of porn). And he needed to stay out of the shopping centre bookstore — which, in any case, didn't buy books from individuals.

Jerome, exasperated, looked at Fradette without saying a word.

"You'll agree that we have placed you in a position of maximum advantage," Fradette continued in a presumptuous tone that grated on Jerome's nerves. "*Primo*: you will be working in your own language. *Secundo*: the two books will appeal to quite different customers, doubling your chance of success. *E tertio,* they both deal with very popular subjects—money and sex. What more can I say?"

"And what if I don't sell them in an hour?"

Fradette gave a little shrug, as if to say the decision wasn't his to make.

"And the point of this stupid test is what, exactly?"

"I just told you, my friend. My bosses have the highest regard for education and degrees, but they also know that a person can have a suitcase full of doctorates and still not know how to strap on a pair of boots—and I mean no offence, it goes without saying."

"All I have is a B.A.," Jerome said testily. He took a sip of his coffee, immersed in thoughts that brought a variety of expressions to his face, from amusement to disdain.

"So?" said Fradette. "The clock's ticking."

Jerome replied with a grunt.

"Come on, man, show a little courage. I'm positive you'll pass the test. I've got a nose for such things."

Said Jerome warily, even antagonistically, "And I am one of how many that has taken the test?"

Fradette scowled, and stood up.

"We're wasting time," he said. "Are you going to do this or not? I've a lot of work I could be doing back at the office."

Now it was Jerome's turn to stand. He picked up the books.

"Do you have a bag? I don't want to be accused of stealing."

"Yes, of course."

Fradette handed him a heavy-duty plastic bag with cloth handles. Jerome slid the books into it and waited at the door of the café as his torturer paid the bill.

"I'd prefer it if you didn't watch me," said Jerome in a surly tone when Fredette joined him.

"Whatever you say, boss. I'll vanish like a puff of smoke. We'll meet back here in an hour. Good luck!"

He gave Jerome a pat on the shoulder and, smiling conspiratorially, disappeared around a corner.

"Son of a bitch!" muttered Jerome between his teeth. "Now what do I do?"

Stage fright robbed him of his better instincts, and irritation took care of the rest. He moved off in the opposite direction to the one his curious trainer had taken. It was almost noon. Customers and window shoppers streamed by, adding their number to numerous old men sitting on benches, busying their days of leisure in conversation and staring at beautiful women.

He strode along, bag in hand, eyebrows furrowed, looking about in search of an opportunity, or at least the seed of a strategy, and came up with neither. If he tried to sell his merchandise he'd be taken either for a thief, a drug addict needing quick cash for a fix, or some weirdo strung out on coke. The triad of possibilities sapped his courage and replaced it with a sickening feeling of humiliation that left him weak in the knees. Ten minutes had already gone by! He had to get moving—or give the whole thing up and get the hell out of there like a beaten dog with his tail between his legs.

He saw two adolescents bantering on a bench and decided, chancily or not, to sit down next to them. The boys—one blond and the other with nut-brown hair—were about sixteen or seventeen, neatly dressed and the epitome of young, white, middle-class francophones. Jerome was a little surprised to see them about at a time of day when they ought to have been in school. Pretending to consult his notebook, he eavesdropped on their conversation. The blond was talking about a certain Guillaume, who'd been working part-time for a couple of years at the Quartier Latin cinema on rue Émery and had been able to buy himself a sweet little Nissan 2000 as a result.

"It's barely got 20,000 kilometres on it, and it's in great shape, no shit, clean as if it just came out of the factory. He took me for a ride in it yesterday. It purrs like a kitten, man, but if you want a little pep it's got all you need and then some, crushes you against the back of your seat. Next winter, Guillaume's driving to Miami with his girlfriend during the Christmas vacation. That's some way to break up a long winter, eh?"

His companion looked skeptical.

"Sure, but how many hours did this Guillaume guy have to work for minimum wage to buy it? What a mug's life!"

The discussion heated up, with the blond protesting that taking a part-time job, even badly paid, was "better than sitting on your hands dreaming." His companion took the opposite view — that "crappy jobs lead to a shitty life," and working as an independent contractor paid a thousand times better and was a hundred thousand times more interesting. In his view, it was the only dignified way to work, and he'd never let himself do anything else.

Jerome, intrigued by the conversation, put his hand in the bag and, turning to the boys, showed them one of the two books.

"Hey, guys, sorry to bother you, but I couldn't help overhearing your conversation," he interrupted. And then, looking at the youth with brown hair, he said, "You know, you're right. I even have a proposal to make that might interest you: a great book—and at a bargain price. *How to Succeed in Business from Scratch*. I'm willing to part with it for, let's say, seven bucks. It's still in its wrapper. At that price, I'm practically giving it away."

The teenagers, surprised, looked at each other and exchanged shifty, wary looks.

"*What?*" yelled the brown-headed boy, jumping to his feet. "*Give you a blow job for twenty bucks? You fucking pervert!*"

Jerome froze for a second, then walked away as quickly as he could, red as a beet, as the two louts behind him laughed uproariously and gave each other high fives. Shoppers walking in the mall stopped and stared in astonishment. An old woman holding the hand of a small boy licking an ice-cream cone stepped in front of Jerome, arm outstretched to halt him, her expression apoplectic.

"You should be ashamed of yourself!"

Jerome fled as if from a swarm of wasps, his heart beating so hard he was soon out of breath. To think he'd wasted ten precious minutes on those little bastards! He might as well throw in the towel, this sort of "test" was not for him. He wouldn't even bother to wait at the café for Fradette and inform him of his decision, he'd just bugger off. One humiliation was enough.

A minute later he was in the food court. A ring of fast-food outlets surrounded dozens of tables and seats attached to the floor by steel uprights, the air thick with a greasy, tomatoey miasma. At this time of day business was brisk. People were lined up at most of the counters, and almost all the tables were occupied. The steady hum that filled the vast hall calmed his nerves. He stopped to look at the diners bent over their paper or plastic plates and saw a vacant table twenty feet away from him. In the next instant, he was sitting at it, setting down his bag of books. How good it felt to lose himself in the anonymity of the crowd, and to feel as though he no longer existed. His morning had seriously knocked the stuffing out of him. He could barely stand, his head was like a ball of lead, and his ego had been reduced to nothing.

He realized that he absolutely had to return to the café where Fradette was waiting and give the books back to him: failing to sell the books was humiliating enough, without seeming a thief on top of it all.

Then, to his surprise, he realized that despite being so profoundly irritated, he was hungry. The smell of pizza was titillating his salivary glands — how insatiable his guts were. No wonder buffet lunches were served in funeral parlours, and survivors of the wreck of the *Medusa* had ended up feasting on each other. Looking up, he tried to identify the outlet that was issuing such a tantalizing odour, and in doing so his eye met that of a man sitting at the table next to him who, from behind his newspaper, had been staring furtively at Jerome's bag of books. The stranger went hurriedly back to reading. Their eyes had met for no more than a fraction of a second, but Jerome's brain was functioning at full speed. His ears were burning. Clearly the contents of the bag, partially open, had attracted his neighbour's gaze. The man, in his forties, looked like a salesman — what with his pocket handkerchief and flowery silk tie — and had just finished eating.

Perhaps he'd be able to salvage the situation. But he'd have to act quickly.

Jerome stood up, whistling a breezy tune, and, leaving the bag on the table, made his way towards one of the outlets. Instead of heading to the pizzeria — too far away — he opted for the sushi counter, conveniently close. Two enormous women were chatting as they waited for their orders. With a few quick steps, he joined them and, although he had nothing to say to them, took part in their conversation, dispensing banalities that they received with civility. From time to time he glanced at his table and saw, to his joy, that the stranger, still half-hidden behind his newspaper, was appearing increasingly restless.

The two women were served their orders, said goodbye to Jerome, and left. Then it happened. As Jerome was in the process of placing his order, the man rolled up his newspaper, stood up slowly, approached Jerome's table, and, with a quick look over his shoulder, picked up the bag and moved nonchalantly and then more and more speedily away.

"Hey, mister!" shouted the Japanese waiter as Jerome headed off. "Your sushi! You don't want it?"

"Yes, yes, I'll be right back," replied Jerome with a wide grin. Then he took off in pursuit of the book thief. The crowded room made his task easier. Twice the man turned to see if he was being followed, and both times Jerome was able to hide behind a pillar. The man slowed his pace, turned down one aisle, then another, and finally, sure of his success, sat down on a bench and discreetly examined the contents of the bag with a satisfied smile. *Love in Paris in the Roaring Twenties* seemed to appeal to him.

"Bad luck, sir," said a voice behind him. "I'm a security officer."

The thief jerked around with a kind of hoarse gasp and stared at Jerome, his eyes wide with terror. He no doubt wanted to flee — but that would have meant leaving his coat behind, Jerome holding it firmly by the collar — and must have concluded that running would only make the situation worse.

"What's going on?" he babbled, getting to his feet.

"You have just stolen those books from me, sir," Jerome said coldly, pointing to the bag.

The three other shoppers sitting on the bench stood up and, retreating a little, observed the scene, simultaneously curious and frightened. A low murmur, sprinkled with indignant exclamations, started to build in the small group that had formed around them. The arrest had become a spectacle and Jerome was afraid a real security guard would appear and spoil his plan.

"Follow me, sir," he ordered, taking the thief by the arm. "Come on, quickly . . . and don't try any funny stuff," he said, showing the man his cell phone. (Oh, how his fertile imagination amazed him.) "At the first sign of trouble, I'll set off the alarm. Got it? Good. I'll be easy on you and let go of your arm, but you've been warned, all right?"

"Where are we going?" the man stammered, keeping his head down and staring at the ground ahead of him with a doleful look on his face.

"To the security office, sir, to call the police."

Now what was Jerome going to do? He had no idea where the security office was, or even if there was one!

They passed a supermarket and turned down a less frequented aisle in which the windows of several unoccupied boutiques were covered with kraft paper.

"I'm fucked," said the man gloomily.

Large drops of sweat ran down his forehead.

"Well, sir, that's not my fault. All you had to do was conduct yourself honestly."

"What a mess! I have to tell you, it's the first time —"

"The way you behaved just now, I doubt that very much."

"But I'm telling you, it's true! I'm a respectable person... I've always made an honest living... I don't know what came over me, I swear... For the past two months I've been going through a rough patch... a *really* rough patch... enough to make me lose my head, I'm not kidding... You can give me another chance, can't you?"

Jerome slowed almost imperceptibly and looked at his watch: still twenty minutes before he had to meet Fradette at the café.

His silence seemed to provide hope to the thief with the flowery tie. He stopped and turned to Jerome with an imploring look.

"Let me go, please... I beg you... I'll give you anything, sir, if you let me go. Everyone deserves a second chance, don't they?"

A young woman went by, pushing a wheelchair in which an elderly invalid sat, nervously turning a pack of cigarettes in her fingers. Then two maintenance men showed up, tool boxes in their hands, laughing at someone named Réjean who had just done something stupid.

"Right, how much do you have on you?" asked Jerome, harshly. He felt his cheeks reddening. The path between villainy and the accomplishment of his goal was a rotten one. But a sort of rage pressed him on.

"How much?" said the thief.

His eyes started to brighten, his relief pitiful.

"Let me see, sir, give me a minute."

He took out his wallet, his hand shaking as he opened it, and began counting in a low voice.

"Er... a hundred and twenty bucks," he said, looking up as if begging for alms. "And a bit of change. Is that enough?"

Jerome pushed the coins away with disdain.

"Just give me eighty and get out of here," he said. "Go on, get lost. I've seen enough of you."

The man gave him an ambivalent look and walked off rapidly. In an instant, he had disappeared around a corner. Jerome left in the opposite direction and, as he was no longer sure where the café was, stopped at a manicure boutique to ask for directions and then hurried the rest of the way at a slow jog. He had only four or five minutes to spare.

When he finally arrived, Fradette was just sitting down. He welcomed Jerome with a big smile.

"Mission accomplished," the candidate announced happily.

"I know."

"You can tell by how I look?"

"I'm a born observer, my friend... Come, sit down. I'll buy you lunch. You must be famished."

Jerome dropped into a chair and stretched his legs.

"And how! I didn't have time to eat. At first, it didn't go so well, to say the least! I almost gave up."

He glanced over the menu, licking his lips.

"I know," said Fradette.

Jerome looked up quickly.

"You know? How do you know?"

He stared at Fradette for a moment.

"You were following me?"

"You're pretty good at being evasive, but I'm pretty good at following," replied Fradette with a twisted smile.

"You were following me," Jerome repeated. He was surprised and more than a little annoyed.

"No need to take that tone," said Fradette. "Monsieur Sicotte asked me to keep an eye on you. If you'd known I was following you, it would have cramped your style."

"So, you know how much money I got from that poor prick?"

"You should have taken it all — never let a thief off lightly! But no, no, keep the money. It's yours. You've earned it."

"I don't want it."

Jerome put the bills on the table. Fradette pouted sardonically and picked them up.

"Your ethics do you credit, my friend."

Jerome replied with a small grunt and went back to reading the menu.

Looking up, he asked suddenly, "Do you think I passed the test?"

"Hands down! I'd even go so far as to say . . ."

Fradette halted himself.

"Do you mind if I call you Jerome?" he asked, "This 'sir' business gives me the creeps. After all, I have an idea we'll be seeing a lot of one another. Obviously it isn't up to me to decide, but in my humble opinion your bag is in business and this business is in the bag."

"I just got lucky," observed Jerome, modestly.

"Yes, but you made your own luck." And turning to the waiter who stood patiently at the table, hands behind his back, he said, "Linguini Alfredo, please."

"I'll have the same," said Jerome.

"And let's have the wine list," said Fradette.

SITTING ACROSS FROM Jerome, Charlie felt the sort of shiver that typically precedes a heart attack. The two friends were in Jerome's kitchen, later the same day. Jerome, trying not to sound like he was bragging, had just related the avalanche of events that concomitantly had transformed both his love life and professional career. And never, never, had

Charlie listened to a recounting of such extraordinarily bizarre events: after spending the night in bed with his mother hen and her chick—which, why beat around the bush, was in somewhat dubious taste—Jerome had transformed himself into a crook in a mall and shaken down a kleptomaniac, thus earning himself the job of assistant lobbyist with a starting salary of fifty thousand smackers a year!

He'd never heard anything like it before in his life. It was also the kind of thing that sooner or later could bring a shitload of trouble down on his head and make the problems Jerome had had so far seem like a Shangri-La.

Jerome put up his hand.

"Hold on, pal! I think you're spreading it a bit thick. Let's take it one point at a time, if you don't mind. First of all, Eugenie and I didn't make love while her little girl was in bed with us, we did it *beforehand*. Let's get that straight. I'm not a pervert, pal, and I have no intention of letting the kid back in bed the next time I'm with her mother, okay? It was our first night together, and I couldn't very well play the dictator and put my foot down in *her* home. A guy has to know how to behave. Secondly, the shakedown. Sure, I agree this Fradette character is a little weird, but Sicotte, his boss—my boss—strikes me as an okay kind of guy. He was as taken aback as I was by this test Fradette put me through; I got the feeling it wasn't his idea and that he wasn't too happy about it. In any case, in a couple of days I'll no doubt have a better sense of the situation."

Charlie looked at him for a moment without speaking, reached for the stein of beer in front of him, took a long swig, then spoke in a strained, anemic voice—one his friend hadn't heard before.

"As for your good woman, I don't know, Jerome, she might be legit—"

"She's great!" Jerome interrupted enthusiastically.

"Let's say she is, let's give her that. You know, if you tell me stories about kids having nightmares in the middle of the night, I'll take your word for it. It's not my world, really isn't. I've never had kids and I'm an only child. But this Sicotte character..."

Looking up, gazing into the distance, he gave the impression of a seer having a horrific vision.

"Your Sicotte, his wife, their drug-addicted son and the whole shebang—Jesus, I'd get the hell out if I were you. You never know!"

He took another long draft of his beer, burped into the palm of his hand, and then, leaning towards his friend with his elbows on the table, displayed the fervour of a Raelian in recruitment mode.

"Why don't you go see my psychologist, Jerome? You need to take stock of your life, it's plain as day, and *rebirth* is perfect for that. It's a treatment that puts you back in touch with your true roots. And Joëlle Frémont is extraordinary at it. Go see her. I mean it. You'll thank me for the rest of your life."

Jerome sneered and got up.

"I'd prefer to consult with someone in Outremont in a treatment two people do together and that, frankly, works wonders, even if it isn't the latest thing. Now if you'll excuse me for taking off on you, chum, I have a long métro ride ahead of me."

"Still," said Charlie, leaving the apartment with his friend, "I've never seen anything like this. Your story stinks to high heaven. Whatever happens, don't say I didn't warn you."

Jerome was content merely to smile, and they parted at the entrance to the Côte-des-Neiges métro station, Charlie deciding on the spur of the moment to pop into the Renaud-Bray bookstore a few steps away. His decision may simply have been a pretext for cutting short a meeting that had verged on the tempestuous, and as the subway carried Jerome towards his night of love (at least he hoped that was what awaited him), he found himself staring off into space, deep in thought. In the heat of arguing with his friend, and for the pleasure of winning whatever contest their conversation had been, he had slightly modified the story of his encounter with Sicotte after his trip to Place Versailles. Or, more the case, he'd been a little selective about the details: expected at eleven, Sicotte hadn't shown up at his office until late in the afternoon, and when he did so it was with the harassed but satisfied expression of a man who'd just accomplished a difficult task. But what task? Jerome never found out.

Fradette, accompanied by Jerome, had entered Sicotte's office to share the good news about their new employee. Sicotte's shock and surprise at the curious test to which their recruit had been subjected struck Jerome as phony. It had not suggested displeasure, so much as secret satisfaction.

In the end, after frowning, furrowing his brow, and letting out a few grunts, Sicotte had broken out into peals of laughter.

"Well, Olivier put you through a strange sort of test, my friend, and I'd go so far as to say one that may not have been in the best of taste. But I have to admit it was conclusive. You showed remarkable resourcefulness and presence of mind. I don't see how I could do anything but take you into my service."

He held out his hand.

"Congratulations. See you tomorrow morning at nine."

"Thank you, sir," Jerome stammered happily. "Until tomorrow, then."

But as he was leaving his new employer's sumptuous office, he had sensed a silence of a curious density settle in the room — one that endured for as long as it took him, ears pricked, to walk the length of the hallway. It seemed, he thought, the kind of silence observed by two people waiting to be alone and able to talk about the person who'd just left.

FOR THE NEXT several days, the episode at Place Versailles filled Jerome with a muddy sense of irritation. Charlie's warning came back time and again. Who exactly was this Severin Sicotte? Was he simply an employer with a strange way of selecting those who worked for him — or was he a crook? A telling detail: despite the brilliance of his victory in the test imposed on him, he'd never said a word about it to Eugenie, always putting it off until later. Two or three times, showing up for work after a sleepless night, he'd been on the verge of submitting his resignation — but each time he had second thoughts. After all, the salary was good. In truth, he'd never earned so much money and, so far, the boring work they'd given him struck him as nothing untoward. Three days into the job, he bought a small Honda — his first new car — and he was very proud of it.

Weeks passed, and his anger over the Place Versailles incident subsided. To prepare him for his real work, he was told to organize a pile of documents that rose almost to the ceiling of a small, windowless room known somewhat grandly as the Archives.

"Yes, I know it's not exactly exciting work," said Sicotte

when Jerome expressed his surprise, "but I think it's a good way for you to prepare for your future responsibilities."

From time to time, Sicotte or Fradette — but most often the latter — came to see him and chat about this and that. The questions sometimes bordered on quite personal topics; Jerome felt his probationary period was going well.

During this painstaking work, Jerome did not come across a single document that struck him as suspect, though the majority of papers, he had to admit, were Greek to him, and he often needed to consult with Fradette about how to file them. Two or three times a day, the boss or his assistant would summon him and dictate a letter or an email they judged particularly important, neither of them seeming comfortable with the written word, whether in French or in English. There again, the content of the messages aroused no suspicions in him.

"How lucky we are to have you," confided Fradette one day, after sending off an email that had needed several edits and corrections. "I wish I were as cultured as you!"

"It's not a question of culture, Olivier, just basic knowledge. What did you do before I was here?"

"Ah, well, if I needed it, I'd see Francine. Her French is pretty good, too."

But from the expression on his face, going to Francine was a last resort, used only in extreme cases.

"You don't seem to like her very much," Jerome remarked, giving the frankness demanded by the house rules a go.

"I'm not being paid to like her, I'm being paid to work for her," chuckled Fradette maliciously.

Jerome pushed his enquiries no further.

Since being hired, he'd had only brief encounters with the woman to whom he owed his employment. He'd arrive in the mornings, and she would call out a warm "Hello, Jerome. Everything going well? Still liking the job?"

"I'm learning, I'm learning," Jerome would answer, infusing his voice with as much enthusiasm as he could muster. They'd exchange a few platitudes about the weather, then go their own ways.

Husband and wife conducted their business lives entirely independently. During working hours, they never saw each other one on one except over lunch, on the rare occasions when one or the other was not eating out. Alma, meanwhile, seemed to have donned a cloak of invisibility; occasionally, if Jerome passed the door to Francine's office and it was open, he'd hear her voice — a low murmur with singsong intonations that sounded oddly out of place. By a curious association of ideas, the voice reminded him of *The Lady from Shanghai*, that peculiar thriller Orson Welles had made for Rita Hayworth before their divorce. Something about its troubled and mysterious atmosphere, although of course Alma, delicate and diminutive Alma, with her long, black hair, was nothing like the gorgeous redhead with the voluptuous figure.

One morning, he arrived and found himself face to face with Alma. She looked at him with a curious smile in which irony and sensuality seemed at once interwoven and separate. She dipped her head, which increased his embarrassment, and said: "Good morning, Monsieur Jerome, I see you are well," in a faintly Hispanic accent — as if she were rolling small balls in her mouth.

"Yes, thank you," he replied, trying to mask his discomfort. "I hope all's well with you too, Alma?"

"Francine would like to speak with you," she said, not responding to his comment. "Would you follow me, please?"

At the door to her employer's office she stopped and backed away, bowing her head again. Francine Desjarlais, wearing a business suit and perched nonchalantly on the edge of her desk, was having a fiery telephone conversation in Spanish. With an animated gesture she pointed to a chair. Alma was about to leave when Desjarlais said, "*Momento,*" to whoever was on the other end of the line. She put a hand over the mouthpiece.

"Stay here, Alma," she said.

"Do I really have to?" Alma replied, wrinkling her nose.

The look her boss gave her was transparently eloquent. Alma leaned against the wall and stared at the carpet, while Jerome, lost in conjecture, studied his fingernails. The telephone conversation resumed, but ended almost immediately with an exclamation from Desjarlais, who replaced the receiver with a look of profound irritation.

"Filthy country!" she said. "And they speak of the revolution of the people, justice for all and all that rigmarole. It makes me sick!"

"You mean...Cuba?" Jerome hazarded.

"What other country would I be talking about?" she said, agitated. She took a deep breath that seemed to suck all the air out of the room, walked behind her desk, fell heavily into her chair, and threw her head back on the headrest.

"I'm sorry," she said, "I'm being dreadful this morning. But what a way to start the day! Oh, Lord! Do you know what's happened?"

Jerome raised his eyebrows inquisitively.

"They're demanding your extradition!"

For a moment, silence fell upon the room. Desjarlais, though, was staring at a fly and following its flight path as if she'd forgotten the presence of the young man who—pale as a piece of chalk, fingers digging into the arms of his chair—seemed on the point of fainting.

"You...you're serious?" he finally managed to say.

"My poor friend," she said dourly, "no one is more serious than I am this morning."

"But, Madame Desjarlais, what happened?"

"Francine, call me Francine. I don't know the whole story—or maybe, damn it, I know the story too well. Someone in the police or the government down there wants more money. They always want more money. For three days now I've been trying to sort the bloody problem out. I didn't mention it until now because I didn't want to upset you. What good would it have done, anyway? But now we must talk about it. I've just been in touch with a lawyer in Havana, a Maître Augusto Herreras. We have to put an end to this business, we can't have it hanging over our heads. As if I don't have enough problems with Felix already. Do you know that he tried to check out of Portage two days ago?"

"I don't give a shit about your Felix and his drug problems, my fat friend," answered Jerome in his head. He raised his hands from the armrests and saw that they were burning red, then cleared his throat to control his voice.

"And what did the lawyer say?"

"Oh, you know, being a lawyer down there is a strange business. Their situation is not the same as ours, as you can well imagine. When you can buy a judge as easily as I do a bottle of wine—well, let's say a particularly good bottle of wine, and perhaps in this case, that's to our advantage... But evidently it's still a risky business. In a dictatorship, my dear, judges have three eyes: two in their face and a third in the back of their head that they use to watch the authorities. And the authorities are unpredictable."

She heaved another sigh and began tapping the fingers of her right hand on her desk; her nails were painted dark red and made dry little clicking sounds that drove Jerome nuts.

"Anyway, Herreras implied that it would be good if we greased the palms of one or two functionaries in the Ministry of Justice, but at the same time he strongly recommended that we come up with an iron-clad alibi for you — and that's where you come in," she said, addressing Alma.

Behind him came the sound of sliding feet, and a cough, before silence established itself again. Jerome didn't dare turn his head.

"What role would that be?" he asked in a low voice.

"At first I thought the lovely payment I sent to your room that night would settle the matter."

A small, stifled laugh made itself heard from the end of the room. Jerome didn't turn; his cheeks were burning as well as his hands.

"I thought it would be enough for Hilda to swear on oath," continued the businesswoman, "that on such and such a day and at such and such a time, she was in your company making — aah, an alibi, no? But her occupation, you understand, doesn't give her a lot of credibility. So I thought of Alma."

"How sweet of you," murmured the assistant, scoffing slightly.

Jerome, livid, jumped to his feet.

"What? You want me to return to Cuba for that little prick Felix? And with the prospect, if things go wrong, of rotting in one of Castro's prisons for God knows how many years? No way!"

His hands spread on the desk, he shot her a ferocious look.

"*Calm down,*" she ordered, articulating each word and

entirely unimpressed by his display of temper. "First of all, my dear boy, let me point out that no one asked you to get in a fight with the man."

"Your son would be dead," spat Jerome, "if I hadn't."

"Second," she went on, raising her hand, "no one has said anything about going back to Cuba. For now, all we need to do—"

"For now?" sneered Jerome.

"Listen to me, little man," she hissed, her turn now for anger. "I've already spent a small fortune on your behalf, and it still isn't settled! I am responsible for *nothing* you did that day, nor that my son did. Agreed? Good. I want that to be crystal clear. I'm trying to extract both of you from a very delicate situation, and it isn't easy. I'm bending over backwards for you and, under the circumstances, I'd expect acknowledgement, if not a little respect, in return."

Jerome, admonished, looked at Francine for a moment and then sat back down. Alma remained at the back of the room. She coughed twice. Jerome wanted to turn around but stopped himself. Impossible to know if those coughs expressed discomfort or amusement.

Francine Desjarlais threw herself back in her chair, stretched her legs out under the desk, and, letting out another deep sigh, said, "I'm sorry... This business has me as upset as you, Jerome, not to mention the fact that the 'little prick,' as you call him, has caused me sleepless nights ever since—"

She raised her hand theatrically and let it fall again.

Jerome lowered his head and sighed, studying his fingernails again.

"All right," he said after a while. "What do you suggest we do?"

"All that's needed is for you and Alma to sign a declaration, under oath, stating that on the afternoon of April 10, between two and four in the afternoon, you were together in your room, Jerome's — or Alma's, it doesn't matter — saying that you were, well, *talking*, if you like. In any case, the details are unimportant."

"Was Alma in Cuba?" he asked, surprised. "No one told me that."

"I hope that's as far as the alibi goes," said Alma, emitting a little laugh that grated on Jerome's nerves.

This time he turned to look at her. She seemed to be finding the whole business extremely amusing. Was she heartless, he wondered, or just silly? Perhaps both?

"Where do we go to fill out this...declaration?" he asked sternly.

"I'm calling the consulate now," said Desjarlais. "No doubt we can get the whole thing settled tomorrow before noon. I'll let you know as soon as I've spoken to them."

She stood and cast a look towards the door: the meeting was over.

IT WAS GENERALLY assumed that it was Francine Desjarlais who had persuaded her husband to hire Jerome on a trial basis. At first, she was pushed to do so by her knowledge of him: after all, had he not saved her son from almost certain death? And he'd done so with a cold-blooded pugnacity that, upon reflection, struck her as potentially useful to their own business ends. Perhaps she also took into consideration the attraction she felt for the handsome young man; wicked tongues might have had it that, in paying for the services of the enticing Hilda, she was sleeping with him by proxy. There are some pleasures the very wealthy can give themselves, even as they wait for better ones.

Severin Sicotte had agreed to take Jerome on without giving it much thought, but he'd needed guarantees, and those were not easy to obtain. For two years, his business had prospered, work was pouring in, and a strong, dynamic acolyte would certainly be useful. He could count on Olivier Fradette's dedication, but his assistant lacked class and, considering the new developments in his business, he needed someone with plenty of it. Jerome was such a man: a young university graduate with impeccable manners, who expressed himself extremely well, but did not appear too cool. Nevertheless, the tasks he intended to give Jerome demanded a particularly elevated skill set.

Thus he had ordered Fradette to put Jerome's ingenuity to the test, and the latter's performance at Place Versailles had exceeded all expectations. There was something of the pit bull in this young man, and one didn't see that every day. In this day and age, a lot of young, middle-class people were like pink-nosed little rabbits; their lives were arranged to suit them, they were naive, and many were only starting to understand that high principles were no more than ornaments hung on official speeches, sermons, and other such nonsense, designed to fool good people and ensure social peace. In the case of his recruit, Sicotte needed to guard against a surfeit of indignation that would harm his business dealings, as university graduates and similarly spoiled children could easily become gossips, and nothing gave them more pleasure than to make a spectacle of themselves in the media.

By saving the life of their good-for-nothing son in Cuba, Jerome, without knowing it, had delivered himself into their hands on a silver platter. The whole episode was more ingenious than anything they could have arranged!

Of course the minor drug trafficker Jerome had beaten up in Varadero had long since left the hospital and gone back to his life of petty crime. And it was in talking over the tiresome affair with her husband that Francine had come up with the story of involuntary homicide and Cuba's demand for Jerome's extradition. She was very proud of her scheme, since the chance of Jerome trying to verify it was practically nil!

Her husband had been opposed to the idea at first, remarking that it was too dirty a trick to play on someone who'd done them such a great favour. But Francine, never mind her show of being a caring mother, was in fact as tough as leather and, in the end, had convinced Sicotte that prudence was paramount and nothing prevented them from revealing their subterfuge when the time was right — when they could count on his loyalty. His reaction might be jaundiced, at first, but soon enough he'd be laughing along with them.

Near the end of May, Sicotte invited Jerome to lunch at the Beaver Club, in the Queen Elizabeth Hotel. The young man had never set foot in that gastronomic temple of the Canadian bourgeoisie, in which the filmmaker Pierre Falardeau had, in 1985, shot *Time of the Buffoons* — a short, merciless exposé of an evening in which the federalist elite had, in the two-hundred-year-old club, celebrated their privilege in period costume and with grotesque pomposity. Jerome, startled and vaguely ill at ease, found himself sitting at a table with his boss in front of a fireplace in which burned three maple logs that would no doubt have won prizes for their design. On their way to the table, Sicotte had stopped to say hello to a prosperous-looking man, bald as a billiard ball, accompanied by a woman using Botox to appear thirty but who instead looked embalmed. He introduced Jerome in elegiac terms in which the words "relief" and "youth" figured largely, accompanied by little pats on the back in the appropriate places.

"*Really?* Wonderful!" exclaimed the woman with a cascading laugh while her companion nodded gravely, like a connoisseur before a putative Van Gogh someone had found in an attic.

"Do you know who that was?" Sicotte whispered in Jerome's ear when they were seated. "No? It's Marc Lalonde. He was a cabinet minister under Pierre Trudeau, one of the most powerful men of his day, lad. The woman, I can't place her..."

Sicotte insisted that Jerome order the venison steak garnished with a potato soufflé, fiddleheads, and wild mushrooms. And breaking his habit of never drinking alcohol at noon—it clouded his thoughts, he said—Sicotte ordered a Bordeaux Champmeslé-Dutrisac 1998, which the sommelier had recommended with an emotional paean.

It would seem he's about to make some kind of announcement, Jerome said to himself.

The conversation got rolling with talk of current affairs. Jerome, trying to hide his uneasiness, drifted off into speculations about what had compelled his boss to invite him to such a posh place. Animated by his third glass of wine, Sicotte dipped his head towards Jerome and, lowering his voice, said, "I know I told you I was a lobbyist, and it's true— and it's also not true: in fact, I'm not listed in the Registry of Lobbyists, which, by law, I should be."

"I suspected as much," Jerome couldn't help saying. The wine was affecting him, too.

"You suspected?" said Sicotte, his chin lifted in an ironic

pout. "Oh well, a point in your favour, I suppose. In our line of work, your antennae need to be tuned as finely as silk... And that appears to be so in your case."

"So," said Jerome, "what exactly *do* you do, Severin?"

Just at that moment the waiter came to refill their glasses and ask them if everything was satisfactory. He was a tall, thin man of indeterminate age, with smooth hair and the expressive range of a sphinx. Sicotte waited until he left and then, apparently having forgotten Jerome's question, launched into a long monologue, tinged at times with nostalgia.

"When I left Laval University in 1981 with my lawyer's diploma under my arm, I went back to Farnham, my hometown, and opened a law practice there. For twenty-two months, three weeks, and two days I nearly starved to death. O naive youth! as the poet says. Farnham already had all the lawyers it needed, and I was the one too many. I'd never been so thin or so long in the face. My girlfriend at the time thought I'd come down with tuberculosis! I was about to go back to Quebec City when old Dr. Ostiguy, who'd delivered all of my mother's children, came to see me one day because he was having problems with the Radio Shack chain, which was trying to buy his Victorian house on the main street so they could put one of their electronics stores in it. That's when I realized there was a lot of money to be made out there, especially when your client—in this case, poor Dr. Ostiguy was beginning to get a little shaky in the head—didn't really know the true value of what he had to sell—no, no, my friend, don't frown at me like that. There was never anything to reproach me for, because my training in the law always kept me on the right side of the fence. And for that I bless my father, who pushed me into becoming a lawyer."

"And so," said Jerome, feeling increasingly in his element, "you made a pile of money."

"That's putting it a bit bluntly, but let's say that if for the previous two years I didn't have a pot to piss in, now I could afford the pot and a lid to go with it. After three or four good deals like that, though, I realized Farnham was too small for me, I needed to move on to bigger turf. So I went back to Quebec City and, after a few months working sixteen-hour days, I was in a position to convert old mansions and similar buildings into pharmacies, video shops, funeral parlours, bakeries, Tim Hortons, McDonald's — whatever came along. But always within the rules of the game, my friend."

The detached smile on Jerome's face was diminishing, and in its place appeared an attentiveness filled with curiosity.

"So what then?"

"Then," sighed the lawyer, "came 1985, the year the Vieille Ville in Quebec City was named a UNESCO World Heritage Site, and the market became totally stagnant, even outside the Vieille Ville. From then on, the order was to not change a thing, or to change as little as possible. For example, if there was an old church somewhere that wasn't being heated in winter because there weren't enough parishioners left to pay the heating bills, oh my stars! You had to argue until you were blue in the face to convince the authorities to replace it with something useful, something that would improve the economy — and sometimes it took so much time and effort that your project went belly up. The dreamers and so-called artists who lived off the government tit were beginning to piss us off royally!"

"And then?"

"And then I saw it was time to move to Montreal. Our hands were less tied here: Old Montreal was already far too messed up to be of any interest to UNESCO — it was no more likely to become a World Heritage Site than a chicken was to have teeth in its beak and dandelions growing out of its ass."

A brief silence followed these picturesque metaphors. Jerome found Sicotte's language as ornate as the furnishings of his office.

"Anyway," the lawyer continued, "from Montreal we spread out everywhere, anywhere we wanted. Thanks to the Internet, we could shine from Saint-Middle-of-Nowhere, right? So then, with time, my business became much more diversified. Much more. Now I'm in the big leagues, my boy." Raising a hand to his mouth he let out a happy digestive burp.

"What leagues are we talking about, if you don't mind my asking?" asked Jerome, half amused, half anxious.

"When you're down to your last nickel, you start to understand a few things, no? Of course you do. I'd be very surprised if a young man like you didn't get it...Listen, Jerome, I'm going to speak to you the way I speak to myself when I'm alone. That shows you how much confidence I have in you, eh? In any case, we were bound to get to this point sooner or later: I'm an 'agent of influence,' like any good lobbyist." He puffed himself up like a peacock. "For example, I make myself the link between politicians and certain businessmen, and vice versa. Politicians need money to get elected, and businessmen need government contracts so they can conduct their — their businesses. I try to create *harmony* between these two needs, if you will. When all's well, the economy runs smoothly, salaries are paid, everyone gets what they deserve, and society purrs along contentedly. Do you understand what I'm saying?"

"I understand," answered Jerome, managing to say as much without looking away. He wanted to add, "A strange way of seeing things, though," but sensed that he should not — and that, of course, he never would.

The waiter returned, signalled to the busboy to clear the table, and presented the dessert menu. Without even glancing at it, Sicotte, slightly drunk, pushed it away with the back of his hand and ordered digestifs.

Decidedly, this was a special occasion.

"Jerome," said the lawyer very seriously, "the moment has come for me to train you . . . Oh, yes! My wife did me a great service when she told me about you. I've been watching you progress since the day I hired you, I see the way you act and react, and believe me, I'm blown away. Blown away! And, as you have no doubt seen for yourself, I'm not a flatterer. I've always made of point of giving my employees their due, as I expect them to do with me. And, to be totally honest, I'd rather have my son, not you, at my side —"

He let out a deep sigh, which he then had to combine with a friendly salute to Lalonde, the former minister who'd raised his hand to wave goodbye from the table he and his fossilized friends were leaving.

"But Felix," said Sicotte with a sombre expression, lowering his voice, "it's all over. He's a smoker! If he'd stuck to tobacco, that damned poison, but no! The disaster had to run its course — pot and hash, and no doubt a good many other things have fried his brain. Yes! When I hear him talking about getting into the vaping business . . . My God! Is it possible he could have sunk so low? My wife still has hopes for him, but not me, it's over. And when I say a thing is over,

Jerome, I only say it once. That's a lifetime of experience talking: never waste your time on hopeless cases."

There was both anger and sadness in the axiom he spat out like an admission of defeat, but then his mind galloped on to new thoughts, and his good humour returned.

"Enough! I have some good news for you, Jerome. At least, I hope you'll find it good news . . . As of now, your days of filing old papers are over. I'll be minding your apprenticeship personally. To start off, you'll accompany me as a simple observer — in my line of work, I meet a lot of people, necessarily — as a way of getting the hang of it in a hurry. But, if I know you, it won't take long. From then on, my friend, you won't be working for a salary, but for a *percentage* — and you'll find that a lot more interesting!"

Sicotte leaned back in his chair, his chest swelled, and a broad smile spread across his chubby cheeks. He was the very picture of charitable deeds practised in the service of his own *joie de vivre.*

"So," he said, "what do you think?"

As if to emphasize the unexpected nature of the offer, a log in the fireplace gave off a joyous crackle and shot a shower of sparks against the protective screen in front of it.

Jerome stared at him wide-eyed. A sort of vertigo came over him that made Sicotte and the room around him a little fuzzy. Was it the wine? Was it the unexpected vista that suddenly opened before him? He thought he heard a flutter of banknotes, whisperings, muffled laughter, the faint tinkling of glasses, and at the same time a vaguely suspicious odour rose to his nostrils and made him nauseous. He was condemned to breathe it in, because it was part and parcel of all the rest. But what worried him most was the contentment and curiosity his boss's offer had awakened in him.

He leaned his hands on the table and took in a deep breath.

"Thank you for the confidence you are showing in me, Severin," he said, as colour rose in his face and his forehead moistened.

"You accept, then? Bravo, my boy! You'll never regret your decision. Obviously, you'll have to work hard, nights will sometimes be short, and in this business you will, from time to time, run into a few real assholes. But when all is said and done it's a good life, as you'll see.

"Gary," he said to the passing waiter, "bring us another couple of calvados."

BACK IN THE office, feeling his lunch, Sicotte took a few messages, had a brief conversation with his wife, then went into his room for a siesta in preparation for an important meeting.

"Off you go, my boy," he called to Jerome, "you look like you have a hangover. Take time off and I'll see you tomorrow morning. Leave your car here, I'll pay for a taxi. This is no time to be arrested for drunk driving."

On the way back to his apartment, Jerome swore he'd tell no one about his new career: not his parents, not Eugenie, and especially not Charlie, who would deluge him with sermons until the two of them came to blows. At any rate, until he was no longer under this threat of extradition, it was important to show himself a willing collaborator: the hand that flattered him and opened doors today could just as easily slam them shut tomorrow. Rebelling would be idiotic.

And yet he had to acknowledge that it was a tempting adventure they were offering him. Was his a desire for retribution after all the bad things that had happened to him over the course of the previous year?

"Maybe this is the way you become an asshole," he told himself as he fell into bed. "A question of circumstances."

Despite the choleric reasoning, within thirty seconds he was snoring like a lawnmower.

EUGENIE MÉTIVIER WAS by far the most remarkable woman Jerome had ever met in his short career as a lover. The biochemical phenomena that accompany, or so we believe, the beginnings of a relationship, and that help make two individuals a couple, must have been working in him with a rare intensity, because the idea of not seeing her again was as ridiculous to him as it was horrible — and this feeling seemed to be shared by his new lover.

Calm and reserved, Eugenie was a methodical, determined woman. She tended to see herself as an organizer, but also had a taste for pleasure, and that meant the blinders so often found in people like her were reserved for administration and commerce. She loved travel, literature, often went to the cinema, and listening to people talk politics didn't automatically make her fall asleep. Six years earlier, after studying to be a dietitian, she had received a bachelor's degree in business administration from the École des hautes études commerciales. The Metro supermarket made her manager of the chain's health-food sections. As with all human beings, life had inflicted its wounds on her, some of which still bled, as Jerome discovered when he asked her about her ex-husband.

"He was Belgian," she replied curtly. "And he's gone back to Belgium. He never should have left it."

Jerome was about to ask more questions, but she gestured for him not to.

"Please. I'd rather not talk about it."

It was a Saturday morning. Andrée-Anne was at a friend's house until four o'clock that afternoon. They'd had a quiet lunch, a few coffees, and made more love than a colony of rabbits. Eugenie couldn't get enough of certain techniques she'd taught Jerome, and practised plenty of her own with extraordinary focus and passion. For Jerome, it was like discovering a new country.

"Eugenie," he said, emerging breathless from a particularly intense bout of ardour, "how do you send me up in a balloon like that?"

She laughed. "I have a lot of helium, that's all. And I must say, you're pretty easy to get off the ground, Geronimo." (Geronimo was her pet name for him.)

She laughed again as he covered her face with kisses.

"God," he said fervently, "I was lucky to meet you. And you? Do you feel that, too?"

She took his head between her hands and looked him in the eye.

"What a question... You have saved my life, Jerome... Even Andrée-Anne sees the difference."

He chuckled with pleasure and, in that moment, almost broke the promise he'd made to himself not to speak to her of his new job.

"I saved your life?" he answered quietly, somewhat startled by the words she'd used. "Someday I may need someone to save mine."

He traced the tip of her chin with his finger.

"What do you mean by that?" she said, taking his hand.

He paused, a shiver running through him. But it lasted only an instant and, teasingly, he imitated her tone. "Please, I'd rather not talk about it."

She wondered for a moment if he was evading the

question, but he laughed so heartily she changed her mind.

"What a joker, you are. So, what are we going to do today?"

WHAT JEROME HAD experienced the day before had all the elements of the oddest and juiciest story imaginable.

But in the two days since his lunch at the Beaver Club, nothing particularly unusual had happened. On the morning of the first day, Fradette, with a complicitous smile, had given him a thick folder with instructions from the Big Boss to read through it carefully, "because of its instructive contents." Jerome got down to it right away. The collection of documents seemed random, most of them covered in indecipherable notes; after two hours of solitary immersion in them, all he was able to conclude was that some entrepreneurs specializing in the construction of sidewalks seemed to have discussed among themselves a call for tenders from the City of Laval.

On the afternoon of the second day, Francine called him into her office and, in a maternal tone, told him that his Cuban affair "had taken an encouraging turn," but that she still had to exert a great deal of effort to have a definitive answer. Then she asked him how his new job was going.

"To tell you the truth, Francine, my new job seems to be a lot like my old one."

"Give it time," she said, laughing.

Sicotte, who'd been detained out of the building by an unexpected bit of business, appeared in Jerome's office the next morning. "My boy," he said solemnly, "come with me. I want you to meet someone very important."

And then, to be sure Jerome understood, he added,

"I consider him my mentor. Yes, nothing less. And I'm not the only one who can say that, believe me."

"And what's this person's name?" asked Jerome, following his boss.

"Joseph-Aimé Joyal. He was known as Jo-Jo in his day, but we never called him that to his face. Good Lord, no! He would have made us eat our shoes."

"Was known? He's not working anymore?"

"Will you still be working when you're eighty-eight?"

"If I was still in good shape, sure."

"A young man's reply."

When they were outside, Jerome let out an exclamation of surprise. An imposing cream-white BMW sedan was parked near the little Honda he'd just bought and which looked forlorn in such august company: the prestigious car hadn't been there when he'd arrived an hour earlier. Until then, Monsieur and Madame had each contented themselves with Cadillac Coupe de Villes, sky blue for Madame, olive green for Monsieur; adequate vehicles, but hardly showy for residents of a city as fancy as Mont-Royal. The cream-white sedan, fashionably chic in its understatedness, was more like a trumpet blast celebrating the progress of a career.

"There are better cars, but this one's not bad," said Sicotte, his air of detachment unconvincing, as he led Jerome towards the vehicle.

"Wow! Pretty luxurious!"

Jerome looked admiringly at the interior.

"It must have cost a fortune . . ."

"Nothing is expensive when you have the means, my boy," replied Sicotte professorially.

He paused to savour his pompous truism, then said, "Come on, get in. We don't want to be late getting there."

"Where?"

"Westmount. Curwood Street."

The BMW rolled smoothly through the gate and, turning right, picked up speed. It seemed to float silently above the pavement, its interior exuding the smell of new leather. Head erect, a satisfied smile on his face, the lawyer reached out with his fingertip and pressed a button; the airs of Bedrich Smetana's *Moldau* filled the vehicle, which began to vibrate like a cathedral. Jerome, dumbfounded, turned his head from side to side.

"It's too beautiful," said Sicotte. "It distracts me."

He turned off the music.

"Not a bad sound system, though, eh?"

"I've never heard a better one...not in a car, anyway," he added, not wanting to sound déclassé.

"It's great art," declared Sicotte.

Jerome watched Sicotte out of the corner of his eye. He seemed so puffed up with contentment, so stupidly consumed with his success, that Jerome was furiously grinding his clenched teeth.

Jerome shook his head to rid himself of thoughts that, in the present circumstances, could only do him harm. He sensed that their meeting was an important one, perhaps critical—a final test to which he was to be submitted.

Houses of the entitled, fancy and at times arrogantly sumptuous, continued to line each side of the street. Who has not dreamed, at one time or another, of owning such a house, all the while knowing that he never would? Among certain people, the dream nourished base envy, rampant jealousy, venomous frustration—and worse. Jerome thought of those who, come the revolution, fought in the streets, ransacked houses, and set fires everywhere. With a grand gesture of disdain, one of his history profs — an old right-wing ass — had called them "populist peat," a handy expression when you want to avoid reflection. Perhaps the richer parts of the city produced the seeds of their own destruction?

Sicotte turned his head.

"You look pensive, my boy. Something wrong?"

"No, no," Jerome sputtered. "Just a small headache, that's all, it'll pass."

He turned red, annoyed that he'd let himself be overtaken by such confrontational musings.

"He's still in good health, this Monsieur Joyal?" asked Jerome, wanting to show an interest.

"The last time I saw him he was on fire, despite problems with his knees. But that's going back more than six months now. Okay, we're here."

On their left there stood a house with stone gables, quite large though neither distinctive nor exceptional by Westmount standards. Sicotte stepped out of the car and, after glancing at his watch, walked rapidly up the driveway, twice turning back to beckon Jerome, who had stopped to straighten his tie and clean the toes of his shoes with a Kleenex.

"Come on, Jerome, hurry," ordered Sicotte impatiently. "You're not going to a fashion show, for Pete's sake! We're almost three minutes late. He'll scold us for that, just you wait and see."

He was about to ring the bell, but the door opened to reveal a portly Haitian woman wearing a maid's bonnet.

"Good day, gentlemen. Monsieur Joyal's been waiting for you," she said, her tone a little grating. "Follow me, if you will."

There was a reproach in her "waiting for you," and Sicotte winced, cleared his throat, and cast an unhappy glance at Jerome, as if he were the one responsible for their being late.

They crossed a room with violet drapes and imposing, massive furniture, and Sicotte asked, with concern that seemed a bit forced, "How is he, Clementine?"

"Oh, not too bad, given his age, but it's been a hard winter, it sure has! Jus' before Christmas he caught such a bad cold, and it lasted so long, that we thought he'd have to go to the hospital. Luckily, it went away by itself—luckily!"

They came to a large oak door. Above the architrave, sculpted in relief, was the head of an angel with small, plump wings looking down at them with a mocking smile. The maid opened the door, stepped back, and held out her arm. "He's in his office. You know the way."

They found themselves in an antechamber onto which several other rooms opened. From behind one door, slightly ajar, came a frail but imperious voice: "In here, Severin! I've been waiting for you."

A large, bald man with black horn-rimmed glasses, broad shoulders but a slightly enfeebled body was leafing through a newspaper lying open on his desk. Jerome noticed that he was sitting in a wheelchair.

"I've been waiting for three and a half minutes!" said the man with a large smile as he extended a hand to Sicotte, and then to Jerome. "At my age, if I may remind you, every minute is worth its weight in gold, as you'll see for yourselves one day."

"It was my fault, Joe. I just received my new BMW and it's the first time I've driven it."

"A BMW? What model?"

"Gran Coupe 6 Series."

"Oh! Now, that's a car, that is. Your excuse is acceptable—but only the once," he added, winking mischievously. "You've brought your *dauphin*?" he said, indicating Jerome.

"Allow me to introduce you to Jerome Lupien, Joe. He's a young man of considerable talent. Francine and I have great hopes for him."

Jerome nodded, embarrassed, and felt like an idiot.

"Don't blush like that," said the old man, with jovial severity, Sicotte quietly laughing. "If he sings your praises, you probably deserve them. In life, you should never be afraid to show your worth. If you don't you'll never get anywhere. Leave the humble pie for the poor."

"It's because I've only just started in this job, Monsieur Joyal," Jerome said. (What job? he asked himself.) "It's good of Monsieur Sicotte to place so much faith in me, though I'm not sure that if I were in his place, and he in mine, I'd have done the same thing."

Joseph-Aimé Joyal turned to Sicotte.

"He doesn't lack nerve, your boy, but I find his mentality more than a little Catholic. You still have some work to do, Severin."

"Count on me."

"There are two or three things I taught Severin that he now understands pretty well. The first is that you should never be led anywhere by sentiment: it's a luxury no one can afford. The second is simple common sense: it's not a case of anybody or anything getting you the same good result. You need to be careful, tenacious, and work hard. But by far the most important thing"—Joyal, staring intently at Jerome, held out his hand, its short fingers deformed by arthritis, and knocked three times on the desk with his signet ring—"is imagination, lad. That's what makes the difference been an ordinary seaman and a captain."

"Well, he has no lack of imagination," interrupted Sicotte, laughing. And he told the story of the episode in Place Versailles.

"Good, very good," said Joyal after listening to the story attentively, uttering occasional grunts of approval. "Very promising, yes... You seem to have what it takes."

Jerome, who was about to classify his host as a pain in the neck, dotard section, put off his verdict.

"Thank you, sir. I'm flattered."

"You see," said Sicotte, beaming as he extended his hand towards Jerome, "on top of it all, he has good manners and expresses himself very well. That's not always the case, as we know."

"Indeed not, indeed not," replied Joyal with paternal congeniality. "It's a plus, no doubt about it..."

Jerome smiled, embarrassed once again. He felt like one of those young girls of good family paraded at balls so they could make their "debut" and find a suitable husband. The situation was becoming crazy.

"But I can see from your expression," continued the old man in his gravelly voice, "that I am beginning to bore you with my advice... No, no, no, don't say I'm not, I can see I'm right, I'm not blind or gaga... It's normal, young people don't like being given advice, they're so full of vitality they think they're infallible... And very often they trip over their own feet, too! So sorry for the advice, but what can you do? At my age I can no longer teach by example. Has Severin told you my story about the Champlain Bridge?"

"No, Joe, I wanted to leave that pleasure for you."

"Would you be interested in hearing it, young man?"

"Of course, Monsieur Joyal," said Jerome, nodding enthusiastically.

"Very well," said the old man, an air of evident satisfaction spreading across his yellowed, deeply lined face. "They began talking about constructing a new bridge between Montreal and the South Shore in the early 1950s. This was when Louis St. Laurent was prime minister — some bridges, as you know, come under the jurisdiction of the federal government. There was an incredible economic boom happening on the South Shore, everyone wanted a car, and the three bridges they had at the time weren't enough to handle all the traffic. I was in my thirties at the time, and I owned a paving company, and another in cement, plus two or three other small businesses. The going was good, but I was ambitious and wanted to do better, see my businesses grow faster. My work put me in touch with engineering offices pretty well everywhere, and I was getting along well with the political parties of the day — which is essential, as we all know, if you want to get anywhere with public works."

He stopped, winded, took a deep breath, and continued in a grave, almost solemn tone. "With that, my boy, I'm just setting the stage of my story."

Sicotte coughed excitedly. Leaning forward in his chair, his eyes dilated with enthusiasm, he breathed in the words of the old millionaire like a groupie at a rock concert, fainting with pleasure before their idol singing a hit for the thousandth time.

"August 17, 1955. The Transport Minister, George Marier, held a press conference in Montreal to announce the construction of a new bridge that would connect the southwest part of the island with Brossard. You should have seen the excitement the announcement caused everywhere! Ottawa decided to call it the Champlain Bridge, as a sop to the nationalists, what else. The call for tenders went out. That afternoon I was having lunch at the Kambo, on Sherbrooke Street, with one of my partners at the time, Vic Lamone, and the news came on the television that was suspended about five or six feet above our heads. 'A huge project like that,' said Vic, 'will be worth millions upon millions upon millions. Too bad we're not big enough to bid on it, we could have climbed on the gravy train. You get one of those babies and you're set for the rest of your days.' 'So why don't we go for it, Vic?' I said. 'We know cement, and we're not afraid of hard work. All we need is to find associates.' Vic said, 'It takes contacts, Joe, and we don't have any.'

"Well, that's where we left the matter, but I kept thinking about it. What Vic didn't know was that I did have a contact. Two or three weeks before, at a fundraising dinner in Verdun, I'd met the guy responsible for finances in Marier's riding. We talked for a long time. He seemed very approachable, and quick between the ears. I phoned him, we met up, he listened to what I had to say, he introduced me to some key people, and after that I was able to put together a war machine that meant I was one of the group of *happy boys* able to submit bids. And, right from the start, I understood that we had to avoid the mistake that was made when they built the Jacques-Cartier Bridge."

"What mistake?" asked Jerome, intrigued.

"The mistake of having made the bridge too solid."

"That was a mistake?"

Jerome was having trouble keeping a straight face.

"And how! Look, my boy, they opened the Jacques-Cartier—when, in 1930? And look at the state it's in! Almost like new! All they have to do is paint it once in a while, maybe patch it up here and there, and everything's dandy. We'll never see the end of that goddamned bridge. I certainly won't, and I doubt you will, either. It's built good enough to last at least another two hundred years."

Jerome looked at him with an astonished smile.

"I don't get it, Monsieur Joyal," he said.

"I can see that you don't get it! That's why Severin brought you here, so that I can give you my *business philosophy*."

Instinctively Jerome turned towards his boss, if only to assure himself the two men weren't amusing themselves at his expense. But Sicotte was still drinking in the old man's every word.

"Listen to him, listen to him," he urged Jerome in a low voice.

"And so," continued Joseph-Aimé Joyal, "I twigged to the fact that if you want a prosperous country, generation after generation, then you have to keep the ball rolling for generation after generation, with lots of public work to do — and then redo, in order to maintain a good economic flow. You have to get out of your egotistical shell, my boy, and think about those who'll come after us and take our places in the business world when we've all bit the dust. What's good for us is good for all, isn't that so? Building bridges — or hospitals or highways, whatever — to last too long will bring a country to its knees, economically. The anemia will be chronic! Coin is meant to roll along — and when it doesn't, it rusts. Remember that."

Short of breath, he stopped again.

Sicotte jumped to his feet.

"Would you like a glass of water, Joe?"

"No, no," the old man replied impatiently. "Sit down..."

But, now that I think of it, I'll have a drop of cognac. Will you join me?"

And, without waiting for a reply, he pressed a button and Clementine appeared.

"A little spark-me-up for everyone, Clementine."

His servant walked over to a drinks cabinet built into a library overflowing with antique books with forebidding spines. Then, with a disapproving air, she served the drinks.

"Leave the bottle on the desk, would you please," said Joyal.

"It's your second bottle in ten days," observed the Haitian, her tone surly.

"And with ten more, it'll be my fourth. Off you go, my girl."

"You know what your doctor told you."

"Away with you, go."

She shrugged and left the room, muttering.

"So," Joyal went on, "with patience, diplomacy, and a lot of phone calls made at the right time to the right people, I succeeded in introducing myself to the 'think tank' charged with coming up with the plans for the new bridge and realized there were two factions at war with each other: the pharaohs and the moderns."

He smiled, seeing the astonished look on Jerome's face.

"The pharaohs were fighting for a bridge they could gaze upon and admire for ever and ever, amen — and which would cost a fortune. It was their clan that had won the battle over the Jacques-Cartier Bridge. The moderns, on the other hand, wanted a bridge *suited to the times*. It wouldn't be all that much cheaper to build, you understand, but it would earn money for its investors *after* its construction. You see where I'm going with this? You build the bridge only once, but you maintain and repair it many times. If you build it too well, you pretty well close the tap on maintenance and repair revenues. The beauty of the modern approach is that one day, after having spent a great deal of money on the bridge, the government eventually decides it isn't reparable anymore, and they have to build a new one. And everything starts all over again!"

He brought his cognac to his nose, inhaled the vapours, then took a sip.

"Naturally, I chose to be in the modern faction, and I saw to it, in the alliances I made, that our side would win. The plans went out, the call for tenders was made, I had the time to create a holding company that put me among the big-time players, and we made our submission—though 'submission' is a big word: in fact, we split the cake. Some of us had big pieces, others smaller pieces, and some had no pieces at all, but a lot of icing. Their turn would come around next time. The business was enervating, but everything works out in the end . . ."

Remembering the caustic remark the old man had thrown out earlier, Jerome pasted a large, approving smile on his face in order to conceal the astonishment and distaste that had come over him, and that he adjusted from time to time by touches of amusement and surprise lest his expression be so fixed that it should end up being suspect. Sipping his cognac made the task that much easier.

Setting his hands flat on the table, his arms spread wide, Joyal graced his audience with a satisfied smile that for a second made him appear twenty years younger.

"It was the *modern* approach that ended up bearing fruit. For the past two or three years, as you may have noticed, there's more and more talk of rebuilding the Champlain

Bridge because it's in such a state of disrepair. It's still safe, but it's deteriorating. Sooner or later they'll have no choice, it'll have to be rebuilt. The government will hem and haw for a while, they'll apply all sorts of poultices to the bridge that'll cost the earth, of course—but, sooner or later, Ottawa will have to come to terms with the facts: we need a new bridge! The very thought of being the government in power when the bridge collapses during peak rush hour is enough to make any politician piss his pants. So, there'll be another press conference in Montreal, new plans will be put forward—improved, of course, you can't hold back progress, after all—new proposals will be studied, the work will start, the economy will pick up, and everyone will be happy."

"Everyone except the taxpayers," Jerome said to himself. Worried that his thoughts might appear in his eyes, he hurriedly took another sip of cognac.

"You can't just think about yourself," continued Joyal with the bombast of a clergyman, "you need to think of future generations. Don't you agree, my good fellow?"

The question came as a kind of warning.

Jerome nodded his head vigorously:

"Completely, sir."

He felt, once again, the colour rise to his cheeks, but held the eye of his inquisitor without blinking. The old man's gaze seemed to penetrate deep into his soul. He had to do something, anything, to prove that he was trustworthy.

"In any case," said Joyal glibly, "the incompetents who govern us waste half our taxes as it is."

"There you have it!" said Sicotte approvingly, giving Jerome a slap on the back. "You understand everything. What's the harm if some of that money finds its way to the private sector, eh? At least we know how to use it—and, when all is said and done, the people profit as well."

Joyal took the bottle of cognac and, the goodfella, signalled to his guests to hold up their glasses.

Sicotte raised a hand.

"No, really, Joe, thank you, but we have to go. Duty calls."

Jerome stood up abruptly, set his glass on the desk, and held his hand out to the old man.

"It's been a privilege to meet you, Monsieur Joyal."

"Farewell and good luck, young man. You have a good boss—make the best of it."

And as Jerome moved towards the door, Joyal discreetly looked at Sicotte as if to say, "He looks okay, but keep an eye on him, you never know..."

Clementine appeared in the antechamber and, still with a haughty air, led them out.

"You kept him for some time, Monsieur Sicotte," she remarked as she opened the door. "He'll be exhausted for the next two days, poor man."

"I'm so sorry, Clementine. Very sorry. I didn't know."

"Every day I see him waste away a little bit more, Mister Sicotte. He won't last much longer, I don't think."

"Would that he kicked the bucket today," thought Jerome. "He's already cost us enough as it is."

And, bowing his head, he said goodbye to the servant with a big smile.

The chilly, bracing outside air stunned Jerome. He almost staggered. Was it the cognac, he wondered, or the contrast of the fresh air with the sordid proposals that he'd had to listen to for the entirety of their meeting, and to which he'd added his own?

They settled into the BMW.

"You look done in," said Sicotte as he started the car.

"Yeah, I don't know what it is ... It just came over me all of a sudden."

"Can't hold your cognac, son? Anyhow, it was a Hennessy XO that cost two hundred and fifty bucks a bottle. That'll put hair on your chest."

The well-oiled purr of the motor, the gentle motion of the vehicle, and even the slightly spicy odour of the seats seemed to upset his stomach. He kept swallowing; his head fell forward, he began to breathe loudly, his face turned beet-red.

"Stop the car! Stop the car!" he yelled suddenly, strangely embarrassed.

Sicotte pulled over and hit the brakes. Jerome leapt from the car and vomited, but a viscous trail of vomit hit the inside panel of the door.

"Oh Christ, what the hell have I got myself into?" mumbled Jerome as he wiped his mouth with a Kleenex, leaning against a fire hydrant, just as a woman with silver hair stopped and glared at him with a look of disgust, her lapdog barking hysterically.

"So, feeling better?" grumbled Sicotte when Jerome, out of sorts, returned to the car. "I hope there won't be a stain on the leather. Bloody hell! I wiped off what I could. There's more Kleenex in the glove compartment," he added imperiously as the car began moving again. "Give the door another wipe, will you?"

Nothing more was said during the entire trip back to the office.

EUGENIE STARED AT her computer screen, perplexed. Her closed door cut the noise coming from the offices around her by half, allowing her to follow well enough the rather tense discussion between two advertising designers concerning publicity surrounding the reduction in size of a container of Irresistible Frozen Raspberries from six hundred to four hundred grams without a proportionate decrease in the price. But frozen strawberries, so good for your health, were in this instance the last thing on her mind. Eugenie was reading an email with the subject line "A worried friend of Jerome," from someone named Charlie Plamondon. Jerome had mentioned Charlie on occasion, describing him as his best friend and "a bit of a pedant at times, though he has a good heart," without revealing much more.

She sighed and read the email again:

Dear Madame Métivier,
First let me assure you that it wasn't Jerome who gave me your email address (out of consideration for you, he would have refused it, I'm sure), I obtained it from your employer. I'll get straight to the point, because I know your time is valuable (so is mine, of course, if you don't mind my saying so!). For several days, Jerome has been worrying me and I wouldn't be at all surprised if he's been worrying you, too. Is it possible for us to get together and chat? Awaiting your reply, and wishing you a good day,
*   Charlie Plamondon*

"'So is mine, of course, if you don't mind my saying so!',"
she repeated, keeping her voice down. "A bit of a pedant is right."

Apart from the off-putting remark, there was something in the general tone of the email that made her hesitate before replying. Her experience with people had taught her that the attitude on display was adopted either by authentic pains-in-the neck who saw themselves as successors to Napoleon, by genuinely shy people using bravado as a shield—or by a mixture of the two types, this by far the worst case since you never knew quite how to take them. Whatever the case, dealing with them was usually a nightmare.

But her decision was quick: she replied to Charlie, saying she would be happy to meet. Was the next day at, say, eight o'clock at the Café Prague, 1317 avenue Van Horne, convenient?

Ten minutes later their rendezvous was confirmed. She was relieved. This Charlie Plamondon wasn't wrong about her being worried. In fact, for some time now Jerome had seemed a different person. Moody, distracted, nervous, and sometimes impatient, he would plunge into himself and not surface for hours. If she tried to engage him by asking questions, he'd evade them with pleasantries verging on the sarcastic, or by saying he was tired from all his moving about and his apprenticeship in a new job.

One evening, he said with a sigh, "You wake up in the morning, and before you even get out of bed the day hits you in the face and it takes you half an hour to recover your equilibrium. Rather stressful way to make a living, I'd say."

But about the exact nature of the job she had only a vague notion. One night, fed up with all the mystery, she'd tried to elicit a frank explanation. *Check and mate.* He'd told her that a lobbyist who's not silent as a fish about his work is a lobbyist on the point of needing another job. His career depended on the most absolute discretion, there was no room for blabbermouths.

"Be kind, sweetheart," he'd asked, caressing her as he knew so well how to do, "and please don't ask any more questions. One fine day I might spill the beans—and you'll regret it as much as I will. I promise you my work is honourable. Difficult, but honourable."

So how to explain his sadness? Because she certainly did find him profoundly sad. Sadness that reminded her of her own, when he'd first approached her at the edge of the pool in that hotel in Varadero, where she was mourning her six years of marriage to a man full of good qualities, but with whom she could no longer live.

What was he mourning, this Jerome she could no longer do without? Was she destined to meet only men who were exquisite but impossible? If so, then long live celibacy!

A THURSDAY NIGHT in mid-June, eight o'clock, avenue Van Horne. Torrential rain. The city is immersed in the endless low roar of thousands of cars driving on watery streets that have become mirrors doubling car lights and street lights. Incipient tonsillitis for Andrée-Anne. The third case in eight months, one of the joys of daycare. Eugenie has left her with Kostis, a fourteen-year-old Greek boy who lives across the street; the previous summer, he'd announced his availability for babysitting on the bulletin board at the supermarket. Calm, serious, smiling, he'd conquered Andrée-Anne's heart within five minutes of their first meeting. But on this particular evening another conquest was required. The little girl didn't want anything to do with Kostis and was demanding to be with Jerome. She had transferred her affections to him some time ago: Jerome had since become her storyteller and official colouring book partner. On a recent Saturday, he had taken her shopping at the Jean-Talon market. An hour and a half later she came back with a look in her eyes Eugenie hadn't seen for a long while.

Kostis was almost losing his guru's cool, his eyes revealing his confusion. But it only lasted a flash and quickly he had the situation back in hand. Two minutes later, Andrée-Anne was laughing. It was a tentative laugh, but she was laughing nonetheless, and Mommy took advantage of it to drive off to her date. She likes this Kostis, with his swarthy complexion and a voice that has already broken — and who, with each new encounter, engulfs her in a look that is at once so timid and burning that anyone might think she had become a sex symbol to him.

But now here she is looking for a parking space as close as possible to the Café Prague, the brightly lit exterior of which shines through the torrent of rain like a warm-hearted message of friendship. Luck is with her: a delivery van parked just in front of the establishment starts up and drives off. A moment later she's hurrying into the restaurant, folding her dripping umbrella and looking around the room. No one is there except for an elderly man sitting on the long, wine-red leather bench that runs along the right-hand wall, flipping through an IKEA catalogue with a subdued smile. The owner, seeing Eugenie, gives a friendly wave from behind the counter.

"You're a brave one, going out in this rain," he calls out to her.

He has the mature voice of a man in his forties. His French accent is imbued with the energy of a small shopkeeper struggling to survive.

"Sometimes there's no choice," she replies with a big smile. "I won't have anything yet, I'm waiting for someone."

"Can I bring you a glass of water?"

"Thanks, but I've had all the water I need for one night."

He laughs as she takes a seat at a small table in a sort of

recess near the entrance, under a series of black-and-white photographs — of Old Prague, naturally.

An aroma of grilled cheese in the air reminds her that she has barely had any supper. She looks at her watch: ten after eight. If Charlie gets here soon, she'll order something. If he's still not here after ten minutes, she'll say to hell with it and order something anyway.

Ten minutes go by. She is about to ask for a menu when the door opens, letting in the noise of the rain, a puff of damp air, and a young man wearing a yellow raincoat who stops in the middle of the room and shakes out the coat's hood. A small pool of water forms at his feet. He looks down at it and smiles.

"Eugenie Métivier?" he asks, coming towards her.

"Charlie," she replies, holding out her hand and smiling, trying not to show her surprise at the Mohawk and beard that don't quite hide the fact that his face is severely pocked by acne.

"Sorry I'm late. The truth is, an urgent matter came up at the last minute. I do apologize."

He sits across from her and wipes his forehead with the back of his hand.

"I haven't even had time to eat," he says with an anguished air.

"Well, that's good, neither have I."

The owner, attentive and at the ready, is already at their table, obliging the pair with menus and his suggestions.

"Tonight, we have two servings left of the salad plate, a *magret de canard*, and an excellent poached salmon, also sandwiches, panini, and the usual *croque-monsieurs*. The kitchen closes in ten minutes."

"Is the salmon Czech?" Charlie asks.

The silence that greets his question gives him time to realize how idiotic it was.

"Monsieur, the only thing that is Czech here," says the owner, breezily, "is the name of the café."

"Then why's it called the Café Prague?" Charlie asks, confused, his face red.

"That was the choice of the former proprietor, sir, and as the previous café's reputation was excellent, we thought it best to keep the name."

"I'll have the magret salad," says Eugenie, cutting short the toponymic discussion. She needs to get something in her stomach.

"Me, too," decides Charlie.

And, turning to his companion, he adds, "My treat. After all, it was me who dragged you out into this deluge."

"You had more of a taste of it than I did, by the look of you," she says, laughing. "But thank you. You're very kind."

The impression he makes on her changes continuously: at first disquieting, then he seemed a little silly, and now here he is being nice. She reckons that the needle won't stop oscillating for the rest of the evening.

"Should we have something to drink?" Charlie asks. "Coffee?" He looks at his watch. "It's almost 8:30. A bit late for me for coffee, even decaf, it'll keep me up all night."

"Me, too."

"Wine, then? Suits me . . . You know the place, from what I see . . . How's their house wine? Drinkable?"

"Their red isn't bad," Eugenie says, laughing to herself.

"We'll have a half-litre of the house red," says Charlie, turning to the bar.

"Very good, sir," replies the owner. "Can you take care of it, Roxane?"

Charlie realizes that alongside the *patron* there is also a *patronne*, a beautiful, tall woman in her forties who comes over, lively and smiling, her velvet gaze amplified by mascara and eye shadow.

"Here you are, sir," she says, setting down the carafe and filling their wine glasses. "Everything okay with you, Madame Métivier?"

After a few more words she leaves, quickly having determined her clients aren't just here to while away the time. From the bench, the man with the IKEA catalogue is apparently satisfied with his analysis, asks Roxane for the bill, and takes it to the cash. After contemplating the street with a dour expression at the door, he opens an immense black umbrella and charges out into the storm.

The duck salads arrive with a basket of warm bread, its enveloping smell a snub to the pitiless rain that continues to worsen.

For several minutes, Charlie and his companion are content to satisfy their hunger and exchange a few friendly banalities. Then Charlie stops, knife in one hand, fork in the other, and looks at Eugenie with intense seriousness.

"Can we call each other by our first names?" he asks.

"I was going to suggest it," she says, a little surprised.

"It'll make things easier for me."

He continues to look at her, swallows. Once. Twice.

"For the love of Pete, what's the matter?"

"I think... I think Jerome is in the Mafia, or something like it," he confides in a low voice. "I was really not sure that I should let you know, because I'm probably losing a friend by telling you this, but I had to, you understand... for his own good."

He goes back to eating quickly, as if relieved of a great

burden. Eugenie, suddenly pale, pushes her plate aside: she won't touch it again.

"But . . . what makes you say that? Charlie, please," she begs, "explain what you just said. It's a serious allegation."

She casts a glance to the back of the room and the sounds of clattering dishes and Roxane on the phone. Reassured, she takes the carafe and refills their glasses, waiting for what's to come.

"Last Wednesday night," Charlie begins, "Jerome had dinner at my place. I'd invited him the night before, because I'd not found him in good form for a long time. We drank a lot of wine and, to be frank, I tried to get him a bit plastered hoping it would loosen his tongue, but so far nothing had come of it. Then, suddenly, near the end of the meal, his cell phone rang. He looked at the screen and, from the way he reacted, I could see he'd rather I'd been on a trip to Disneyland or visiting my great-grandmother, than sitting across from him. Well, I wasn't about to do either, though I did get up to go to the bathroom—a good friend knows when to pee. But actually, I had a plan . . . You can't see the bathroom door from the kitchen, so I opened and closed it but stayed in the hallway and listened. Only for about thirty seconds, no more, but in those thirty seconds I learned more about Jerome's work than I had in all the weeks before then."

"And what did you learn?"

Charlie's eyes widen and he assumes an air of importance.

"What did I learn? Well . . ."

He pauses and takes a gulp of wine.

Which is when Eugenie explodes, controlling her voice.

"Look, Charlie, this isn't some television detective series here, this is real life, so come on, get on with it . . . I'm dying of suspense."

And she grabs his hand as the owner looks over from the bar and pulls back just as quickly.

"He was talking to Sam Calvido," Charlie blurts out.

"Sam Calvido? The chairman of the executive committee of the City of Montreal?"

"Yes, that Sam Calvido. Quite the connection, don't you think? For the past month, as you know, people can't stop talking about him in relation to the street light scandal, and two days ago his name appeared — *hello!* — in relation to Faubourg Saint-Amable, a fraud of several hundred million dollars, it seems. And that's got to be just the tip of an iceberg that goes down a few kilometres. I'd bet ten years of my salary that he's about to be fired and dragged into court. Ha! Just wait until that shit hits the fan!"

Now it's Eugenie's turn to look over to the bar. She raises her hand: "Roxane, could you bring us another carafe of red, please?"

The lilt she tries to put in her voice makes her distress so apparent that Roxane and her husband trade glances.

"Coming right up, Madame."

Roxane brings the wine and steps away even faster than the last time, if that's possible.

For a moment, Charlie and his guest are silent. They've already emptied their glasses when Eugenie perks up with a last hope and leans towards her companion.

"You said he was talking to Sam Calvido?"

"Yes."

"Are you sure? There's talking *to* and talking *about*. They're not the same thing."

Charlie gives her a sorrowful look. "Wow," he tells himself, "she really does love him. She'd throw herself under a truck for him! He doesn't know how lucky he is, the idiot!"

"I'm sorry," he says, shaking his head, "I didn't listen very long—but still, long enough to hear him say, 'Yes, Monsieur Calvido . . . No, Monsieur Calvido,' which, to my mind, is what you say only if you're really talking to someone named Monsieur Calvido, wouldn't you say? What's more," Charlie adds, raising a hand to dash her last hope forever, "I know they were talking about whoever that bastard is who's making headlines in the newspapers, because Jerome mentioned street lights. *Twice.*"

"Okay," she sighs, hanging her head, "I guess there isn't much to add. Thanks for warning me."

From the street comes the sound of skidding tires and a low thud. Charlie turns his head and sees his reflection in the dark window. Eugenie seems not to have heard a thing.

"What are you going to do?" Charlie asks.

"I don't have the faintest idea." She sighs again.

"It's unbelievable," thinks Charlie, "how comfortable I feel with this woman. She really gets to me. *Look out, Jerome. If she drops you, I'll be on her doorstep in the next half-hour.*"

She empties her glass with one gulp, reaches for the carafe, and gives him a wry smile.

"My God, I'm getting to be as bad as my ex. Enough."

The moment passes. Now she has only one wish: to leave, go home, take a sleeping pill, and sleep for three years.

"The rain seems to be letting up," she says, looking towards the street. "Did you park very far away?"

"I came in a cab," Charlie says. He's lying: he took public transit.

"Can I drop you off at your place?"

They've had a lot to drink, she more than he. The image of a breathalyzer with its damn balloon cursed by revellers forms in Charlie's mind. In weather like this, fog as thick as pea soup, a collision can happen in a second. He almost sees the police squad car's blue, white, and red lights sweeping the street behind them. But what the hell, forget the police. He feels good with this woman, even when he's half pissed. What's the harm in prolonging their meeting? After all, it's not as if his loyalty to Jerome is in question.

"That would be great," he says, smiling, "if you're not too tired. I live only ten minutes from here."

VILLE-MARIE

SEVERIN SICOTTE HAD had it up to here with Roland
Dozois, chief fundraiser for the New Montreal Party,
who had for years haunted the city's back rooms and any
other place of good or bad reputation where he could line
the party's pockets — and his own. Thickset, paunchy,
with white hair on his mostly bald head; his face creased by
wrinkles that looked as if they'd been carved with a knife;
a great boozer and smoker, Dozois was always in a good
mood and seemed perfectly comfortable in his skin, tire-
lessly hauling himself from place to place and gathering the
spoils of war, something he said as pontifically as if he'd
invented the phrase. An uncharitable journalist once compared Dozois to a tank that would have done well at the
Siege of Stalingrad, describing him as an indestructible ves-
tige of a disastrous era. In his youth, an automobile accident
in which he'd almost died had brought him under the knife
for a trepanning on the left side of his head that left a long
scar that disappeared into what remained of his hair. The
incident earned him the nickname Bled Man, which was

seldom used to his face but amused him all the same.

"This is why I have an open mind," he would say, running his index finger along his left temple. "My brain was able to air itself out for a couple of hours—doesn't happen every day!—and the result is that I can understand a bunch of different points of view at the same time, and take a *larger view* of things... In my job, that's an asset, a real trump card! There's people who are surprised to see I've lasted this long in my job. Well, there's the reason, look no further."

Bled Man's burr hole explained, no doubt, his multiple and ongoing allegiances. In Quebec City, he had worked for the Union Nationale and the Liberal Party, went to Ottawa to fill the coffers of the Social Credit Party (Réal Caouette, alas, kicked his ass out of there), then those of the Liberals, before finally ending up with the Conservatives. He was always careful, however, to keep away from separatists and the left.

"It's a waste of time with those daydreamers," he'd say. "What's more, they're all hypocrites, when you scratch the surface. They make me sick."

Everywhere he went, Bled Man's efficacy was a legend. Power games, internal rivalries, and the winds of fate explained his change of employers, but his enthusiasm remained intact. The substantial revenues he accumulated from his work, it has to be said, were a powerful incentive.

"I live on love, not on water, and good whisky's not cheap."

The phrase, having circulated around the city, made its way up to the highest echelons of power and got a lot of laughs. Some of the laughs, however, rang a little hollow, because it was discovered that Bled Man preferred very expensive whisky. But everyone agreed that he was a *virtuoso*

of good contacts and useful information, and that in his baili-
wick the only events he didn't know about were those that
hadn't taken place yet.

For some time, Sicotte had been among those whose
laughter had rung hollow. That said, several years earlier it
had been thanks to Dozois that he'd been put on the scent
of a project to change the zoning of a huge piece of property
in the city's east end. There, the city council was going to
allow the construction of twelve-storey buildings where pre-
viously only duplexes had been permitted. As a consequence,
he'd been able to join a very select group of speculators who
bought the land before the zoning was changed, and then
ten months later sold it for an enormous profit. It was insider
trading, of course, but who wouldn't have jumped at such
a glorious opportunity?

No sooner had the transaction been completed than Bled
Man showed up at Sicotte's office with his big Happy Face
on and his aw-shucks manners and his voice coarsened by
tobacco: Sicotte had to pay up—and not just once, but twice!
Once, of course, for the Montreal Progressive Party (there
can be no progress if electoral coffers are empty, and the
fuller they are, the more Montreal progresses), and again to
his faithful friend standing before him, the one who'd had
the pleasure of presenting him with a golden opportunity
to make some cash—a lot of cash, in fact—and who had
no qualms about accepting gifts from friends grateful for
services rendered; said gifts to be of the order of fifteen per-
cent of profits, payable immediately, if you please. Thanks.
Until next time.

Bled Man had also been useful when Francine and her
husband had decided to buy the Varadero Iberostar Hotel.
Its Spanish owners had got themselves into a bind and were

forced to sell the property "at a bargain-basement price." Using his contacts in Ottawa, the city in which he had hung about in every possible gutter since the Diefenbaker years, he had simplified and facilitated the numerous and complex formalities imposed upon the Canadian citizen who wanted to buy a building in a communist dictatorship run by bearded cigar-smoker in a military cap.

"I'm only asking you to pay me for my time," Dozois said cheerily to Francine one fine morning when he came to present her with his bill.

She looked at the piece of paper.

"For your time, you say? Holy smokes! Did you start working on this case when you were still in short pants?"

He burst out laughing, and after a while she laughed in turn, though hers sounded somewhat forced.

That said, the purchase of the hotel turned out to have been a good investment. Bled Man may have been greedy, but he was reliable and had provided good counsel, all of which distinguished him from a common thief.

This is how it came to be that Sicotte got in the habit of counting Bled Man among his collaborators; he even let him make two or three trips a year to the Iberostar, *gratis,* and in the company of Madame Dozois, a respectable woman who sometimes brought along her niece in order to have someone with whom to play cards in the evenings, as her husband, faced with the bargain of an open bar, was usually dead drunk by six o'clock.

Everything went well until the unfortunate incident of the street lights. A few months earlier, the City of Montreal— wanting to increase public safety, reduce its consumption of electricity, and improve the look of its streets—had issued an appeal for tenders to supply 30,000 new-generation street lights, the installation of which was to be spread over three years. Word was this would be a $400-million project. The chance of a lifetime! In some city offices, a person with a sharp ear could have heard the sounds of lips smacking.

The manufacturers Beauceron-Luminar had hired Sicotte to act as a lobbyist on their behalf, and the lawyer had naturally turned to Bled Man. After a few consultations in high places, Bled Man promised the earth, on his usual terms, adding with a knowing smile that the installation of the aforementioned street lights would probably go to the engineering firm of Sopin & Vermillard, the reputation of which was well established; in addition, it had its own connections with the Montreal executive committee, as well as with the Ministry of Municipal Affairs.

"Sopin & Vermillard?" Sicotte said, shrugging. "So what? It has nothing to do with me."

"You're right. Me, neither. There are those who make ketchup, and those who make pots to put it in. You and me, we make ketchup."

Bled Man had been giving Sicotte a secret message, and Sicotte had obviously not picked up on it. What the lobbyist-lawyer was ignoring was that Sam Calvido, chairman of the Montreal executive committee, had, thanks to a pseudonym, a financial interest in Sopin & Vermillard. But despite this precaution, rumours had begun to circulate. Some people were gossiping about it, and maliciously. Should bad luck intervene, there was enough substance to the rumours to set off a magnitude-8 earthquake. Bled Man, the money man, was surprised that Sicotte, who was reputed to be a sly old fox, had not got wind of it, but too bad if a scandal broke out and the lawyer came to him with complaints; he could always say that on such-and-such a day, at such-and-such an hour, he had been warned and he thought the lawyer had understood the situation. As for himself, he had already distanced himself for when the shit hit the fan.

Things took their course. Four tenders came in for the job, and as they'd arranged beforehand to divvy up the municipal pie over the long term, Luminar obtained the contract for the city's street lights, to the great joy of Sicotte, who pocketed a healthy commission. Every now and then, Bled Man, in his capacity as messenger for Calvido, would approach Sicotte for legal advice regarding the contract with Sopin & Vermillard—advice he would then pass on to the illustrious chairman of the executive committee in exchange for a few banknotes.

Sicotte and Calvido had crossed paths at social gatherings and political meetings, and twice in television studios, but didn't really know each other. One day, the councillor asked Bled Man to set up a meeting with the lawyer; the next week, the fundraiser invited both Calvido and Sicotte, with their wives, to a box at the Bell Centre to watch a hockey game between the Montreal Canadiens and the Boston Bruins. Messieurs Sopin and Vermillard had also been invited, but excused themselves—the former because he was on a cruise on his yacht in the Caribbean, the latter because he was in Las Vegas, recovering from a bout of too much work.

The evening passed in a happy, relaxed atmosphere, topped off by the flashy appearance of the Minister of Public Works, Normande Juneau, who dropped in to say hello to Calvido and wish him a speedy recovery from a minor operation of an intimate nature.

"You are too kind, my dear Normande," replied Calvido, touched by her concern and kissing her hand.

The minister, a woman in her mid-thirties—tall, thin,

quite pretty, with dark, piercing eyes casting a discreetly sly gaze—laughed.

"I'm only kind to those who are kind to me, Monsieur Calvido, but that's a lot of people! As for the rest, I wish them luck."

"They don't deserve it, madame," said Calvido.

And then he squeezed the politician's fine, velvety hand between his own, fat with short fingers, and she laughed even more gaily.

The respectable Madame Calvido—who, for twenty years now, had been slowly disappearing into her own fat and cellulite—gave a full and toothy smile, all the while shooting sharp looks at her husband. The old pig, despite his age, was still chasing skirt, oblivious to the ridicule it brought him. Had he succeeded, she wondered, in carving the intriguing name of Normande Juneau into his list of conquests? There would be a discussion at the end of the evening.

At this precise moment, Bled Man gave a sign and two uniformed waiters made their appearance, one carrying a magnum of chilled Champagne and the other pushing a trolley laden with platters of hors d'oeuvres, and Madame Juneau, despite having so much to do that night, agreed to remain for a few minutes so that she might enjoy a glass of Champagne in such charming company. It was the apotheosis of the evening—and a triumphant one for the fundraiser who, for once, allowed himself to drink, if only a moderate amount.

Three days later, Calvido found himself pilloried by an article on the front page of *Le Devoir*, in which he was accused of gross conflict of interest by awarding the City of Montreal's contract for the installation of 30,000 street lights to the firm of Sopin & Vermillard, a company in which he was a shareholder.

Terrified that he would be dragged into the scandal, Sicotte tried to arrange a meeting with the chairman of the executive committee, but without success.

"That sonofabitch," muttered Sicotte, his face grey, his tie askew. "I've never seen such a blundering idiot! A schoolboy would have done better. If I'd known, I'd never have involved myself in this business. I risk being washed up with him in the court of public opinion. Damn it, I sent him three pieces of legal advice, and one even had my signature on it. He has to give me those documents back, the bastard. If he doesn't, I'll pull every hair on his backside out, one by one!"

He finally succeeded in reaching Calvido by telephone on the Thursday. But it wasn't a good move: an embarrassing article about Calvido had appeared that morning, the gift of a journalist he'd considered, until that point, a comrade-in-arms. His friends were turning on him like Judas, said Calvido. Would he end up being crucified in court?

Calvido spoke coldly to Sicotte, and Sicotte responded with equal rudeness. The tone of the conversation escalated, each one insulting the other more vehemently. The city councillor hung up. Theirs was a total falling-out, exactly when they needed to stand united if they were to ward off the blows.

"You should have kept better control of yourself," hissed Francine, who had been in the room and listening to the conversation. "Now what are we going to do?"

"It's easy to preach virtue when you don't have to practise it yourself," sputtered Sicotte, his face livid and swollen.

But he knew his wife was right. In his line of work, only

cold-blooded animals got out of corners like this alive. His temper had betrayed him. Was he getting too old for this?

"If," he said in a strained voice, "you were to leave me alone for a moment, that would help me with the work I have to do."

She left the office, slamming the door. Fradette and Jerome, who were in the next room and had overheard everything, looked at each other nervously. A foul atmosphere reigned in the office for the rest of the day.

Sicotte's nights were divided into two more or less equal parts: one was given over to insomnia, the other to nightmares. During the bouts of sleeplessness, he tossed and turned in the conjugal bed, prey to an itch between his toes that sent him into acrobatic contortions; the nightmares, diabolically realistic, ranged from torturous hanging to falling into pits swarming with tarantulas. Eyes wild, he would suddenly sit up in bed screaming an *"Arrgh!"* loud enough to rattle the bedroom walls. His wife, exhausted, would go to sleep in a room on the ground floor, stretched out on a couch, trying to find a solution to their quagmire as sleep, it goes without saying, had abandoned her as well.

It was apparent to Francine that the two men had to settle their differences whatever the cost. Their parting of ways could prove calamitous for both of them. One morning, at breakfast, she suggested to her husband, who was looking like death warmed over, that he send Fradette as an emissary to try to speak to Calvido, present him with apologies, and offer Sicotte's complete collaboration. Which is what happened. Within the hour, Fradette was ready to go. But despite being dressed to the nines and carefully prepped by his boss, Fradette didn't even manage to speak to a third-ranking functionary. The name Sicotte was received by the city councillor's staff like a cholera-infested blanket. Or perhaps Fradette seemed too much himself? But if that were the problem, it had never been so before.

For weeks, the Leader of the Opposition in the National Assembly, Aline Letarte, had been loudly calling for a commission of enquiry into the finances of the Ministry of Public Works. The demand was her favourite refrain, one she issued at any opportunity, as the heady scent of her Chanel No. 5 swirled about her. The media pressure became unbearable. That morning, the premier, Jean-Philippe Labrèche, no doubt shaken by the polls, announced the creation of a commission of enquiry.

Francine — haggard, her hair in disarray, a long run in one of her nylons — burst into her husband's office at 9:15, threw herself onto the sofa, and started weeping silently.

"We're screwed," she moaned, her voice breaking. "It's over. And all because of your stupidity."

Sicotte groaned, coughed a couple of times, and then dismissed the assertion with an indeterminate gesture. When he had got up that morning, he had found somewhere deep in himself a residue of combative energy and so put on the stoic front of a captain of a sinking ship preparing to send one final distress signal.

"A few minutes ago, I tried once more to speak with Calvido. I was treated like a Jehovah's Witness. So I decided to send Jerome."

"Jerome? Are you crazy? Come on, he doesn't have the experience!"

"For one thing, he has more class than Olivier. That counts for something. And he's more intelligent. Not to mention he's an unknown. Almost no one knows him, he hasn't been around long enough to make enemies. Sometimes inexperience is an advantage. Anyway, my dear, we have nothing to lose. If you have a better idea, send it to me by courier."

Then he banged his fist hard on his desk.

"I've got to get those goddamned papers back! I have no wish to be called in as a witness to this commission, my business would be ruined forever…and to think I did the work for that asshole for nothing!"

Francine stared at the Boulle desk she had given to her husband for Christmas eight years before, its corners encrusted with bronze figurines, a gleaming symbol of the family's prosperity. The desk and everything else in the office might be swept away in a tempest that would leave them naked as worms, forever disgraced.

"When are you going to speak to him?" she asked in a low voice.

"I've already spoken to him. He's on his way. I'm waiting for a phone call early this afternoon."

"What instructions did you give him?"

"I told him to do his best."

Then he added, "There are times when you just have to trust your instincts. I found his performance at Place Versailles very impressive, as you will recall."

Jerome had jumped into his car and driven to City Hall, seized by a sequence of contradictory emotions: fear of failing in his assignment, pride at having been chosen for it, but also a profound distaste for the whole business and the world of crooks into which he was being dragged. Sicotte had described with brutal frankness the thorny situation in which he found himself. Curiously, his distaste instilled in him a sort of amused detachment that gave him the aplomb that had been eluding his boss for days.

"And if the boss doesn't like my work, to hell with him," Jerome said to himself as he approached City Hall. "I'll throw my resignation right at his head and it'll be *adios, amigos*! I've got a bit of cash in hand, enough to give me time to change horses. After that, who knows? Maybe that lawyer of mine will succeed in making that goddamned guide pay me the money he stole. Who would have guessed," he said to himself with a disillusioned smile, "that one day I'd be working for crooks myself?"

After successfully working his charm on one receptionist, two secretaries, and an information officer (who seemed particularly receptive), he managed to get a certain Aurélien Dumais, Sam Calvido's political adviser, on the phone and he finally agreed to meet with him for thirty seconds at the end of a corridor later in the afternoon.

"So, how can I be of use to you, Monsieur Lupien?" Dumais asked Jerome haughtily. He had the kind of thin moustache that made him look like he just came in from hunting with hounds. "I'm very busy," he said, "and Monsieur Calvido is even busier, if that's possible. And I believe he and your boss have already said all they have to say to each other, no?"

"Perhaps not," replied Jerome, looking the man straight in the eye and all the while wriggling his toes in shoes soaked with sweat. "First of all, Monsieur Sicotte has charged me with conveying his apologies to Monsieur Calvido. He profoundly regrets the turn their conversation took the other day, an unfortunate development that he attributes to nerves and his being overworked."

"Very well," said Dumais, with a condescending smirk. "I'll tell him as much. Anything else?"

"Monsieur Sicotte also asked me," Jerome went on, his

cheeks burning as he improvised, "to — to present an offer to Monsieur Calvido, in order to get back some documents he urgently requires."

"I don't know what you're talking about," replied the other, drily.

"Would you be so kind as to pass on my message anyway, sir?" said Jerome, dropping his head deferentially. "I assure you I'm talking about an offer that Monsieur Calvido will find interesting. He would be disappointed if he didn't know it was being made."

"I'll see what I can do," said Dumais with a shrug. He turned slightly away, indicating that their discussion was over.

"Here's my card, Monsieur Dumais. I am entirely at Monsieur Calvido's disposal. Is it all right if I wait here for an answer?"

"You'd be wasting your time, my friend. Monsieur Calvido will call you if and when he thinks it appropriate. Good day."

Dumais disappeared behind a door that closed with a dull slam.

"Hoodlums like to surround themselves with classy types, it seems," thought Jerome on his way out. "Severin told me that at their meeting Calvido behaved like a hooligan."

He returned to the office to report on his mission to Sicotte, and they waited for the chairman of the executive committee to call. A day went by, then another.

At Sicotte's request, Jerome waited in a café a short distance from City Hall in order to be ready to meet with Calvido as soon as the councillor indicated a desire to do so. Restless, taciturn, stuffing himself with pastries and knocking back coffee after coffee under the intrigued gaze of the café staff, he would phone Dumais's office from time to time, but received only vague responses if any at all. He informed Sicotte, fulminating and pacing in his office, while Olivier fearfully hid in his own, frantically chewing gum.

Finally, on the afternoon of the third day, driven half mad by stomach ache (the excess of pastries he had eaten was taxing his liver), he returned to City Hall, if only to stretch his legs and rid himself of an intolerable sense of inertia.

All morning a radiant sun had been calling him outside. Hands in his pockets, Jerome strolled for a while on the promenade adjoining the imposing building, then went inside and walked the hundred paces of the immense, echoing foyer. The space seemed gloomy to him. He peered at everyone he passed, hoping to come across Calvido, who never appeared. His behaviour finally drew the attention of a security guard. In his early twenties, overweight, and assuming an air of importance beneath a cap too large for him, he asked:

"Can I help you, sir?"

"Er...no...I'm just waiting for some...oh, actually, yes...can you show me where the accounting department is?"

The guard frowned severely.

"The accounting department or the tax office?"

"Er...both, actually."

The guard, suspicious, nonetheless provided directions, which Jerome found incomprehensible. Hands on his hips, he watched Jerome move off and then, taking out his cell phone, the guard made a call.

After crossing the foyer, Jerome went down one corridor, then along another, and another, before finding himself in front of an elevator, the doors of which opened to discharge a half-dozen secretaries chatting happily and spreading about themselves the elixir of youth. (One blond woman smiled at him and, taken by surprise, Jerome looked down at his feet.) "Hmm," he thought, going into the elevator, "not bad, that one. I think I may have seen her the other day when I met with Dumais."

He pressed the button for the fourth floor, but the elevator descended and then stopped with a jerk; the door opened onto a basement corridor in which, so often the case in underground parking lots, the bitter fumes of car exhaust lurked. No one appeared to have summoned the elevator. Robotically, he stepped out—after all, he had to go somewhere and had no need to go either to the accounting department or tax office—turned to his left, took a few steps, and almost immediately heard a murmur of male voices behind him. He turned. Four men appeared, and he recognized Sam Calvido among them: short and bloated, his face flushed, wearing a grey toupé to cover his baldness, and carrying an overcoat folded over his forearm. He was, apparently, in a very good mood.

Jerome felt something like a blow to his midriff, his vision clouding slightly as he walked towards the approaching group in a kind of trance.

"Monsieur Calvido!" he said, his voice strained. "What luck to find you here! Did your adviser, Monsieur Dumais, give you my message? I'm sorry, let me introduce myself: I'm Jerome Lupien, sir, here on behalf of Severin Sicotte. Do you—"

The group stopped and was silent. With a slight motion of his head, Calvido signalled to the others to move on. Slowly, as if he were alone in the corridor, he put on his overcoat without looking at Jerome.

"Do you..." Jerome said again, stammering.

"Move on, my friend," murmured the councillor, still not looking at Jerome. "I'll call you at six. On your cell. So go on now, move away, move away," he said, even giving Jerome a slight poke.

And then he hurried off.

Jerome returned to the elevator and soon found himself back in the foyer, now brightly lit; a catering crew was setting up a buffet for a reception. He left City Hall and, contemplating rue Notre-Dame and its rush-hour traffic, a heavy fatigue came over him like a flood of ice water, liquefying his calves and making them tremble. With his eyes closed, feeling a little dizzy, he lost the thread of his thoughts, though the sensation lasted only an instant. Jerome's watch said twenty after four. "He won't call, the bastard, I know it," he thought, "he only said that to get rid of me." But he returned to the café anyway, in case he was wrong, and also to put himself beyond any possible reproach.

An hour later he'd emptied a half-bottle of red wine and felt comfortably disassociated from any earthly contingencies. He'd not yet called Sicotte to tell him about his unexpected encounter with Calvido when the cell phone he'd slipped into his shirt pocket sounded its melody. It was Eugenie.

"I can't talk now, darling, I'm on a job in Old Montreal. I'll call you back at seven, I promise." Under the spell of a supercharged erection, he couldn't help adding, "My God, how I love hearing your voice!".

"Jerome!" Eugenie laughed. "Have you been drinking, by any chance?"

"As a matter of fact, I have. A half-bottle of red, for now. A real binge, isn't it... But I've got to go, my love, much as

I hate to, I assure you. I'm expecting an important call. See you later, my dear. Kiss-kiss — all over."

He put his cell back in his pocket and decided to give up on the wine. If Calvido did call, he needed to be coherent and in control of himself.

"A double espresso, please, and make sure it's well-tamped," he added as he turned towards the counter.

From the snarky expression on the face of the waiter who was sorting cups, and that of his barista colleague, he realized that one of the effects of the alcohol he'd been consuming was an involuntary raising of his voice. A quick look around the café confirmed as much: the seven customers who had heard him were chuckling quietly to themselves.

He drank his espresso with an embarrassed smile, paid the bill, and left. It was ten to six. He had only just sat down behind the wheel of his car when his cell phone emitted its New Wave jingle again.

"Calvido here," said a gruff voice. "What do you want? Be quick, I'm in a hurry."

A whirlwind of ideas was spinning in his head; he grabbed one at random.

"Monsieur Sicotte would be happy to . . . to compensate you for returning his documents. He has charged me with . . . discussing the matter with you."

Jerome's words were met with a hearty laugh, then silence.

"'Compensate'?" said Calvido. "Not bad! Lawyers always choose their words so carefully."

"That was *my* choice of words, sir," Jerome corrected him. He was a little annoyed, but regretted his rashness immediately.

"Well, better watch out, then," the councillor said

mockingly. "You're in danger of becoming a lawyer yourself!" Jerome thought Calvido must have knocked back a few drinks, too — maybe a few more than he had done. "How much is he offering, your boss?"

Jerome, flabbergasted by the crassness of the councillor, was silent for a moment.

"Twenty thousand dollars," he said, picking a figure out of a hat.

"Peanuts, my friend. He knows the situation as well as I do, maybe even better...If not, he wouldn't be shitting bricks like he was the other day...I've never seen a guy behave like that...He didn't exactly make a friend of me then, oooh no! And you can tell him that."

"So, how much do you want, Monsieur Calvido?"

Jerome heard a long clearing of the throat, followed by some muttering and finally a bit of gurgling; times were hard for the chairman of the executive committee, it seemed.

"Me, anything less than fifty thousand, young man, and I don't move."

Jerome remained silent for a few seconds. Was it possible that society was directed by such hoodlums? But this was no time for such socio-political considerations. He needed to respond immediately.

"Shall we say forty thousand, Monsieur Calvido?" said Jerome, trying to maintain a light and disinterested tone. "With all due respect, I should let you know that is double what I was instructed to offer. I'm accountable for my actions, you understand...and I have no wish to go on the dole."

Calvido laughed.

"You don't mince words, do you? Okay, let's make it forty-five."

"I'm sorry, sir," said Jerome, who sensed a weakening

in the councillor's voice, "but I'm going to have all the miseries in the world trying to get you forty thousand. That's a lot of money, you'll agree, for a bit of legal advice that—no offence—my boss gave you pro bono."

"Okay, fine, it's a deal. I'll need the money in cash no later than tomorrow noon. And in twenties and hundreds, half and half. Got that?"

"Got it, monsieur. Have a good evening."

Jerome, torn between the hope that he would be praised to the skies for his work and the fear he'd be yelled at, drove to Caledonia Road to report on his mission. Alma met him at reception: the boss, indisposed, had gone to bed and Madame, needing to clear her head, had gone to the movies with a friend.

"So, all is well, eh?" she concluded, subtly pushing her hips forward and curiously smiling.

"I absolutely have to speak to Severin, Alma," Jerome said, his expression severe. "It's urgent."

They heard footsteps in the hall and a door opened. Sicotte, who had heard Jerome's arrival, appeared in his dressing gown. He looked defeated, grey, and ten years older.

"My office," he ordered Jerome, without giving him time to open his mouth.

When he heard how much money Calvido wanted for the return of the documents, the lawyer, sitting on the couch, went into a kind of shock and Jerome thought he was going to fall to the floor. But the reaction lasted only an instant.

"Ahh . . . ouf . . . okay," he said, wiping his forehead with the sleeve of his dressing gown, "it's a lot of money, obviously . . . but when you're dealing with trash that's what you have to expect."

He heaved a deep sigh, stretched out his legs, and stared

at a point in space above Jerome's head. Then, returning his gaze to the young man, he offered up a feeble smile.

"Thank you for your good work, Jerome, the worst has been avoided. At least I hope so. Except we'll have to ask that jerk for more time: forty thousand dollars in twenties and hundreds isn't something you find under a rock, is it. In things like this, we have to act with discretion."

"I have a small question I'd like to ask you," said Jerome, relieved and flattered by his boss's praise.

"Just a minute," Sicotte interrupted as he stood up with renewed energy. He went over to the cabinet with the gorgeous clock, opened one drawer, then another, and returned with a crystal decanter and two wine glasses.

"Nothing like a good cognac to sharpen the mind and purge the brain of negative emotions."

They clinked glasses.

"Ronceau-Legardois 1937, my friend, $675 a bottle. For special occasions only. Too bad Francine is at the movies. She's probably turned off her cell phone, otherwise I'd call and tell her the good news."

He smiled at Jerome.

"And your question, what was it?"

"Aren't you afraid that Calvido will keep a copy of those documents so that he can play a dirty trick on you later?"

The lobbyist shook his head.

"Not to worry. Those papers are a lot more . . . compromising for him than they are for me. He's probably already destroyed them. But I didn't want to risk it, you never know."

"Then why this messing around, all this haggling?"

"He wants to teach me a lesson, that's all. That's the way he is. He's a pig."

Jerome, exhausted by his mission, drank out of politeness

and forced himself to appreciate the precious elixir. He had the feeling he'd eclipsed Olivier Fradette in the lobbyist's estimation. His job was proving itself tumultuous and not without danger, but promising. Though it was not anything like he'd hoped it would be.

Arranging for the payoff kept Jerome busy for the next two days. He had to phone several times in order to plead for Calvido's patience, and the latter, no doubt overwhelmed with work, called twice to change the date of their meeting for the delivery of the money.

It was one of these calls that Charlie overheard on the night he'd invited Jerome to his house — and it caused him alarm.

JUNE WAS A splendid month for Jerome. On the money front, Sicotte acknowledged the skill and resourcefulness with which Jerome had handled the Calvido affair and, under pressure from his wife, nearly doubled Jerome's annual salary, bringing it up to $90,000. And that was before his commission percentage was paid! So much money at the age of twenty-five! He thought he was dreaming.

"And that's just the beginning, my boy," the influence-peddler assured him with a self-congratulatory smile.

But that was the extent of June's favours: it didn't take Jerome long to notice that his success as a negotiator had turned Fradette — who, until then, had been friendly and helpful enough — into a competitor sick with jealousy. A week or so after the Calvido business, Jerome happened to overhear a conversation between Alma and his colleague in the latter's office.

"It's easy to spend other people's money," said Fradette, fractiously, in response to Alma's vaunting Jerome's performance. "I could spend millions, I could, with one hand tied behind my back! You want some money? Here, here, take it! Catch! You too, you could do the same thing, anyone can. It's nothing to get excited about."

His hissing, outraged voice was that of frightened jealousy, the darkest and most ferocious of jealousies, the kind the survival instinct wakes up to defend one's vital interests. Fradette felt outclassed and feared for his job. The game had changed. It was him or Jerome.

This explained the coldness Fradette had been exhibiting for quite a while: his sarcastic smiles; his ambiguous remarks and the times he'd declined to go with Jerome to lunch, citing too much work.

From now on, Jerome would have to keep an eye on his former mentor.

June was also notable for other troubles, even more painful: a falling-out with Charlie and something very similar with Eugenie. Both were consequences, of course, of the Calvido affair.

It began one Friday evening, usually the glorious beginning of a weekend and its sense of endless freedom—at least until the miserable wake-up call on Monday morning. Eugenie had invited him for dinner and he'd been counting on—a reward for his hard work—one of their "4F" Soirées (Fabulous Food, Fantastic Fucking), to use a phrase invented by Charlie a few years before, when Charlie was dating a very nice but rather bizarre psychologist, whose other favourite pastimes were parachute jumping and playing vinyl records on vintage turntables. But of the 4Fs, Jerome was favoured, alas, with only the first two, the other two evaporating after a discussion at the end of the meal concerning the precise nature of his profession.

"Jerome," Eugenie said hesitantly, a bottle of Cuvée Julien having diminished their usual inhibitions, "I have a question to ask you about something that has been bothering me for a few days now."

"You want to know how I'm doing with my AIDS treatments?" asked Jerome. "Or maybe you're curious about my status with Opus Dei? Go ahead, my love, ask away. I've got nothing to hide tonight. I'm ready to strip myself naked before you right now, if you like."

"Jerome," she resumed, evidently deaf to his jokes. She looked him straight in the eye. "Is your boss a part of the underworld?"

There was a moment's silence.

"Why are you asking me that?" Jerome said quietly. His voice had changed.

"Because it's important for me to know."

He twirled his glass of wine in his fingers for a moment, then took a gulp of it.

"He's not in the underworld. If he was, I wouldn't be working for him. All the same, he's not exactly a choirboy, either. Nor am I, for that matter. It's real life we're talking about, life without the frills and lace . . . You have to fight hard if you don't want to be flattened by the next guy in line, and it's not always pretty. You know that as well as I do."

Reaching under the table, he took her hand.

"What's going on, Eugenie? What's happened?" he asked. "I've noticed you haven't been yourself for the past few days. Why not?"

He felt as if he had a rock in his stomach, the euphoria brought on by the wine suddenly vanished.

"Jerome," she said in a stifled voice, "last Thursday, Charlie called, and we met that night in a café."

Calmly, she told him about the telephone conversation with Sam Calvido that Charlie had overheard, the shock he'd felt, his troubled thoughts, and then the decision he'd made to tell her about it — not to gossip, but because the commitments of true friendship compelled him to do so.

"The fucker," Jerome muttered under his breath.

"Is it true you spoke with Sam Calvido?" she pressed. "Is it true that you're mixed up in this street light scandal?"

"I've talked with the man several times, and I've even met him three times — because Sicotte asked me, I should point out — but I am not in any way involved in that rotten street light business. I can even say that I'm delighted not to have anything to do with that bastard, who I hope will go to prison someday — and soon!"

"Then why associate with him?"

"I'm *not* associating with him," said Jerome, sharply. "If my boss hadn't forced me to meet with him, then I'd never have set eyes on his pig face or tolerated his boorish ways. He's a disgusting man, believe me. Having to put up with someone like that is one of the worst parts of my job."

The cries of a child torn from sleep filled the apartment, forcing them to lower their voices. Jerome fiddled with the edge of the tablecloth while Eugenie, looking down, seemed tormented by dark thoughts.

"In any case," she said in a troubled whisper, "he sends you off to some dubious meetings, this boss of yours. Which is the least you can say."

"We don't always get to choose our encounters, Eugenie. You must know as much from your own experience."

His voice definitely lacked conviction; her expression soured.

Andrée-Anne, after a sigh and a brief murmur, went back to sleep.

"If you're not in some mess yet, Jerome, it won't be long before you are, believe me. Your boss is trying to push you over the edge of a pit, I'm sure of it, and when he succeeds, you'll slide down to the bottom with no hope of climbing out again. It's a classic case."

He said nothing, turned his head away; she saw that his eyes were filling with tears.

"Jerome, I went through a relationship with a man who made me suffer more than you can ever imagine. He was an honest man, I believe, but he got caught up in something he couldn't see his way out of, and no amount of help, no one's good advice, could make him turn himself around. We lived through hell, and Andrée-Anne suffered terribly. I promised myself I would never go through that again, do you understand? I'm not trying to preach moral behaviour to you, Jerome, I'm simply trying to save my own skin. And because I love you so much, I want you to save yours, too. Because they'll end up skinning you alive, one way or another. Your famous Sicotte and his wife don't care a bit about you or anything that happens to you. All that counts for them is money, you know that, don't you? And the minute you become an embarrassment to them, they'll cut you off in thirty seconds flat, you can be sure of that."

He was mechanically spinning a knife back and forth on top of his crumpled napkin, his distraught gaze flitting from object to object in the room and settling, from time to time, on Eugenie's face before looking away again uneasily. He was filled with shame, despair, but also a strange irritation—as if his girlfriend was suddenly transformed into a mother trying to correct his behaviour and instill noble principles in him. She was a good four years older than him, but he hadn't perceived her that way before, and he didn't like it.

"So," he said bitterly, sarcasm in his voice, "you want to stop seeing me, is that it?"

She looked at him for a second, disconcerted, then, after a brief hesitation, said: "No, Jerome, it's not about that at all. I love you—haven't you noticed?—but you have to stop working for these dubious types who are going to get you into deep trouble—who have already started to, it's pretty obvious."

"Oh, really?" he replied with a sneer. "I can be that easily fooled! I didn't know that about myself."

But it was only a brief show of defiance, and his face quickly became sombre again.

"It's easy to give advice when you have a good job that pays well...My money, I earn it, I'm not stealing from anyone. You can't say as much about a great many of the people you see walking around with honourable faces."

He could have come up with a stronger argument, but didn't dare. The hellish matter of his possible extradition to Cuba would only tarnish him more in her eyes, thank you very much!

"If I leave this job," was all he decided to say, "I have nothing to turn to. Not a pretty picture!...And if I decide to stay?" he said in a defiant turn. "Well, you'll kick me out, is that it?"

She closed her eyes and looked exhausted.

"I don't know, Jerome, I don't know...But the idea of going through the same again...You have to get away from them, Jerome," she said with more force and then, looking up at him, "If you really love me, you'll leave...Tell me you're going to quit, please, I beg of you..."

Seeing her in such a state of distress gave him a repellent kind of pleasure, and that made him feel ashamed. Desirous, he rose, went over and began kissing her. She stiffened, shook her head, and said, in a tortured voice, "Jerome, no, not now, please...I'm really not in the mood, truly not..."

He caressed her more boldly for a moment, but it had no effect. He stopped.

"Well, what about some dessert, then?" he said, his voice cold and tense as he drew a plate towards himself, then another. "At least we won't have wasted the entire evening..."

"Stop, stop," she said, smiling weakly and halting him with her hand.

He turned away and moved towards the front door.

"You'll forgive me," he said, "but I'm going to sleep at my place tonight. I've got a very early meeting tomorrow morning with a car dealer" (which was not true), "I've decided to buy a new car" (which was true).

She followed and placed a hand on his shoulder.

"You're angry with me, aren't you?"

"I don't see things the way you do," he said drily.

She looked at him for a moment, and he felt himself turning red.

"What are you going to do, Jerome? You have to make a decision."

"I'll let you know when I've made it, Eugenie."

And he left without kissing her.

HE NOW HAD only one desire: to get to Charlie's and beat him to a pulp. Friends like Charlie he could do without; in fact, they were a ruinous luxury.

Charlie's apartment was on rue Marie-Anne, near Saint-Denis. Jerome called him from his car: it was a Friday night, half past midnight, he would surely be in. The phone rang five times, then went to voicemail.

"I still think he's home," muttered Jerome, furiously, as he started the car. "He's hiding. He's scared of me. Informers are always cowards. As you'll see in just a few minutes, my fine fellow!"

Fifteen minutes later he was on Marie-Anne. Luck was with him, it seemed: a rare thing, there was a parking space free right across from the small building in which the traitor had an apartment on the second floor. Standing beside his car, hands on his hips in the pose of a righter of wrongs, he saw Charlie's windows were dark. However, Charlie was a homebody, and congenitally indolent on weekends, when he would stay up watching movies or reading mystery novels until the wee hours of the morning.

"He's playing possum, or else he's flown the coop," said Jerome, kicking his foot against the pavement.

A couple of buffoons appeared at his right and sneered at him indignantly as they passed, cigarettes hanging from their mouths, then moved off with bursts of laughter, leaving in their wake the heady odour of marijuana.

Jerome went into the brightly lit vestibule, neon lights glaring overhead, and rang the bell. Once. Twice. A third time. On the fourth, he kept his index finger on the bell for a full minute. No sign of life came from the apartment. It was like trying to contact the XG 19444 nebula. So the spendthrift was out: but sooner or later he'd be back.

"And I'll be here to welcome him," Jerome promised himself. "If I must, I'll spend the night in my car. He won't get away, oh, no!"

His wait was short: as he left the vestibule, he almost bumped right into him.

"Ah ha! There you are, finally!" roared Jerome menacingly.

Charlie's face turned circumspect, though he replied calmly enough.

"I knew you'd be here. I'm just come from a friend's house. She was intending to spend the night here, but I thought it best if you and I were alone to talk."

There was a hint of defiance in his careful words.

"Thanks for your discretion," said Jerome snidely as his friend unlocked the apartment building's door and went towards the stairs to the second floor. "Too bad you didn't show any earlier!"

Charlie turned towards him with a finger to his lips.

"People are sleeping here," he whispered. "Calm down a bit, if you don't mind."

With fury in his eyes, Jerome shook his fist in front of Charlie's nose, but made the rest of the climb in silence.

Surprisingly, instead of the usual chaos, Charlie's apartment was as orderly as a compulsive old maid's — surely proof that he'd been expecting a quiet night. But Jerome hardly noticed. No sooner had the door closed behind them than he planted himself in front of Charlie and spoke to him in glacial tones.

"I didn't know I was hanging around with a spy. And that he'd rat me out to my girlfriend."

Charlie blanched, then reddened, then blanched again.

"I was going to tell you about it tonight, Jerome...And then Martine came over this afternoon, and it sort of slipped my mind, you know how it is...I should have talked to you sooner, I know...But when the opportunity was there, my heart wasn't in it. I'm sorry."

"That's what they all say, people caught with their pants down."

"Hey, my friend. *Moderato*, okay? You see betrayal everywhere."

"I am *no longer* your friend, chum. That's over. Jesus may have forgiven Judas but me, I don't want to end up being nailed to a cross. I'm not into pain."

"Let me explain, Jerome, or would you rather go the totalitarian route? I have zero interest in this whole affair, none whatsoever! If I went to see Eugenie, it's because I was worried about you — very worried — and because, as happens any time I try to have a civil discussion with you, you're about as approachable as a Sherman tank. So I thought Eugenie would probably have more influence than me. Period. End of story."

His voice had risen a bit. The same arguments Jerome had heard from the mouth of his lover were now coming from Charlie's, and he met them with the same responses. But this time he felt he was more justified.

"Is it bad conscience or just cynicism that makes you like that?" asked Charlie, exasperated. "Don't you realize you're setting yourself up for a long time in jail? Your 'boss' and his scumbags can afford to pay lawyers who'll find all kinds of loopholes that will see them out or at least buy them more time. But you? What do you have, eh?"

"What the hell does this have to do with you?" Jerome replied, his hand on the doorknob. "We don't even know each other anymore, Charlie... Goodbye!"

And he left, slamming the door. A neighbour noted Jerome's departure by banging on the wall with his fist.

THE END OF June arrived. The pleasures of *far niente* were at
hand—at least for those who were in a position to be able
to do nothing. Jerome hadn't seen Charlie since their nighttime row on rue Marie-Anne. The falling-out between them
seemed deep-seated, perhaps permanent. Jerome pursued
his relationship with Eugenie, but their evenings together,
already irregular, occurred at increasingly longer intervals.
Something in their relationship was broken, the proof being
that they never again mentioned the differences dividing
them. Love turns silent before it dies. Their physical relationship seemed, at least for the moment, to be a stop-gap.

On June 28, Eugenie phoned Jerome to inform him she
was flying to Paris to attend a conference on industrial food
production taking place during the last week of July. She was
taking advantage of the trip to hop down to Barcelona and
visit a friend she hadn't seen for a long while, and wouldn't
be back until mid-August. There wasn't much time between
now and then to get together, she added, what with work and
making the arrangements for the trip. Jerome, surprised that
she'd told him so late in the day, made a few jokes to hide the
hurt, said the timing worked out well because he, too, was
so swamped with work that he would likely postpone his
own holidays until autumn (which was not true, of course).

What would happen when Eugenie returned from
Europe after being away for three weeks? He didn't even
want to think about it.

Jerome had sold his Honda in order to buy the Mitsubishi
convertible he'd been dreaming about for ages, and was
thinking of buying a condo in Notre-Dame-de-Grâce; real
estate, his father always said, was the best investment, the
safest and most profitable. Forgetting his disdain for bourgeois dressing, which always struck him as old-fashioned or

the style of the *parvenu*, he espoused jackets and ties, which obliged him to buy an entire wardrobe. His view of things changed. It was the job, he told himself. You don't go fishing with a hammer.

The Calvido troubles for the moment contained, Sicotte seconded Jerome to Fradette and had them work together on a delicate and complex case: the allocation of part of the assets of a rich Algerian family, the Afnalis, who had been in Canada for a few months as investor immigrants. The Afnalis were living discreetly in Saint-Lambert, waiting for their permanent resident status to come through. Two hitches had complicated their case that required a particular adroitness to address: they were under investigation by the tax authorities in their native country ("The taxman, that predator," said Sicotte with a shrug) and were also accused of illegally removing treasures belonging to the national heritage of Algeria — specifically, a set of bas-reliefs dating from the Roman era (another shrug from Sicotte: "None of our concern"). The Afnalis had invested considerable funds in the Alberta tar sands, and this seemed to have bought them a certain amount of favour with the federal authorities, but even so, the necessary channels had to be followed.

Meanwhile, working with Fradette was becoming increasingly unpleasant for Jerome; his colleague was uncooperative, easily irritated, and sometimes openly argumentative. Two times, Jerome suspected him of setting him up for embarrassment. On the first occasion, a meeting had been arranged with Salem Afnali, the head of the family, for 9 a.m., but Jerome was told it was at 10. Fradette denied everything, of course, and pretended that Jerome had simply misunderstood, but Jerome subsequently received a dressing down from his client such as he'd never experienced before.

Then, a few days later, during a meeting with the family of the millionaire, he'd been the butt of a so-called joke. Fradette had turned to Jerome after Salem Afnali accepted a condition that at first he'd met with resistance.

"You see, Jerome?" said Fradette, grinning cheek to cheek. "Contrary to what *you said the other day*, wealthy Arabs *can* be reasonable."

Jerome had turned scarlet and needed a few minutes to recover from the effects of the comment, all the while under the indecipherable gaze of Afnali, sitting across from him.

During their drive back to Montreal, the incident provoked a lively discussion between the two men. Fradette argued that Jerome lacked a sense of humour; Jerome retorted that his colleague lacked good judgement. He'd left it at that for the time being but, furious and worried, he'd reported the incident to Sicotte in Fradette's presence.

All the lobbyist would say was "I pay you two enough, friends. Work this out between yourselves, for heaven's sake. My God, this isn't a kindergarten, after all. Come on, shake hands right now, in front of me, and we'll say no more of this nonsense."

But on the twenty-ninth, an event took place that allowed Jerome to rid himself of the colleague who was proving such an impediment, one with serious consequences for his career—and his life.

On that day, at eleven in the morning, the prime minister of Canada, Sydney Westwind, flanked by his Heritage minister, Chuckly Colslaw, held a press conference in Ottawa to announce the creation, in Montreal, of the Museum of Canadian Culture in the French Language. The date of the announcement had been carefully chosen. Five days had passed since June 24 and Saint-Jean-Baptiste Day—Quebec's national holiday — so that the patriotic fervour of the inhabitants of la Belle Province had time to abate. And there were two days to go before July 1, Canada Day, which provided a fresh opportunity to discuss Canadian unity, a topic flourishing pretty well everywhere.

"We anticipate a budget of $675 million for the new institution," the prime minister announced in impeccable French stymied by his notorious rubber accent. "The Museum of Canadian Culture in the French Language will attest, for today's citizens as well as for future generations, to the bilingual nature of Canada and the commitment of this country to one of the fundamental aspects of the national character."

He droned on this way for several long minutes, surveying the crowd and the cameras with his dead-fish eyes, stringing worn clichés together to the point of their becoming totally impenetrable, then turned the podium over to Colslaw, who repeated the same blandishments only in different words. The journalists' faces drooped more by the second; six were stifling yawns. Don Macpherson, on the other hand, the redoubtable columnist for the Montreal *Gazette*, was scribbling madly in his notebook and smiling wickedly, enthralled by this supply of fresh ammunition.

Which was when a young woman raised her hand with an air of disingenuous innocence and asked if Quebec had been consulted for a project with which it was so vitally concerned. With a rapid motion of his hand, Westwind signalled to the minister that he should field this one.

"I am pleased to say that discussions between our government and Quebec's are underway as we speak, and we have good reason to believe they will prove fruitful. It would only be natural, of course, that Quebec, the principal seat of French life in North America, become a major partner in a project that aims to celebrate the work of the descendants of Samuel de Champlain, a contribution that is so precious to Canadian culture..." (and so on and so on).

Ottawa was aware the announcement would raise cries of protest in Quebec—especially from those eternal shit disturbers, the separatists: the federal government would be accused of meddling in a provincial jurisdiction, wasting public funds, Machiavellianism, and all the rest of it.

The choice of June 29 for the press conference provided another advantage: the turmoil created by the news would quickly dissipate in the heat of summer, as citizen unrest over political issues always goes down when the mercury goes up.

The next day, caustic commentary appeared in *Le Devoir*: "Are Québeckers Objects in a Museum?" asked columnist Michel David; an editorial by Josée Boileau made a similar point. For several days letters poured into the newspaper offices from citizens either outraged or delighted with the Westwind Project (as the museum came to be called). Facebook and Twitter buzzed for a while, the issue was discussed briefly on television, a stand-up comic achieved a certain notoriety with a joke about a stuffed Quebecker, and there was a small demonstration in front of the Sulpician Grande Séminaire de Montréal on Sherbrooke Street: rumours were circulating that the order was planning to sell the garden adjoining the venerable institution to the federal government as a site for the museum.

In Quebec City, Opposition Leader Aline Letarte made mincemeat of the project—until July 1, that is, when she and her family flew to Costa Rica for a well-deserved holiday. "The name of the museum," she declared so forcefully that her bangles shook, eyes ablaze with anger, "is an insult to the men and women of Quebec. It should at least be called the Museum of *Québécois* Culture — with all due respect, of course, to the valiant francophone minorities of other provinces that have shown such resilience," etc., etc. And that being said, she went on, Quebec, not Ottawa, needed to oversee the project, culture first and foremost being Quebec's domain. "In a pinch," she added — this, the sort of conciliatory gesture that is the mark of the seasoned politician, "some form of collaboration with the federal government might be considered — one that takes into account culturally specific factors such as … (etc., etc.)."

Jean-Philippe Labrèche, the Quebec premier and, truth be told, a fervent Canadian, was more or less in favour of the project as announced by Westwind, but preferred that it be called the Museum of French-Canadian Culture — a name more representative, he thought, of our history and that had the further advantage of acknowledging Canada's flourishing diversity, *blah blah blah*. The assiduous observer, however, would have noticed that the debate was fairly uninteresting to him as he, too, was in a hurry to take a well-deserved vacation.

A poll to determine the name of the future museum appeared in *La Presse*, suggesting that the name proposed by Aline Letarte enjoyed a three-percent advantage over that favoured by Jean-Philippe Labrèche. The subject became a contentious one and everyone watched their step. Public opinion was a volatile (not to say fickle) thing, and it was impossible to know which side would win. In discussions held by the highest ranks of the Opposition party, an ex-minister lauded for his subtlety made the point that "French-Canadian," despite being an outmoded term ("and rightly so!"), was still more inclusive than "Québécois," what with the significant number of francophones living outside Quebec and Québécois living inside the province who saw themselves as Canadians first. Their opinions needed to be respected. It was therefore decided, through the democratic process, that a neutral attitude be adopted and for the whole business to be resumed only if and when the conditions were more favourable.

Severin Sicotte followed the debate attentively, but for completely different reasons. One of his sources in Quebec City had leaked to him that when the fall session of parliament resumed, Premier Labrèche would endorse Quebec's participation in the museum project. The exact terms were still to be worked out, but the government's financial involvement would be significant. In effect, Westwind and Labrèche had already concluded an unofficial agreement three months beforehand, hoping that such a spectacular example of collaboration would promote Canadian unity.

Neither the subject of Canadian unity nor the question of Quebec's ultimate destiny kept Sicotte awake at night or even made him sleep uneasily. On the other hand, the idea of colossal sums of money two levels of government were prepared to spend on a project that was nothing but pure propaganda prompted *frissons* of pleasure to pass through his body that sometimes kept him sleepless at night for hours on end.

But it wasn't enough to lie awake pleasantly trembling; he needed to act.

He made numerous phone calls and, though the most inept of golfers, took part in two tournaments at a select club on the West Island and invited not one but two executives of an architectural firm to dinner at the Beaver Club. (The bill gave him a bout of acid reflux.) In turn, he was invited to dine by others (and thus able to take his revenge) and went with his wife on a pleasure cruise on the private yacht of a construction-company owner who seemed to no longer know what to do with all his money, still less with his principles. On July 9 at 3 p.m., he convened Jerome and Fradette in his office — the latter purely for form's sake, as he had no intention of conferring any particular task on him, though he always wanted to cultivate love and loyalty in his staff. Team spirit, as he was fond of saying, was reinforced by the sharing of important information.

"My friends," he began in a solemn tone animated by a hint of emotion, "if things go the way I hope, the coming months will be particularly fruitful ones. There's a good chance — ha! — that soon we'll be relishing some top-quality bacon. If you know how to handle your luck, boys, you'll be thanking me so hard your throats will be sore. First of all," he said, turning to Fradette, "there's the Afnali file, which you are handling very well, though it hasn't yet netted us all the profit in its potential. And, on the other hand, there's a new file very much in the wind these days..."

"You mean the *West*wind!" said Fradette, grinning.

"Exactly! It's because of it that you haven't been seeing much of me around here this past little while. But, with a bit of luck, I won't have been absent for nothing. Quite the contrary! This particular file," he said, turning this time to Jerome, "is one the two of us are going to be looking after. We won't be wasting Olivier's time, he's got enough on his plate with the Algerians. Grasp all, lose all, or something along those lines. Don't forget it."

"What do you want me to do?" asked Jerome.

"First, take two weeks off, get yourself in good shape. That goes for you, too, Olivier, as long as the Afnalis permit it."

"I'll sort it out with them," replied Fradette, attempting to hide his annoyance.

"No, I'll sort it out with them myself," Sicotte decided on second thought. "I'll call the great Salem shortly to tell him you're going to be unavailable for a while, and if anything urgent comes up he can contact me directly. You need some down time like everyone else, my friend. I'm every bit as concerned about my team members' well-being as I am about my own. Understood?"

"Understood, chief."

"One more thing: Francine is leaving for Varadero this afternoon to take care of a few things at the hotel. She'll be back on the ninth of August, when we'll be welcoming Felix, who is coming back to stay with us. Finally."

"Will Alma be going with her?" asked Fradette.

"No, not this time. She has work to do here."

The telephone rang. Sicotte lifted the receiver and made a gesture indicating the meeting had come to an end. As the two were leaving, Fradette invited Jerome for coffee in his office and, to make an occasion of it, he took from his desk drawer a tin of chocolate biscuits imported from Switzerland and offered them to his colleague with a big smile. ("Go on, take one, don't be shy! They're delicious!") The offer surprised Jerome as he had, over time, concluded that Fradette was a tightwad. It had been a long while since he'd seen his colleague being so considerate. Perhaps the compliments he'd received from Sicotte had put him in a good mood.

"What are your plans for your holidays?" Jerome asked him amiably.

"To get as far away from Algeria as possible," replied the other, laughing.

"No, but really."

"I might spend a few days on my uncle's farm in the Eastern Townships, and then maybe indulge my belly in Ogunquit. What about you? Are you still raising your girlfriend's daughter?"

The question, collegial as it was, stunned Jerome as he'd never spoken at work about his private life. Perhaps he'd made some vague allusion to Eugenie, and his clever colleague, jumping to conclusions, had retained the information.

"No chance of that," he said, with a disenchanted smile. "I'm as free as a bird."

"Ah," was all Fradette said, and the conversation went in a different direction.

AFTER THREE DAYS, Jerome began to find his vacation deadly dull. Eugenie's absence, his worry about their relationship and the falling-out with Charlie, who seemed to have disappeared from the face of the earth, all became mixed up in his mind with painful reflections about what he was becoming. Pointless to kid himself; he was about to swell the ranks of scoundrels. In a Dickens novel, he'd be one of the despised characters, Murdstone and company, characters he'd always thought of as contemptible; in a Balzac novel, he'd be hanging out with the horrible Vautrin and the rotten Lousteau. His only consolation was the comfort and excitement of working in the shadows, behind the scenes. This was new and required him to be constantly vigilant. He often felt as though he was living in a crime novel — a thriller infused with toxicity, but each episode paid so well! And the best, said Sicotte, was still to come.

Despite the-best-is-still-to-come, his vacation seemed about as restorative as being washed up on a desert island.

He'd telephoned Eugenie a few times and exchanged two or three emails with her, all of them strictly neutral and factual. For the past few days, silence had reigned, as if they no longer had anything to say to each other. No, things were not going well between them. Something had broken, perhaps irreparably.

On the afternoon of the fourth day, Jerome went to visit his parents, who welcomed him with affecting exultation. His mother was in the middle of giving a piano lesson to a young student (she looked pretty but seemed a bit thick) but interrupted the lesson to greet him and make him a latte with their new espresso machine.

"Well? Do you like it?"

"Yes, it's delicious, Mom, really delicious. Is it a Ravina? I wouldn't mind having one of those myself."

"I'll tell you where I got it. It was quite the bargain. Now, you'll have to excuse me, dear, I've got to get back to my lesson... I'm coming, Odile!"

There was no summer *far niente* for Claude-Oscar, who'd decided long ago that September was the best month to take vacations, despite the inconvenience it caused his wife and, above all, young Marcel. At Jerome's arrival, his father came up from his basement clinic in a lab coat covered in splotches.

"Well, if it isn't my beloved son, finally deigning to pay us a visit."

And, eschewing the traditional handshake stipulated by the Code of Masculine Behaviour, he took his son in his arms. Then, still holding Jerome by the shoulders, he stepped back to look at him.

"How are you? You look good, anyway. My, my, you're becoming a man. Still happy with your Mitsubishi?"

"For now, yes, Dad."

"Come and show it to me, I can't wait to see it."

His father was as excessively high-spirited as ever, though Jerome found him older. Her piano lesson over, Marie-Rose reappeared in the kitchen to make supper (there was no question of his not staying) and whispered to him that Claude-Oscar had been diagnosed with diabetes. "Don't say anything to him . . . When Dr. Groulx gave him the news he blew his top."

"At who?"

"At life, I guess."

"Does he give himself insulin shots?"

"No, he's only pre-diabetic. For now he's been put on Glucophage, but he has to follow a strict diet and, as you can imagine, it isn't always easy."

Around five o'clock Marcel burst into the house with a friend, and Jerome was obliged to show them his new Mitsubishi in all its glory, and then take them for a spin around the neighbourhood with the top down.

"Wow!" Marcel exclaimed, looking at Jerome with wide eyes. "It's a millionaire's car."

Jerome broke out into laughter.

"*Are* you a millionaire?" his brother asked in all seriousness.

"No, no, not even close! Why are you asking me that?"

"The other day, Dad said you were making pots of money."

"Well, yes, I'm doing all right, but I'm not making millions."

And he gently ruffled Marcel's hair.

Despite his spontaneous visit, Marie-Rose, adept at accomplishing a lot in a short space of time, produced a first-class dinner: cream of mushroom soup, salade Niçoise, sweetbreads, scalloped potatoes and, for dessert—because of the diabetes—a fruit salad doused with just a splash of port. The welcome they showed Jerome touched him deeply but, at the same time, saddened him a little. Their display of affection concealed a gentle reproach—that he'd been neglecting his parents. But one detail struck him even more painfully: not once was he asked about his job, as if it were a taboo subject—even suspect. His parents must have sensed something was not right and were hiding their uneasiness.

He left the house around nine, tried calling a friend from his CEGEP days, then another, without success. July seemed to have emptied Montreal. He even thought of phoning Lucy, but then told himself not to stray into the ridiculous. Besides, she was probably in Istanbul or Fiji with some sugar daddy.

He decided to check out a discotheque downtown. Around two in the morning he returned home alone and hot, and felt like blowing up his apartment.

When he woke up the next day it was midmorning, and he was in the best of moods, which astonished him. "Good Lord," he told himself as he made breakfast (he was starving), "are we nothing but clusters of hormones and cells, a kind of machine that watches itself work but has no idea how or why?" Seated by the window, he drank his café au lait and feasted on toast generously spread with raspberry jam and thought, "Yes, that Ravina is tempting. I think I'll go out and buy one this afternoon."

Who knew? Maybe his change of mood had to do with the weather? The sky was grey, but a luminous grey that made the world appear peaceful and pleasant. It seemed impossible that somewhere on the planet people were trying to kill each other.

Suddenly the New Wave tone of his cell phone went off in his bedroom.

"That'll be Charlie wanting us to explain ourselves," he thought as he hurried to pick up.

He managed to find the cell in one of his pant pockets. "Hello?"

His lips curved downwards as he frowned in disappointment. It was Fradette, calling from the office. A load of shit had been dumped on their heads. Could he come in to lend a hand, pronto? No, he couldn't say anything more on the phone. He was very sorry to disturb Jerome while he was on holiday, but he had no choice. He'd make it up to him somehow.

"Yeah," said Jerome, "the timing is bad, to be frank." *When it comes to you*, he thought to himself, *it's always a pain in the ass.* "Is it going to take a while? You don't know... Hmmm... Well, okay. I'll take a shower, put some clothes on, and come down." *Shit!* he added as he hung up. *I don't need this! He's the one who's supposed to have the experience. Son of a bitch!*

Driving to the office, he mulled over their rivalry and how Fradette was peevishly jealous of his standing, but couldn't figure out why he would call Jerome for help when doing so would only weaken his position. Maybe this was the beginning of the end for Fradette? "That would be good for me," he told himself, although, curiously, concluding so gave him no satisfaction.

When he arrived at 27 Caledonia Road, he found Fradette frantically going through a pile of papers spread about his desk, while Alma, crouched in a corner, was piling up folders.

"Ah, here you are at last," sighed his colleague. "With three of us, I'm sure we'll find it."

Alma gave him a big smile.

"It's good of you to come, Jerome."

The pest seemed to have mucked up her day, too. He'd almost always seen her in more casual clothes, but today she was dressed to kill, with a midnight blue dress and matching high heels.

"What do you want me to do?" he asked sullenly.

Fradette gave him a somewhat confused explanation. Sicotte had called that morning; they had to find a specific document as quickly as possible—a contract with a certain Robert Rémillard, a Quebec businessman. This Rémillard had signed the contract, and Sicotte was supposed to have signed it, too, but for God knew what reasons he hadn't, which was actually a good thing because the deal looked like it was going to blow up in their faces. The document was on very pale blue paper—or maybe green, but very pale—and Francine had handled it last, though she had nothing to do with the deal, and that's what had caused the mix-up. She'd misplaced it about it a week ago, or was it two weeks? In any case, Alma thought so, she had seen it lying on Francine's desk for a while without giving it much thought. Now the boss, in a real panic, had telephoned from she did not know where, asking them to find it, and they'd bloody well better hurry up about it because he sounded extremely agitated, regardless of anyone in the room having done anything to be worried about.

"Okay," said Jerome, the calmness of his vacation evaporating at the speed of light. "What was it about, this contract?"

"He said he couldn't tell me," answered Alma in her reedy voice. She gave Jerome a strange look.

"So what do I have to do?" asked Jerome, impatiently. "If I understand rightly, all we have to go on is the colour of the paper, is that it?"

"Blue or green, but not necessarily all the pages."

"Even better!" said Jerome. "And how many pages is it, if I may ask?"

"Listen, pal, if I knew more I'd have told you...Maybe a dozen," Fradette went on in a more agreeable tone. "You should've heard the state he was in. He was babbling!"

"All right, let me ask a third time: what do you want me to do?"

Olivier pointed to a large cardboard box, overflowing with papers, in a corner of the room.

"Look through all the contents, *file by file, page by page*, and if you turn up anything that seems relevant, put it to one side. I'll give them a look when you're done. There are three more boxes just like that in Madame's office," he said, with a contemptuous snigger. "They should have gone to the shredder..."

Jerome took a chair, sighed heavily, and went to work. For several minutes, the only sound in the room was of the shuffling of papers and shifting of folders, and words muttered under the breath by one or other of the unhappy investigators.

"Does anyone want coffee?" Alma asked after a while.

"I don't need coffee," said Fradette, "I'm jittery enough already."

"I'll have one," said Jerome. "I didn't get much sleep last night."

Alma stood before him and looked his way with a mischievous smile; he'd never seen her act this way before.

"Busy night, Monsieur Lupien?"

"I wish."

Her carefree attitude surprised him, but then he'd always found the comportment of the young woman strange, if not incomprehensible. What kind of life did she lead? He didn't know if she had a boyfriend or not. She lived with the Sicottes as if she were their daughter, but the comparison ended there.

Fradette looked up.

"Go, Alma, get a move on, girl. We've got to find this damned contract. Severin might call any minute."

She left the room with a bit of a skip and came back a few minutes later carrying a tray with two cups, some sugar packets, and a carton of cream. Jerome held out his hand for a cup and their eyes met; she frowned as she pointed her chin in Fradette's direction, as if to say "What a shithead!" then went back to her corner.

More and more astonished by her behaviour, Jerome, too, went back to work. Half an hour later, his left foot and calf had gone to sleep, and his neck was beginning to hurt. Suddenly he cried out: "I think I've found it!"

He held up a set of pale blue pages encased in a sleeve that was pale green.

"Give it here," Fradette cried gruffly.

He flipped quickly through the pages, sometimes backwards, his face muscles twitching, while Jerome and Alma awaited his verdict.

"Well, my friend," he said quietly, heaving a huge sigh of relief, "I was right to call you in . . . you have in fact found it! *Yippee!*"

The two men exchanged high fives. At the very same moment, the telephone rang. Fradette grabbed the receiver.

"Yes? Severin, we just found it! Yes, just now! That's right . . . the option on Hôtel-Dieu is clearly stated . . . Perfect. I'm on my way."

Fradette hung up and turned, triumphantly, to his two companions:

"Mission accomplished! Thank you, friends. And a huge thanks to you, Jerome. I'm going to take the damned thing over to him now."

"Where is the boss?" asked Jerome, a little miffed that he'd not been credited with the find.

"In a hotel out by the airport. Thanks again. See you later. Enjoy the rest of your vacation."

Fradette hurried out of the room and ran down the hall. Soon after, they heard his car start up.

"*La commedia è finita,*" murmured Jerome, with a sigh.

He moved behind Fradette's desk and sat down with a satisfied air, took a sip of his coffee, and stretched his legs out in front of him.

"It wasn't exactly a *comedy,*" Alma said, leaning against a file cabinet and watching him intently.

Jerome laughed.

"I was using a classic Italian phrase," he said. "I thought you'd know it."

They looked at one another in silence. A sort of uneasiness came over Jerome.

"You look pretty great today, Alma. That dress suits you perfectly . . . Are you going out?"

She shook her head.

"Not really. My evenings out, they happen here," she laughed.

Outside the window, a blue jay was calling as if his life depended on it.

"There's more coffee if you want it."

"No, thanks. You're very kind, but I have to go."

He stood up and she gestured for him to wait. "Can you stay for a minute? I want to show you something."

She smiled ambiguously.

"It won't take long, you'll see."

Then she left, turning at the door with a fresh smile.

Jerome sat back down and finished his coffee. It was luke-warm, but still delicious. They made good coffee here. But what did this curious woman want him to see? He found her more peculiar and concerning with each passing day.

He heard her voice from the other side of the office partition.

"Jerome, can you come in here for a second?"

He went into the corridor and entered the kitchenette. It was empty.

"I'm in the next room," she called in a slightly muffled voice. "Open the door."

He pushed the door open and froze on the spot. Alma stood in front of Jerome, staring at him with a strange intensity.

"Yes?"

She said nothing, just continued to stare. Imploringly, thought Jerome.

"You're so handsome," murmured Alma, as if in ecstasy.

A slightly mocking smile rose to his lips that quickly dissolved into an expression of smug pleasure. He took a hesitant step forward. She remained where she was, not moving, her stance of such dizzying abandon that he could not help but be overcome. It was then that he realized Alma had undone the top buttons of the dress she was wearing. She shuddered and the dress opened, falling a little from her shoulders and revealing a good portion of her breasts. Their rosy flesh made his head swoon.

In the ensuing moment, they embraced each other passionately. Alma set about sucking his tongue so fren-etically that Jerome winced in pain and retreated slightly. But in no time at all, their clothes were falling to the floor until, almost naked, they had found each other.

Alma started to let out little whimpers that struck Jerome as affected and silly. But he came almost immediately and then, breathing hard, halted. Seconds passed. Stretched out beneath him in the mess of their clothes, she was smiling up at him languorously. He lifted himself up by the elbows and collapsed at her side.

"Sorry," he said sheepishly. "I came too quickly. You took me by surprise."

Alma turned her head and winked at him.

"It was fine. Don't worry about it. Thank you."

"I can do better."

"We'll see about that," she said. She reached out towards him with her free hand and caressed his ass and they started to embrace again, kissing each other hungrily.

"You really did surprise me," Jerome repeated a few minutes later. "Really, I wasn't expecting that."

"I know," said Alma. "I'm like that. I like surprises... creating scenes."

She looked at him, smiling. He wanted to put his boxers back on. If this was a scene, it wasn't intimate. It was something else. He didn't know what.

"Have you given Olivier surprises like this? Or maybe the boss?"

"In your dreams," she said with a dismissive laugh. "I only like surprises when they amuse me."

She stood up, patted her hair in place, and straightened her dress.

"Would you like another coffee now? There are also some mille-feuilles in the fridge that I bought this morning. They're really good... After going through all those boxes, we deserve one, don't you think?"

"Sure, why not? All this rummaging around makes a person hungry, don't you find? Tell me," he continued as he pulled up his jeans, "you planned all this, didn't you? Don't say you didn't..."

She looked shocked and shook her head.

"Not at all. But when I found out you were coming in, I promised myself I wouldn't let such a good opportunity pass me by, that's all..."

"So you did plan it."

"Well, if that's what you call 'planning'..."

"Well, me, I didn't see it coming, I swear."

"'Well, me, I didn't see it coming, I *swear*,'" she repeated, mimicking his tone and tweaking his nose. "Men are so sneaky, I can't believe it..."

She was right about the mille-feuilles; Jerome had never tasted any so delicious. They ate two each with their coffee, then went upstairs, and made love in Alma's room, the office floor striking them as too hard for what they had in mind — and, besides, Fradette's sudden return was always a possibility.

When Jerome finally left Caledonia Road that afternoon, it was with a measure of relief that he couldn't quite explain. He and Alma had agreed to keep their adventure to themselves. What good would it do anyone if it were known?

"It would only cause complications," the young woman observed. "And in our line of work, there are enough complications already, no?"

They were, therefore, in perfect accord, a rare thing in such matters, Jerome thought as he drove back to his apartment. So why did he feel such relief to be leaving? And why was it so hard to sleep when finally, after surfing the Internet for the evening, he went to bed? Despite his efforts, thoughts of Eugenie kept nibbling away at the satisfaction the escapade with Alma gave him. True, he had succumbed so easily...But who wouldn't have, faced with a lovely ass such as hers, offered up so unexpectedly? The surprise of it all was like a wave coming up from the deep, sweeping away everything in its path...And he'd succumbed again, right away, and for a longer time! Was he counting on seeing her again? No doubt yes, but why? To punish Eugenie for having poured ice water on their relationship by running off to Europe for most of the summer? Or because of their differences concerning the increasingly suspect life he was leading?

A feeling of irrevocable doom suddenly took his breath away: he was on the verge of throwing away real love for a meaningless fling...

At three in the morning, in the weak light from his bedside lamp, he was in the midst of reading a sixth Chekhov short story when finally he felt a welcome heavy-lidded drowsiness and sweet suspension of consciousness that finally allowed him to put an end to the strange day he had just lived through.

FOR SIX DAYS Quebec broiled under a ferocious heat wave that drained Montreal of every citizen able to flee the city. On July 23, news broke that shook the media: it was leaked that three months earlier, the Westwind government had come to a secret agreement with the Sulpicians, who'd ceded some of the lands of their estate for the purpose of constructing the much-touted Museum of Canadian Culture in the French Language. The old priest factory had been functioning below capacity for a long time, mostly due to the lack of raw materials, and it was incumbent upon the order, after all, to cover its operating expenses. All that was missing was the endorsement of the Quebec Minister of Culture, and that was more or less a foregone conclusion. The few thinkers who hadn't yet slipped into their summer coma began to grumble. Christian Rioux, the Paris correspondent for *Le Devoir*, wrote about the treason of the clerks, "in which the term is used in its original sense." Yves Boisvert, a pundit at *La Presse*, ended his column by noting that "the conceivers of this plan so injurious to Quebec have proven that one can be both a mongrel and a cynic at the same time." A press release from the Société St-Jean-Baptiste clamoured for the society's indignation. But, in the summery furnace, everything melted away. The Opposition maintained radio silence; its leader, Aline Letarte, was no doubt completely absorbed by thoughts of suntan lotion and beach reading or perhaps, ear glued to her smart phone, she was trying to prioritize her ideas with the help of a counsellor.

So, what would have been a bomb if it had gone off in the fall sounded more like the chirping of a cricket.

The next day, Sicotte reappeared at the office with a cruise aficionado's swarthy tan and a new lease on life: a discreetly handled cabinet shuffle in Quebec City had placed Normande Juneau, formerly in charge of public works, at the head of the Ministry of Culture.

"Things are moving along for us like they're on wheels, lads," said Sicotte, jubilantly, to Jerome and Fradette, who were back in harness that morning. "Everything's falling into place. Normande Juneau is extremely approachable, as you know. In fact, I have her in my pocket. All we have to do is keep our nose to the wind and try not to step in any cow patties, and you'll see what we shall see. This new

Museum of Franco-Canadian-Québécois, or whatever the hell they call it, is going to be our museum of money! So, as we agreed earlier, Jerome, you'll be handling this file with me."

Then, turning to Fradette, he said: "You had a good vacation, champ?"

"Not really. I had to meet with the Afnalis three times, and old Salem phoned me about his investments practically every day."

"You should have referred him to me, like I told you."

"I did, but he wasn't able to get hold of you, either by telephone or email."

Sicotte looked away, to some place where chaos and cunning intermingled.

"I admit I have my little weaknesses," he said. "You'll have to excuse me. We're all human, right?"

But he seemed about as regretful as a man who'd won the jackpot at Loto-Québec.

"Some more than others," replied Fradette, acidly.

The lawyer broke out laughing, and Fradette followed suit. His riposte was the only indication of any discontent over his truncated holiday.

There were three light taps at the door, and Alma came in carrying a platter with the boss's steaming pot of coffee. Sicotte consumed great quantities of the stuff. "I'm no Balzac," he was fond of saying, "but when I take up my pen, great things sometimes happen . . . especially when I'm dealing with numbers."

"Be careful there, my dear," said Sicotte as Alma set down the platter. "The last time you made a huge ring on my desk. It cost me in the three figures to take it out."

She responded with a mutter and, as she left, passed

Jerome without looking at him. He held back a smile. Ten hours earlier, in his apartment, she'd comported herself quite differently.

"A coffee, boys?"

Fradette shook his head and left, knowing that his boss needed to speak to Jerome.

"And all's well with you?" Sicotte asked, when they were alone.

As soon as Jerome nodded, Sicotte quickly moved on to more important topics.

"I seem to have a weakness for cruising the Greek Isles," he said, "but you'll never guess who I met there."

"I have a feeling you're about to tell me."

"None other than Ernest Rouleau, Normande Juneau's riding secretary. An amazing man! The most interesting person in the group, by far! We exchanged a lot of useful information that I'll pass on to you in a memo. It partly explains why I'm in such a good mood. I didn't want to mention it in front of Olivier—I trust him, of course, quite a lot, but there are some things we want circulated as little as possible. It's a matter of not muddying the waters, you understand... Normande really wants to be re-elected, but she has a few little problems in her riding. She has no intention of adding to them, people gossip too much, so I offered my help—through an intermediary, of course. That's just the way I am, I have a generous nature, you see."

"I see."

"Westwind also wants to be re-elected; his lust for power keeps him awake nights. He has it in his head to strengthen his position in Quebec. Hence this museum project, which is far more advanced than we thought. He's a sly one, this Westwind, he hasn't believed in Santa Claus for a long time..."

The plans and specs for the museum are pretty much in place, and the call for tenders will probably go out in October. That's when our game will be afoot, Jerome. Because we're talking about a Canada-Quebec-Canadian-Unity-*unité-canadienne* partnership type of project, there'll be plenty of bacon for everyone, by which I mean everyone who has a fork long enough to skewer the meat. Long forks are expensive, but if you have one you can spear yourself some bloody big chunks! The plans and specs have to be approved by Quebec City, which is in part financing the project, but that's not the problem. They'll be approved, you can bet on that. Labrèche is *Canadien* in his soul, though even more so a 'Canadian,' if you see what I mean. That's why Normande Juneau was just made Minister of Culture. She's a woman you can trust, and the premier has her well in hand—unless it's the other way around? In any case, she's the one he's picked to handle this. Are you getting my drift?"

"I am."

"As effective lobbyists, we are to be the intermediaries between the working guys who want the contracts and a minister who needs money for her campaign expenses."

"Yes, yes, I see."

"It looks simple enough, but it's not as easy as it seems. We have to apply the WED principle."

A question appeared on Jerome's face.

"I haven't told you about that rule yet? You know it without me having to tell you, my boy. WED: Work, Elegance, Discretion. Repeat it to yourself ten times. It's always a good principle to keep in your head."

"Elegance?" asked Jerome, smiling sardonically. "That's hardly the word that comes to my mind when I think of Bled Man."

"He's old school. You, you represent the future."

Jerome nodded.

"Thanks, boss."

Below the name of Bled Man, thought Jerome, Sicotte might have added his own, despite the Boulle furniture and the law degree and the increasingly highfalutin language in which he indulged. A vague irritation ate at him again, but he kept it from showing and listened to the lawyer attentively. There'd be plenty of time to reflect on all of this later.

"You'll have your chance to apply the WED rule, starting this afternoon. We're meeting with Freddy Pettoza, head honcho of Simo Construction, at three o'clock."

"But didn't you say the call for tenders wasn't going out until October?" Jerome said, surprised.

Sicotte gave him a commiserating smile.

"Come on, Jerome, I see I'm really going to have to take your education in hand. Forget about the call for tenders, dear boy. That's for the general public. The submitters have already agreed among themselves that Freddy will get the contract to build the museum, it's his turn. And I have even succeeded, slaving away, to secure him an advanced copy of the museum plans, so we'll know what we're dealing with when we draw up the tender. That's the kind of service he won't forget. So then, three o'clock, Café Vicky, on rue Stanley."

Reaching to the floor, Sicotte picked up a heavy leather briefcase and set it on his desk.

"Here," he said, handing Jerome a thick file. "Here's a copy. Give it a quick glance. It doesn't matter if you don't understand everything. We have to get going on it right away. Pay particular attention to clauses covering cost overruns. With all the limits imposed on us in other areas, that's often the most lucrative part of the contract."

AT FIRST GLANCE, Freddy Pettoza was a difficult individual to classify — or, to be more precise, to subclassify, as by all appearances he belonged to the category of "businessmen most likely to have to appear before a commission of enquiry." In his early fifties, he was short, stocky, not too overweight, with heavy overhanging eyebrows that gave his face a certain Neanderthal aspect. His full head of salt-and-pepper hair hung down over his forehead, and his three-day beard wasn't the kind that had become popular in recent years, but was that of a man who had far too much to do to be able to spend time at the bathroom mirror. In animated discussions, his upper lip curled malevolently, but an instant later, the expression beneath his cavernous brow might brighten, take on a tender glow, and he'd smile like a five-year-old who'd just been handed a kitten, without even seeming to notice the change. He was a hard man but without rancour, an excellent liar but one who detested hypocrisy (unless it served his purposes), who was intolerant of tardiness and given to declaring that time is money — and applying the old adage to himself as much as to others. Experiencing this made Jerome see how difficult it was to consider even the most proven assholes to be of one type.

When Sicotte and Jerome showed up at the Café Vicky at five minutes past three, Freddy Pettoza was sitting at a corner table with a half-empty stein of beer and a vegetarian hamburger in front of him: along with hypocrisy and lack of punctuality, an excessive appetite for meat and an interest in taxidermy were among the objects of his loathing, as he loved animals and made generous donations to the SPCA (for which he received large tax deductions).

"You never said you were bringing someone," he declared

right off the bat once he and Sicotte had exchanged the usual handshakes.

He spoke with the slightly rolling accent common to certain second-generation Italian-Quebeckers.

The lawyer took the high road immediately.

"Monsieur Pettoza..."

"Call me Freddy, that's better."

"Okay, Freddy, if I didn't have the utmost confidence — and I mean the *utmost* — in the young man you see before you, well... you wouldn't be seeing him before you."

Pettoza made a subtle sign to speak more quietly: he might own the café, but he didn't screen its clientele and wanted to maintain a measure of confidentiality.

"I'd still have liked you to have given me the heads-up, Severin. We're not here to play cards, you know."

"Holy moly," Jerome thought, "I'm in the presence of a real ball buster."

But nothing of the kind happened. During the *sotto voce* conversation that followed, Pettoza thanked the lobbyist again for securing the museum plans; they would allow him to pull in even greater profits and cause him a lot fewer headaches.

"I'll remind you of that," said Sicotte.

Then, snapping his fingers, he called the waiter and ordered a bottle of Salice Salentino 1988, which he described as "the elixir of Venus." After which, they went seriously to work; the selection and evaluation of false cost overruns for a project that hadn't even been started yet smacked of fantasy, but it was imperative to substantiate the fantasy with a degree of technical finesse that sometimes demanded long preparation.

"The farther ahead you see delicate questions coming

up, the less chance you have of tripping over your answers to them," Sicotte had explained to Jerome.

In the little time he'd had at his disposal, Jerome had prepared for this meeting with enthusiasm because — whether out of pride or a taste for the challenge — he was anxious to make a good impression. With the plans spread out on his desk, he had studied them carefully, sometimes consulting a lexicon of construction and architectural terms that he'd discovered in the company archives during his first days on the job. Then, putting aside his dislike of Fradette, he'd sought him out to learn the meaning of certain graphic symbols. As a result, during the meeting at the Café Vicky he was able to ask two or three pertinent questions about the analysis of the site, the time it took for cement to cure in cold temperatures, and the implications of that for the work schedule. He'd even found an inconsistency between two of the drawings. In short, while not trying to hide his lack of experience, he revealed himself to be an astute observer motivated by a deep desire to learn. This pleased Pettoza and delighted Sicotte, who congratulated himself on having unearthed such a brilliant collaborator.

An hour and several glasses of wine later, they had satisfactorily determined the "zones" in which unforeseen expenses were going to oblige the country's taxpayers to spend a little more of their hard-earned cash; the next step was to establish certain understandings with the inspectors — at least with those who were not already in the game — so that the horn of plenty would tip its pots of money in the right direction. Sicotte was aware that Pettoza had no need of him to secure these arrangements, but as the lawyer was working for a percentage, not by the hour, he wanted to come to grips with the operation in its smallest details.

When the time came to break up the meeting, Pettoza, in a charming frame of mind, gave Jerome a friendly pat on the shoulder and winked with satisfaction at Sicotte.

"This is a good start," he said. "I think we have a god-damned good chance at scoring a bull's eye with this museum. I owe you one, Sev. And never fear, I never forget a service rendered."

Then he turned to Jerome.

"Glad to have met you, my friend. Keep on like this, and you'll go far in life."

And, for no apparent reason, he added: "I can see you doing well in the café business. You have the right style for it... And of course there's nothing to stop you from engaging in other activities... But I'm joking," he hastened to explain to Sicotte.

It was a good thing he pointed it out. The lawyer hadn't appreciated the joke at all.

WHEN HE GOT home at the end of the day, Jerome was so pleased with himself he decided to have dinner at a good restaurant, something he rarely did, since he usually found eating alone in public depressing. Hands in his pockets, he whistled as he walked towards Côte-des-Neiges. A sweet odour floated in the air, like the scent of lilacs, even though the season for lilacs was long past. The pedestrians he passed at the beginning of this evening seemed to be an appealing bunch, and most of the women, up to the age of about fifty, struck him as attractive, and some of them frankly desirable. He found himself thinking fondly of Charlie, convincing himself that his former friend must also be having similar thoughts about him. All in all, he was in a very good mood.

He'd checked his cell phone for text messages before

leaving the car; two had brought a smile to his lips. The first was from Alma.

"Would you care to extend your hospitality to me tonight? I need something to cure my insomnia. I can be at your place by 9:30." He'd replied: "Come, my lovely, I can't wait to see you. But don't expect me to cure your insomnia."

It was a strange adventure he was having with this fiercely sensual but at the same time cool-as-a-cucumber woman. Each time they made love, a kind of friction settled between them, despite the alcohol and pleasantries, and it made him long for Eugenie. If Alma was able to come to his place tonight, it was because there'd be no one at Caledonia Road. God knew where Sicotte had got to.

The second text was from . . . Charlie, and it was with a smile of retribution that he read its few words.

"Are you still alive? Call me if you have the strength."

Well, well, was Charlie as susceptible to boredom as the rest of the human species? Curious, that a man so inclined to brag should be so earnest. Did pure souls need to roll in the mud from time to time?

He'd call him tomorrow.

He arrived at the corner of Édouard-Montpetit and Côte-des-Neiges, so hungry that he felt his body was going to split at his navel. After hesitating for a moment, he crossed to the east side of Côte-des-Neiges; almost across from the Renaud-Bray bookstore was an excellent Thai restaurant where the service was quick, which on this night was vital.

Four minutes and forty seconds later he was wolfing down a bowl of tom yum soup and waiting for a pad Thai and a bowl of mushroom rice.

Having to eat by himself did not in the least diminish his good mood (the prospect of a night with Alma went a long way towards explaining this) until a familiar voice made him look around. To his left, in the middle of the room, Jacques Parizeau, the former Quebec premier, was sitting at a table with a man in his forties who looked perfectly at ease. Jerome was almost startled. That said, during his university years he'd often seen the famous politician having lunch in a local restaurant—alone, on one occasion, an ordinary citizen reading his newspaper.

Parizeau had been his father's idol. "He's the real deal!" Claude-Oscar was in the habit of passionately declaring. "Unlike so many other politicians who think of nothing but their own petty careers, who smile as they screw us over every chance they get, that man *really* works for Quebec. We'd be our own country today if it wasn't for those cheats who stole the referendum from us in 1995." Jerome remembered his father closing his denture clinic for three months that year, while he went door to door distributing pamphlets in L'Assomption, where his idol was the candidate.

As he ate, Jerome snuck furtive glances at the former politician. He'd aged and was bent over, his grey hair almost white, yet the familiar intelligent energy and aristocratic presence that, among journalists, earned him the nickname "Sir Jacques" still emanated from his eyes, face, and smallest gestures. Simply seeing him made one forget the sordid aspects of human nature. So why then, Jerome asked himself, was this sudden, cloying depression coming over him and ruining his appetite?

He asked for the bill and left. Alma, always punctual, would be at his apartment in exactly forty-five minutes, and the two would turn to more important things.

At least that was what he tried to tell himself.

At 9:30 on the dot she arrived at his flat, smiling, wearing a touch of makeup, in tight jeans that made her ass irresistible, and urgently wanting to get started on the spot and move as quickly as possible to the bedroom. Jerome was happy to oblige. She was, in sum, that hot bunny dreamt of by adolescents and salacious young men, a few sighs shy of porn star and all but insatiable. After their third bout, Jerome, a little out of breath, gently suggested they get some sleep given that she had, as she'd said, joined him to be cured of her insomnia. She readily agreed. That got them all the way to ten past four in the morning, at which time Jerome was jolted out of a mystifying dream about a pipe that was about to melt Greenland. It took him a long time to get back to sleep, trying as he was to reconcile the quiet, evanescent Alma he'd always known with the torrid Amazon stretched out beside him.

In the morning, they shared a silent breakfast of cinnamon porridge, toast and jam, and drank coffee after coffee. The impassive, articulate voice of a radio announcer brought them up to date on the most recent atrocities plaguing the planet. Alma had already showered and dressed and was punching in a number on her cell phone.

"Who are you calling?"

"A taxi."

"So soon?"

"I want to get to the office before he arrives."

"Who? Sicotte? But he was probably home last night."

"No, I called there last night. No one was home."

Jerome looked at her, perplexed.

"But you were asleep. It was just before the pipe..."

"I think it's absolutely crucial that no one at the office knows about us. You too, no?" she added with a calculating laugh.

"What are you going to do when Francine gets back from Cuba?" asked Jerome.

She shrugged.

"Your girlfriend will also be back, darling." Then, pushing the thought away, she said, "I don't know...We'll just have to look for times when we can get together alone. It might take a while...I really don't know."

A wave of spite came over him.

"It seems to me you're getting pretty messed up about this. Do you like fucking me or not? What are you going to do? Take cold showers until our situations change?"

"Something like that."

"Maybe there's someone else at the office who'll take care of your beautiful ass," he chuckled.

"Stop your nonsense."

Her calm, detached tone angered him.

"Wait, I just had a thought," said Jerome. "Alma, do they pay you to sleep with me? Isn't that just the kind of thing the boss would do?"

"More nonsense."

"Are you sure?"

"My ass is not for rent, darling."

She stood up and, with a light and dainty step, made her way to the door, picking her purse off a chair as she went. She looked out the window.

"The taxi's here," she said gaily. "Okay, so see you later, Jerome...and thanks for your hospitality."

Jerome, tight-lipped, hung back a few steps behind her and felt a strong urge to reach out and slap her.

THAT DAY IT was as if every truck in Montreal was idling on his chest. People had to ask him questions twice for him to respond; if anyone spoke to him for more than two minutes he needed to make a superhuman effort not to fall asleep on his interlocutor's nose; going up four steps felt like he was climbing a stairwell of forty. He and Alma crossed paths twice and, as she warned she would do, she adopted her just-a-colleague-nothing-more comportment. She'd looked as fresh as a spring tulip and once, in front of Sicotte and Fradette, had amused herself by commenting on how tired Jerome looked, asking him tongue in cheek whether he had a cold or a touch of the flu. He looked at her without saying a word. "You, my lovely, are acting the perfect cow. I'll remember this," he thought.

Towards noon, skipping lunch, he locked himself in his office to take a nap on the floor. His condition was beginning to worry him. "Okay, so last night I made love five times and got four hours' sleep. But I'm only twenty-five! What'll I be like in ten years, for Christ's sake?"

At one o'clock Sicotte knocked on the door and Jerome jumped up to open it, rubbing his face to remove any traces of sleep.

"Things are going down faster than I expected, Jerome," said Sicotte. His words were charged, though his tone was edgy.

He said, "Rouleau, Normande Juneau's riding secretary, wants to meet with us right away. Turmel, her chief of staff, might be there, too. I get the feeling Pettoza has been in touch with them. But he's in too much of a hurry, it's all too soon...It seems he wants to give them their donation right away, in order to be sure of getting his piece of the museum pie. Only the money should go through me, and in the form of cheques signed by different people. He knows that. I tried to call him but I couldn't get through.

Something's happening that I don't understand. We have to go and straighten things out with Rouleau. Come on, they're waiting for us."

Minister Juneau's riding office was in Laval, on rue Vaillancourt. Although it was early afternoon, the streets were congested with traffic and it took them almost an hour to get to their destination. Jerome took advantage of the time to sleep, hoping to get back his strength. Sicotte, lost in thought, hardly said a word the entire way.

Ernest Rouleau, perky but agitated, was almost over-bearing in his welcome — "Delighted to see you," and "The pleasure's all mine," a few ad hoc references to the unusual warmth of the weather and the absence of rain since the beginning of summer, and so on. He was in his thirties, his figure tall and thin and a little stilted, with a face that was also long and thin, his gaunt cheeks marked by long, vertical ridges that made him look like an ascetic; he talked a lot, without ever taking his eyes off his interlocutor, attentive to the other's every reaction and showering whoever it was with niceties, even going so far as to move Sicotte's chair because it was too close to the air conditioner — the blast of cold air, he said, could give the lawyer a stiff neck.

"I'd rather be stiff somewhere else," Sicotte replied, laughing at his own joke. Jerome found it juvenile, but it kept the riding secretary in stitches for some time.

"Monsieur Turmel won't be able to join us, sadly," Rouleau said, getting the meeting underway. "A matter of some urgency has kept him in Quebec. But we can get in touch with him soon."

"So, what's up with our friend Pettoza?" asked Sicotte in a concerned tone.

The riding secretary had received more information since their call, and what had seemed confusing and unlikely to Sicotte then suddenly acquired a distressing clarity.

"Freddy Pettoza, contrary to what I led you to understand, doesn't want to make a single, large, er... donation to the riding organization," Rouleau said, crossing and uncrossing his legs. "He knows how inconvenient such a procedure would be."

"I should think so," said Sicotte. "He's not an idiot, after all."

"He wants to make his contribution in the form of a hundred and forty-seven cheques from his employees and certain of his acquaintances — he'd reimburse them, of course — but we've found in the past that such a process carries certain risks; a hundred and forty-seven donors, all of them working for the same company? You understand?"

"Of course! Surely he knows that. Compiling fictitious names isn't new."

"Monsieur Turmel offered to provide him with another list, one that was more secure, but he turned it down."

"Where did it come from?"

"From Arthur Boniface, Madame Juneau's campaign manager."

"Did Pettoza say why he wouldn't take it?"

The secretary shook his head.

Sicotte sputtered his discomfort, gripping and releasing the arms of his chair.

"Maybe they had a falling-out," suggested Jerome.

It was his first contribution to the conversation. He felt he needed to make one.

"That's what I was thinking," said Sicotte. "Unfortunately, I've not been able to get hold of damn Freddy. He must really hate the guy to make him eat his balls" — the secretary recoiled slightly — "and act like this! Freddy's risking losing the contract, the idiot!"

"Which means you'll lose it, too," thought Jerome, carrying the thought to its conclusion.

"We can't accept Monsieur Pettoza's list, unfortunately," said Rouleau, politely.

The telephone rang. It was Adrien Turmel, Juneau's chief of staff. The riding secretary listened, uttered occasional monosyllabic responses in an increasingly deferential tone, then handed the phone to Sicotte.

"Monsieur Turmel wants to speak to you."

"We can't use Pettoza's list," barked a strong, deep, gruff voice. "Too risky. As you well know."

"You're completely right, Monsieur Turmel," said Sicotte. "I'll speak to him this afternoon."

"I don't know why he won't take our list. Do you? No, well . . . people who like to complicate things needlessly end up getting left in the lurch. Tell him I said that, in case he's forgotten. And call me as soon as you've straightened this out. Good afternoon."

They made the return trip in the same silence that had taken them there. From time to time, Jerome, still recovering from his previous night, glanced at Sicotte with the intention of speaking, but the sullen expression on his boss's face told him it was better to wait. They'd just turned onto Papineau when a traffic bottleneck forced them to slow to the speed of a hearse. At the third stop, Sicotte lost his temper:

"Are we going to get there today, for Christ's sake? I've got to talk to him, the asshole! He's going to scuttle everything!"

He spun the steering wheel, turning the car to the right, then stopped in front of a service station and took out his cell phone.

"Ah, so I reached you at last! What's going on, Freddy? Don't you realize you're about to mess up the whole deal?"

From the receiver, Jerome could hear a loud crackling sound through which he made out a fairly expressive fragment — "*. . . don't use that tone of voice with me, okay?*" — followed by a long rant punctuated by a few particularly strident syllables that had the effect of dampening Sicotte's rage.

Sliding his phone into his pocket, he turned to Jerome. "We're going to meet with him."

"Are you sure I should be there?"

"Oh, I'm sure."

Sicotte made a U-turn and drove back north on Papineau. The traffic changed from the consistency of glue to that of caramelized apple pie. Three-quarters of an hour later, they entered the underground parking lot of a building that rose thirty-four floors above the noise of boulevard Metropolitain; an elevator took them up to the twenty-eighth, the entirety of which was occupied by Simo Construction.

A brunette who could have been a model (and perhaps was) escorted them to Freddy Pettoza's office. In one of the classic poses of an uncultured parvenu, Pettoza was waiting reclined in his armchair and with his feet up on his desk, smoking a cigar that filled the room with the aroma of vanilla and honey. He stood up and came over to shake their hands. His temper seemed to have cooled.

"Terrible, this traffic, eh? I think someday I'll move to the Yukon."

This time around, he took no notice of Jerome's presence and gestured for them to sit. He went back to his chair behind his desk.

"I'll get straight to the point, Severin. No more diddling around with the puck."

"I agree completely," said Sicotte in an almost obsequious tone.

"This Arthur Boniface, Juneau's campaign manager, do you know who his father is?"

Sicotte indicated with a movement of his eyelids that he did not.

"Arturo Benedetto Bonifaccio."

A short silence ensued.

"Is that name supposed to mean something to me?" the lobbyist wanted to say.

"And so?" he said.

"When I was a kid, that fucking piece of stinking dog shit *ruined my father's life!* In fact, you could say that he killed him. I'll spare you the details. Arturo Bonifaccio, who now calls himself Arthur Boniface, is the eldest of Benedetto's four sons. In my whole life I've seen him for maybe half an hour—and that was a long time ago—but it was enough for me to see that the same rat's blood runs in his veins. He's a carbon copy of his father, even worse than him if that's possible. Understand this: there's no way I'm working with him, not even indirectly. Don't waste your time trying to make me change my mind, it's N-O *NO*, end of story."

Sicotte fidgeted, trying to put the situation into perspective. But the more he employed his powers of persuasion, the more he panicked and lost ground, and the more severe the businessman's face became. The light emanating from the face beneath that imposing brow took on a ferocious intensity. Jerome, left out of the discussion, observed the scene in silence. The most elementary common sense seemed to have abandoned both men; they were heading for a collision and, all said and done, neither was applying the brakes. The simple solution that a five-year-old might have come up with in thirty seconds didn't seemed to have crossed their minds.

So, putting a hand on his boss's shoulder, Jerome intervened in a light, carefree manner — as though he considered the entire discussion amusing:

"But look, all we have to do is come up with another list of donors, isn't that right? You don't need a Nobel Prize to see that!"

Silence ensued.

Sicotte stared at his knees, overwhelmed. Jerome had never seen him in such a state. Did he belong to that category of men who were effective only when everything was going well? If that were the case, he was in the wrong business.

"Obviously," replied the lobbyist, "but it's not that simple. We can't just take anyone. There could be consequences. Juneau's campaign manager" — he didn't dare mention his name — "already has his list ready. You can't just come up with another one overnight, and they seem to be in a hurry in Quebec."

He looked up, suddenly cheery.

"But maybe we can try anyway, eh, Freddy? Surely you must have a few safe names on your list?"

"Er...I can look it over," replied the contractor, mollified, crushing the end of his cigar in an enormous marble ashtray.

"For my part, I can come up with a quick fifty or so... And if need be, I can contact Dozois."

"Bled Man?"

"Yeah."

"Don't go near him, my friend...What? You haven't heard? We've smelled the ground burning round him for a week. I hear the police are on to him...But hey, what's the matter?" he said in a suddenly cordial manner. "You look tired, Sev. A good whisky should do us a bit of good, no?"

And without waiting for a response, Pettoza pressed a button on his intercom.

"Jennifer, bring us three whiskys, with ice...That's right, ice on the side."

IN THE PARKING garage, Sicotte turned to Jerome and handed him the keys.

"Do you mind driving? I don't feel up to it this afternoon...as you may already have noticed."

Jerome looked at him, surprised and a bit worried.

"Are you sure? I've never driven a big boat like this before. I don't want to bang into anything."

"It drives like any other car, my friend."

With sweat suddenly running from his armpits, Jerome, driving with his eyes wide open and infinite precaution, manoeuvred the imposing BMW through the maze of the parking garage as his boss, half asleep and heaving occasional deep sighs, seemed no longer aware of where they were. Even though he'd had only one whisky, and hadn't even finished that.

Once on the street, Jerome became more confident, and the way the luxurious vehicle handled brought an easy smile to his lips. They drove this way for a few minutes.

"Life isn't always easy," said Sicotte out of the blue, and wearily.

Since the statement was irrefutable, Jerome answered with as convincing an "Er, no, it isn't" as he could muster.

"My son's driving me crazy," said the lawyer in the same tone.

"Oh?" said Jerome, surprised.

"He's leaving Portage next week...It went all right, I suppose, more or less...I haven't slept for four days...What that little bugger has put us through . . . I can't wait for Francine to get back . . . She has more control over him than I do . . ."

After each sentence, he stopped and heaved a weighty sigh. Jerome filled the silences with "Ah, I see," "Oh, really?" or "Yeah," as seemed appropriate, keeping his eyes on the road ahead of him, imbued as it was with the spectre of his making the wrong manoeuvre.

"And I had such hopes for him, my only son!" said Sicotte, obviously disillusioned. "Where are those hopes now? In the trash can!"

Jerome, stunned, felt a measure of compassion stirring within him for the lawyer; that was a first.

"No, no, your Felix, he'll take himself in hand, you'll see. He probably already has . . ."

The sudden appearance of a tractor-trailer moving erratically forced him to concentrate on his driving. The gentle sound of snoring was soon heard in the BMW.

IN THE DAYS that followed, Jerome again felt compassion stirring within him, but now it was compassion for himself.

The morning after their meeting with Pettoza, Sicotte, consumed with a deluge of tasks, handed the responsibility of establishing the new list of fictitious names over to Jerome. To get the project started, he gave him a list of seventeen names that he'd carefully vetted himself, plus another twenty-eight names provided by Freddy Pettoza and guaranteed to be secure. Finally, Jerome was given a page torn from a notebook containing the names of five subcontractors—from which the name Bled Man had been redacted. Jerome needed to find another hundred names of reliable, amenable people who, for a fee, would bring the total to the magic number of one hundred and forty-seven.

For the next three days, Jerome was on the phone or at his computer from eight in the morning until ten at night (after that, the number of unpleasant or frankly hostile reactions went up alarmingly). He went to bed and got out of it like an automaton, groggy with fatigue. On the third day, he slept at the office, not even having the will to call for a taxi to take him back home. From time to time, Alma brought coffee and sandwiches. Once or twice she gave him a friendly pat on the shoulder to encourage him, and once her caresses were considerably more familiar. He hardly noticed.

The list was completed on a Thursday and approved at the end of the day by Juneau's chief of staff, and the production of cheques signed over to the riding—reimbursements paid on the spot from a box of cash supplied by Freddy Pettoza— was finished by midafternoon on Tuesday, August 6. Most of the signatories seemed to Jerome to be completely ordinary people, unsuspecting or ignorant of the ends to which their names were being put. He functioned like a mailman, speaking to each as little as possible and evading questions when there happened to be any. When, mission completed, he returned to the office, dark bluish circles ringed his eyes. Sicotte, who seemed to have refound his vigour, took Jerome aside and handed him $2,000 in twenty-dollar bills, a gratuity to which Freddy Pettoza had also contributed.

"Now, get the hell out of here, boy! I don't want to see your face here for at least two days. You deserve a break."

With every intention of devoting his break to catching up on his sleep, he drove to his apartment barely able to keep his eyes open and driving so erratically that he prompted several drivers to angrily honk their horns.

An email from Eugenie and a voicemail from Charlie put paid to his plans to get some sleep.

"I've been checking the obituary columns for three or four days," was Charlie's acerbic message, "just to see if your name came up. I didn't see it anywhere, so I suppose you must still be alive. I deduce that, since you haven't returned my call, you don't want to see me. If I'm wrong about that, disabuse me. Goodbye."

The email from Eugenie put him through a panoply of emotions.

I hope you are well, Geronimo. As for me, I've hit a snag but don't worry, nothing too serious. I'm emailing you from the emergency room of the Plato Hospital, in Barcelona. Laura brought me here. For two days I've had a fever, been shivering, feeling nauseous, headachy, muscle pain, and so on. Probably just a virus, but a really bad one. Long story short, I have to delay my return. I can't even think of travelling like this. Can I ask you to do me a favour? Andrée-Anne is very bored at my mother's. She's doing all she can to take my place, but she's 70. The day before yesterday ma petite burst into tears over the telephone and then asked where you were. Can you go see her? It would make her so happy! Please don't say anything to her about me being sick (or to my mother, for now). In spite of everything we said to each other before my departure, I think about you a lot, Jerome, and I'm looking forward to seeing you when I get back.

Eugenie

The address and contacts of Madame Yvonne Lacerte, a widow living on boulevard Gouin, near Rivière-des-Prairies, were attached. He'd never met her.

The tone of the email and the unexpected request within it brought tears to his eyes. Was there a chance then, despite everything, that their relationship might survive? Her request seemed to imply, anyhow, that some arrangement might still be made between them. What form would it take? He hadn't the faintest idea, but for now, that was simply a detail.

"As long as she comes back," he said out loud, "I'll take care of the rest."

He wrote a quick reply to her email, then called her mother. A woman with a somewhat dry, cracked voice replied, though it took on a warmer tone when he gave his name. That augured well. They arranged for him to come out the next afternoon. Andrée-Anne would have absolutely loved to speak with him right away, the elderly woman said, but she was visiting one of her little friends.

So, his spirits buoyed, he pushed on and called Charlie despite a fatigue so great that it left him struggling for words. Charlie was "hard pressed" at work—as he was any time Jerome called (you'd think he worked in a steel plant)—but this did not stop him from having the following conversation with his good friend:

"So, you aren't dead after all."

"Very much alive, old buddy, but me too, would you believe, I've been completely swamped at work. In the last three days I've had so many phone calls to make it's a wonder I don't have elephant ear."

"How are you?"

"Dead tired but happy to be talking to you, Charlie."

"Me, too. Are you free tonight?"

"My loss, chum, but I doubt I've slept eight hours total these last three days. I'm afraid I'll fall flat on my face. Tomorrow work for you?"

"Yeah, that's fine ... Where?"

"Come over to my place for dinner. I'll make something simple and guaranteed non-toxic... But Charlie?"

A trace of apprehension had affected his voice.

"Yes?"

"We're not going to have a repeat of the last time, are we?"

Charlie chuckled in a manner that was difficult to decode.

"Oh, that... it's not just up to me, Jerome... But let's say that since I've been getting my 4Fs with Martine, my nerves are under much better control."

JEROME WAS EXPECTING a more venerable and tony house at 1992 boulevard Gouin Est, as the neighbourhood was known for its heritage architecture. What he found, instead, was an ordinary duplex, if well maintained, clad in faded white aluminum siding and set back from the street on a lot that left plenty of room for a backyard bordered on three sides by luxuriant cedar hedges. Madame Lacerte lived on the ground floor; the upstairs was rented.

Getting out of his car, he heard the shouts of children coming from the back yard, followed by two large splashes. One of the voices was unmistakeably that of Andrée-Anne and, without quite knowing why, he was happy to hear it.

He went through a low wooden gate, walked up a path of flat stones, climbed two steps to a porch that seemed to have been freshly painted, and rang the bell. After a third unanswered ring, he figured that Madame Lacerte was outside with the children. He walked around the right side of the house and came to a yard in which an inflatable swimming pool had been installed that was almost the size of a large wading pool. An old woman in a long, deep purple dress of flowery cotton and a wide-brimmed straw hat was sitting in a folding chair, a book open on her lap, watching the nautical romping of two little girls. Stretched out in the water, the children were kicking their legs and making loud splashing noises and hadn't noticed his arrival.

The woman turned her head and saw him.

"Ah, it's you."

She rose with a nimbleness only slightly wavering. Tall, slim, elegant, she gave the impression of a former diva fighting off ossification.

"I suppose you rang the bell? I should have put a note on the door telling you to come straight out back."

"Jerome!" one of the girls called loudly.

Andrée-Anne bounded out of the pool, dripping, threw herself against Jerome, and wrapped her arms around his legs as the grandmother, horrified, chided her. But Jerome laughed raucously, surprised and delighted by the child's welcome.

"Oh Andrée-Anne, come on, you're soaking wet! Now look at his pants! Good Lord, how could you do such a thing!"

She grasped Andrée-Anne by one arm and gathered her up—making herself a second victim.

"No worries, ma'am," said Jerome, still laughing. "In this heat, it'll cool me off."

He leaned over Andrée-Anne and patted her head.

"You seem to be having a pretty good time with your friend, here. I'm glad to see you."

Her little friend, still stretched out in the water, her chin propped on the edge of the pool, was watching the scene solemnly.

"Me, too, I'm happy to see you," replied Andrée-Anne, looking up at him with a serious expression.

Then she added, "Have you seen Mommy?"

"I haven't been able to see her, Andrée-Anne, she's still travelling. And I have to work in Montreal, as you know. But I'm looking forward to seeing her. Just like you are."

"She's home in a week, my darling," said Madame Lacerte, signalling to Jerome to change the subject. "The time will pass quickly, you'll see."

"What's your friend's name, Andrée-Anne?"

He turned towards the little girl who, intimidated, crawled farther away in the water.

"Jacinthe. She lives over there in the house with the red roof, where there's a dog that barks."

"What would you say to having iced tea on the porch?" proposed Madame Lacerte to Jerome. "The sun is brutal this afternoon. With all these UV rays, we have to be careful...And there are orange and raspberry Popsicles for the little misses."

"Yes! Yes!" shouted Andrée-Anne. "I want a raspberry one, Grandma. Come on, Jacinthe, hurry up!"

The other girl, a small, plump child with a round nose, dark skin, and magnificent brown eyes with long lashes, came out of the pool. She averted her gaze and approached slowly, the struggle between shyness and a taste for Popsicles apparently raging within her. Shyness was losing, but not by much.

Madame Lacerte handed each of the girls a beach towel.

"Dry yourselves well, okay? I don't want a single drop of water in the house."

They towelled themselves carefully, especially their feet, those sworn enemies of floors and carpets, and then everyone went onto the porch. Andrée-Anne immediately took Jerome's hand, and he bent over her and smiled, surprised by her tender gesture. What had he done to deserve this?

"So," he said to her, "have you enjoyed your vacation with your grandmother?"

"Yes, but I want my mother to come home."

"So do I. I miss her too, you know."

"I know."

And she squeezed his hand. Jerome, increasingly moved, gave her a wink. What would happen if Eugenie were seriously ill? If she died? Good heavens, he mustn't even think such a thing! But trying hard not to have such thoughts sometimes serves to bring them on more. So young, this little girl, and so advanced in age, the grandmother...

The iced tea was served, with gingersnaps, and the swimmers were allowed two Popsicles each. Jerome suspected the extra treat was on his account. Lively, energetic, seeing to everything, Madame Lacerte came and went with a slight limp. Jacinthe, who'd not said a word so far, leaned in towards the ear of her friend.

"We're going back to the swimming pool, Grandma!" announced Andrée-Anne.

"Fifteen minutes, no more, Andrée-Anne. Your skin is getting a little red."

Jumping down from her chair, Andrée-Anne noticed that one of the straps on her bathing suit had come undone. She went up to Jerome, turned her back to him, and, as if it were the most natural thing in the world, asked him to do it up for her.

"She likes you very much," remarked Madame Lacerte when the girls were in the pool.

He turned to her with a somewhat troubled smile, his cheeks flushed, trying to hide the strange emotion that had come over him.

"Yes, so it seems... I'm really very touched."

"Children never give love out of calculation," she said, pitcher in hand. She refilled their glasses. "Only when someone deserves it...And sometimes you don't even see that you've won their hearts. A strange thing, don't you find?"

Driving back to his apartment at the end of the afternoon, Jerome could not say for sure whether he had enjoyed his visit.

THE DOORBELL WOKE him up. He jumped out of bed and moved like a sleepwalker to the door.

"Shit," he said, looking at his watch, "it's 6:30. I've been asleep all day."

"A good thing I saw your car parked across the street," said Charlie, with a broad but uneasy smile, "or I'd have thought you'd been kidnapped. That's the fourth time I rang the bell!"

"Come on in, come on in. I'm sorry, old man."

They shook hands. Jerome noticed that his friend's acne had almost disappeared.

"When I said I was exhausted," said Jerome, heading to the kitchen, "I'd just come home from visiting Eugenie's mother, she's looking after Andrée-Anne..."

Charlie's eyes widened in astonishment.

"You went to see her daughter?"

Jerome, disregarding his unease, gave Charlie a brief account of the afternoon, downplaying its significance. For the time being, he was uninterested in analyzing his feelings.

"So, when I got here, I opened the door—and my tiredness hit me like a cord of hardwood. I dragged myself to bed and poof! Out like a light."

"Well," Charlie said, sniffing the air, "I can tell we won't be eating here tonight. I'm hungry."

"No, no, no! My invitation stands. I've got two excellent pizzas in the freezer."

"Thin crust?"

"Yes, noble sir! Thin crust. We think only of your pleasure, as you well know. I put them in the oven at 425 degrees, leave them for twelve to fourteen minutes, and *voilà*! We eat. Meanwhile, you can assuage your hunger with a beer. I have some Belle Gueule and some Tremblay. And of course the Belle Gueule is a blond beer on a bed of dregs, your favourite. All is well?"

Charlie, satisfied, smiled. He nodded and then threw himself onto a chair, stretched his legs out, and looked anxiously about the room as Jerome, after turning on the oven, uncapped two bottles and handed one and a stein to Charlie. (Charlie drank beer only from steins or pilsner glasses, believing they made the beer taste better.)

"I won't drink too much tonight," he said.

"No?" said Jerome, bent over the stove. "Were you planning on getting drunk?"

"Not really." He took a swig, then said: "After a certain amount of alcohol, you could say my personality changes, and I don't like that... It makes me say stupid things, as you well know... And Martine mentioned the other day that I was getting a gut."

"Things seem to be serious between you two."

"Yeah... she's a lovely girl."

"A psychologist, isn't she?" he asked, a trace of irony in his voice.

"No, not even close. She works in administration at the National Comedy School."

"That's great," Jerome said, sitting down across from him. "Can only be good for your sense of humour, no?"

Charlie pursed his lips and his eyes shot darts like a rooster in a cockfight.

"So, is that it with the bad jokes for the evening? Can we move on to more serious things, now?"

"Sorry, Charlie, I didn't mean to upset you." Jerome took a long drink of beer and wiped his lips with the back of his hand. "What serious things?"

"You know very well what I'm talking about," said Charlie, exasperated. His fingers played the piano on the edge of the table. Then he looked up. "Bah! Forget it. I don't feel like getting into any heavy discussions tonight...I'm hungry. I could eat a barrel of nails."

Jerome stood up, checked the oven temperature, and slid in two pizzas.

"In twelve short minutes, Your Honour's hunger will be satisfied. At least we hope so."

"Hmm...Not hard to tell you've been to university... What kind of pizzas are they?"

"Three-cheese with mushrooms."

"Bada-boom, bada-bing!" said Charlie, drumming his hands on the table. "Okay, forget what I said earlier. I'll have another beer—if you don't mind, that is."

"Your wish is my command, good sir."

A couple more bottles lost their virginity. The two friends drank, exchanged commonplaces, then started horsing around. Charlie was decidedly convivial, though his mood seemed a little forced—the sort of high spirits one uses to hide anxiety. And, true to the principle of communicating vessels, Jerome subsequently felt his own level of anxiety increase.

The delicious aroma of melted cheese slowly filled the air, becoming harder and harder to ignore.

"Pizza! Pizza!" shouted Charlie, knife and fork in hand.

The pizzas were finally ready, their cheesy topping blistering with quivering bubbles intent on swamping the little islands of delicately browned mushrooms. They attacked them with theatrical enthusiasm, in the faint hope that the food would function as a way of avoiding the conversation that seemed to be coming anyway.

Jerome gave an account of his visit to Madame Lacerte's house, how it had been at Eugenie's request, and of the welcome he'd received from the child.

"I felt like her father. It blew me away, I can tell you."

"Well, well," scoffed Charlie. "You've got yourself a little family, I see."

"We're not the Holy Trinity, believe me."

"I cannot believe what I do not know," Charlie observed. "I need more details."

There was a short silence.

"Never mind," said Jerome. "We'll save it for later, okay?"

But prurient curiosity had taken hold of the technician.

"So you're hard at it at work, I take it?"

"And how! About to blow a gasket."

"What exactly are you working on, if you don't mind my asking?"

They'd both finished their beers.

"What would you say to moving on to red wine?" asked Jerome. "It goes better with pizza, no? I've got a very nice Juan Gil, a Monastrell from Spain. I came across it this summer."

"Monastrell? Wow!" Charlie was enthusiastic. "You've become a connoisseur with all the money you're raking in."

"It wasn't all that expensive. Even you could afford it."

Charlie, who seemed to have forgotten his promises of temperance, raised an arm in salute.

"Go for the Juan Gil. Down the hatch!"

But a slight tremor in his voice suggested he was following a plan.

"So," he continued once the wine, much appreciated, had been poured. "What's making you so exhausted at work, pal?"

"A case I find repellent, but which has been . . . thrust upon me, let us say."

"What case?"

"You'll never guess . . . No, really, you won't believe it . . . it's this goddamned Museum of Canadian Culture in the French Language."

Charlie turned beet red.

"You're working on that! You, the separatist?"

"Oh, I'm just on the sidelines, nothing big," said Jerome defensively. "But I'll be asking them to give me something else to work on."

'Twas ever thus, my friend, Charlie thought, *when you work for pigs, it doesn't matter what you do, you get covered in shit.* But rather than revealing his thoughts, he contented himself with saying, "A project like that would never have gone ahead under Parizeau, that's for sure. He knew where to draw the line, that one."

"Speaking of Parizeau," said Jerome, happy to change the subject, "I saw him the other day, in a restaurant. I thought he looked older, but he was still very much alive and the big man."

"You should have gone up to him and asked his advice," Charlie said slyly as he grabbed himself a slice of pizza.

"Really? Advice about what?" asked Jerome, feeling trouble coming.

"About this case of yours with the museum, about your career, about your employers, I don't know...He's a man of good judgement...at least most of the time...Except I think you know what he would have said."

Jerome stared at Charlie without saying a word. His upper lip began to tremble. He picked up his glass and took a large gulp of wine.

Charlie continued, "He would have said—in his own words, very politely, because he was very well raised, wasn't he, and has seen a lot—he would have said your bosses are scoundrels. He wouldn't have been far wrong, I think. And he would have added that when you work for bastards, you end up becoming one yourself. Maybe he wouldn't have said it, but that's how he would have seen it. Don't you think?"

Jerome kept on staring at him, flabbergasted. Curiously, small red spots started to appear on his face; his hands gripped the table, he was breathing raggedly and could feel an avalanche of emotion tumbling inside him, a blind, piti-less avalanche tearing up everything in its path.

"But I don't want to become a bastard!...I only want to be successful, to have a good time...Except that they've got me, Charlie! *Ah*, you have no idea how much they have me in their grip!"

And he broke out into sobs.

Charlie jumped to his feet, almost knocking over his glass and righting it at the last second. He looked at his friend, who was wiping his eyes with a napkin. He didn't know what to do, but had a very good idea of what *not* to do. He couldn't pat his friend on the shoulder or hold him in his arms; Jerome would have punched him in the face, and that would have been that.

He settled for a cough and a sigh.

"Anything I can do to help?" he ventured after a moment.

"Buzz off, Charlie... Please, just go," pleaded Jerome, still wiping his eyes. "I want to be alone. We'll see each other another time... I need to get some sleep. If you only knew..."

"Okay... if that's what you want... But I'm worried about you all the same... I didn't mean to..."

Jerome had calmed down somewhat and pushed Charlie gently towards the door, but just as his friend was about to leave, he took him by the shoulder and forced him around.

"Eugenie didn't ask you to come see me, by any chance, did she?"

Charlie braced. "I don't need permission from Eugenie to come and see you, Jerome," he said matter-of-factly. "I'm capable of making my own decisions. I haven't spoken to her since we met at the café on Van Horne."

Jerome watched him go down the stairs, then closed the door.

He was headed to the bathroom for a shower when the phone rang. To his great surprise, it was Alma.

She offered up some pleasantries, asked about his day, talked about this and that, then came to the point.

"The boss is about to leave and won't be back until tomorrow afternoon. Do you want to come over?"

"Frankly, Alma, it would give me great pleasure, but I'm completely tanked. I'm going to bed."

"Too bad," she said with a little laugh. "I was hoping you'd take *me* to bed. Ha-ha. Ah well, sleep tight."

And she hung up.

He shrugged off his resignation, got undressed, and spent a quarter of an hour under the shower thinking of nothing, plunged into a state of animal torpor.

Then he went to bed.

A half-hour later, he still hadn't closed his eyes. Crazy, cruel, anguishing thoughts raced through his mind, all of them feeding the desire that had tormented him since the phone call from that diabolical Alma.

He hadn't seen Eugenie since the end of June and here it was, the second week of August, and illness was delaying her return for God knows how long. What if all of it was a trick and a ruse to gain time? Who knew? Maybe she'd renewed her relationship with the Belgian. Or had found another lover? And all the while, he, the perfect turkey, would be busy looking after her daughter and moping around by himself, waiting for Madame to come home and announce their separation was permanent.

He was ashamed of having such thoughts, but in the very next instant all his worries and suspicions flooded back again, only to give way yet again to remorse.

Finally he got up and, after pacing back and forth for several minutes in his apartment — changing his mind from one room to another — he called Alma.

"Come on over, my lovely, I can't sleep for thinking about you, you little vixen."

He heard a squeal of triumph at the other end of the line.

As he waited, he put on his dressing gown, went outside and, sitting on the porch steps, looked down the street. It was almost midnight. A warm, humid breeze carried the rumbling sounds of the traffic on Côte-des-Neige. Were he a smoker, he'd have smoked several cigarettes while contemplating the slings and arrows of life. Dejection came over him. He needed some good news, it didn't matter what kind, but could not imagine where it might come from.

Suddenly, despite the lateness of the hour, an old man

appeared on the sidewalk with a small dog on a leash. The animal trotted along quickly, purposefully, nose to the ground, delighted by the unexpected late-night excursion, while its owner walked stiffly, staring straight ahead, lips pursed, and taking slow, calculated steps as if he were crossing over a precipice on a high wire.

Despite the difference in their ages, Jerome saw the man as a brother.

THREE DAYS LATER, Francine Desjarlais arrived home from Cuba with a dark tan, four kilos heavier, and her wrists and fingers loaded with silver rings and bracelets "picked up for a song." Her abundance of energy quickly turned into a feverish restlessness, and for good reason: Felix was coming home! She had his room repainted to rid it of any hint of the evil weed that had almost destroyed his life, filled the fridge with his favourite foodstuffs (he was crazy about seafood and maple ice cream) and — a surprise gift — bought him the *ne plus ultra* of LED flat-screen TVs.

And that Wednesday, August 14, towards the end of the afternoon, Felix drove up in the avocado-green Corolla that had been waiting for him in a parking garage in Portage. He'd refused to let anyone come pick him up and had refused to attend the ceremony traditionally held to mark the departure of patients who'd successfully travelled the long, hard road to detoxification.

He'd hardly put a foot on the ground when his mother rushed out of the service entrance of the house and, with a shrill cry, ran towards him with open arms.

"How are you, my pet? How are you? You look great!"

"Yes, I'm fine, Mother, I'm fine."

And, with an embarrassed smile, Felix gently tried to extricate himself from her embrace.

"Dad!" he said, seeing Sicotte by the door. He looked pale, his cheeks were deeply creased, and he was holding his hands folded over his sternum in a pose that made him look strangely like a priest.

"Here I am, Father," said Felix. "Back at last!"

Sicotte approached, shook Felix's hand for a long time, and then, holding him at arm's length, managed to say in a voice heavy with emotion, "Well, well, I'm... happy to see you again, my boy... You've put on a bit of weight, I think... How are you?"

"I'm fine, Dad... Mother, stop crying like that, for heaven's sake, it's ridiculous."

"Ridiculous, ridiculous," babbled Francine, "I'd like to see what you'd do if you were me..."

And she cried even harder.

"Okay, enough of this," ordered Sicotte as a general would. "He's right: we're putting on quite a show, and it's really not necessary. What'll the neighbours think?"

"They'll think what they want to think," said Francine, "and anyone who thinks badly of us can go jump in a lake!"

And, as she guided him towards the house, she tenderly gathered her son to her side.

Jerome, Fradette, and Alma had been following the scene through a window and returned swiftly to their desks when the family entered the house and retired to their rooms. Jerome had been able to observe the young man; he thought he looked a little stronger, toughened, with a curiously inexpressive face. But perhaps he had only imagined that last trait, having anticipated extraordinary changes in Felix, when in fact there had been none.

Ten minutes later, absorbed once again in his work, he'd all but forgotten the prodigal son's return. Towards six o'clock, a call from Barcelona made him forget everything else.

"Am I speaking to Mr. Jerome Lupien?" asked a female voice that layered every syllable with a veneer of olive oil that made them ring like bells.

He felt a huge punch to the base of his stomach, and his mouth filled with acid.

"Yes, that's me."

"Hello, monsieur, my name is Laura Esteve," the voice went on. "I'm calling about Eugenie. I'm a friend of hers. She asked me to telephone."

"Right, right. What's happened, ma'am?"

"Eugenie needs to stay in the hospital for some observation. She has a fever, she's throwing up a lot, she has cramps and all the rest of it. The doctors don't know yet what kind of illness she has and they need to give her more tests. Going back to Quebec isn't possible at this time, you understand. That's why she asked me to call you."

"Okay," said Jerome.

A void expanded in his brain, and his breath came in short gasps. He stared at a porcelain cup on his desk with a coffee stain on the lip.

"Hello? Hello? Are you still there?"

"Er... sorry, ma'am," Jerome stuttered in a troubled voice. "Is she... is she suffering very much?"

"Call me Laura, it makes it easier, don't you think?" said the woman, whose status as Eugenie's friend seemed to make her a friend of Jerome's, too. "Yes, she's suffering in the way that someone with a bad case of the flu would be. And she's very worried about Andrée-Anne. She wonders if you might see her again. You can do that, can't you?"

"Yes, yes, of course, with pleasure. She can count on me. Where are you now, ma'am? Are you calling from a hospital?"

"Yes, I'm calling from the Plato Hospital. But please call me Laura," she repeated, "it makes things simpler, no? Now I must go, please excuse me, someone is waiting to use the phone. I'll give you my number so you can call me whenever you like. But there's no need to worry too much, Jerome — I can call you Jerome, can't I? — the doctors here at the Plato are very good and they will discover what's wrong with Eugenie and find a cure, I'm certain of it."

"Yes, of course," he replied, swallowing with difficulty. "We're not in the Middle Ages, after all, are we?" He was pouring as much optimism as possible into his voice.

She had to repeat her telephone number two or three times — she kept switching, a matter of habit, back and forth from French to Catalan — and he asked her to give Eugenie a thousand hugs from him.

"Well, that's a lot of hugs," said Laura, laughing. "I don't know if I'll have enough time and, besides, she might be contagious, you never know. But I'll do what I can, I promise."

"I'm counting on you," replied Jerome, jauntily.

He hung up, devastated. He stared at the porcelain cup in front of him and felt himself sliding into a morass of sickening, suffocating images. His trysts with Alma now haunted him and were making him retch. What kind of low-life was he, anyway? Yuck! The man no person wanted to be, that was who! Unworthy, a thousand times unworthy of poor Eugenie who, though she'd made him unhappy, nevertheless had confidence in him — and all this despite the rotten mess he was sinking deeper and deeper into with each passing day. And now she might be dying! It was a possibility he was powerless to avert... He'd adopt Andrée-Anne and show her the road to virtue, like those Mafia types who sent their daughters to school at high-class convents. Money can buy anything, after all, even respectability.

"You're a stinking pile of shit, Jerome," he muttered, biting into his lips as he leaned his head on his fist. "Who knew you could smell so bad?"

He decided to go outside and get some air in the yard behind the house, something he'd do sometimes to clear his head after a particularly boring task or an arduous phone call. In the corridor, he ran into Fradette, who stopped and gave him a strange, sideways glance that could have been taken two ways. It was a new habit of his, adopted back when they were speaking to each other.

"Anything wrong?" asked Fradette.

"No," said Jerome, striding on. "Quite the contrary, everything's great!"

The yard was a pleasant, verdant sanctuary, shaded by old lilacs and a magnificent oak. A fountain with a pink marble basin, which had been installed at great expense by Francine earlier that summer, gurgled in the middle of the lawn. He sat on the stone bench that faced it, stretched out his legs, filled his lungs with fresh air, and closed his eyes. When he opened them again, he could make out Alma's head as she watched him from a ground-floor window. Quickly, she withdrew.

"I'll bet they're in cahoots, those two," he muttered to himself, with a venomous scowl.

After twenty or so minutes he went back inside, not feeling any better; he'd come to no decision and felt a kind of dark rumbling within himself. He went back to reading an indigestible summary of a technical report on the foundations of the future Museum of Canadian Culture in the French Language, obtained thanks to a leak sourced by Sicotte—who suddenly appeared at Jerome's door, beaming.

"The signs are promising!" Sicotte announced. "I think they did a good job on him in Portage...I mean...I think *he* did a good job in Portage...In fact, I don't know who did what, but that's not important...He's decided to finish CEGEP and then go to business school—to the École des hautes études commerciales—unless he decides to...anyway, it doesn't matter."

"No, of course not, he has lots of time to think about it," said Jerome, forcing himself to be polite. "I'm very happy for him. I'd like to say hello. We haven't seen each other in donkey's years."

"He just left to go for a stroll in town. It'll do him good. It was like being in the army out there, my friend, iron discipline, endless chores, physical training every day, and then his studies, mandatory lectures, discussion groups, no one had time to sit around dunking doughnuts, you can bet on that! In the beginning he was calling us every night, bawling like a calf that lost its mother!"

Then, suddenly serious, he pointed his index finger at Jerome.

"Ah, I almost forgot...Write this in your daybook: Thursday, September 5, five o'clock, fundraiser for Minister Juneau at the Grand Palais restaurant on rue de la Montagne. You'll come with Francine and me. It's very important—and I'll pay, of course."

Jerome responded with a slight nod.

"Okay. I've got to run. Now about this report," said Sicotte, resting his hand on the thick folder, "is it okay? I haven't had time to look at it."

"A bit of tough sledding for a newbie, but I'm making headway."

Pen in hand, he plunged back into the work and, for a good hour and a half, covered the report with notes, queries, and cross-references, until huge yawns began to stretch his jaw and flood his eyes with tears. Eventually he pushed the file aside and wrote a long email to Eugenie, words of love and encouragement pouring out of him. He assured her he would look after Andrée-Anne as if she were his own daughter. "To be honest," he wrote, "it's as if she already is."

It was going on five o'clock. He took care of a few pressing phone calls, then, famished and happy to be leaving the office, he exited the building and walked towards his car. He was about to get into it when a loud honking from an emerald-coloured Cadillac made him turn around.

"Hey! Don't leave! I need to talk to you," shouted Bled Man as his car screeched to a halt beside him, skidding over gravel. The door swung open and the fundraiser stepped out of the car and confronted Jerome, gasping for breath.

"Tell me what the fuck's going on!" he clamoured. "I've been trying to get hold of your boss for three days, and all I get is a run-around! I know he's here, the fucker!"

Facing Jerome was a man who, livid and gasping for breath, his dishevelled hair revealing the ravages of baldness, was braying like an ox.

"I don't know anything about anything, Monsieur Dozois. You'll have to speak to Sicotte — except," Jerome added, remembering the instructions he'd been given, "he's not here right now."

"He's not here but his car is," shouted Bled Man, pointing to Sicotte's BMW. "What do you take me for? Some kind of idiot?"

"He's gone, Monsieur Dozois...he left in his son's car."
Jerome himself was confused. "Felix came home today, did
you know that?"

"Oh, did he?" Bled Man mumbled, casting a haggard eye
up and down the street.

He leaned on the hood of his car.

"Is he going to have a heart attack on me, the bully?"
Jerome wondered.

"Are you all right, Monsieur Dozois?" he asked. "Are you
okay?"

Dozois — without looking at Jerome, his mouth half-
open, a baleful eye fixed on the lawyer's house — nodded.

"I'll tell him you were here when I see him, first thing
tomorrow morning. I promise."

The man waved his hands at him, as if to say *Don't take
it personally, you haven't done anything.*

"They're throwing me under the bus, the bastards," he
muttered, looking down at the ground, "Sicotte and all the
rest of them."

Then, turning sharply towards Jerome, his eyes filled
with fury, he said sourly, "You, too, young as you are. You'll
be in my shoes one day. I hope to God you will be! Then see
how they treat you!"

There was a moment's silence. The money man returned
to staring at the house.

"Would you mind moving your car, please?" asked
Jerome, who'd decided the exchange had gone on long
enough. "You're blocking the drive and I have to go home."

"Move my car?" Dozois said derisively. "Sure thing, big guy!"

The next moment he was in his car, backing up with
a ferocious grinding of gears, provoking a shrill cry from
a woman on the sidewalk whose Pomeranian had come

within inches of being transformed into a crêpe. Jerome ran over, fearing the worst.

"That man is crazy!" the woman yelled in English. "Utterly crazy! Who is he? Call the police! What are you waiting for? *I'll* call the police!"

It was too much. Had Satan unleashed all the shit-storms on the planet on their heads? He offered the fifty-something woman, now as hysterical as her dog, a gesture of apology. He suddenly felt faint, his legs as weak as those of a rag doll. He slid into his car and slowly drove off, careful not even to slightly incite the Englishwoman and her dog, who were both yapping in his rear-view mirror as he pulled away.

His hunger had altered his plans for the evening, and he drove down Mont-Royal, the primary restaurant route on the Plateau, looking for a parking spot not too far from The Avenue, a congenial bistro known for its generous servings. Charlie had discovered it a year ago. Suddenly his cell phone started to sing in his jacket pocket.

"Christ!" he muttered. "Not now, I've got to eat!"

He was still speaking when, just in front of him and to his right, a yellow convertible edged out of a parking space just a hop and a skip from The Avenue. He pulled into the space, killed the engine, and, feeling much better, took out his still-ringing cell phone.

"Is this a good time?" said a voice he didn't recognize. "It's Felix."

"It's a great time, old buddy," said Jerome. "How are you? I'm glad you called, after all this time . . . I saw your arrival this afternoon, but thought it best to leave you alone with your—"

"Yeah," interrupted Felix, "four months of my life I'll never get back."

"Where are you?"

"On Saint-Denis, somewhere between Marie-Anne and Rachel."

"Good. I'm very close, on Mont-Royal. Have you eaten? No? I'm just going into The Avenue, do you know it?"

He gave Felix the address and, ten minutes later, they were vigorously shaking hands. Felix sat across from Jerome and stared in amazement at the small mountain of spaghetti bolognese that Jerome had just dug into.

"Sorry," said Jerome, a little embarrassed. "I was hypoglycaemic and couldn't wait, I've been dying of hunger for hours. It happens to me sometimes these days."

"No need to apologize, I get it. Is the spaghetti good?"

And, understanding the nod of his companion who, cheeks stuffed, was delivering the *coup de grâce* to his hunger, he looked up at the waiter who was approaching with a menu and ordered, "The same, please."

From the meal's outset, Jerome's impression of Felix had been confirmed: he was no longer the same young man he'd briefly come to know in Cuba. And the change was not only physical. The handsome but frail blond boy he'd pulled from disaster by throwing himself into the same was not only more dynamic, but seemed to be wiser, mellower. There was a composure in him that he'd lacked before—that of the traveller who comes back from a dangerous trip about which he prefers not to speak. His voice had dropped, his eyes taken on a gentle gravity. He listened more than he spoke and there was a slight droop to the corners of his eyes, the beginnings of crow's feet suggesting his life was no longer as easy as it had been. Was this the "fresh start" parents so earnestly desired for their wayward offspring but so seldom saw?

"How are things with you?" asked Felix, attacking the

spaghetti placed before him. "Are my parents giving you any space?"

"Oh, me, I'm still alive and kicking, though I can't say the same for my girlfriend, who's had to stay over in Spain because of some kind of illness she came down with. They've put her in hospital. It sounds serious."

Felix shook his head and pursed his lips.

"She'll be all right, you'll see . . . Knock on wood," he added, tapping the tabletop.

"Your father tells me you're going back to school?" said Jerome, changing the subject.

"Yeah. I'm finishing my CEGEP and after that I want to go to university. I haven't yet decided what to major in but, as they say, there's plenty of time . . ."

Jerome was beginning to catch glimpses of the bottom of his plate and stopped gorging himself; any more and he'd be stuffed. His companion ate more slowly, but with appetite. Why had he called, Jerome wondered. Did he need to confide in someone? Or did he simply want to renew contact with a friend who'd done him a good turn, to ease back into daily life?

"How was the food down there?"

"It was . . . adequate."

There was a pause.

"Obviously, it wasn't a five-star hotel," he added.

"Was it hard?"

Felix cast his eyes about the restaurant. The room was full of people and noise; plates carried by the wait staff whisked by like flying saucers. A small smile appeared on his lips. He seemed overjoyed to find himself in such a place.

"Hard?" he repeated, returning his gaze to Jerome. "Sure, I found it hard. The first few weeks I called my mother I don't know how many times and begged her to come and get me. It was a good thing she didn't listen. I had a desert to cross. I had to cross it in bare feet on burning sand, that was part of the deal. Those who refused were shown the door, simple as that..."

Felix rolled the last strand of spaghetti around his fork and brought it to his mouth.

"I've just told my parents that I want to move out and find an apartment. They weren't too happy about it, but too bad, I've made my decision... The odour of shady deals, I've been breathing it ever since I was a kid. I want to clean it out of my lungs."

He noticed Jerome's face darken.

"Sorry about being so frank," he added. "I didn't mean to make you feel bad. Did I go too far?"

"Not at all!" replied his companion with a smile that he hoped would hide his irritation. "So, I'm looking at a new man, is that it? No more electronic cigarettes, I gather... Have you joined the Jehovah's Witnesses or something? You talk as if you've been converted. Have you had a vision of the Holy Virgin changing Baby Jesus's diapers while Joseph plays with his flowering stick?"

Felix shrugged.

"I don't give a fuck about religion... In four months, you have time to think about a lot of things... Truth is, I wasn't going anywhere, even though I was absent. And my father was the same, in his own way... Say, are the apartments in your area very expensive?"

"For the most part, yes. But your parents will pay the whole shot, no?"

"They'll need to," he sighed.

"Tell me," Jerome said, wanting once more to change the subject, "how did you get my cell phone number?"

"From Alma. Does that surprise you?"

There was an ironic inflection in his voice, a hint of subtext. Jerome was afraid he was blushing, and to hide it he picked up his water glass and took two long drinks.

Felix started to quietly laugh.

"She told me everything, Jerome... No need to get upset... I slept with her a few times. Be careful with her, she's a little whore. I never understood her games. My mother hired her four years ago; she always says she's not sorry she did, but at the same time she doesn't exactly think she's a darling. Quite the opposite! Bloody Alma. She was a baby when she came here from Chile with her parents, who were political refugees, although no one has ever seen them... I've always had a hard time swallowing that story, or anything else that's come out of her mouth, for that matter. On the other hand, I've never known anyone like her in bed. When she has an orgasm, man! Quite a performance! With me, in any case."

"With me, too," said Jerome, drily.

Felix smiled, his eyes half closed, no doubt retreating into his own voluptuous memories. But he came to almost immediately and looked at Jerome.

"Only I sometimes wondered, since we're being honest, if she wasn't putting on a show. She lies about everything else, why wouldn't she lie about that? What do you think?"

"Hmm... I don't know... You'd have to be in her head."

This meal is ending badly, Jerome thought. He raised his hand and called for the bill.

"No, no," he said, seeing Felix put his hand in his pocket. "It's on me. I asked you here, and I'm happy to pay."

He managed to accompany the words with a cordial smile.

THAT NIGHT JEROME had a lot of trouble falling asleep. Felix's revelations tormented him. Bizarre Alma, who shared confidences too easily. Their little adventure may have been no more than bedroom antics with no tomorrow, but if Eugenie found out about them it would be the end of their relationship. What if the "little whore," as Felix called her, had set him up somehow? The idea could have been her own, or due to the machinations of someone else. Blackmail had always been one of the best ways to turn a person into a puppet. He felt as though he were walking over an ice floe breaking up beneath his feet; at any moment a crack could open up and swallow him. How could he get out of this damned job that had become a trap? But first things first. "I'll straighten things out with Alma first thing tomorrow morning," he told himself for the tenth time.

Sparrows were chirping all up and down Côte-des-Neiges when, finally, he fell asleep.

At twenty past eight he was at the office, looking haggard but with a determined step and coolly resolved to remove the weird secretary from the prospect of screw-ups facing him. The stars, that morning, seemed to be aligned: when he opened the door, Alma was taking an armload of files into Archives. He greeted her as if nothing was up, then followed her into the little room, the walls of which were covered with shelves crammed with files. He shut the door behind them.

"What's going on?" she asked, surprised.

"Keep your voice down, okay?"

He stepped in front of her.

"I heard you were gabbing with Felix yesterday."

She frowned and tried to smile, but turned her face away.

"What if I was? Don't I have the right to speak to Felix?"

"Talk to whoever you like, I couldn't care less. I have no control over you or your ass, Alma, you can wave it in front of a giraffe if you want to. But you must never tell Eugenie about us, do you understand?"

He put his hands on her shoulders and squeezed so hard she gave a little yelp.

"If you ever do, I'll rip your head off."

He pushed her back against a shelf and left.

She let herself slide onto a chair and began to cry.

A minute or two went by. Then the door half-opened and Olivier Fradette silently entered.

"Something wrong, Alma? Is there a problem?"

But from his solicitous and satisfied expression it was clear he knew everything.

A WEEK WENT by. Jerome and Laura Esteve spoke on the phone every day. Eugenie had fallen into a semi-coma, but her condition appeared stable. The fever had diminished, her bouts of nausea were gone. The tests showed the presence of a rare virus that, according to the doctors, had probably been transmitted in something she ate. "But she couldn't have been poisoned by food, Jerome," Laura exclaimed, "I don't like restaurants much, I find them too loud and they get on my nerves, and we ate mostly at home. So I would have been sick, too, wouldn't I? But I'm not, I'm perfectly healthy! Nervous, maybe, and worried, sure, tired, oh my God! But in perfect health."

Doctors still had much to learn about viruses, as well as a lot of other things.

Laura had read Jerome's email to Eugenie; she'd managed a weak smile in response. Eugenie barely spoke these days, but she'd found the strength one afternoon to ask if her daughter was all right and if Jerome was visiting her. "Yes, of course," Laura had told her, "he sees her almost every day and she's fine, don't worry about her."

The very sick sometimes need their dose of reality embellished.

For in fact, Jerome had been to see Andrée-Anne only three times — with his heavy workload, even that was remarkable — and in truth Andrée-Anne wasn't doing well at all, nor was Madame Lacerte much better. The abandoned-child syndrome had transformed the little girl into an anxious, irritable, and capricious crybaby. Her mother's days of twenty hours of drowsiness seemed to mimic those of the daughter, who spent her nights unable to sleep at all — and neither could her grandmother.

"I'm exhausted, Jerome," admitted Madame Lacerte one evening. "I don't know how much longer I can hold on. If that worthless Bénédict" — he was Eugenie's ex-husband — "hadn't taken off so heartlessly to Belgium, I'd have handed this poor little girl over to him, at least long enough for me to get some rest."

On the evening of August 22, Laura Esteve finally had encouraging news to give Jerome. For the first time since her hospitalization, Eugenie had been showing signs of improvement: her fever had diminished, then disappeared, and her appetite returned. The previous evening, she'd been able to talk to her friend for twelve minutes and seemed to be resuming an interest in life. If her recovery persisted, there was reason to believe she'd be out of hospital in four or five days.

On August 27, Eugenie finally left the hospital. She was extremely weak, but in such a jubilant state that she chattered away like a magpie. Her doctor told her she must have complete rest for three weeks, followed by a slow return to normal activities, and it took all of Laura's powers of persuasion and a show of temper that almost ended their friendship before Eugenie was convinced to stay another three days in Barcelona. (Eugenie, despite the fact she could barely stand, had been determined to fly to Montreal the very next morning.)

The day of her release, Jerome had spoken to Eugenie on the phone for twenty minutes and found her excitable, autocratic, and irritable.

"It's the cortisone, my love. I don't know why they gave me such a large dose, but I suppose I have to take it, don't I? I spent so much time sleeping in the hospital, now I can't even seem to take a nap! But you'll have to excuse me, Geronimo, I must phone Andrée-Anne now; I promised her I'd call her three times a day. The poor thing, she misses me so much— and I miss her too! When I called this morning, I could hardly get a word in edgewise! She cried and cried...If tears could travel over the telephone, I'd have been inundated! Okay, I have to go...I love you and can't wait to be with you. Do you still love me, my love?"

"Like never before," he said tenderly.

Then he winced.

"Swear?"

A loud smack of his lips made her laugh.

Sitting at his kitchen table with a second cup of morning coffee cooling in front of him, he was nevertheless glad he'd called her from home. The blush that spread across his face would not have gone unnoticed by prying eyes at the office.

"LISTEN JEROME," SAID a capricious Sicotte, "all I'm asking for is a bit of your time, two or three hours at most. Stop giving me grief! You'll have worse things to put up with in life, for Christ's sake! For the salary I'm paying you, you should be a little more flexible, my friend."

They were in the BMW on their way to Le Grand Palais, the chic restaurant and bar where a fundraising dinner for Minister Juneau was being held. This time, Francine Desjarlais had decided not to go; she wanted to spend the evening with her son, whose moods were worrying her.

"This bloody dinner couldn't have come at a worse time," said Jerome. "Eugenie and I haven't seen each other all summer, Severin."

"You have the rest of your lives to see each other. With the minister, opportunities are altogether less frequent, wouldn't you say? I absolutely insist that you meet her, because you're going to be reporting to her — if not directly then at least through someone in her entourage."

He noticed Jerome's stubborn expression.

"Look, I understand how frustrated you must feel, but if ever you're going to prove to me that you have the interests of the office at heart, then tonight's the night. Understood?"

"Okay, okay, I understand," groaned Jerome. "I'm here in the car with you, aren't I? It's not like I'm going to jump out the window."

He stretched out his arms and took a deep breath.

"It's okay," he repeated.

Five days earlier, he'd gone to the airport to welcome Eugenie home. He'd greeted a convalescent still enfeebled by illness and held her in his arms for a long time. They'd driven straight to her mother's house on Gouin, where Madame Lacerte and Andrée-Anne had been waiting with an impatience hard to contain. On the drive over, Eugenie had given him a long account of her misadventures in Barcelona, and then the conversation had flitted about superficially, neither of them feeling brave enough to broach sensitive subjects quite so soon. Eugenie and her daughter's reunion surprised him. When she saw her mother, instead of flying into her arms with cries of joy, Andrée-Anne had frozen on the spot, the expression on her face inscrutable. Then, without saying a word, she'd run to hide in the back of a closet and it had taken all the negotiating talents of the three adults to coax her out.

Obviously, Andrée-Anne was not ready to put the summer behind her. Neither was Madame Lacerte, whose role as grandmother-cum-babysitter had tested her to the limits. Nevertheless, she insisted that her daughter stay with her until her recovery was complete. The decision made a lot of sense and, after a few hours, Andrée-Anne began purring like a kitten. Cuddled next to her mother, thumb in her mouth, she let herself be swaddled once more in the delicious depths of childhood. Her revolt had been short-lived.

Mother and daughter stayed at Madame Lacerte's for four days, where they were pampered in the elderly woman's austere but effective way. Jerome came by to see them every day after work and made Eugenie talk about her long sojourn in Europe—relieved, if truth be told, that the presence of Madame Lacerte prevented the conversation from taking a more intimate turn. But he was well aware of what was hanging over his head, and sometimes, as he listened, he couldn't help looking down at her legs, which were so very beautiful.

On September 4, Eugenie, speedily recovering, decided to return to her own apartment.

"How about coming over for dinner tomorrow night?" she'd said to Jerome on the phone.

"What a coincidence," he said. "I was just going to invite myself."

The "tomorrow night" turned out to be the fifth of September, the night of the fundraiser for Minister Juneau. Jerome had gone to see Sicotte and tried to get out of it, but the lobbyist wouldn't have it. They had words. The tone escalated. Sicotte remained adamant. The discussion continued in the car, with the same result. Jerome, disgruntled, stewed in his frustration and gently tapped his foot on the car's carpet.

The lawyer watched him from the corner of his eye.

"Listen, if after two or two and a half hours I see that you can leave, I'll give a little sign. Make your excuses—say something, anything—and you can hop in a cab and fly to your paramour's arms. Get a receipt from the taxi and I'll reimburse you tomorrow."

"Come on," grumbled Jerome, "I'm on the job so I won't be paying for the taxi as it is."

But his face started to brighten.

Their silence reasserted itself, although this time it was less oppressive. They seemed to have negotiated the terms of a just peace. The lawyer didn't want to be introducing a bad-tempered Jerome to the minister, well known for her ability to sense half-hearted enthusiasm and with a penchant for turning a cold shoulder to anyone not genuinely overjoyed to be in her perfumed company. Truly, it made people wonder why she'd gone into politics . . . Sure, journalists and those in the know called her a sly fox endowed with a particularly keen intelligence, adding that she didn't always choose to show it—but, they would continue, her most significant asset by far was her relationship with Premier Labrèche, whose ear she notoriously had; this relationship was inevitably embellished by gossipmongers. Was she a former mistress? Current? An aggressive seducer? A much-sought-after prize? (Cupid's arrows flew in all directions, depending on the teller's imagination.) Sicotte had even heard one overconfident journalist report that she was the illegitimate child of the premier, who'd kept the fact hidden but cherished her the way Santa Claus cherished his elves, watching over the auspicious beginnings of her political career with paternal solicitude. But of course that could only have been muckraking speculation; no one could imagine such generosity from a man as dry and calculating as Jean-Philippe Labrèche.

In order to break the silence that had really become a bit much, Sicotte brought Jerome up to date on the various rumours surrounding the minister. Jerome seemed amused.

They stopped in front of Le Grand Palais and a valet-parking attendant promptly came up to the car.

Sicotte leaned towards the ear of his adjutant.

"Okay, my boy, it's time to put a smile on your face. The game is afoot."

Le Grand Palais was such a swell restaurant that it was impossible for a normal mind to imagine one more so. But jealousy and spite are omnipresent, and there were those who, keeping their voices down, murmured that the white marble columns were an unintentional reminder of the laundered money that had backed the restaurant's construction. The managers, with an exquisite sense of the formulaic, had chosen for its slogan:

LE GRAND PALAIS
RENDEZVOUS OF GREAT PALATES

A bald colossus in a tuxedo tailcoat bowed and smiled as he opened the door, the enormous handles of which were of polished leather in the shape of the letters G and P. Sicotte and Jerome found themselves in a vestibule that, despite its small size, did its best to rival the Hall of Mirrors in Versailles. Two delightful hostesses were waiting and — judging from the smile with which they addressed the lobbyist and his assistant — clearly believed that after searching for so long, they'd finally found the Holy Grail. Sicotte, as congenially as he could manage, handed the women two business cards bordered in gold; these were immediately relayed to a young doorman in a black tricorn hat decorated with a huge red feather.

"This way, please," said the doorman, bowing very low.

As guests filing in behind them introduced themselves and the hostesses thrilled to yet more dates with destiny, they passed into the famous hall of marble pillars resonant with the conversation of a hundred people. Guests were circulating from table to table, flutes of Champagne in hand, as others congregated in small groups. Four imposing marble statues, copies of works by the great Michelangelo — *Moses*, *David*, *Rebellious Slave,* and *Pope Julius II in Prayer* — had been installed, one in each corner of the room, watching over the effervescent goings-on with impassive eyes. On the left, a well-stocked bar displayed a row of glittering bottles and decanters. On the right was a small stage on which a screen had been mounted.

Sicotte had to stop every three steps, accosted by one person, greeting another, and he introduced Jerome as often as occasion permitted. The poor doorman charged with escorting the pair to their table waited patiently as they made themselves available to innumerable displays of friendship.

And as happens in such a demi-monde, the evening wear of the men — in the majority that night — ranged, according to the age of each, from the formality of the "noteworthy bourgeois" to chic "ostensibly casual but very much on trend." The women took a more classic line, their hair and makeup serving either to highlight the lures of youth or to mask, as much as possible, the effects of biological wear and tear.

Jerome, hard on the heels of his boss, greeted, smiled, shook hands, all the while switching from French to English (this was a Liberal function) and feeling overwhelmed by innumerable faces, only a few of which were vaguely familiar. They finally arrived at their table, over which loomed Michelangelo's *David* in all his triumphant virility, and to the left of it they heard a woman say, "No, I don't think I've had the pleasure of making his acquaintance, Monsieur Brébeuf, but I would very much like to meet him, you know."

Sicotte gave Jerome a flurry of jabs in the ribs and, tugging him by the sleeve, almost knocked over a large woman in a pink pantsuit as he cleared a path towards the voice.

Jerome had already guessed the voice belonged to Minister Juneau. A dozen or so people were surrounding her, all vying for her attention.

"We'll go up to her quietly, as if we're just happening by," the lobbyist said silkily into Jerome's ear. "If I've spent two thousand dollars tonight, my boy, it's for the chance of having the couple of minutes of light banter with her Monsieur Gino Brébeuf over there just had. As soon as we're near, try to make a decent impression, okay?"

From his vantage point, Jerome could see the minister in three-quarter profile. She was attractive enough, the features a bit angular but quite distinguished, and her velvety skin was—from time spent in the tropics?—the colour of honey. Her expression intrigued him; she was smiling as she listened to her interlocutor, attentively but at a remove, though nodding slightly as if to say, "Yes, yes, I know all that, let's move on." Jerome deduced that it would take a lot of skill to monopolize this woman's attention for even a few minutes.

Suddenly there was a flutter in the minister's entourage, a breach in the ranks opened up directly in front of them, and Sicotte charged into it with his assistant in tow.

"Madame Minister, what an honour!" said Sicotte, hand outstretched and interrupting the conversation of a thin, stooped man with a furrowed brow he'd judged unimportant. "Such a pleasure to see you again!"

"Hello, Severin," replied Normande Juneau, causing the lobbyist to blush with pleasure at this sign of familiarity. "I was just thinking about you yesterday."

"If I weren't so shy, Madame Minister, I'd reply that I'm *always* thinking of you—but that would perhaps be lacking in propriety."

Polite laughter rippled around them. The minister smiled, but barely.

Sicotte worried that he'd committed a faux pas and resumed, "If you were thinking of me, it must be because there's some way in which I can be of use to you. Your word is my command, ma'am; I am at your service."

"There'll be other occasions for that. Aren't you going to introduce me to your associate? I assume he's one of your employees?"

"Yes, of course, I almost forgot...What an idiot I am... You make me forget my manners, ma'am."

And Sicotte introduced Jerome, trying to say as much

about him as he could in thirty seconds.

"An honour, Madame Minister," said Jerome, who bowed and quickly shook the hand that was offered him.

"Your name is familiar, Monsieur Lupien," said Juneau, who was looking at him with noticeable interest.

"A few days ago I met with your riding secretary, Minister, and I've spoken two or three times with your chief of staff. Perhaps they mentioned me in your presence."

"Ah, yes, I see... It was you they were talking about so favourably. I hope we meet again, Monsieur Lupien. Thank you for coming. Have a good evening."

She held out her hand again, again looking at him intently.

Sicotte led Jerome back to their assigned table. He was jubilant.

"You hit her like a ton of bricks, Jerome. I've never seen her so friendly... You managed yourself very well and that has given us the edge! Ask me for anything you want and it's yours!"

"I want to go now," replied Jerome, goading him.

"Soon, my boy, soon. I'll give you the heads-up when the moment is right. Ah, Gino!" he exclaimed, turning towards a ruddy-faced man wavering slightly as he approached. "How are you? When did you get out of hospital? You look as if you're in terrific shape, my friend!"

"Yeah, I've been doing okay for a week... They let me out the first of the month. But you wouldn't have been saying such nice things about me the night of the accident! The other day I bumped into one of the ambulance drivers who got me out of my Jaguar. He said I looked like a busted-up apple."

Even in his weakened state Brébeuf looked like a man

who could choke an ox with his bare hands. He seemed a fairly unremarkable sort and hardly stood out in the room, but for the exclusive leather Chevignon jacket he was wearing, which would have dignified even a prince consort on the job, and went some way towards explaining his presence.

The constant flow of drinks offered by the servers, who circulated through the crowd with platters in hand, saw the volume of conversation steadily rising. Sicotte had to shout to introduce Jerome, then patted Gino Brébeuf on the shoulder. "Well, good luck, old friend! Try to be a bit smarter next time. We only have one life, you know."

"Speak for yourself. When I was born, my mother wrapped my ass in a rosary blessed by Brother André, and that gave me nine lives. Like a cat."

And off he limped. Vigorously.

Small coughs were heard over the loudspeakers; a tall, chubby man in a tailcoat, looking distinguished but also half asleep, appeared on the stage and invited the guests to take their seats. Five musicians followed and, as everyone moved to their tables, played music that, alternating between semi-classical and world jazz, spread throughout the room, floating just above the considerable noise of the crowd.

The round tables were set for ten places each. Jerome had Sicotte to his right and, to his left, a woman who introduced herself as Betty Watson, a Liberal senator and daughter of a senator who, alas, was no longer with them. She spoke competent French but had a marked preference, it seemed, for her mother tongue; Francine Desjarlais was absent; her place remained vacant. Jerome didn't know any of his six other table-mates, two women and four men. Sicotte knew three of them, and two others by reputation. In any case, it was almost impossible to have a conversation with anyone the least bit at a remove, which meant that the exchanges Jerome initially participated in took place largely between himself, his boss, and Betty Watson. She was a jovial woman in her sixties, heavily perfumed, with beefy, masculine features showing the signs of a recent facelift (the others at the table were provided a primer on her fourth glass of wine). Jerome found her rather funny. But on her fifth glass, she launched into a long account of her exploits in support of Canadian unity during the referendum over Quebec's independence in 1995, and Jerome was the only one at the table who did not break out into peals of laughter. After that, though he remained polite, he chatted mostly with his boss and the fellow on his boss's right, a certain Gérard Jolivet, an engineer with SNC-Lavalin who loved to go on safaris.

After an hour, he was so bored he could barely keep his eyes from watering.

"May I?" he whispered into Sicotte's ear.

"After the speeches."

"How many are there?"

"All you can think about is getting laid, my God . . . Do I have to nail you to your chair? There are three, usually."

Jerome looked at his watch and heaved a sigh of despair.

"Having trouble?" Betty Watson asked him in English. She was on her sixth glass. "Can I be of some help in any way?"

Sicotte assured her in the impeccable English he'd learned in Farnham and perfected in Montreal that everything was dandy.

"Really?" she insisted in a playful tone. "This young man looks miserable."

Hoping for an ally, Jerome explained that his girlfriend had just returned from spending several months in Europe.

"No kidding! What are you doing here? She needs you! You need her!" she exclaimed with the sudden, warm familiarity of the tipsy. *"Alléé, parthez thoutt sweet, mon ami, for God's sake!"* she added in a touching spurt of bilingualism.

Jerome and his boss exchanged embarrassed looks, but Jerome remained in his seat.

Dessert and coffee were served. Whether as a result of general fatigue or boredom, the buzz of conversations began to diminish. Suddenly the music stopped, and once more coughs were heard over the loudspeakers, and the master of ceremonies, with his unctuous, somnolent voice, again thanked the participants for the evening's success, which would allow one of the most extraordinary ministers Quebec had ever known to continue doing her extraordinary work for the greater benefit of... blah blah blah...

"Mesdames et messieurs! Ladies and gentlemen!" he thundered. "I now have the pleasure and honour of presenting to you a citizen dedicated to the public interest... an exceptional woman, an irreplaceable minister... and I'm referring to *MADAME NORMANDE JUNEAU!"*

The thunderous applause caused small cracks to appear in the room's painted walls, fortunately almost indiscernible.

Minister Juneau was under no illusions about her talents as an orator and had decided not to add to the work her supporters had so obligingly endured up to this point. At any rate, the goal of the evening, essentially pecuniary, had been achieved and even surpassed beyond all expectations, so it would have been counterproductive to wax eloquent about ideological or social considerations no one in the room wanted to hear. Papineau, Jaurès, de Gaulle, Bourgault, and Lévesque were dead and buried, Fidel Castro was effectively so, and we were now in the era of the short and sweet. After a few obligatory pleasantries that warmed up the crowd and put them in a good mood, Juneau provided a brief survey of current events, damned the opposition party for never understanding a single thing and then, modestly but assiduously, gave a succinct description of her past accomplishments and those she intended in the future as a Minister of Culture driven by an unrelenting desire to serve Quebec's interests. She thanked the donors for their generosity and graciously relinquished the microphone.

The cracks in the wall spread into tiny networks.

Then came the inevitable thank-you speech, relegated this time to the Minister of Health, Laurent Lirette, a huge and overbearing man with a big mouth, the subtlety of a nightclub bouncer but the smarts of an old crow. Climbing the five short steps to the platform left him short of breath for some time; he'd been forced to wait in the wings for a while so that he might deliver his speech without the asthmatic gasps that public address systems amplified so disagreeably.

Seeing him appear, red and sweating, jowls quivering, his body bulging everywhere despite the well-cut suit intended to make him look slim, Jerome recalled that cruel but amusing comment of the moralist Chamfort: "It might be said of the former bishop of Autun, who was monstrously fat, that he had been created and placed on Earth for no other purpose than to show how far human skin can be stretched."

"My dear friends," he began in a loud, full voice that immediately commanded the attention of every attendee, *"mes chers amis*, thank you for coming tonight to Le Grand Palais, a place, it must be said, that does little to help my weight-loss program, believe me!" (Prolonged laughter from the audience.) "Thank you for showing your support for Madame Normande Juneau in such large numbers..."

He took a deep breath and yelled, *"ONE OF THE BEST MINISTERS THE QUEBEC HAD EVER KNOWN!"* (Warm applause.)

"It's thanks to your help, my dear friends," he continued, "and that of all those active in the Liberal Party of Quebec, that we're able to relegate Aline Letarte and her gang of separatists to the Opposition benches, as we look to the day — it will come soon, I promise you — when we can kick the whole lot of them out of the National Assembly once and for all!" (Long applause and a few bravos). *"Never,* once we are in power, *never,* you understand, will Quebec leave this beautiful country of Canada, of which we are the birthplace and the cradle, and which the separatists want to destroy and turn each and every one of us into welfare bums!"

Jerome turned to Sicotte with an imploring look. Sicotte discreetly indicated that he could leave. Jerome stood up quietly and nodded to his neighbours at the table. Betty Watson gave him a knowing wink. The others, facing the speaker, hardly noticed his departure.

As he was leaving the room, a man with salt-and-pepper hair and a distinguished air blocked his path.

"Monsieur Lupien," the man said, keeping his voice low, "Minister Juneau asked me to give you this."

He handed Jerome a small card, nodded again, and rapidly moved away. Taken aback, Jerome looked at the minister's professional card on which a telephone number had been scrawled in tiny characters. He shrugged, smiled vainly, slipped the card into his pocket, and left the restaurant.

SHE STOOD IN the doorway in the night's lukewarm air, delighted and fearful.

"Finally, you were able to get away! I'd almost given up hope, my love."

He smiled when he saw her in a tempting orange negligée. The message was clear, and Jerome was both overjoyed and relieved that she was setting the tone: their first night together would be devoted to love, their problems put off a little longer. They stood holding each other for a long time, then she disengaged herself from his embrace, which was becoming more and more insistent.

"Let's go inside," she breathed. "People can see us."

"I don't see anyone," he said, laughing. "The street is deserted. I see no one but you."

He went in and closed the door behind him. In the living room, bathed in soft light, she appeared as a beautiful wraith upon whose drawn features death had tried its damnedest to leave its mark. "In two months she'll be back to normal," he told himself.

"You must find me changed," she said, turning to him.

He shook his head.

"I still see the lovely bird I first espied that morning beside the pool in Varadero...Don't worry, in two weeks you'll be your old self again...And I know a very effective treatment for speeding your recovery..."

He began to tickle her with feverish ardour. She backed away, head thrown back and laughing quietly, and soon they found themselves on the sofa; he whispered heady endearments and, as he did so, they managed to more or less undress. Their love-making took on a feral intensity. She quickly reached orgasm, her thighs raised, emitting a stifled moan. He attained his own pleasure soon after, then let himself fall onto her, out of breath.

For a long time they didn't move.

"I'd almost forgotten how good that feels," she murmured, running her hand over his head.

Face upon her shoulder, he stayed silent, covering her neck with tiny kisses.

"I missed you so much," he said, finally. "The summer was interminable. But now you're here, and I'm going to bring you back to health, you'll see."

She said nothing, which made him uneasy.

"Is everything okay?"

"Yes, everything's fine," she said in a lazy voice. "So how did you manage to do without me all that time, lover boy?"

"By spending a lot of time with my busy wrist, my love."

She laughed, but he thought he heard a hint of skepticism in the sound of it. So, his head still pressed against her shoulder and glad she couldn't see his face, he tried changing the subject.

"It's a good thing Andrée-Anne didn't wake up..."

"Since we've been home she's been sleeping like a log, my poor baby. She's exhausted. At suppertime she fell asleep in her plate. I could change the bed she was in and she still wouldn't wake up... And my mother, looking after her all that time! They spent so many white nights together while I was away... Tantrums, nightmares, it was endless. I got back just in time..."

"Yes, you did."

They lay on the sofa in each other's arms and, despite the discomfort, dozed off for a while. Suddenly Jerome opened his eyes.

"Yes, it's about time you got back," he whispered, and then he planted on her lips a heady, imperious kiss — an invasive one giving new meaning to his phrase.

"No, no, wait, my love," she implored, disengaging

herself. "Let's go to my room, we'll be more comfortable. Andrée-Anne might wake up, you never know . . . And I need to freshen up. You too, no doubt. Come and take a shower with me."

And so, the night passed peacefully. It was hunger that awakened Jerome in the early morning, and with it an onslaught of luminous and gloomy thoughts all mixed up together. Leaning on one elbow, he tenderly contemplated Eugenie, who was still asleep; her face was a little thinner and reminded him of the look of distress that had struck him so forcefully the first time he'd seen her, beside the swimming pool. This time, however, he knew what was causing it. She let out a lengthy sigh when he left the bed, despite his many precautions, but didn't open her eyes. He had to go to his own apartment to change before going in to work. He'd grab something for breakfast on the way.

He was just about to leave when little footsteps made him turn around.

Andrée-Anne was standing in the middle of the living room, staring at him with the sleepy, brooding look children often have when they first wake up.

"My, already up, are you? How do you feel?" he said, bending down and holding out his arms. "Come give me a hug."

She stared at him without reacting, as though she hadn't heard him. Then something clicked in her and the next second she was hugging him fiercely. "Are you leaving?"

"Yes, my little peach. I have to go to work."

"Did you sleep with Mommy?"

"Yes."

"Are you coming back soon?"

"Of course."

He stroked her hair.

"I'm hungry," she said, pulling away. "I'm going to go eat some cereal."

"Do you want me to make it for you?"

"I know how."

She gave a little pout that, pushed, might have passed for a smile, then ran into the kitchen.

As he drove to Côte-des-Neiges in traffic that grew heavier by the minute, he relived the events of the previous evening. His reunion with Eugenie had, all things considered, surpassed his every expectation but still hadn't erased the memory of the quarrel that had erupted between them before her departure for Europe, nor had it made him forget that she'd chosen to spend her vacation six thousand kilometres away from him. What should he expect in the future? Sooner or later there would no doubt be a rupture, since the gulf between them could only grow wider. Unless... You never went very far in life with "unless" and its eternal indecision. What he needed was a complete break from everything, and that required courage. A lot of courage. Did he have it? Would he ever have it? His adventures with the bizarre Alma only served to prepare him for the inevitable.

"Oh, well, that's life," he sighed.

But the bouncy aphorism didn't make him feel any better; in fact, it made him feel sick.

A CASCADE OF events would change his state of mind.

That afternoon, Sicotte called him into his office to show him a new version of the plans for the Museum of Canadian Culture in the French Language, and they had a lively discussion about the meaning of certain architectural terms used in them — so lively, in fact, that the lobbyist telephoned Tony Petozza and asked him to send over a technician to settle the matter. Sitting side by side behind the sumptuous desk conceived by the illustrious Boulle, they were continuing their discussion as they waited for Petozza's man to show when Jerome noticed his boss recoil slightly, suggesting to him that the previous night's fundraising dinner had left him with a bit of morning breath. He stuck his hand into his jacket pocket to find a stick of chewing gum when his fingers found the business card that had been given to him by Minister Juneau.

With a certain braggadocio, he tossed the card on the desk and told Sicotte about the messenger chasing him down after the dinner.

"My eyes were as big as saucers, Severin. Why do you think she wants to see me?"

Sicotte scrutinized the card, then said with a smirk, "This is her personal number, Jerome. Don't play the innocent with me. You know as well as I do why she wants to see you ... Madame the Minister has the reputation of a grand seductress of men. If you didn't know that before, you know it now."

He slapped his thigh with a satisfied laugh. "Hah! I see I was right to bring you to that fundraising dinner."

"What if I don't want to sleep with her?" countered Jerome, turning red.

"My friend," replied the lobbyist, his eyes glimmering with a salacious twinkle, "we have to take advantage of every opportunity. You have to admit that that's not the hardest part of our job, right? Call her back, for pity's sake! You'd be crazy not to. She's a beautiful woman, after all ... And you, at your age, you're no babe in the woods! Where's

the harm in pleasing a minister who wants to unwind a little? It can only be good for us. And you won't make it into
the papers, either."

"She may have given me her card for some other reason,
Severin."

"All the more reason to follow it up, then, see if there's
anything in it. It's your job."

The technician's arrival cut off their discussion. Jerome
returned the card to his pocket and didn't mention it again.

Two days went by. Sicotte seemed to have forgotten their
conversation. Jerome thought it just as well. Perhaps the lobbyist had done some asking around to find out if, as seemed
likely, they were in fact in the minister's good books. Still,
Jerome wanted to be sure, so at the end of the afternoon he
asked Sicotte straight out.

"Yes, hard to say," Sicotte answered off-handedly. "I made
some calls, but I didn't learn much. She has a so-called lover
in Quebec City, but obviously that doesn't mean anything.
In the end, it's you who has to make the decision, Jerome,
I can't very well call her in your place."

Jerome was content to shrug it off. Let someone else
climb onto the conveyor belt of men satisfying Madame
Minister's voracious sexual appetite! He was enjoying
his second honeymoon with Eugenie. Not once since her
return had she alluded to the shadowy work in which he
was engaged; it was as if she had forgotten all about it. His
own life experience and his reading — mostly, he had to
admit, the latter — had taught him that love, when it wasn't
blind, was easily forgiving. Might as well take advantage, he
told himself. This didn't mean he was about to review his
decision not to quit the job he despised, but it did let him
procrastinate for a while.

The last time he'd seen Eugenie had been on the Wednesday. On Friday, towards six o'clock, he turned up at her place as usual without phoning beforehand and was looking forward to another glorious weekend. She wasn't there. In her mailbox he found a hastily scribbled note saying that she'd gone to see her mother, who wasn't feeling well. She would be there until Monday morning. That she hadn't called to tell him during the afternoon surprised and annoyed him a little. He stood at the door and phoned Madame Lacerte; she herself answered and informed him rather drily that her daughter was out shopping and she didn't know when she would be back. She didn't sound like someone who was sick, but he didn't dare ask anything else, and hung up.

"What's going on?" he muttered, his anger turning to worry, then to dejection. "I don't understand this at all. Someone's done me a bad turn, I'm sure of it."

He returned to his apartment, drank a beer and ate a bag of peanuts, then flopped down in front of the television. After ten minutes of not following a single thing on the screen, he turned it off angrily and got himself another beer.

Around nine o'clock he called Madame Lacerte's number again. This time there was no answer. A third beer in hand, he began pacing about the apartment. Three scenarios of betrayal played themselves out in his head. The first involved Alma; the second, Fradette; and the third, Charlie; the big galoot might still be caught up in his Boy Scout idealism.

The previous evening after work he'd asked Charlie to accompany him to Mariette Clermont, a high-end furniture store on rue Saint-Hubert. He'd decided to get new furniture for his living room and bedroom, and given that Charlie was constantly browsing magazines and catalogues, paper as well as online, he was a good person to have on hand. Jerome went over in his mind every minute of the evening, but nothing led him to suspect that Charlie was the master-mind behind whatever this double-cross was. On the other hand, nothing was impossible when it came to that odd little twerp, and it was better to check with him before turning the city upside down.

When he phoned, Charlie laughed in his face.

"I learned my lesson the last time, chum, and I promised myself never again would I get mixed up in your love life. Right now, my own is more than enough!"

Simple friendship should have led Jerome to ask if "more than enough" was meant in a positive or a negative way, but he didn't even think of it, gnawed as he was by his need to know just what was going on.

He left the apartment and drove to Caledonia Road. Alma would no doubt be home. At first, he'd thought of telephoning Felix to find out for certain, but Alma may very well have been in Felix's bed and his call would have ruined the surprise of his arriving. As for Fradette, he'd recently moved and Jerome had no idea where to find him. He was, by far, the more formidable opponent, besides which he was very likely to be in cahoots with Alma.

"If ever I find out it's you, you little rat," muttered Jerome with a frown, "I'll turn your skin inside out so fast you'll choke on your own asshole."

Anger raged through him like wildfire.

He left his car a few doors down from his bosses' house and went the rest of the way on foot. The driveway was empty. So Felix had gone out, either alone or with someone, Sicotte and Francine too. There was a light in an upstairs window. Two months earlier, Sicotte had given him a key to the building, along with the security codes, proof of the trust he'd taken several shrill minutes to avow. It also meant that, as his employee, Jerome was able to work overtime when no one else was on the premises.

He entered the house without making any noise and stopped for a moment in the hall with its grotesque, pretentious chandelier. No sound came from the ground floor, which appeared to be deserted. A vague suggestion of music, perhaps Oriental, came from upstairs. Ears alert, he proceeded softly up the stairs, which was covered in a thick rose carpet. His rage was now mixed with apprehension, as his patrons would not at all appreciate such an intrusion into domestic space to which he'd only very infrequently been invited.

But he needed to know.

At the top of the stairs was a long corridor leading to several rooms; a vase lamp sitting on a marble pedestal table cast a dim light. Alma's room was at the far end of the corridor, above the company offices, but the music wasn't coming from there. He moved forward, intrigued. The infrastructure of the house was built of concrete, so that the hardwood floors were almost completely silent. Through the half-opened door of one of the bedrooms, a spectacle greeted his eyes that filled him with astonishment. Alma, dressed only in a half-slip, naked from the waist up, was completely absorbed in a kind of dance, a solitary *baladi* that looked almost gymnastic. She turned suddenly towards the door and uttered a cry.

"So sorry," he said with a wry smile. "I should have called first. But I love surprises, don't you?"

She stared at him without saying a word, lips tight, her face rigid with fear. She crossed her arms over her breasts, a gesture he found comical.

"What do you want?" she asked dispiritedly.

The techno-Eastern music lent an exotic, almost surreal atmosphere to the scene.

"Is there anyone home except you and me?"

She shook her head.

"Good."

He added, "I'd advise you not to lie to me, Alma."

"They left early this evening... Can I put on a T-shirt?"

Her voice, though still trembling, was a little more confident.

"I never thought of you as timid," said Jerome, mockingly. "Where is this T-shirt?"

She pointed to a chair at the end of the room. He replied with a nod. It surprised him that he'd become so indifferent towards her. It had to be said, she was a terrific lay, and perfectly built for it.

The music stopped. Her T-shirt on, she came up to him with a light step and gave him a look she tried to make suggestive. "You poor thing," he said to himself, "do you think you can get out of this by fucking me?"

He was a good five inches taller than she, so small and lissome. He took a step towards her, leaned his head above hers so closely that their breaths mingled, and looked her straight in the eye.

"So tell me, Alma, have you been up to any dirty tricks, by any chance?"

"Dirty tricks?" she stammered, backing away. "What are you talking about?"

"I warned you."

"Warned me about what? I haven't done anything."

"That's what they all say when they're caught."

"I haven't done anything, I tell you... Do you mean... our sleeping together?"

"What else would I be talking about?"

"Who would I be talking to about that?"

"Good question...Not the mayor of Montreal, I imagine."

"I don't know your girlfriend, I don't even know her name. Why would I tell her anything? Why?"

He noted with pleasure that she was flustered again.

"Oh, I don't know...There could be a lot of reasons... For revenge, or to help someone else get revenge...or simply for the pleasure it would give you."

He began to squeeze her arm, smiling.

"Leave me alone!" she cried, pulling away. "You're hurting me!"

There was a moment's silence. Standing in front of him, panting, she looked down and rubbed her arms convulsively. Jerome began to feel ashamed of his behaviour.

"Listen, Alma, I'll explain. It isn't complicated; my girlfriend came back from a long trip, we hadn't seen each other all summer, and the homecoming was great, like we were floating on our backs in a sea of happiness. And then all of a sudden, pouf! She won't even speak to me, it's like I've suddenly become a complete stranger to her — or worse, an enemy. So I ask myself why. What did I do to deserve that? Only one thing: I slept with you. And who knows about that, except the two of us? No one. Oh, sorry, there's also Felix. But Felix would never do anything to hurt me like that, I'm sure of it. So that leaves you, Alma. What do you have to say to that, my sweet?"

She started to sob, then raised a face to him that was flushed scarlet and running with tears. A thread of snot dripped from her nose.

"I've done nothing!" she yelled. "Nothing, do you understand. Nothing at all! I'd never have dared! Even if I was tempted to, I wouldn't do it. Do you want to know why? Because I'm scared of you! There! Are you satisfied? Now get out! If you don't leave, I'll call Francine!"

She ran out of the room and down the corridor, and Jerome heard a door slam behind her.

AN HOUR LATER, Jerome was sitting on the stairs outside his apartment building, reflecting calmly. A great chill had descended from the dark sky, a blessed coolness after the torrid September day that was gradually appeasing the overheated city. In the distance, the low rumble of traffic, punctuated from time to time by a honking horn, snored softly along Côte-des-Neiges, but the side streets were quiet.

Since the start of the evening Jerome had sent Eugenie three emails, none of which were returned. She'd burned her bridges. Beer in hand, he tried to unravel the mysterious betrayal to which he'd been subjected. He forced himself to think in as measured a way as he could, the celebrated Sherlock Holmes his inspiration, he who knew that an excess of emotion in any enquiry worked in the criminal's favour. Sensing that alcohol, given his fatigue, was beginning to dull his analytical faculties, he stretched his arm out through the banister and poured a long stream of foamy beer down to be lost in the grass.

There were accomplished liars, he told himself, who pushed the art of deception to such an astonishing degree of perfection that they ended up believing their lies themselves. Such people could be found everywhere, they were crooks and charlatans of the highest order, but also politicians, men of the cloth, businessmen—as well as the most ordinary of people. Sooner or later you were going to cross paths with one of them. Alma, was she one such professional liar? He now doubted it. Her distressed reaction had shaken him. Besides, what motive would she have had to act in such a fashion? Unrequited love? He'd never felt that she loved him. They'd been together for a single reason: to make love. The manner of their first coupling had proven that conclusively.

Charlie was eliminated, too. That left Olivier Fradette. It wasn't hard to guess the motives inspiring him. For a long time now, Jerome had replaced him in their boss's esteem, and his jealousy had become more and more apparent. Fradette's reaction was typical of the impotent: unable to eliminate a competitor, they could at least take some satisfaction in doing them harm, hoping that the setbacks would do enough damage to their work that some day they'd be rid of them.

But before Jerome confronted Fradette, he had to obtain concrete proof that he was the author of his downfall, and only Eugenie could provide that. He decided to wait for her the next day as she left her office, and wrest the truth from her.

This resolution calmed him even more, and he began to think he just might get out of the wasteland in which he'd been wandering. Fatigue came over him and he went inside to bed.

But when four o'clock rang from St. Joseph's Oratory, he'd still not closed his eyes.

AT FOUR O'CLOCK the next afternoon, Jerome was at the headquarters of the Metro chain of grocery stores, on boulevard Maurice-Duplessis in Rivière-des-Prairies, north of the city. Eugenie, who had gone back to her old job, never left the building before five, and he wanted to be sure to catch her as she left. Withdrawing into a quiet corner of the lobby, cell phone to his ear, he pretended to be absorbed in conversation with an inexhaustible babbler while monitoring the comings and goings around him. Every now and then he would smile at the security guard, who was keeping an eye on the premises.

After forty-five minutes, despite the exemplary comportment of the young man and his numerous smiles, the security guard began to feel suspicious, even worried, and, hands clasped behind his back, he approached Jerome.

"Can I help you in any way, sir?"

"No, no, everything's fine," replied Jerome amiably.

"Do you mind if I ask who you're waiting for?"

"Certainly, you may ask, sir, but as it's supposed to be a surprise, you'll have to—"

A severe expression consumed the guard's reddening face. He seemed to grow four or five centimetres, the stress of it all forcing him to stand on the tips of his toes.

"The rules don't permit surprises here, sir," said the guard. "In fact, they're expressly forbidden."

He was about to courteously ask Jerome to leave the building when Jerome let out a muffled cry and ran towards Eugenie, who'd just appeared at the other end of the lobby and hadn't yet seen him.

Everything happened quickly, though not at all the way he'd hoped.

"Eugenie," he asked, "what's going on? Why are you keeping away from me? I need to talk to you, I don't understand a thing!"

For a second she was frozen to the spot, turning pale. Then, looking straight ahead, she started to walk off.

"I don't want to talk to you," she said.

"But that's not possible, you're driving me crazy!" Jerome

cried as he fell in behind her. "At least tell me who—"

People were starting to stare. A balding man in his fifties, heavy-set but in good shape, stopped and looked their way indecisively. The security guard, more conscious than ever of his social and strategic responsibilities, followed them, ready to help the woman should the occasion demand it.

Eugenie stopped again and raised her hand so that the guard kept his distance. Then she turned to Jerome. He'd never seen her look so resolute.

"Stop this spectacle, you're embarrassing me," she commanded, her voice low but adamant. "I have nothing more to say to you. You know better than I what you deserve, and it isn't much, believe me. I've already lived with one imposter, and two is too many. Go about your business as you have every intention of doing, and don't try to see me again. I'm afraid I might catch something from you."

Flabbergasted, he watched her exit the door, then disappear. His heart was beating so violently that his surroundings started to undulate, like a veil shaken by the wind. But the sensation lasted only an instant, and he threw himself after her, ran down the front steps of the building, and looked for her in the parking lot. The heavy-set, fiftyish man followed him and was watching the scene with interest, gently rubbing the top of his head as he did so.

Suddenly Jerome saw her pearl-grey Prius leaving one of the lanes. Without stopping to think he ran in front of the car; it stopped with a jerk, a window rolled down, and a terse Eugenie leaned out and ordered him out of the way. "You're wasting your time . . . and you're making us both look like fools. Go away, or I'll run you over."

Knowing she wouldn't, he took the few seconds remaining to him to make his desperate entreaty.

"Someone has slandered me, Eugenie! I don't know what you've been told, but I have the right to give my version! All I ask is that you hear me out! I know I have faults, but it's not what you think!"

"I don't think anything anymore," she said. "Go away."

And, taking her foot off the brake, she forced him to leap aside.

"I'll redeem myself!" he yelled at the top of his voice. "And it'll be you who'll come to me saying you're sorry . . . and crying!"

But by then she was too far away to hear him.

HE WOULD HAVE to strike fast and decisively, because that piece of shit Fradette was obviously on his guard. First, of course, he'd have to make the best case possible — then take it to Sicotte and demand his dismissal. Free of him, he'd see to the rest. Because this was only the beginning: Jerome had decided to quit the infested swamp in which he was working, gradually losing any reputation he had and what little remained of his self-respect. His romantic ordeal was giving him the opportunity and the will to do so.

All this incurred considerable risk, since denouncing an enterprise built on shady wheeling and dealing and in which he himself had been wheeling and dealing for a number of months was to invite complications. But he wanted redemption, and if there was a price to be paid, he would pay it.

Spying on Fradette would not be easy, as they no longer worked together and, despite there having been no up-front quarrel between them, they avoided each other whenever possible.

Jerome met with Charlie and asked for his help. Was he able to tap his colleague's phone lines, for example?

"Jesus! You don't ask much, do you! Sure, I work in computers, but that doesn't make me a CIA agent."

"Come on, Charlie, for a nerd like you there has to be a way—I can give you all his phone numbers."

"I'll think on it," Charlie replied grumpily. "I'll see what I can do."

"Think on it quickly. My ass is on the burner."

Charlie shrugged, but there was a touch of compassion in his voice when he said, "So you want to expose this guy and your secretary, is that the idea, Jerome?"

"Well, for a start, she's not *my* secretary. Secondly, do I have to tell you again how all this came about? I'd like to have seen you in my place, Charlie. Anyone would have cracked!"

Two days passed. Jerome was working hard, and pretending to do so with zealous application, but was keeping his eyes peeled. Two or three times he invented pretexts for going into Fradette's office, but gained nothing from his efforts except sore cheeks from so much forced smiling. His nights were awful, but he was able to sleep a little. Every so often he ran into Alma in the corridor; she nodded mechanically, as if nothing at all were up.

"I find you a bit distracted lately, Jerome," said a concerned Francine Desjarlais one morning as he passed her office. "Come in and sit down. Are you having problems?"

"Not really. It could be worse."

"What's the matter? If you don't mind my asking."

"Nothing in particular, I assure you. It's just life, good old ordinary life." He changed the subject. "How's Felix? I haven't seen him for a while."

Francine's expression became sombre.

"He wants to live in an apartment somewhere. You didn't know?"

"Bah, he said something about it the other day. That worries you?"

"A bit, yes."

"Why? In my opinion, it might do him some good. Everyone needs their independence at a certain point, no?"

"Okay then," she said with a sigh. "I was going to ask you to try to persuade him to put off moving until some time later. He has a lot of respect for you, Jerome. Anyway . . . let's just say I didn't ask."

"Sorry, Francine, but I wouldn't make a very good lawyer."

He hurried out of the room.

Later that morning, having drunk coffee after coffee, he came upon Minister Juneau's business card as he was rummaging in his desk drawer. He contemplated it for a moment and felt a strong sudden urge to call her. He turned the card over in his fingers, rubbed his nose, and cleared his throat, torn between curiosity and guilt. If he called her, wouldn't he be giving credence to Eugenie's suspicions? But an imperious voice inside him whispered that under the circumstances it was the only thing he could do.

"Oh, man! What harm can it do?" he finally said to himself. "I should have called her ages ago, if only out of politeness."

To his considerable astonishment, thirty seconds after giving his name, he had the minister herself on the line.

"What a lovely surprise, Monsieur Lupien!" said Normande Juneau with a tinge of irony in her voice. "You haven't vanished from the face of the Earth after all!"

"I'm so sorry, Madame Minister," he babbled, blushing, "but . . . these last few days I've had . . . a few small problems to deal with."

"Well then, you'd better not go into politics," said the minister in an agreeable tone. "Small problems are our daily bread here, small problems and big problems...I'm delighted to be speaking with you this morning, believe me, but I have to make it short, Monsieur Lupien, because I'm late for a meeting. But I'd like to see you to discuss a very important file. When are you free?"

He swallowed with difficulty.

"I am at your disposal, ma'am."

"Perfect...Let me look at my calendar..."

There was a silence; over the receiver, he could hear the murmur of a conversation between two women.

"Here I am again, Monsieur Lupien. How does the twenty-fourth of this month at four o'clock sound? Can you come to my office? I mean, of course, my Montreal office, at 480 boulevard St. Laurent?"

"With the greatest pleasure, ma'am."

"Good. I've got to go now. Have a nice day. See you soon."

He hung up and spun around in his chair.

"With the greatest pleasure, ma'am," he muttered under his breath. "I overdid it, I'd say. I sounded like a real boot-licker."

Which is when he realized that the back of his shirt was soaked with sweat and making him cold. For several minutes, his mind blank, he stared at the ceiling, sucking in huge breaths of air. He suspected that something very significant had just happened, and that if he rose to the occasion, even bigger things were lurking on the horizon.

THAT AFTERNOON, JUST before five, a frantic Fradette had to leave the office in a hurry to get to Saint-Lambert after an unpleasant telephone conversation with Ahmed Afnali, the patriarch of the rich Algerian family of investors. Afnali had accused him of having swindled them and had even called him a *ventriloquist*—an insult the precise nature of which Fradette could not quite grasp, this offending him all the more.

"A ventriloquist, he called me! I'll shove that so far down his bloody throat it'll come out his ass. A ventriloquist! That degenerate Bedouin! And Severin's gone God knows where with Francine and I can't get hold of him! What a bloody circus this place is!"

Jerome had listened without saying a word, occasionally nodding with faked sympathy and noticing that, in his haste to be off, his colleague had forgotten to lock his office door.

Two minutes later, he heard Alma go upstairs to her room; she was sure not to come down again until the next morning.

He was alone.

Jerome had been offered an unexpected chance to snoop around in his colleague's office. Who knew, maybe he would find some proof, or at least evidence, of his betrayal?

Quietly, he went into Fradette's office, closed the door behind him, and listened. A soft rushing noise from the upstairs plumbing told him that Alma was taking a shower. Satisfied, he sat behind Fradette's desk, where he saw to his delight that none of the drawers was locked. He needed to act quickly, as Sicotte and his wife might show up at any moment, and he also had to work with care for Fradette not to know he'd been there. *Festina lente*, as the Romans used to say: *Hurry slowly*. He opened the middle drawer first, took a mental photograph of the arrangement of the objects inside it (ballpoints, felt-tipped pens, Post-it notes, etc.) so that he'd be able to return them to their places. He inspected the contents of a small cardboard box, then another, ran his fingers over everything, and then closed the drawer.

Nothing.

The large, deep drawer on the right was full to bursting with hanging files.

"I'd be really surprised to find anything interesting in here," he told himself, "but you never know."

He'd skimmed through a half-dozen dossiers without finding anything of value and was about to open another when a small cough made him look up.

Standing in the doorway, Felix was watching him with a big smile.

Jerome, caught in the act, stared at Felix for a moment with the feeling that the game was up. An idiotic joke came to his lips:

"Oh, hi. The cleaning lady's sick, so I'm taking her place today."

"So I see. Good of you to start with your best friend's desk. He'll be touched."

"You're quite right," answered Jerome, straightening the papers in the folder he had in his hand. "He's my very *best* friend. I'd give my life for him."

He started to leave the office.

"And if I had nine lives to give, I'd give them all. And now," he added, stopping in front of Felix, who was still standing in the doorway, "I suppose you're going to report me to your papa? Good timing, as I was just about to quit anyway."

Felix furrowed his brow.

"What do you take me for, you jerk. A snitch? Come on," he said, "I need to talk to you, but not here."

Jerome, still in a state of shock and wondering what was coming, nonetheless took a moment to inspect the room and make sure he'd left no trace of his visit. Then he followed his companion, who was striding swiftly towards the exit.

"What's up, Felix?" he asked.

"I feel like a beer" was all he said, once they were outside. "You?"

"Why not?"

He didn't think he had much choice.

A half-hour later they were in a brasserie on Jean-Talon.

"My treat," said Jerome, sinking into a leather chair that so many fat behinds had occupied during its long tenure that it was finally collapsing under the strain.

Despite the hubbub, animated by strobe lights and a mixture of blues, Greek ballads, and country and western music, the otherwise dimly lit room seemed dismal and airless.

"When you hear what I'm about to tell you," replied Felix with a somewhat boastful air, "you'll want to buy me more than one beer, Jerome. You'll want to buy me a dozen cases, at least."

A waitress in a leather miniskirt, a fringed vest with a plunging décolletage, and a cowgirl hat decorated with a red ribbon came to take their orders, provocatively batting her eyes.

"She's not bad, eh?" remarked Felix. "Wouldn't mind straddling her saddle for a while."

"So," said Jerome, impatiently, "what is it you want to tell me? I'm listening."

"Last night," replied Felix with sudden gravity, "at about one in the morning, I was sound asleep in my bed, lights off, when my parents came home from who knows what reception, and went upstairs to their room just down the hall from mine. They were a bit drunk, and arguing loudly about something, which is not unusual. All of a sudden I heard your name so I started to listen. They'd left their door partly open, but my mother came to close it so I got up without making any noise and eavesdropped . . . and you'll never guess what I heard, old friend!"

The cowgirl came back with a tray held at shoulder height in one hand, her voluptuous chest thrust forward, the very personification of an erotic Wild West.

"What did you learn?" Jerome asked impatiently, once she'd gone.

"You promise to keep this *entre nous*, right? If my parents ever found out it was me who told you, I'm done for."

"For fuck's sake, Felix, tell me what you heard. Deliver the goods."

Felix leaned over the table and looked his companion in the eye, his bold expression tainted with fear. In a low voice he said, "That guy in Varadero you clobbered when you came to my defence —"

"Yes, that guy?"

Felix's eyes started to shine and a childlike joy gave his face the look of an angel.

"He's not dead."

"Not dead?" Jerome repeated like an automaton.

He slammed his glass down on the table with such force that it spewed beer into the air.

"No . . . in fact, he's in great health — and that extradition order that Cuba is supposed to have issued against you?"

"It doesn't exist," said Jerome.

"Right."

There was a moment's silence. The two men simultaneously lifted their glasses and gulped down a long swig of beer.

"That's what they were arguing about last night," said Felix after wiping his mouth. "Dad wanted to tell you, because he really does think very highly of you, and the little trick they played has been bothering him for a long time."

"Little trick?" sneered Jerome. "Obviously it wasn't you they played it on."

Felix looked at him for a moment. "They've played other tricks on me that weren't quite so funny, you know."

Jerome groaned and lowered his gaze.

"Sorry… What you've just told me is so… disgusting… They're no saints, your parents, I know that, but I never thought them capable of such a low blow."

He looked around the room. Three tables over, a man in his sixties, with a grey beard and a withered face and wearing a checkered shirt, was chatting with the cowgirl, trying to rub her thigh. She let out a loud peal of laughter and dodged his hands. What a shitty job she had, thought Jerome. The smell of french fries and grilled beef hung in the air. He pinched his nostrils.

"They wanted power over me so they could buy my silence in case their own unscrupulous dealings came to light… or for some other reason, who knows…"

"Like I said, Dad didn't think their deception was necessary anymore. But Mother, she refused to open the trap. I'm not sure I understand why."

He paused.

"I told myself that after the favour you did me in Varadero, I'd be a real shithead not to tell you what I heard."

Jerome was hardly listening, overwhelmed as he was by a deluge of thoughts that made him breathe fitfully and robbed him of all strength. But he returned to the present with a jerk, stretched his hand across the table — almost knocking over his glass — and warmly shook that of his companion.

"You're a special guy, Felix...I was right about you all along."

Felix, flushed with pride, chewed his lips and gingerly laughed.

NOT LONG AFTERWARDS, they left the brasserie. Twenty minutes later, Jerome was home. Parking the car, he almost banged into another vehicle, and twice he tripped going up the stairs to his apartment. He was practically delirious with rage. Every fibre of his being cried out for vengeance. Sicotte's contrition, so pathetically late in the day, changed little.

He imagined himself bursting into the office at Caledonia Road, revolver in hand, and exacting his revenge on the scumbags—Fradette along with the rest of them. But that would be silly. Worse, it would be disastrous. He had to keep a cool head and analyze the situation.

But there's no containing such rage with impunity; one way or another, it will find its way to the surface. In Jerome, it took the prosaic form of a bout of serious indigestion that kept him on the toilet until two in the morning. It was as if his body were trying to void itself of all the villainy, baseness, and turpitude he had already committed or seen committed in his short life. And that was a good thing, as his indisposition prevented him from communicating with his employers on the spur of the moment and using up all his ammunition in a single burst of gunfire, reducing his ability to manoeuvre to zero. Above all, it allowed him to think, to arrive at certain conclusions and put together the beginnings of a plan. One thing was certain: things could not remain as they were.

It was clear to him now that the lousy turn he'd been done

when Eugenie was told about his relationship with Alma (it couldn't have been anything else) hadn't been orchestrated by Alma or Fradette. It had to have been Francine Desjarlais, the bitch who'd so perfidiously manipulated him with the trumped-up story of homicide in Varadero. She must have taken a great deal of pleasure in having her little tête-à-tête with Eugenie, and if Alma or Fradette had been involved it would have been on her instructions. There was no use bothering about those two, he needed to focus on the engine behind the deception. From now on, a total shutdown was his goal.

His stomach cramps and heartburn gradually diminished, and he was eventually able to get some sleep. At 9 a.m. he telephoned the office to say he wouldn't be in that day as he wasn't feeling well. His call was answered by Alma, who hardly recognized his voice.

"Nothing serious, I hope?"

The concern in her voice surprised him; surely he didn't deserve it.

"No, no, I'll be fine. Probably something I ate. I'll be back on my feet tomorrow."

A few minutes later, over a breakfast of herbal tea and a slice of whole-wheat bread, a second realization came to him, half-formed and uncertain as it was. To the question he'd posed himself a hundred times about what could possibly have been his employers' motivation to engineer his break with Eugenie, he suddenly discerned a thin thread leading to Minister Juneau. But that brought him up against an enigma: why on Earth would the minister's sex life be of any interest to Sicotte and his wife? Were they working for her or on her behalf?

He filed it all away in his mind's trunk of hypotheses and went back to bed.

Come noon, his cell phone woke him up. His device was on the kitchen table and he dashed naked across the apartment, stubbing the little toe of his right foot against the leg of a chair, to reach it. When Jerome finally picked up, what Sicotte heard was the near-death voice of someone saying, "*Oui*, hello?" in three unelided syllables.

"Good Lord, Jerome, you sound a mess. Alma just told me you're not well."

"Just a stomach bug," said Jerome, sweat running down his forehead as he watched his bruised toe balloon before his eyes.

"Good," sighed Sicotte. "Take care of yourself. We'll see you tomorrow?"

"I don't think I'll be able to come in tomorrow, either," Jerome said, suddenly consumed by an urgent desire to be left alone.

"Your call, lad," replied Sicotte in the solemn, gravelly voice he used when trying to sound kind. "Do what you think best. You're the one who knows how you feel."

But the man sounded highly put out.

JEROME MADE HIS way to the pharmacy and bought a splint for his toe, then returned to his apartment and plopped himself in a chair, his right foot stretched out on a hassock to ease the stabbing pain, and spent a good hour trying to think of some reason for their sabotaging his affair with Eugenie.

In whatever variation of the hypothesis he did eventually construct, the name Juneau was in the picture.

His phone rang.

"Hey, how's it going?" said an exuberant Charlie.

"I'll live."

"Which means you thought you might not," Charlie translated. "What's up, old chum?"

"I'll tell you some other time. I don't have the stomach for it right now."

"As you wish," replied his friend, knowing how useless it was to insist. "Anyway, there's a Hitchcock festival on at the Cinéma du Parc this week, and tonight at eight they're showing *Vertigo*. Feel like going?"

Jerome hesitated for a second, then decided he would. They agreed to meet at the theatre ten minutes before show time.

Charlie had seen the film three times, but Jerome, who owned the DVD, had lost count of how often he'd watched it. On the big screen of the cinema, however, Hitchcock's work reminded him of his childhood with incredible force. The two friends watched in silence, like pilgrims fascinated by the appearance of the Holy Virgin. For a few precious moments, Jerome even forgot about the ball of thorns spinning around in his brain. As they left the theatre, he decided to share the fruits of his deliberations with his friend.

They went to a Spanish restaurant in the neighbourhood, and Charlie, after listening attentively to his companion, posed many questions and asked for a few clarifications, widened his eyes in astonishment a gratifying number of times, and finally uttered the verdict Jerome had been awaiting with impatience.

"Hmm... what you've deduced is very reasonable... though you are assuming that everyone involved is crooked as a corkscrew. Still, there's no dearth of people like that on this planet... When you think about how they conned you with that Varadero story, it seems to make sense."

In fact, everything had fallen into place like the pieces

of a jigsaw puzzle. And the picture that emerged was not a pleasant one!

On the one hand, there was a minister with whom Sicotte wanted to collude in a scam involving bogus contracts for the construction of a "French Canadian" museum. They knew she was ambitious, sly, and as forbidding as a frenzy of sharks, but they also knew her weak spot: a certain resemblance to Catherine the Great—who, it was said, had taken to her imperial bed every soldier in the royal guard—and more than a few others—to assuage her insatiable appetite for the phallus. So far, nothing special. Gossips feed on the private lives of all and sundry, and rumours of the minister were titillating and shameless but effectively harmless, given the liberality of the age. But then along comes what should have been a run-of-the-mill fundraiser organized for said minister in Montreal: Sicotte brings Jerome, his favoured employee, presents him to Madame Minister, and *thwap!* Cupid's arrow buries itself deep in the minister's heart. She scribbles her private phone number on her personal business card and has it brought to Jerome who, caught off-guard, doesn't get the message right away, because he's unaware of the minister's voracious libido. He relates the incident to his boss, who laughs and jauntily encourages him to take advantage of a fortuitous development in his professional career—given that a lobbyist lucky enough to lie in bed with power leaves his competitors in the dust. Jerome, alas, already has a girlfriend with whom he is very much in love; but curiously, for various reasons, she spends a good part of the summer alone in Europe. He finds his hot, solitary summer interminable, and thus does not deprive himself of the pleasure of sleeping with the office secretary—and not just once. How interesting! And now the girlfriend is home again and he still hasn't responded to the minister's clear come-hither, the clueless dawdler. So the boss, increasingly concerned, decides to nudge events along and informs the girlfriend about his employee's adventures with the office secretary. Bingo! The way has been cleared. But there's no time to waste: Jerome, after all, isn't the only fish in the sea, and Madame Minister might any minute stop pining for him.

"Pretty sickening," said Charlie, sighing and shaking his head.

He raised his decaf cappuccino to his lips, giving himself a thin white moustache that he removed with his tongue, then smiled. *Vertigo* and Jerome's story had melded in his mind, giving him the impression that his life had become an adventure. The thought put him in an excellent mood.

"What do you plan on doing?" he asked.

"I haven't decided yet. But things can't stay as they are, that's for sure. I have wet dreams about seeing the lot of them sinking in a vat of cowshit and slamming the lid on their heads."

"Well, for now don't let on that anything's amiss, Jerome. Gather the evidence, gain some time. And above all, for crying out loud, find another job!"

But almost immediately Charlie's analytical mind, possessing him like a demon, went into gear.

"That being said, I think you've been a bit naive, don't you? That little test they put you through in Place Versailles, didn't that tell you anything? I warned you at the time. Sicotte and his wife had to be crooks, and since all crooks are by definition manipulative, then they were manipulating you — and boy, did they ever!"

"Thanks for your support . . . and for your extraordinary insights," replied Jerome coolly, his feet tapping the floor beneath the table. "You're a big help. I absolutely needed someone to remind me that I'm naive, even a bit stupid. Keep going, I'm dying to hear more."

Embarrassed, Charlie half-rose from his chair and patted his friend's shoulder, assuring him he had the greatest respect for his intelligence. His was an extraordinarily astute mind to have come to the conclusions he'd just expounded.

"All you need now is to test your theory," he said, with an equivocal smile.

"Yeah... and that's a whole other quagmire."

"Really? I don't find this Minister Juneau so bad. She won't eat you. And you'll have some wonderful memories to share when you're old and grey..."

"I don't give a flying fuck what I'll have to talk about when I'm old and grey, Charlie. If I see her, I'll just get deeper and deeper in the shit with Eugenie. Have you thought of that? You say one thing and then the opposite: three seconds ago you wanted me to find another job, and now you're advising me to sleep with Juneau?"

Charlie, caught short, opened his mouth to speak, closed it again, and then managed to blurt out, "Why not sleep with her? Whatever happens, you and Eugenie are finished, right? So what's wrong with having a bit of fun while you're on this secret mission of theirs? And there's more, my friend. This might provide you the means to avenge yourself on your paymasters, you never know. So sleep with the minister!"

"I think that Martine of yours has turned you into something of a pervert," said Jerome, laughing bitterly. "And by the way, when am I going to meet her? I could practise on her before going to see Juneau."

Charlie, offering up a saccharine smile, gave him the finger. Then he glanced at his watch, took a final gulp of his cappuccino, and stood up.

"Shall we go? I have to work tomorrow."

Jerome dropped him off at his place. Charlie, careful with his money and a fervent advocate of public transit, refused to buy his own car. Jerome leaned over to shake his buddy's hand and noticed a woman's profile in one of the windows of Charlie's apartment.

"Is that Martine?" he asked. "Why didn't she come to the movie with us?"

Charlie looked a little embarrassed. "Because she, er... she hates movies with violence in them... They give her nightmares."

Jerome patted him on the shoulder.

"Go comfort her. She needs you."

Charlie stepped out of the car and turned towards Jerome.

"I'd introduce you to her now, but it's a bit late, you understand. She gets up at six to go to work."

"Go, old friend, Eros is our master in all things."

During the drive home, Jerome reflected on their discussion and, by the time he'd reached his apartment, had come around to Charlie's point of view. All things considered, his friend had seen things correctly. The bridges between him and Eugenie were completely burned. Everything he could have lost had been lost. But from this loss he'd wrest glorious revenge. How? For the moment, he had no idea.

"Sicotte, you can piss off," he mumbled as he stepped into the shower. "Tomorrow, I'm going back to work."

A PHONE CALL on the Thursday night from someone calling himself Olivier Fradette had intrigued Eugenie. It was the beginning of September, she'd been back from Spain barely a week, and her luggage was still piled in her bedroom. The unknown caller said he was a colleague of Jerome's.

He apologized for calling her at home, but he had something important to discuss with her, a matter that concerned them both.

"Both of us?" she'd said, surprised and dubious. "I don't even know you."

"No, but we have an acquaintance in common," replied the unknown voice, calmly and politely.

"First of all, how did you get my phone number?"

"I had to make use of certain means at my disposal," answered the caller. "Believe me, ma'am, I'm not calling on a whim. It required a great deal of effort to make this call."

"So what's it about?"

A harrowing sense of apprehension came over her; she suddenly felt as though her bra had become too small for her.

"I'd rather we spoke in person, ma'am. You'll understand why right away. Obviously," he quickly added, "I'll leave it up to you to decide where."

Eugenie hesitated. The receiver almost slid from her moist fingers, and she had to grip it more firmly. First a friend of Jerome's had asked for a meeting to discuss him, and now here was another of his colleagues asking for his turn.

"You must have my address, too," she said, her tender voice causing the caller to smile. "When can you get here?"

"In less than twenty minutes, I figure."

"I'll be here."

As Eugenie went into her daughter's bedroom — Andrée-Anne had been woken by the sound of the telephone — Fradette returned whistling to his car, impatient to experience one of the most delicious moments of his career: one in which professional duties and personal interests coincided. That didn't happen often.

Earlier that summer, Sicotte had asked Fradette to install a tiny surveillance camera in Alma's bedroom; at the time, he hadn't wanted to tell Fradette why. All he'd said was it had to do with an "exploratory" project, and he'd demanded absolute secrecy. The camera had caught some truly satisfying scenes: Alma in a pink nightie masturbating in front of the television while chewing gum; Alma lying across her bed, shaken by a fit of tears—and best of all, and this is what enthralled Sicotte most of all, two long episodes showing her in bed with Jerome. (During the second, she'd had to help the young man get an erection, Jerome obviously having had too much to drink.)

Sicotte, watching the two assignations, slapped his thigh and laughed out loud. And then, giving Fradette a friendly poke in the ribs, handed him a hundred-dollar bill. Still, the first episode ran a bit long for his liking and had to be cut by three or four minutes.

"I want it to have maximum effect, you see... Don't get me wrong, I'm not a voyeur." Then, with a perverse and cheerful smirk, he asked, "Do you know whom I want you to show this cinematic masterpiece to?"

His bulbous eyes half-closed, Fradette mulled over the question for a few seconds.

"Ah, the girlfriend!"

"Hole-in-one, my boy!"

"May I ask why?"

"If my plan works out," replied Sicotte with a wink, "you'll know soon enough."

That evening, Fradette edited the recording. He enjoyed the task as it provided an opportunity for him to perfect his technical skills. But he had another reason for savouring the success of his mission; sexual revenge was equally his motivation.

Fradette had never had much of a prodigious libido. Fucking once or twice a month usually satisfied his needs and, for a short while, a discreet understanding with Alma had taken care of that. On either a Friday or Saturday night, he'd invite her out for dinner or to the movies—but never both on the same date, as it would keep him up too late—and afterwards they would end the evening at his place. Alma had always insisted on being back at Caledonia Road before midnight; she called it her Cinderella Clause, and it defined the relationship for both of them.

But then, one day, the little tart had fallen for Felix, Papa's little pothead. But after Felix went to Portage, Fradette had made several advances to Alma and all of them had been rebuffed. The reason was soon apparent: she was sleeping with Jerome! He hadn't let on that he knew, nursing his anger like a cow chewing its cud, but he promised himself the revenge he could never have taken on the son of his employer. Ever since, he'd been obliged to content himself with the services of a massage parlour, fortunately not too far from where he lived.

The next day he showed the fruit of his labours to Sicotte, who congratulated him and asked that he arrange for a meeting with Eugenie as soon as she got back to Montreal, to let her know about her boyfriend's shenanigans.

Never before had the prospect of a meeting given him so much pleasure. Fradette outdid himself in his artifice, perfectly controlling his intonation and ceding to the young woman no more information than was strictly necessary to pique her curiosity. The semblance of goodwill he put on was emotionally detached, and so much so that if his employer had asked him to strangle her—a preposterous assumption, of course—he might well have done so, what with it being an even more effective way of revenging himself on his odious colleague.

It was twenty minutes to nine when he rang the bell of Eugenie's apartment.

"Sorry I'm late," he apologized, after introducing himself. "I had to take a detour. There was a traffic jam on Jean-Talon, probably an accident."

"What's that you're carrying?" asked Eugenie right off the bat, pointing to the briefcase in his hand.

He bowed his head to look.

"My computer, ma'am. There's something I need to show you."

Seeing her turn pale, he added, "Believe me, I'm enjoying this no more than you are."

She bade him come in and, without a word, led him into her study and shut the door. He set his briefcase on the desk, took out his laptop, and turned it on. She stood behind him silently, her arms crossed, breathing erratically. He was disappointed, realizing his mission was bringing him much less pleasure than he'd anticipated.

"This is it, ma'am," he said, starting the video. "I should point out that the woman you see here is my wife, or might as well be — I'm sorry, but I had to let you know."

Seeing Jerome, she let out a stifled gasp. Eyes stretched wide, hands pressed against her mouth, she observed the cavorting of the couple for ten seconds or so, then seized the computer to shut it down. The device slipped from her hands and fell to the floor with a loud crack, and the screen went black. Now it was Fredette's turn to let out an anguished cry. He bent over to pick up the computer and their heads banged together in a farcical scene, though no one seeing it would have laughed.

"Get out of here," said Eugenie tersely.

She didn't seem to have felt any pain from their collision, but Fradette was rubbing a large red bruise on his forehead.

The next instant, he was gone.

JEROME WAS FACED with what was undoubtedly one of the greatest challenges of his life: to seem calm and full of friendliness towards people he would gladly have throttled. He'd classified them in descending order of contemptibility. First, of course, was Francine Desjarlais; coming a close second was her meddling husband; and bringing up the rear was his loathsome colleague, Olivier Fradette, that louse with a human face willingly seeing to the first two's dirty work. He'd more or less exonerated Alma, feeling now that he'd been judging her too harshly.

His first day back at work had been relatively easy to get through because he was able to blame his lack of enthusiasm on the gastrointestinal troubles that had kept him home the day before. But no one suffers from a simple bout of indigestion indefinitely, and after that first day back he went through a period of "pretending to do" that went hand-in-hand with the no less taxing "what to do?" To take his revenge by denouncing his boss to the authorities was better than nothing, but the role of stool pigeon didn't sit well with him, and he needed to take into account the not insignificant fact of his having been an accomplice of those he'd be denouncing. He needed something more satisfying; his sorry, deflated ego needed pumping up.

Which is when he remembered his appointment with Minister Juneau eight days hence—unless there was a cancellation, of course. On the surface, their meeting didn't seem to open up any interesting avenues for his vengeance project; on the contrary, it might even make it more complex and hazardous. But after all, you can only play the cards you're dealt, and leave the rest up to chance and instinct.

He hadn't yet informed Sicotte about the meeting. He decided to do so right away, and went to Sicotte's office. The door was closed but he could hear his employer in conversation with Fradette. The two men were speaking in such hushed tones it sounded conspiratorial. What could they be up to?

He knocked.

"Come in, Jerome," said the lawyer heartily.

"I see you're busy," Jerome replied as agreeably as he was able. "I'll come back later. I have some important news for you, Severin."

Sicotte looked up at Fradette, who was standing beside him, bent over what looked like a sort of ledger, lying on the desk.

"We've covered everything, haven't we?" said Sicotte.

"Just about."

Fradette closed the book, slipped it under his arm, and began walking to the door.

"All is well?" Jerome asked him.

"Tickety-boo," he replied with a somewhat apprehensive smile.

"Good," said Jerome, "hang in there, my friend."

He gave Fradette the thumbs-up but in his mind, added: "You piece of shit. Wait until you see what's in store...I'm going to flush you down the toilet, pal."

"Well, Jerome," said Sicotte, pointing to a chair, "what's your big news?"

"I'm meeting Minister Juneau on the twenty-fourth," he said, assuming a modest countenance.

"Wow!" cried the lobbyist, his face lighting up with a jubilation so intense he resembled a beach ball. He thrust *two* thumbs up in the air.

"But it's only a meeting, Severin. At her office."

"Trust me, I know how things roll. You didn't expect her to invite you into her bedroom straight off, did you?"

He giggled like a schoolboy and the look he gave Jerome was filled with warmth and pride — like that of a coach whose trainee has just won a gold medal.

Jerome detested him, though he was also surprised because he was feeling a measure of sympathy for someone so ignoble.

The sound of a car starting up and driving off came from the parking lot: Fradette must have just left.

"You're a smart lad, Jerome," Sicotte went on. "Smarter than most. If things go well with Juneau, if only for a few months or even weeks, it will be *in-com-par-a-bly* good for us, believe me."

"We don't want to bite off more than we can chew, Severin."

"You've got the teeth for it, my boy . . . So why are you looking at *me* like that? Like you want to chew on *me*!"

Jerome forced a laugh.

"I'm looking at you as I always do, Severin."

But his cheeks had started to burn.

"Well then, I, too, have news for you, and I don't think it'll upset you."

Severin let a few moments pass, as if to secure maximum possible effect.

"Olivier is leaving the office. We're sending him to Varadero to run our hotel operations there."

"Oh good" was all Jerome said.

He busied himself by staring at a bronze statuette of a water nymph standing on one foot on the Boulle desk.

"Francine and I have noticed for some time now that all has not been a bed of roses between the two of you...No, don't shrug it off like that, my boy. Good relations within a team like ours is *pri-mor-dial*, I've said that often enough."

He picked up a coffee that had gone cold beside the stapler, took a sip, and went on. "But that's not the only reason we're sending him to Cuba. Olivier made a mistake. A huge mistake—one that concerns you, in fact."

"Oh, good," Jerome repeated, though he was increasingly uneasy.

Sicotte, suddenly serious, coughed and took another sip of coffee.

"How long has it been since you saw your girlfriend, Jerome? Her name is Eugenie, if I'm not mistaken."

The young man turned crimson.

"That's my personal business, Severin," he hissed, his expression suddenly nasty.

"I understand, my boy, but I'll tell you what happened, anyway. I've been obliged, go figure, to settle a matter of jealousy between you two. Over Alma, who, it seems, you *stole* from him over the course of the summer. I don't judge anyone, Jerome, the only thing that matters to me is business, keep that in mind."

And he told Jerome about Fradette's visit to Eugenie, modifying a few details to hide his own involvement.

Jerome blanched and listened with mounting agitation, then leapt out of his chair.

"I'll kill him, the son of a bitch!"

Sicotte rose to his full height behind the desk.

"You'll do nothing of the kind," he thundered. "He

doesn't work here anymore, do you hear me? I've exiled him to Cuba. Isn't that enough for you? He behaved badly, yes, but all you needed to do was sow your wild oats somewhere else, for Christ's sake!"

Jerome stared, dumfounded. He tried to reply, but all that came out was a kind of gurgling. He spun on his heels, almost tipping over the precious Boulle chair he was sitting on, and hurried out of the office shouting as his eyes instinctively turned to Fradette's office door, where the tiny click of a bolt sliding into place told him the door was only now being locked. He hadn't left?

"*Fradette!*" he yelled. "Come out of your office, you bloody coward! I need to talk to you!"

Everything happened quickly. Sicotte, then his wife, then Alma appeared in the corridor to watch the epic scene: Jerome, wild with rage, had thrown himself against the door, which broke open with a splintering crack. Fradette, livid, was sitting behind his desk and holding a paperweight as a weapon. He threw it at his assailant and missed his target, entirely the wrong thing to do as Jerome then rushed towards him, fuming with rage, and landed a punch so hard it knocked Fradette back against the wall, his lip spurting blood. That blow was followed by a second, even more carefully directed, and no one knew how the scene might have played out had Sicotte not thrown himself upon Jerome and immobilized him, allowing Fradette to flee through the open door.

Jerome and his employer looked at each other without speaking; the only sound was that of their breathing.

"What a mess," sighed Francine, standing in the doorway. "I've never seen the like . . . and in my own house!"

Jerome laughed wickedly.

"This is only a taste," he said. "The rest is still to come."

Sicotte took him by the arm.

"Don't make me do something I'll regret... Enough of this, do you understand me?"

Jerome shook him off and left the room, heading towards the door. Alma, who'd wisely stayed at a distance by her office door, winked as he passed.

"You didn't miss," she whispered.

He rubbed his fists and didn't so much as glance her way.

Then came the sound of a second car starting. Jerome had left the premises.

Sicotte, after contemplating the room in frustration, went back to his own office. His wife quickly followed him.

"Now what?"

"You saw what happened. He's gone."

"Why didn't you wait until Olivier had left before giving Jerome the news?"

"I thought he *had* left! I heard a car start up in the parking lot."

"That was Felix."

He sighed, dropped back into his chair, and stretched out his legs, looking dejected.

Francine came up behind him and rubbed his neck.

"Don't worry, he'll be back, your Jerome. I'm sure of it. He doesn't have a choice..."

She observed him a moment, then said, "I have to go take care of Olivier now — and get that door fixed."

On his own again, Sicotte nervously ran his hand through his hair with a harried look on his face. He took another sip of cold coffee, and spat it back into the cup: now the liquid tasted vile.

TWO DAYS PASSED. Jerome went to ground in his apartment. Ten times, he came close to telephoning Eugenie, always hanging up at the last second. What could he say? That he'd been so despicably betrayed by a colleague didn't mitigate for a moment his own act of betrayal.

Early in the afternoon of the second day, his father called to find out what was up. Claude-Oscar rarely phoned, and this call surprised and moved him.

"What are you doing, son? I just called your office and they say you've been away for a while. Are you not well?"

"I decided to take some time off, Dad. We work hard at the office, you know."

"So what are you doing?"

"I'm rereading Balzac's *Lost Illusions*. Have you read it?"

"Yes, a long time ago. Back when I had all my hair. Apart from reading, my little one, *quid novi?*"

"I'm catching up on some lost sleep."

"Then come over for supper. It's been light years since we've seen you. I'm beginning to forget what you look like."

Jerome said nothing, suddenly incapable of speech, and his eyes filled with tears. In the background he heard a student learning to play Schumann's *Träumerei* on the piano and making a clumsy job of it. Jerome himself used to play it a lot better than that.

"So, will you come? Your mother would love to talk to you, but she's with a student."

"Yes, okay, Dad," he said after clearing his throat, "I'll be there around six. See you soon."

He took a shower, made a stab at tidying his apartment, so chaotic it looked like a tornado had gone through it, made some coffee, and reimmersed himself in *Lost Illusions*. Curiously, the story of the decline and fall of Lucien de

Rubempré, a brilliant but vain and fallible young man trying to make a go of it in Paris, comforted him. It allowed him
to distance himself from the immorality of the human condition—the core element, it seemed to him, of all societies.

The previous evening he'd called Charlie and brought
him up to date on the treachery of which he'd been the
victim.

"Come on, let's go out for a beer," Charlie had immediately proposed. "We can talk about your problem and I can
introduce you to Martine, since I've been telling you about
her for so long... She'll join us later on."

"Thanks, Charlie, but for now I'd rather stay here."

"And what are you doing there?"

"Hanging out with a guy named Balzac."

"The writer?"

"The same. A formidable fellow, and all the more so
because I don't have to put up with his defects. He's been
six feet underground for a hell of a long time."

"Whereas me, Martine, and all the rest are still very
much alive, with all that that implies... Fine, take the solitary cure, old pal. Call me when you need some contact with
this poor human race, but don't wait too long."

Then, in a more serious tone, Charlie added, "Your story
interests me, and I might end up very worried about you."

"I'll call you shortly, I promise, as soon as I've got
all my ducks in a row. You have to understand what I'm
like, Charlie... I need to be alone in order to recharge my
batteries."

JEROME FOUND THE evening at his parents' house very pleasant. Spending a few hours with people who seemed to have
no other earthly purpose than to see to his wellbeing perked

him up, despite the fact that he'd kept them completely in the dark about what was happening to him and had no intention of enlightening them. Buoyed by the spaghetti carbonara and two helpings of raspberry parfait in his stomach, he sat down at the piano and tried to make his fingers remember *Träumerei*. Not long after, to his great astonishment, he was able to play it.

"You should take lessons again," his mother suggested.

"I'm going to buy you a piano," said Claude-Oscar.

His little brother Marcel — who was becoming less and less "little" and seemed destined to be several centimetres taller than Jerome in a year or two — asked if he wanted to see his comic-book collection (a privilege accorded to very few people). Off they went to Marcel's room and spent a long time there, finishing up with a wrestling match from which Jerome emerged with a bruised tibia, but his mind refreshed, clarified, revivified.

On the way home, he decided to call Charlie. They arranged to meet that night, and it was during the course of their late-evening get-together that a plan, still vague in its details, of breathtaking audacity, was hatched.

Charlie was with Martine and came to the door in his dressing gown, as if to make the nature of his relationship even clearer than it had been. The young woman, however, decided it more appropriate to get dressed and redo her makeup. She was very pretty, with lovely skin, pink cheeks and long, nut-brown hair. Quite petite, she wore a very short skirt that allowed Jerome to admire her legs, which were magnificent. But she had a purposeful air and he sensed right away that she was much more than a piece of arm candy.

Charlie, glowing with pride, introduced her as the person "responsible for running the National Comedy School."

"Responsible?" she said, laughing. "Maybe one day, Charlie, but for now, I'm merely the assistant."

She offered her hand to Jerome, her expression engaging and full of assurance.

"Charlie's told me a lot about you," she said in a high-pitched voice that had a lively, crystalline timbre. "From what I understand, you're his best friend and I gather the two of you have something important to talk about. Don't worry, I'll make myself scarce."

"No, no," Charlie protested. "The fire hasn't reached the house yet, Martine, there's plenty of time. Stay a while. Would you like a beer, Martine? Jerome, I've got some Blanche de Chambly."

"I'll split one with you, Charlie," said Martine, "and then I'll leave. Bro stories don't interest me all that much."

Eight minutes later, she tossed back the last of her beer, gave Charlie a long, full-mouthed kiss, and said goodbye to Jerome with a polite smile. The stairs echoed with the sound of her heels; in the time she'd spent with them, she'd been able to give Jerome an encapsulated version of her life, thrown in a few leftist political opinions, and arranged her next rendezvous with Charlie.

"Tell me," said Jerome, a little subdued, once they heard the downstairs door close, "how did you meet that little marvel?"

"Oh, in a café nearby. One night when I was feeling depressed I went there for a latte and to read the newspaper, sure I was in for a sleepless night by having caffeine so late. She came in with a friend and the two of them sat at a table close to mine. I heard them laughing, athough I couldn't tell what they were laughing about. I didn't care, it was just good to hear someone laugh. Then Martine told her friend a joke and it was so funny I couldn't help laughing, too. I apologized, and Martine said she didn't mind at all, and it was so much better than when you tell a joke and it falls flat. The next minute I was sitting at their table and we were talking about all sorts of things and nothing in particular. After twenty minutes, it felt like I was gabbing with old friends. Laurie — Martine's friend — got a call and had to leave. Martine and I went on talking, but it was getting late and I could see we had to go. I don't know what got into me, because it isn't like me at all, as you know, but I told her I lived just down the street, and I'd never met anyone as extraordinary and pretty as she was, etc. etc., and that I'd be the happiest guy in the world if she'd come back with me and spend the night. I was expecting a polite refusal or, maybe worse, to be made fun of...but she said yes! It was written in the stars that I wouldn't get any sleep that night."

"You've never told me that story," said Jerome. "Getting secretive in your old age?"

"We all have our private lives, my friend. We don't all walk in the same shoes."

"That I have to admit."

Then he added, "She must lead you about by the nose."

"She leads me by something, but it's not my nose," said Charlie, laughing. Then, abruptly, he changed his tone: "But from what I know you didn't come here to listen to me talk about my love life. What's up?"

"Well, what's up is..."

And under the effect of a strange mental shortcut, he proposed to Charlie an inchoate plan that quickly metamorphosed into an irreversible decision.

"In two days, I'm meeting with Minister Juneau. I'm going to play the role to the hilt — well, as far as she'll let me, anyway. And when I've gathered enough proof, I'm going to blow Sicotte's operation sky high."

Charlie looked at him without speaking, his high spirits dampened and prey to an apprehension that tightened his lips and creased his cheeks. "Blow his...is a figure of speech, I hope?"

Jerome laughed skittishly.

"What, you think I don't mean it?" he said. "Well, I'm not a member of Al-Qaeda, as you know. I'm using a metaphor, Charlie—from time to time I like to remind people I have a degree in literature."

"Right."

Charlie put his hands on his knees, dropped his head, and thought for a moment.

"Another Blanche de Chambly?"

"I wouldn't say no. It's warm in here, don't you find?"

Charlie smiled wryly. "Only in the last twenty seconds, Jerome."

He went to the fridge, came back with two beers, and set them on the table.

"You know what you're getting into, don't you? It's a dangerous game you'll be playing, old chum...more so because you were an accomplice to Monsieur and Madame...If your plan works too well, they won't spare you and neither will their friends. Be ready to find yourself in the headlines and dragged into court...maybe even to jail."

Jerome started to laugh. The longer the list of consequences, the more it galvanized him. The need to be a hero or a martyr—or both at the same time—had suddenly become a reason to live. Never had he felt so good. To recover his self-respect by wreaking vengeance, what a tonic! It justified any risk he might have to take.

"Listen, Charlie, if I don't do what I've just said I won't be able to look at myself in a mirror anymore. You understand, don't you? I'd end up being like that rubby, you'd find me on a street corner somewhere."

Charlie threw up his hands as if to say, "All the same, all the same, don't do anything stupid!"

"Let's drink to my plan!" cried Jerome.

Carried away by the moment, he clinked his bottle so hard against Charlie's that the glass almost smashed in their hands. The noise frightened Charlie's elderly upstairs neighbour so much that he took himself to bed.

"Hey, easy!" Charlie protested. "You're splattering beer on my dressing gown!"

"Baptism by fire — or at least by beer!" said Jerome happily.

He stood up and, taking Charlie by the shoulders, looked deep into his friend's eyes.

"You know, Charlie, I'm probably going to need your help with this . . . This'll be when I'll see if you really are my friend. Are you my friend, Charlie?"

"Funny question, that," babbled Charlie as he released himself from Jerome's grip. "Really, after all these years? Calm down, old chum! Have you been drinking?"

WHEN HE ARRIVED at work the next morning, there was a message waiting for him from Minister Juneau's office, confirming their appointment for the following day but pushing it back half an hour, to 4:30. A little shiver ran down his spine. The euphoria of the previous night had waned somewhat, but the morning still went fairly well. No one mentioned the incident of the day before; it might as well not have happened. Fradette had vanished — God be praised and let the devil take him!—too busy with preparations for his transfer to Cuba to come to work, they said. His office door had been repaired and the room put in order. Sicotte was strangely amiable; three times he came into Jerome's office to ask for clarification about some minor technical issue concerning the future museum. The last time, he even complimented Jerome on his way out, saying he valued Jerome's keen memory and acuity. This was not something he was in the habit of doing. Around 10:30—oh, what a surprise!—Francine came in with a café au lait and a plate of warm chocolate biscuits smothered in butter.

"Try these, my boy, I'm sure you're hungry. I just discovered a wonderful patisserie in Westmount Square. Run by some Moroccans who learned their trade in Bordeaux. Heavenly! And not too expensive, either."

Jerome's employers' cozying up to him didn't disturb him at all, because he had come to consider them as future victims. And when, a half-hour later, he encountered Alma in the hallway, he put on a big smile. He felt sorry for her now, a poor little nympho who'd no doubt been taken advantage of in a perfidious Machiavellian plot to which she was not privy.

At noon, Sicotte, a broad grin chiselled into his face, invited him to lunch. But this was too much, way too much. Sitting in close quarters with him would have been torture, so Jerome begged off, saying the *pains au chocolat* Francine had given him "weren't sitting well." And from that point on, he found the very sound of their voices insufferable: he was developing an allergic reaction to phoniness.

He needed a change of scenery. He went into Sicotte's office and found him on the phone.

The lawyer interrupted his conversation and put his hand over the receiver.

"Yes, Jerome?" he said, forcing a smile. "What can I do for you?"

"I'm meeting the minister tomorrow, and—"

"I haven't forgotten, my boy!"

"—I need to make a few purchases first. Can I have the rest of the day off?"

"Take all the time you want, my boy, you have my blessing *urbi et orbi*. If I need you for anything, I'll give you a buzz."

Jerome bowed his head and was headed for the door when Sicotte stopped him with a wave, suddenly serious.

"Yes?"

"Good luck, my man. You have class and you comport yourself well. Don't forget, fortune favours the brave."

Jerome laughed, but was uneasy.

"It probably won't be what you're thinking!"

The lawyer dismissed the thought. "My little finger has its own ideas about that . . . Get in her good graces and great things can happen."

"You can count on me, my crocodile," mumbled Jerome as he left. "If my plan goes the way I hope it does, you'll soon be hauling your Boulle furniture out to a yard sale!"

HE'D NOT BEEN lying about the need to buy a few things. He visited a chic store in the west end of the city and bought a half-dozen shirts, a pair of pants, some sexy underwear (he chose them with a sly smile), and a brand of after-shave lotion he'd always denied himself because of its outrageous price tag. "Sicotte's paying, so go nuts."

He'd decided to spend the night in his apartment, but this time Balzac was no help because he just could not concentrate. He turned on the TV and began channel surfing, but everything was stultifying. The evening was agreeable

and warm, so he decided to go for a walk in the neighbourhood. He ran into an old friend from university with whom
he'd hung out for a while (they were both into swimming
and crossed paths fairly often at the university pool), so they
headed to a brasserie. In the intervening few years, Richard
had lost some hair and put on weight but retained his jovial,
almost childlike good nature; he was teaching literature at
a CEGEP in Old Montreal, was going to be a father for the
second time, and was the co-editor of a dictionary of syno-
nyms for a publisher of scholarly manuals.

After catching up on their news, and recalling a few old
anecdotes, the two former friends found little else to say to
each other.

"I've got to go," Jerome announced. "Big day tomorrow.
Shall we get the bill?"

Twenty minutes later, he was in bed, staring at the ceiling. Come midnight, he was still staring at it.

"This is crazy," he said to himself. "I'm a nervous wreck!
For Christ's sake, she's just a woman like any other woman,
with the same limitations and idiosyncracies as anyone
else. I'm swimming in a fantasy world... And even more so
because nothing is likely to happen."

He was surprised by just how intimidating was the power
of her position, even for those on the circuit. He remembered how Sicotte, who'd been hanging out with politicians
for years and knew all their secrets, was so nervous he was
practically stammering, the night he'd been introduced to
Minister Juneau.

And it was during his reflections on the vanity of human
affairs that he abruptly fell asleep, not opening his eyes again
until mid-morning, when he was awakened by his telephone.
It was Felix.

"It's really not going well with my folks," said the young man in a stifled voice, as if he were out of breath. "I've got to get the fuck out of here. Can you put me up for a day or two, till I find myself some digs?"

Jerome frowned. He wanted to say no, but knew it would be churlish of him to refuse.

"Come on over, Felix. What's going on? Total war? Are you burning your bridges?"

"I'll tell you when I get there. But if I stay here one more day I swear I'll murder one of them. Jesus!"

"I'll be here."

"You're a lifesaver. I'll owe you."

"You've already paid me, Felix."

"Is there parking at your place?"

"Montreal is Montreal, but at this time of day you shouldn't have any problem."

He hung up. Talk about bad timing. He'd set aside two or three hours to bone up on the Museum *d'la belle province* (as he called it) since, after all, that was the official reason he was seeing the minister—and could well be the only reason. But poor Felix seemed genuinely upset.

He suddenly felt as if a sliver of ice had been thrust into his stomach. Maybe Felix had inadvertently let slip some unexpected news. During an argument with his parents, for example, perhaps he'd uttered a sentence or two of the nighttime conversation he'd overheard between his mother and father regarding their duplicity about the incident in Varadero. Perhaps he'd revealed that he'd divulged what he'd heard. If that was the case, *then they knew that he knew*! Not only would that put an end to his plans for revenge, but he'd find himself in a very awkward situation. He'd have to clear off, and fast!

He paced about the bedroom, muttering and swearing, his hands shaking, his back in a sweat. Then he rummaged frantically through his pants pockets looking for the notebook in which he'd written down Felix's cell phone number.

He found it, but no one picked up. So, rather than tying his nerves in more knots, he took a shower, shaved, got dressed, made coffee, put some bread in the toaster, and waited for the sound of the doorbell. Felix was taking his time. After a while, Jerome managed to calm down. He breathed more easily — at least until the bell rang, which startled him so much he dropped a jar of peanut butter on the tile floor, where it broke. He was grumbling when he opened the door. Felix, though, was all smiles, a cigarette dangling from his mouth. He held out his hand.

"Thanks again, eh?"

Seeing the cigarette, Jerome pursed his lips. He'd stopped smoking at the age of twenty-two, after eight years of servitude and three relapses. At the time, it had been the hardest thing he'd ever done, and it had made him a sworn enemy of tobacco. But he decided to say nothing for the moment; Felix would have found it an indelicate welcome.

The poor man looked drawn and unfocused, like someone in hard times, and was carrying a travel bag filled to bursting with all the personal belongings he could stuff into it.

"Come in," Jerome said, leading him into the kitchen. "I was just about to have breakfast."

"Already eaten," said Felix, thinking it appropriate to be frank. "Yikes, what a mess in here." He looked about the kitchen and at the sticky debris of the peanut butter jar on the floor and let out a heartfelt sigh that escaped his lips like a cloud of compassion.

"Some mornings are like this," Jerome said. "Let me just wipe the floor and I'll be right with you. Pour yourself a coffee, if you want. The milk is in the fridge."

As he finished the sentence, he cut his finger on a shard of broken glass from the peanut butter jar.

"So tell me," he said, sounding a little irritated as he came out of the bathroom with a bandage on his finger, "you haven't come to bring me more bad news, I hope?"

"I gave you the bad news on the telephone," said Felix, surprised. "I've left home. Can't stay there anymore! What more do you want?"

Jerome, taken aback by Felix's acerbity, poured himself a cup of coffee and sat down at the table across from his guest.

"I didn't mean that," he said. "I was wondering about... what you told me the other day... you know... Your parents still don't know... that I know, right?"

"Why do you think they'd know?" said Felix, a little testily. "You think I told them?"

He'd turned beet red. Jerome was afraid he was providing exactly the indelicate welcome he had hoped to avoid.

"No, no, forget I asked," he said, placing a friendly hand on the young man's arm. "All I meant was that maybe — you know, by accident, without meaning to..."

"I would have told you, old man. I'm not a complete idiot, you know... You want to know what went down? Last night, during dinner, they started needling me again about my studies. They'd found out I was skipping classes at CEGEP, and fairly often. I told them I only skipped the boring classes, and that they'd do the same in my shoes. In any case, I have friends taking notes for me, and all that really counts are final exam results, isn't that so? Well, my father launched into one of his sermons about the value of hard work and discipline and so on and so forth, my mother started throwing in her two cents' worth, and my nerves just gave out. I told them I didn't think I needed lessons from their sort. 'Oh, I see,' said my father, 'and what sort are we, then?' His face turned as red as a tomato and my mother, she just stared at me, her mouth hanging open like she was having a stroke. 'Does the word Mafia ring any bells?' I asked, which is when my father picked up a salt shaker and hurled it at me, and if my reflexes weren't so good it would have caught me right on the forehead. My mother began howling and yelling, and my father pounded the table so hard our plates jumped into the air, and then he stormed out. So I went upstairs and began packing ... Twenty minutes later, Alma came in and tried to calm me down — my mother sent her, I'm pretty sure — but I ended up convincing her to lend me a travel bag, because all my suitcases were jam-packed."

He paused.

"Are you relieved now?"

His tone was grating. It was time to change the subject. Looking for an apartment seemed like the right diversion.

"Case closed, Felix, I won't even think of it again. Now, about finding you some digs. How much are you willing to pay?"

"No idea," he said, shrugging his shoulders. "I've never rented before."

"It's fairly expensive in this area, because of the university."

"No problem. My mother's paying."

Jerome tilted his head to one side and opened his eyes wide as if to say, "Are you sure, after everything you just told me?"

"She'll pay, she'll pay, don't worry. I know what she's

like. And it'll be a nice change for her, spending her money on a worthy cause." He laughed. "Do you have an ashtray?"

"You can use a saucer."

He stubbed out the butt of his cigarette and lit another. He took a long drag and then, eyes half closed, said, "I really must stop smoking."

He looked up at the ceiling and lifted his hands, palms open, in a tragic pose. "But with things the way they are..."

Jerome bit into the last mouthful of toast, took a sip of coffee, and stood up.

"The easiest way to find an apartment, I guess, is to go on the Internet..."

He pointed to the door of the small room next to his bedroom that served as his office. "My computer's in there. I'll boot it up and you can do all the browsing you want, okay?"

"Yes *sir!*" said Felix, his good mood suddenly restored.

"I have to leave now," said Jerome once the computer was up and running. "Don't know when I'll be back, probably not till early evening."

"I see I'm disturbing you," said Felix, a bit embarrassed.

"Not at all, I assure you. I'm happy to help."

He took a ring of keys from his pocket, detached one, and handed it to Felix.

"Make yourself at home, my friend. You'll find clean sheets for my bed in the closet in the bathroom. I'll sleep in the living room...No, no! Really, don't worry, I sleep anywhere these days. I must be descended from nomads."

They returned to the kitchen. Jerome picked up the leather briefcase containing the files he wanted to brush up on and headed for the door, followed by his guest, who cast him a warm and grateful look.

Seeing that Felix was his old self, Jerome asked him as

casually as he was able, "Would you mind very much if you smoked outside, Felix? I've been feeling a little asthmatic lately."

"You have only to ask, my good man! Of course, no problem."

Happy with his little lie, Jerome shook his hand, bounded down the stairs, and went to his car. It was almost noon.

THE MINISTRY OF Culture's Montreal offices were located in a building vaguely inspired by art deco, at 480 boulevard St. Laurent, in the centre of the historical district—or what was left of it.

Felix taken care of, Jerome checked his cell phone and decided to have lunch in a Vietnamese restaurant, Saigon 27, just across the street from the ministry. The establishment, a half-floor below street level, was quiet and spacious with lots of corners in which he could sit alone and enjoy some privacy. He chose a table near a window with a view of the ministry, ordered a bowl of beef-noodle soup and a spring roll, then perused the files. But after ten minutes, he realized he was wasting his time: he already had the necessary details firmly in his head, and the meeting would almost certainly be more about strategy than building codes.

By the time he shut his briefcase he'd drunk a considerable quantity of green tea and it was barely two. The waitress, who, until then, had treated him with exquisite Asian deference, discreetly signalled that his departure would be greatly appreciated. He still had a lot of time to kill.

He paid the bill, took his briefcase out to his car, and decided to go for a walk in Old Montreal. He headed first to the old Bonsecours Market, its silver dome glinting in the sunlight. A bulletin board advertised an exhibition of

Victorian bicycles that had received a lot of reviews. He strolled down the aisles of the market for twenty minutes, then left.

Near rue Saint-Claude, a clutch of people gathered around a calèche caught his attention, and he went over to see what was happening. A horse had hurt a leg, apparently by stepping into a pothole, and, with its hoof raised, was neighing and whinnying, shaking its head and refusing to move despite curses from the coachman, evidently furious at his loss of revenue from the steady stream of tourists.

"Git' along, there, *tabernac*, you. Fuck'd if I'm gonna spend all day standin' here, dammit!" shouted the driver. A short fat man, wizened by age and weather, he was whipping the horse mercilessly.

Old or tired, perhaps both, the horse continued to neigh loudly and kept shaking its head, its eyes wide with fear. It danced around weakly on three legs, enfeebled, its master arousing the indignation of passersby.

"Can't you see his leg's broken, you numbskull?" shouted a stentorian voice.

"Mind yer own business, ya bugger!" replied the coachman. "I know what I'm doing."

Women were crying, and a small boy asked his mother questions hysterically.

Out of the blue, Jerome remembered the barbaric scene in Dostoevsky's *Crime and Punishment*, in which a coachman, mad with rage, flogs his horse to death. Suddenly he was Raskolnikov in the middle of Moscow during the time of the czars, only this time he could do something! (Was it the effect of the tea? he wondered.)

Ignoring the spectators, he leapt onto the calèche and grabbled the whip from the driver's hand.

"Stop this at once, you, or I'll call the police!"

For a second the man stared open-mouthed at Jerome, while the crowd roared its approval, and applause burst out all around. Suddenly, drawing himself up to his full height, the man threw himself at Jerome so violently that the younger man was thrown from the carriage and would no doubt have been seriously injured had he not fallen into the arms of the man with the stentorian voice, who caught him, stood him on his feet, took the whip from his hand, and held it against the coachman's chest, glaring at him menacingly. The driver tried to grab hold of the whip, but such a deafening cry arose from the assembled crowd that the coachman decided to play the role of the victim.

"You're stopping me from earning a living!" he cried in a tearful voice.

"We're stopping you from going to jail!" replied a bystander to a chorus of laughs from the others.

The horse, shaking and sweating, still refused to move, but was no longer dancing about.

"You should be ashamed of yourself, sir!" shouted a pretty jogger in a strong English accent. "Mistreating a poor animal like that!"

Jerome called the police, but three or four of the spectators had already done so. A squad car squealed in from rue Bonsecours, lights flashing, and came to a halt at the scene.

"Tell them what happened," said the Stentorian Voice, gently nudging Jerome in the direction of the officers climbing out of their vehicle.

Explanations were provided. Discussions were held. By the time the affair was dealt with, the horse unhitched and taken away in a trailer to be tended to, it was almost four o'clock, and Jerome noticed with consternation a small tear on his right pant leg; it must have happened when he fell from the calèche. Obviously, it was too late to go home to change.

He went back to his car, retrieved his briefcase, and made his way to the ministry. The lobby was connected to a couple of fast-food restaurants in the adjoining building. The minister must eat in them from time to time, excellent for her PR. Since he was still twenty minutes early, he went into one of them, a bakery and café, and ordered a cappuccino, which he drank while keeping an eye on his watch and reading a newspaper left behind by a previous customer.

At 4:25, beginning to sweat and somewhat short of breath, he returned to the lobby. It was a grand, circular space paved with polished granite squares with a giant egg surrounded by a black band for a motif. There was something austere about the place, deserted as it was at this time of day. He pushed the elevator button to take him up to the sixth floor. There, he'd been told, a receptionist would conduct him to the minister's office.

That day the receptionist was a security guard and amateur bodybuilder who, as soon as the elevator door opened, welcomed him, retreated to his cubicle, and asked Jerome to identify himself. Then, saying nothing more, he led him one floor up and left him.

Jerome found himself in an empty waiting room and, as there was no one else to greet him, was about to sit down in one of the empty chairs when a woman's voice called him.

"Monsieur Lupien, come in, I'm on the phone."

The voice came from a door on his left. He went to it and entered a sumptuously furnished if solemn, democratically minded office, designed with wood, steel, and water — Quebec's primary natural resources. Water was represented by a superb illuminated aquarium in which a few haggard-looking fish swimming about and constantly opening and closing their silent mouths were no doubt meant to symbolize the electorate.

"Excuse me, I'll only be a few minutes," said Minister Juneau, covering the mouthpiece of her phone with her hand. "Have a seat, please," she said, smiling charmingly and indicating a chair.

Jerome set his briefcase down and tried to appear calm and slightly nonchalant, but it wasn't easy, and the rip in his pants didn't help. Juneau, wearing a stunning pearl-grey designer pantsuit, spoke on the phone cheerily and speedily, but it was impossible to determine the subject of the conversation.

She seemed tired. After several minutes, she hung up and sighed.

"Case closed...like so many others...But that's part of the job, isn't it? How are you doing, Monsieur Lupien?"

"Very well, thank you, Madame Minister."

She examined him assiduously, as though assuring herself that her memory had not misled her.

"Let's drop the titles, shall we?" she said, smiling. "Or we'll never get anywhere. It was kind of you to take the time to see me. Your work must keep you as busy as mine does me."

"Please, madame, it's of no importance whatsoever."

As he spoke, he felt the minister staring at his right pant leg and lost his train of thought.

"I...Excuse me coming here with my clothes in such a state...I had a bit of an accident a few minutes ago...or, to be more precise...I tried to stop a calèche driver from whipping his horse to death, just across from here. We got into a bit of a tussle, and before I knew it my pants were ripped when he pushed me off his carriage. But I called the police and they took him down to the station."

"Well, what do you know," said Juneau, laughing heartily, "you have the blood of a musketeer flowing in your veins! It doesn't surprise me, though. I'm a pretty good judge of character—a trait I find useful in this business, as you can imagine—and I sensed in you, when we were introduced at the fundraiser, something…Well, let's leave your street-fighting tale behind and talk a bit about this museum project, shall we?"

"Yes, of course, ma'am," said Jerome, reaching for his briefcase and taking out the files.

The story of the calèche driver seemed to have established some familiarity between them, and Jerome began to feel more at ease.

"This project has raised a lot of hackles, as you know," said the minister. "And to complicate matters even further, the Westwind government has dropped a bombshell on our heads. I just found out that they're thinking of cutting the budget he announced with such pomp and circumstance last June. The reason? It's always the same: the bloody zero deficit that he's determined to achieve before the next election. It's Ottawa's latest obsession; announcing the museum budget was obviously premature. So—and I'm telling you this in strict confidence, you understand—the reaction in Quebec City hasn't been good. There was a pretty lively discussion in cabinet two days ago, and I was more or less put on the defensive. Some of my colleagues even wanted to withdraw our support for the project, saying it's been receiving bad press and why should we finance our own unpopularity? The premier, he listened to all this without saying a word. As for myself, I consider the polls, and they're not good. But, in my view, all of this is first and foremost a question of strategy: public opinion comes and goes. So I'm trying to defend the project as best I can. Which is why, my dear Jerome, I'd like to review some of the details and numbers."

The minister had delivered her little exposé in velvety tones, casting plenty of smiles in his direction.

"There are plenty of people in the ministry who can do that," said Jerome. He'd always thought the idea of a "Museum of Canadian Culture in the French Language" was ridiculous and even insulting to the Québécois. There was something funereal about it, something sinister, a sort of official recognition of the province's collective agony. But he had taken it on as if he were in a sewer conduit at the end of which there was — or at least he hoped there was — fresh air, freedom . . . and triumphant vindication.

He was also acutely aware of the "my dear Jerome," with which he'd been shown the gratitude of a minister who was very influential — and, in the full bloom of her thirties, very attractive.

"Let's go into the conference room, shall we?" said the minister, getting to her feet. "We can spread out the plans and documents you've brought along. Word is that the federal government wants to delete two exhibition halls on the main floor. I'd like to take a closer look at that."

"And there's something else I'd like to take a closer look at, Madame Minister," thought Jerome, following her. Could it be that his plan was falling into place?

They went into a large, windowless, rectangular room furnished in mahogany. A half-dozen chairs were aligned on either side of a long table as smooth and bare as the memory of a suspect witness at a commission of enquiry.

"So, let's see these famous plans of yours, Jerome," said the minister, casting a particularly friendly glance his way.

He blushed at the use of his name again, but, nervous as he was, his hands were steady as he placed the plans and papers on the table. The minister stood beside him so they could look over the documents together, and he began answering her questions, providing numbers and specifics with confidence. Their eyes met often. Truly, she was an "ice queen" type (though surely easily warmed up) and a beautiful woman; her face might have adorned a Greek statue, were it not for her forehead, which was a bit stronger than that. Her magnificent black eyes, heavily made up, had a lively and mercurial gleam filled with aplomb. She was in excellent shape—from diets and working out in the gym?—with the body of a teenager and full breasts of astonishing lift that may have owed something to a surgeon's skill. But all of his critical assessments vanished from his mind once the perfumed scent of her gorgeous black hair, gently undulating as she asked her questions and made her remarks, reached him.

It soon became apparent that her questions were posed only for appearance's sake; her own grasp of the file was as good as if not better than his, and her interest in the museum was fading second by second.

They fell silent. She turned and looked at him with an almost imperceptible smile, as if waiting for him to make a decision. The moment had come: he had a window of just a few seconds that might never come again, and so, without a word, he took her by the shoulders and pressed his mouth against hers. She sighed, closed her eyes, and responded fervently to his kiss, then took his tongue in her mouth and sucked on it so ardently he almost cried out in pain. But his attention was already required elsewhere: through his trousers he felt her hand squeezing his hard penis and pulling it vigorously. Inspired by her flagrant familiarity, he gently turned her around intent on taking her right there on the conference table among the documents. What a story this would make later on!

"No! Not here, Jerome," she said, disentangling herself. "Never. It wouldn't do, would it..." she added in a softer tone, arranging her clothes. "Maintenance staff, the cleaning lady, you understand... My apartment is very close, just over on rue Saint-François-Xavier. We can walk. I've given my chauffeur the day off."

She put a hand on his cheek.

"Come and have dinner with me, you beautiful boy."

For the first time in his life he felt like a puppet. Bizarre, but not disagreeable.

Within minutes they'd left the ministry. They walked almost in silence, she with a rapid and determined step, head held high. Two or three times she was compelled to stop and speak to a citizen who was daring and bold enough to ask her a question or make a comment. She was always warm and attentive, almost maternal. Jerome kept his distance, pretending to look at something on the street.

The limestone building at 409 Saint-François-Xavier was a former warehouse that had been converted into condominiums. The minister's was on the fourth floor, and Jerome admired its flashy elegance before bringing himself back to the task at hand. After briefly surrendering to the young man's increasingly passionate caresses, the minister, who seemed constantly to keep her cool, suggested they refresh themselves in one of the apartment's three bathrooms.

Jerome looked at her in surprise.

"We don't know each other well enough yet, my beautiful boy."

Smiling, she handed him a bathrobe.

Jerome decided that beneath her penchant for order and control lay an exuberant, sensual woman. By eleven o'clock, they had made love three times — a light dinner forming an intermission between the first and second acts — after which, despite her full day, the minister required his services twice more during the night. Jerome could not remember having been so tired.

But it had been exhilarating to attain the summits of power, even if he had done so by the service stairs.

He left her at 7:30 in the morning; she saw him to the door after an espresso he'd gulped down in a couple of swallows as she listened to the news on the radio. Another trepidatious day awaited her: the telephone was already ringing, and emails and texts were flowing in.

"Shall we see each other again?" he asked after a final kiss.

"Of course," she replied with a smile. "I'll call you."

WHEN HE ARRIVED home, Jerome found Felix sleeping on the sofa despite his having offered his bedroom. Felix's sensitivity surprised and touched him because, despite certain displays of courage (his rehab in Portage having been one), Jerome had lumped him in the category of Daddy's Boy, a more or less degenerate type assuming as a matter of course that the universe existed to serve him.

His arrival did not wake the sleeper, who sighed and turned towards the back of the sofa. Jerome smiled and quietly made his way to his own room to prolong by a few more hours a night that had been, at the very least, eventful.

He was about to unhook the telephone so that he could sleep in peace when it rang. It was Sicotte.

"Finally got you. About time. I left three messages last night."

He sounded tense, worried, and cross.

"Sorry. I turned off my cell phone . . . for professional reasons," he added equivocally.

Sicotte, seemingly not catching his innuendo, was brusque.

"Is Felix with you?"

Felix appeared at the doorway in his boxer shorts, a finger to his lips.

"No, why?"

"Are you sure?" the lawyer replied caustically. "Last night I sent Alma to check the streets in your area and she saw his car parked near your building."

Jerome grimaced. "So Alma's a detective now, is she?"

"Let me repeat the question: is Felix with you?"

"Just a minute."

Covering the receiver with his hand, he turned towards Felix. "He knows you're here. Alma saw your car last night."

"That bitch!"

"Never mind her right now . . . Listen, all this is putting me in a shitty position. What do you want me to do?"

"Tell him I left."

"I can't do that. He knows we're talking."

Felix was leaning with his hand against the jamb of the door. He crossed his feet, looking dejected, as Jerome resumed the conversation.

"Okay, Severin, yes, he's here . . . Sorry, but he asked me to keep it between us. Now, if you'll allow me to say so — and I mean no disrespect — your family quarrels are not my concern, I've got enough on my plate as you well know. I've had a very busy night, you'll be happy to hear, and I'm dead tired and just want to get some sleep. So, if it's all the same to you, I'm going to let you deal with your family problems without my help."

There was a silence at the other end of the line. "Okay then," said the lawyer, mollified. "Sorry to have burdened you with all this. Let me speak to him, please."

Jerome handed the phone to Felix, who waved his arms in a frenzy and disappeared into the living room.

"He'll call you back, Severin," said Jerome, taking it upon himself to convince Felix to do so. "Right now, he can't."

"What do you mean, 'he can't'?" said Sicotte in alarm. "He's in no state fit to?"

He could hear Francine Desjarlais starting to wail in the background.

"No, no, nothing like that!" said Jerome. "No need to panic, for God's sake. I promise he'll call either you or Francine before noon. Is that okay? Right now, with your permission, I'm going to bed."

He hung up and went to find Felix, who had dressed and was busy folding the sheets and blanket he'd put on the couch.

"What are you going to do?"

Felix turned, frowning and chewing his lip as if wanting to come to an irrevocable decision in a matter hard to decide.

"I'm going to look at apartments," he said. "Last night I found two or three interesting addresses. And I have no intention of phoning either of those two today."

Jerome stepped in front of him.

"Look," he said, "Felix, you've got to face the facts. You can't have your cake and eat it, too. If you need your parents' money, then you have to talk to them. In a pinch, I can lend you enough to get by for a few months, but what happens after that? I like you and I want to help you, but this business with your parents puts me in a delicate position . . . You heard me: I promised your father you'd phone him this morning. So phone him, please . . . Or Francine, if you prefer. But whatever you do, you're probably going to need one of them to sign your lease. As for me, I'm dead on my feet. I'm going to bed."

He was looking Felix in the eye, waiting for an answer.

"Okay," said Felix with an awkward smile. "I'll call my mother."

"Right away?"

"I'm going out for a bite to eat at a restaurant. I'll call her from there."

ALMOST A WEEK, and Jerome still hadn't boasted to Charlie about his exploits with the Minister of Culture, a charismatic woman many observers considered the rising star in the Labrèche government. Jerome's discretion was due on the one hand to prudence, but also to some extent to shame. He felt as if he'd wandered inextricably into an archipelago of dishonesty, and that he was drifting farther and farther away from the simple, honourable life he'd always thought he would lead — the life of ordinary mortals.

Like Eugenie.

Soon he and she would inhabit such different and distant universes that communication between them would be impossible. They wouldn't even be speaking the same language or having the same feelings.

Twice he dreamed of her. Confused, agitated dreams; all he remembered from them was the image of her beautiful face, stern and smiling as she stared down at him fighting to scramble out of the whirlpool swallowing him. "It really is over between us," he told himself when he awoke, his mouth dry and feeling faintly nauseous.

Felix had taken his advice and was doing well. A tactical reconciliation had been made with his parents, who'd resigned themselves to his moving out. He'd rented, courtesy of mama and papa, a modest three-room apartment on rue Gatineau, a stone's throw from the university and close to Jerome's place. Discreetly, Francine had asked Jerome to keep an eye on her son. He'd promised to do so "as much as circumstances would allow," intending nothing of the sort—or at least very little, as he believed Felix to be coping much better than his parents.

His principal endeavour — to achieve the status of Minister Juneau's irreplaceable intimate — gave him the freedom to do as he pleased, which he very much appreciated as it allowed him to come and go at the office whether his reasons for doing so were valid or not.

Six days after his encounter with Normande Juneau, he received a cell phone call from her in the middle of the afternoon. He was at the office with Sicotte and Freddy Pettoza, discussing concrete, its official price and its actual cost, in an atmosphere charged with that particular tension born of greed, which the lawyer and the businessmen were trying to pass off as good fellowship.

"Yes?" said Jerome a little wearily. "Oh! Hello! How are you?" he said, his face suddenly lighting up and his tone so friendly that his companions exchanged quizzical glances. He stood up, gestured that he needed to be excused, went into his own office, and closed the door.

"I'm leaving Quebec City in ten minutes," she said. "I'll

be in Montreal by late afternoon. I was wondering if you're free this evening?"

"For you, Madame Minister," he replied with clownish sycophancy, "I'm always free, as you know."

"Drop the honorific, my dear, and in exchange I'll drop something else. I thought we might have dinner at the Bonaparte at seven. It's close to my condo. Is that okay with you?"

"More than okay."

"See you at seven, then."

It was only 3:30, but Jerome thought he would take advantage of the situation to leave early. He returned to the boss's office and poked his head in the door.

"Sorry, but I have to leave," he said to Sicotte, as if that settled the matter. "Something's come up."

The lawyer, untroubled, nodded with vigour.

"You'll keep me posted?" he asked.

A salacious gleam flickered in the back of his eye.

"Of course."

Pettoza, suspecting something was up, had a curiously slanted smile on his lips.

Jerome decided to use his free hours to do some shopping. He'd just started his car when his cell phone rang. It was Normande Juneau again.

"Ah, glad I caught you, Jerome. I'm so sorry, but something's come up that I have to take care of. Can we meet tomorrow night instead, same time, same place?"

A brief silence followed.

"Yes, of course," he said.

"What a crazy life we lead sometimes," she sighed. "I hope you're not angry with me."

He laughed. "Why would I be?"

"Okay, I have to run, they're calling for me. *Kiss kiss.* Until tomorrow."

He stayed behind the wheel, surprised at how disappointed he felt, and turned off the engine. But the thought of going back to Sicotte and Pettoza made him restart it and drive off. His desire to go shopping had disappeared. He drove for a few minutes towards his apartment. The sky was turning gloomy. A bank of menacing, dark-blue clouds stretched along the horizon, a storm gathering somewhere far away and approaching Montreal. What was he going to do with his evening?

He decided to call Charlie and pulled over to the curb.

"Hello, who's this?" said a familiar voice—a bit staccato, the voice of a technician who takes care of problems.

"Hi, it's me."

"Oh-ho!" said Charlie, cheekily. "Monsieur Lupien has descended from great heights to mingle with the hoi polloi. To what do I owe this honour?"

"Stop fooling around, Charlie. Are you free tonight? We could get something to eat somewhere and then go see a film?"

"It just so happens I am free, surprise, surprise. Martine has her jazz-ballet class at seven, which means . . . Hey! What the hell is that? What's that noise? Someone firing at you with a machine gun?"

The storm had broken, and heavy rain was pelting the roof of the car.

"Look outside your window, you'll see for yourself."

"What window? There aren't any windows in this place. Oh, I get it, a rainstorm."

The pounding rain doubled in force. They exchanged a few more words, then Charlie was called back to work and hung up. But they had had the time to fix a rendezvous for six o'clock at La Brioche Lyonnaise, on rue Saint-Denis, not far from the Quartier Latin cinema.

And it was there, under the streaming window that looked out over the rear of the restaurant, that they had a conversation so long and so intense they almost missed their film.

"It's a done deal," announced Jerome after a mouthful of mochaccino. He leaned back in his chair, giving himself a feeling of authority.

"What's a done deal?" asked Charlie, his mouth full of smoked-salmon panini.

"Last week I got it on with Minister Juneau."

He had promised to keep their relationship secret a little while longer but was disappointed their meeting had been bumped to the next night (he had worked himself up into quite a sexual lather) and felt a bit riled that he'd been treated like a plaything she could pick up or put down so capriciously. Eagerly and swiftly, he was finding succour in vanity.

Charlie's eyes widened and he stopped in the middle of a swallow, nearly choking.

"No way," he said in a reedy voice.

"Yes way, my good man," said Jerome. "Last Tuesday . . . She's quite the nympho, our good minister . . . You can't imagine! We did it six times in ten hours. It was like a tropical storm!"

"You should give your balls a rest," Charlie said. "You could neuter yourself."

"Don't worry, I've got everything under control."

Charlie picked up his bottle of mineral water and refilled his glass. (He was on the wagon, for the time being.)

"When are you seeing her again?" he asked.

"Tomorrow. Unless she cancels. We were supposed to get together tonight."

"I see. So I'm Plan B."

"Not at all," said Jerome. He tilted his head to one side and raised his eyes to the ceiling as if to say, "Oh, the things I cannot tell you!"

"So how often are you going to bang her this month? Do you have a schedule?"

"There's no schedule. It's more a matter of spontaneity — and Madame Minister's availability, of course."

"You're a gigolo, then?"

Jerome bit his lip.

"I'm not doing it for money, you idiot. Or even for the pleasure of it, although I've got to say she's pretty good between the sheets. As I told you before, I'm doing it to get information. Information that will let me destroy Sicotte's business. And maybe give his goddamned government cronies a poke in the eye while I'm at it."

"Has it occurred to you, my good angel, that from her opposite corner she may be sleeping with you for the same reasons? She's in league with your boss, but as we all know, in their world, no one trusts anyone. Maybe she's using *you* to get the goods on Sicotte, or to verify certain things she's heard. Possible, no?"

"Gee, Charlie, I never thought of that," said Jerome sarcastically. "What an insight! Aren't I lucky to have a friend like you."

"Joke all you want, but you're not dealing with a schoolgirl. She's trouble, Jerome. If I was hanging with her, I'd want an eye in the back of my head."

Jerome leaned over the table, eyes ablaze, and gave Charlie a resolute, penetrating look.

"Charlie, that's what I want to talk to you about. Right now, of course, I have no idea how things will turn out, but the time will come when I'll need your technical expertise. You see what I'm getting at?"

Charlie managed a "yeah" that sounded both flattered and skeptical. "We'll see when the time comes," he said, "if ever it does. Just don't ask me to mike her bathroom or put a bug in her bra."

"You can leave her bra to me."

"On the other hand, I might be able to help you crack a password or open a file, that sort of thing. But I can't give you any guarantees. They're not stupid, these politicians."

The rain had stopped, replaced by heavy winds thinning and dispersing the rivulets of water on the window. Thinking, all of a sudden, that in any friendship it was necessary to look to happier times, Jerome put his hand on Charlie's arm and said, "How's Martine? Still in love with her?"

Charlie lit up like a little boy who'd been given a cream puff. "Ah, Jerome, she's the nicest girl a guy could ever meet! I've never known anyone like her. Really!"

And he launched into a passionate and detailed paean of praise for his girlfriend. Her vivacity, her equanimity, her charmingly easy manner, her gazelle-like grace, the way her sense of humour could make a funeral cortège laugh; it all flourished in Martine. It still amazed him that he'd been more attracted to her friend Laurie the night he'd met them in that café near his place.

"It took me twenty minutes, would you believe, to realize that I was sitting beside somebody so marvellous who'd come to me directly from heaven on earth!"

"That's something."

"We were sitting beside each other, and sometimes, without meaning to, we touched elbows. But I kept hitting on the one across from me. She was okay in her way, of course, but…but when I finally turned and opened my eyes…"

He stopped, choked up with emotion and lost in a reverie that brought an ineffable smile to his lips, a look Jerome had never seen on him before. It made him a little jealous.

"And the forbidden fruit? How did it taste when the two of you bit into it together?"

"Ah, my friend, my friend!" was all Charlie said. "I don't know what else to tell you. No, I don't know…"

But ten minutes later, Jerome had to interrupt his friend's lyrical description of Martine's cute and tiny pink toes, the very sight of which sent him into a trance.

"We're going to miss the film, Charlie. They must be finishing the trailers by now."

Charlie stood up and followed him silently, a smile on his lips.

IN MID-NOVEMBER, NORMANDE Juneau was so wrapped up in parliamentary sessions that she asked Jerome to join her in Quebec City for the weekend. He said yes, and passed the news on to Sicotte. The lobbyist rubbed his hands together, so enchanted was he by the progress of their liaison.

"It looks like love has set in for the long haul, eh? Stay on for a few days, if you feel like it. I'll pay your expenses. So, you're having a good time, my boy?"

Jerome laughed. "Well, I'm not bored."

"They say she's very demanding in bed," said Sicotte, riddled with curiosity.

"Well, a guy has to be in pretty good shape."

"I'm not worried about you, you can take care of

yourself... Don't talk to her about business yet. Sooner or later the subject will come up on its own, obviously... Take your time, let it come. First you have to gain her trust."

"I've already figured that out," said Jerome, looking away. He felt his face turning red. Sicotte's advice, so carelessly given, confirmed, were there any need, that the lobbyist had ruined his love life simply to use him as a pawn in his game of deceit.

Sicotte, leaning back in his chair, stared at him with an engaging smile. Had he been drinking? Jerome wondered. Did Sicotte take him for an idiot? His boss seemed totally oblivious to his assistant's state of mind.

The telephone rang. Jerome used it as an excuse to leave the room.

AS IT TURNED out, the weekend with the minister did end up being extended by an extra three days, and Jerome did not get back to Montreal until the Thursday. Normande Juneau had smiled unreservedly when Jerome told her he'd like to stay on for a few days.

"I need a holiday, and I'd like to spend it with you."

"Nothing would make me happier, Jerome, but we can only see each other in the evenings. I have to work, you know."

His relationship with the minister continued to bring him surprise after surprise. At times, she seemed genuinely taken with him. She was attentive and showed him a gentle and even tender side he couldn't otherwise explain. One evening he told her about his admiration for Émile Zola and how he'd always wanted to purchase a special edition of his complete works. The next morning, while he was lounging in bed after a bout of love-making that had obliged his lover to reapply her makeup before heading off to the National Assembly, there was a knock at the door; a courier handed him a package addressed to him by name. He opened it and cried out with joy. Normande had bought him the five volumes of Zola's *Rougon-Macquart* series in the Pléiade edition.

She never talked to him about politics or business, and he knew very little about her, apart from the fact that she was born in Rivière-du-Loup, an unpretentious port town on the St. Lawrence, that she'd been divorced at the age of twenty-five after having had an abortion, that she had a brother who taught the physically handicapped and a younger sister with whom she was no longer speaking. Any time he tried to find out more, she would furrow her brow and change the subject. In any case, most of the time it was hard to have any kind of flowing conversation with her, except late in the evening, because her life seemed to be little more than a series of comings and goings, of emails sent and received, and conversations over the telephone. "A horrible life," thought Jerome. "I'd rather be a bus driver, for Christ's sake."

It seemed impossible, even given her reputation as a devourer of men, that she was having an affair with anyone else. Where would she find the time? But nothing was to be taken for granted. At best, she was faithful to him for as long as he was on the scene. All the more reason to act swiftly.

For three years she had been renting a beautiful apartment in Old Quebec, on rue Sainte-Ursule, a few steps from the National Assembly. The building dated from the nineteenth century and had been occupied by rich bourgeois families of the period. Then times became difficult, and the apartments were rented to people of more modest means. Slowly, the building deteriorated to the point of being more or less abandoned. But in 1985, a developer had snapped it up, somewhat reluctantly, and he then restored it at great expense in conformance with new regulations laid down by UNESCO due to the old city's status as a World Heritage Site.

The apartment was warm, comfortable, and spacious, filled with all the latest gadgets, and extremely attractive, what with its vaulted ceilings and exposed beams, original woodwork and oak floors. One evening, after they'd had a few drinks, Normande confided to Jerome that for a few nights she'd felt she'd been visited by the ghosts of aristocrats from the building's past, come to continue their interrupted lives.

"Mind you," she added, laughing, "I have no interest in the occult, believe me!"

"Maybe your regrets take the form of ghosts," Jerome said jokingly.

The minister's face froze.

"Regrets?" she said testily. "I haven't done anything I regret."

Her eyes shot him an accusing look.

"Come on, Normande," said Jerome defensively. "I was joking."

That night he vowed never again to venture onto such thin ice.

Charlie's warning—that perhaps the minister was interested in him for the same reasons he was courting her—stuck with him. He might have been willing to betray Sicotte at any time, if that would advance his cause, but so far nothing made him believe she was seeing him for any other reason than his performances in bed. For a while, the ease of his relationship with her, sometimes extending to irreverence, seemed to remind her of the overwhelming duties of her office. She'd even asked him one night, head on the pillow, two or three questions about Sicotte's way of life, and the role of Roland Dozois (aka Bled Man) in the lawyer's and his wife's acquisition of the Iberostar Hotel in Varadero. But it didn't go farther than that, and Jerome decided that she'd asked only out of curiosity.

Weeks passed. November was nearing its end, and whatever spying Jerome had been able to manage had so far yielded scant results. All he'd gleaned from their random conversations, morsel by morsel, was that her rapid ascension in the party was the result of a secret understanding between her and Premier Labrèche that appeared to be linked to some form of blackmail. What was at the bottom of it? He didn't have the foggiest idea.

One Friday night at the end of November, the truth struck him like a flash of lightning. They'd got in around ten o'clock after a well-lubricated dinner at La Bonaparte. Once in the apartment — even before she'd taken off her coat — Normande headed straight to the living room, turned on the television, and plunked herself down on the sofa with a vaguely anxious look on her face. The evening news had just started.

She'd had a difficult week. A clumsily handled declaration that had been made two days earlier to justify the decision of the Sulpicians to sell a part of their land for the construction of the Museum of Canadian Culture in the French Language had put the opposition in a fury. They were demanding the resignation of an "uncultured" Minister of Culture obviously "incapable of insuring the protection of our heritage," one member proclaimed, "because she has no idea what's at stake." Criticisms and insults were abounding on Twitter and Facebook. The newspapers had been more restrained, but had nevertheless launched vitriolic attacks on her. That very afternoon, journalists had cornered Jean-Philippe Labrèche as he was leaving the cabinet meeting, after Normande had refused to reply to their questions. Labrèche had come to her defence, but only half-heartedly and pretty much ducking the issue. His tepid responses had been surprising; some interpreted it as a sign that he would shortly dump her.

Normande, unsmiling, listened to the news. Jerome, slumped on a sofa, didn't say a word, eyes shifting between the television screen and his lover's face.

Ten minutes passed and the minister was beginning to hope she'd be let off the hook that night, but then Labrèche, surrounded by journalists, appeared on the screen — and the controversy was resumed! Normande grabbed the remote and turned off the television with a snap, muttering a few dirty words *sotto voce.*

"Do you think he's going to watch you fall?" asked Jerome.

If he hadn't had so much to drink, he wouldn't have dared to ask such a question.

Her laugh had a sinister turn.

"Don't worry...I've got something here that will keep him from doing that."

"Here?"

"Here...and elsewhere."

She stood up.

"Do you mind hanging up my coat? I'm going to take a shower. I'm exhausted."

He went back to his regular schedule at the office, taking long weekends when Normande Juneau was in Montreal; to have done otherwise would have caused suspicion. Sicotte had him on the Museum file but was talking about bringing Fradette back from Varadero because two new "projects" had come up and there weren't enough people in the office to look after them. The barometer of Jerome's moral well-being had sunk to minus-forty.

One Monday, he arrived at the office around 10:30 in the morning, following another three-day weekend with Normande, and was passing Francine's office when she called him in.

"So, Beau Brummell, how's it going?"

Something in her voice, a trace of insolence perhaps, was also reflected in the exaggerated smile she gave him as she leaned back in her chair, her wrists sparkling with bracelets showily positioned on the armrests.

"Fine, and you?" he replied, trying to hide his discomfort behind a glib manner.

He looked out of the corner of his eye to make sure Alma wasn't in the next room.

"I sent her off on an errand, my dear. Don't worry, no one can hear us."

He shrugged, as if the segue meant nothing to him.

"Did you have a ... busy weekend? You and the minister?"

The prurience of her salacious inference made him open his eyes wide, colour rising to his face.

"Severin would never dare say as much, but we're beginning to find the benefits of your relationship with the minister a bit ... long in coming ... Good heavens! I've never spent so much time in the sack with anyone in my whole life!"

He glared at her, angry to the point of recklessness. "What I do on my weekends is my business, so far as I know," he shot back. "I don't have to account for them to you."

"Yes, I take your point, my dear, but your weekends often begin Friday at noon and end sometime on Monday...Do you realize what time it is?"

With her index finger, she tapped the glass of her watch.

A cold rage seized him. He was on the verge of saying right to her face that he knew all about the plot she'd played against him with her husband, but fear of the harm it might do Felix stopped him.

"I have a simple solution, Francine: find someone else to sleep with the minister."

And, turning on his heels, he left the room, went to his own office, and collapsed in his chair, distraught, eyes filling with tears, his hands trembling.

"Bitch! You old bitch!" he muttered. "She takes pleasure in humiliating me now! You're lucky, you little slut, that you have a son worth ten of you...I won't be festering long in this place, you can be sure of that. So be on your guard!"

He opened his computer and clicked on a file, but two minutes went by and he was unable to concentrate. He rose and stood by the window, hands behind his back, squeezing and twisting his fingers. A stooped old man in a brown cap, cigarette in his lips, was raking the garden, stopping from time to time to watch a squirrel running in circles in a stand of old lilacs. He heard the door open and recognized Sicotte's footsteps, but didn't turn from the window. The lobbyist stopped in the middle of the room and coughed.

"Things not going well, Jerome?"

He'd tried to make his deep, gravelly voice sound warm and compassionate but was not managing it.

A shiver ran across Jerome's shoulders, but he said nothing.

"Listen, I just spoke to Francine. You two had an

argument? Look at me, damn it! I feel like I'm talking to the curtains! Good," he said when Jerome finally turned.

"I don't want to speak to your wife again," said an obdurate Jerome. "She insulted me. For no reason. You can have the minister's file back. Find someone else. I've had it up to here!"

An anguished grimace came over Sicotte's face, as if all of his features had converged on his mouth.

"Come on," he said, "don't lose your head over this, okay? Francine doesn't believe a word of what she said to you. She even sends her apologies. Take advantage, it doesn't happen very often! Do you want to know what's behind all this, Jerome? What's really behind it? Felix. Yes! She's worried sick about him. And she thinks it was you who convinced him to leave."

"That's not true! He came to my place on his own. I had nothing to do with it."

"Yes, yes, I believe you, no need to go into it . . . You know how mothers are, Jerome, they're lionesses defending their cubs."

"I don't like being raked by her claws, then. Especially when I haven't done anything to deserve it. Do you understand? Nothing!"

"I know, you just told me. Let's move on, shall we?"

Jerome returned to staring at the garden. His anger was appeased, but he was trying hard not to show it. Here was a chance for him to reinforce his position. Despite what Sicotte was saying, his sense was that Francine was losing her way and that her apology was only strategic.

"Have we turned that page, Jerome?" Sicotte repeated.

And taking Jerome by the shoulders, he pulled the young man towards him and looked him in the eye.

Jerome, with a contrite smile, gave an acquiescent nod of his head.

"Okay, put her there, my boy!"

And they shook hands, vigorously.

A silence followed.

"Has Oscar finished cleaning up the yard?" Sicotte wondered aloud, feeling in need of a transition. He glanced out the window. "I don't see him anywhere. He must be on the other side of the house."

He turned back to Jerome.

"Say," he said, "can we talk for a minute?"

Without waiting for a reply, he took a seat as Jerome went to his desk.

A quizzical musing served as Sicotte's preamble.

"In my entire career I've never had a personal conversation with *anyone* on my staff like the one I just had with you. It shows how much respect I have for you...And Francine respects you as much as I do, despite what you might think...What can I say? Women sometimes have moods. They'll say anything that comes into their heads. You have to learn to take the bad with the good."

Jerome's expression was scathing. "Where the hell is he going with this?" he asked himself.

Sicotte impulsively put his hand into his inside jacket pocket and pulled it out just as quickly.

"I've been having one of my migraines all morning," he said with a painful wince. "If I'm not careful, I'll swallow this whole bottle of Tylenol...It must be stress, bloody stress... We're not in an easy business, you and I."

"Or Francine either, it seems," added Jerome sarcastically.

"Of course, neither is she...Listen, Jerome. At the risk of repeating myself, I want to be entirely sure that everything is okay between us as far as your mission with Juneau is concerned. I've never expected any specific outcome, do you understand? At least not for now. The only thing that matters to me is the connection you're making with her. Understood?"

"That's what I've always thought, Severin, but I'm not sure Francine is on side."

Sicotte, overwrought, expelled air through his nostrils.

"Leave Francine out of this, okay?" He raised his index finger menacingly. "I'm the one you have to deal with here, not her. *Capisce?*"

Jerome felt he had gone too far. He needed to back off or at least appear to.

"*Capisce*," he said.

"Perfect."

Spreading his knees, the lobbyist pressed his hands on his thighs and slowly raised his chin, a sign that he was about to say something important.

"It's an incredible opportunity, Jerome, you catching the minister's eye. Nothing like that would happen to an old carcass like me, or even to someone like Olivier — not to take anything away from him. I owe this lucky break to your... youthful physique, to your charm, yes, and to your... how shall I put this? To your *know-how*. Yes, that's it, we have to call a spade a spade here, goddamnit!"

He was laughing and, once again, his hand involuntarily slid into his jacket pocket, and he emitted a small, painful groan. He looked worried.

"Impossible to say how long this thing you have with her will last," he said. "But we know that sooner or later your place will be taken by someone else: that's how she operates, our Normande, nothing anyone can do about it..."

A loud noise came from outside the building, followed by a curse. Things weren't going well for Oscar in the shed, it seemed.

"There's been a rumour making the rounds for the past couple of weeks that Labrèche is going to shuffle his cabinet. Normande Juneau is going to be made Minister of Municipal Affairs, which is a much more interesting ministry to us than Culture is, obviously; projects like this museum come along once in a lifetime . . . Has she said anything to you about it?"

Jerome shook his head. There was a moment's silence.

"If I'd heard anything at all, Severin," Jerome said, "I would have told you."

"Absolutely," said the lawyer with a nod of his head. "Good Lord, we've no shortage of problems . . . Imagine that Senator Freddy Peck — a Conservative! — has declared war on Pettoza. He's accusing him of colluding with his Chinese suppliers . . . Another asshole whose palm we haven't greased who's doing his best to let us know it. Has Juneau said anything to you about him?"

Again, Jerome shook his head.

Sicotte stood up. He smiled.

"I'll let you get back to work. We'll talk another time. Maybe we can grab a bite later on?"

"Whatever you say, Severin."

For a long time after Sicotte left, Jerome sat at his desk staring at his computer screen. Behind all the praise and protestations of friendship, he had detected in his boss's words, almost imperceptibly slipped in, a subtle but urgent exhortation for him to get off his ass.

There wasn't much time left to put his plan in motion.

THAT EVENING, JEROME was finishing his dinner in a restaurant near his apartment, a habit he'd fallen into whenever he was feeling low or anxious, when he received a phone call from Charlie that put him into a state.

"I've got a good one for you," said Charlie. He sounded frantic, bursting with joyous stupefaction, as if he could hardly believe what he was going to say.

"What?"

"You'll never guess."

"Go on. Tell me."

"Eugenie just called me to ask how you were doing."

The silence that followed lasted long enough for Charlie to listen to the incomparable Pavarotti, of whom the owners of the restaurant were particularly fond, sing six or seven bars of "O Sole Mio."

"If this is a joke," said Jerome, his annoyance diminished, "then it's one of your worst yet."

"Hey, I'd never joke about this," Charlie protested. "I've got better judgement than that, I hope."

And then he told Jerome about the conversation he'd had with his former girlfriend. The pretext for her call (after all, she had to have a pretext) was that there was some chronic problem she was having with her home computer. Charlie had mentioned, during their meeting at the Café Prague, that he worked as an IT guy at Micro-Boutique, and this was a sufficiently plausible excuse for her to call, right? They talked shop for ten minutes, then fixed a time and place to get together. But right from the start he felt there was something in her voice, a kind of veiled tension, that was different—a pretense of detachment put on to contain a huge well of emotion, like the lid on a pressure cooker fighting against the forces trapped in the pot. And then the question popped out of nowhere, one of those inconsequential questions you'd ask with perfectly amiable but disingenuous indifference to close a business meeting in good stead. "'Oh, by the way,' she asked me, 'how's your friend Jerome doing these days?'"

She had tried to sound casual, Charlie told Jerome, but her question came at him "like a cannon shot."

"What did you answer?" asked Jerome, panting.

"The only thing I could: that you were well, and that you were working so hard we didn't see each other all that often. In other words, nothing. Or nothing much. So that you can fill her in yourself."

"Did she ask anything else about me?"

"No."

A second silence followed, allowing Pavarotti to launch into "Granada."

"I think you've got it all wrong," said Jerome at last. "She asked the question because she knows you and I are friends, simple as that. You're confusing imagination and reality."

"And I think you're giving me the gears. Think about it: there are at least four hundred technicians in Montreal who could have helped her with her computer. She, or someone in her entourage, must know a dozen of them. If not, she could have looked one up in three minutes. But what does she do instead? She calls the *only* technician in town unfortunate enough to know you. Even an idiot could see through that, Jerome."

"When are you seeing her?"

"The day after tomorrow. But you should show up instead of me, Jerome. I'm sure her laptop can wait."

"Count on me!" sneered Jerome. "You aren't by any chance under the influence of any illicit drugs, are you, Charlie?"

"Well, let's see... The only strange thing I've eaten today was a bag of chips I bought at the corner store earlier this evening. Come off it, Jerry-boy!" he cried suddenly. "Aren't you happy to hear good news? The love of your life is thinking about you! Better than that, she wants you to know she's thinking of you! What more do you want? A Nobel Prize in literature? To win a ten-million-dollar lottery?"

At the other end of the line, Charlie heard Jerome's exasperated sigh mingle with the final strains of "Granada."

"Sorry, Charlie," said Jerome. "Thanks for calling... but this only further complicates an already impossible situation."

His voice conveyed a depth of distress to which Charlie was unable to respond. After muttering an almost inaudible "Good luck," he hung up.

THE WEEK WENT by as slowly as a visit to the dentist. Jerome made and received calls, most of which led to nothing; he took part in discussions that generally went nowhere and provided bits of information about this or that to no great effect. And this was fine with him, given that the work was shameful and did harm, and anything he did accomplish would benefit the two people he most wanted to hurt. But what a trying task it was to have to feign pleasure and interest when what he really felt was hatred and disgust! His only motivation was his desire for the vengeance that would allow him, he hoped, to regain his self-respect.

One dread weighed heavily on him: that Sicotte or his wife (whom he avoided as much as possible) would identify the torment gnawing at him; two such virtuosos of duplicity must have gleaned from their trade, a long time ago, how to detect duplicity in others: for them, it was a matter of survival.

Friday night came at last. Normande had been back in Montreal since mid-afternoon. At 5:30, she left her riding office, head buzzing after interminable meetings with her constituents, and was looking forward to joining Jerome, who was waiting patiently for her in the lobby of her condo building.

Jerome would be taken by surprise a few times over the course of the weekend.

He had complained to Normande about having to hang about waiting for her in the lobby like a pizza delivery boy whenever a last-minute holdup kept her at work (which happened fairly often) because he had no key. Each time she'd replied with some pleasantry or changed the subject.

Friday night, she arrived on time. The smile she had upon seeing him immediately erased all signs of fatigue from his face.

"See?" she said. "I can be punctual sometimes, my love."

It was the first time she'd called him "my love" since they'd been together, and hearing it alarmed him. Alone in the elevator, they were locked in a passionate embrace when Jerome unexpectedly felt a metallic object being slipped into his hand.

"There's your key, delivery boy of my heart!" she said, laughing. "From now on, you can put the pizza in the oven while you're waiting for me. Are you happy?"

They arrived at her floor, and if it weren't for an employee running a vacuum cleaner in the hallway, Jerome would have shown her his appreciation with a healthy grope against her door.

That evening, the night that followed, and the next two days were particularly gratifying for both of them. The minister, who'd never been afraid to show her mood swings in

private and sometimes even in public, was quite simply delicious; claiming to be seriously in need of sleep, she'd had her
calls transferred to her chief of staff, with the express order
not to be called for anything but an emergency, and there
were none. Naked in bed, they watched the entire television
series of Bergman's *Fanny and Alexander* on the ultra-large,
high-definition screen, interrupting certain episodes with
sessions of love-making to ward off Bergman's celebrated
northern melancholy. A caterer had been engaged to sustain
them through the weekend, and he did so with incomparable refinement; Jerome drank two or three wines he knew
of by name, but never expected to taste.

"You're crazy, Normande!" he exclaimed, embarrassed,
in the end, by all her lavish kindnesses. "You're going to
ruin yourself."

She laughed: "Well, then, you must take charge."

There could be no greater contrast between such tender moments of pleasure and the infernal week Jerome had
endured at Sicotte's office.

The final surprise came his way came early Sunday evening. Normande was packing for her return to Quebec City,
expecting to arrive by ten that evening. Her driver was due
to ring at any moment. Jerome, wiped out by the excesses
of the past few days, was nodding off in the bedroom, still
heady with the scents of their love-making.

Normande came into the room, makeup on, ready to go,
and sat on the edge of the bed. He promptly sat up.

"Oh, leaving so soon? I'd better get dressed."

"What's the hurry?" she said, pushing him back down on
the bed. "Why do you think I gave you a key, silly?"

And she made him repeat the two access codes to be sure
he had them memorized.

A bell rang somewhere in the apartment: her driver was waiting for her on the ground floor. They kissed, she stood up, and, as she was leaving the room, turned and said to him casually, "Oh, before I forget . . . What are you doing during the Christmas holidays? Some friends of mine have invited me on a cruise in the Bahamas . . . They have a beautiful yacht. Would you care to come with me?"

He stared, immobilized by a stupefaction so profound that she had to laugh.

"What's wrong? Are you having a heart attack?"

"No . . . it's just that . . ."

The bell sounded again.

"We'll talk about it later. Have a good week. Don't forget to be good."

And in an instant, she was gone.

Sitting in bed, knees pulled to his chest and his desire for sleep undermined, he was plunged for a long time in thoughts whose nature was easy to surmise because of the worried pursing of his lips and the wild looks he cast about the room. In effect, Normande had just expressed her desire to make their relationship public. If she hadn't fallen in love with him, then she was certainly showing the signs! And the trust she'd shown in him by providing him a key to their apartment was hardly the least of them.

What was going on? His success surpassed not only his hopes but his needs! An already complicated situation was taking on ever more Byzantine aspects. He leapt down from the bed and, naked, threw himself onto one of the large chairs in the immense living room. Coals were dying in the rose marble fireplace, above which hung a copy of a Canaletto painting, *The Thames and the City of London from Richmond House*. It struck him that he could explore the apartment at his leisure, look for some kind of evidence to unleash a scandal that would ruin Sicotte and his wife, plunge the Labrèche government into turmoil; but that risked collateral damage, bringing his lover down too.

Perhaps the evidence he needed wasn't in the apartment, if it existed at all. He was surprised by how little joy the idea of getting the upper hand was giving him. Avenging a betrayal by betraying someone who seemed, quite genuinely, to love him, seemed repugnant to him. But hadn't that been the plan he'd been following all along? Of course it had been. Except that he'd not anticipated the notorious appearance of love surprises that, from time immemorial, had turned the world on its head.

He should have reread Marivaux, that incomparable playwright and philosopher of love.

What had he done to end up in such a situation? *Nothing.* It was what it was, one of those merciless twists of fate that falls upon us without warning and reminds us of the essential cruelty of living. He congratulated himself, at any rate, for having resisted Charlie's urging him to get in touch with Eugenie immediately. Good Lord! How would he have explained—let alone get her to accept—the utter tangle in which he was enmeshed.

He remained a long time contemplating the embers slowly fading on their bed of grey ash. From time to time, he sighed. He looked up at the Canaletto. The famous painter had abandoned the incomparable light of Italy for cold and foggy London, the capital of an empire within which the Québécois remained, in a way, humble and docile vassals.

He craved a beer. He rose and went into the kitchen.

"All the same, Jerome Lupien," he mumbled—as suddenly he stood still, seized with giddy happiness. "Look at you. You're one lucky son of a bitch! You have nothing to complain about: here it is, a beautiful Sunday night, and you're walking around naked as if you were in your own place, but you're not. You're in the apartment of the Minister of Culture, who has given you your own key and is now on her way to Quebec City in a limousine, a woman of importance. But appearances are nothing, nothing at all! She's crazy about you, my boy, completely besotted! She is at this very moment counting in her ministerial head the number of hours between now and the sweet sixty-nines you'll be enjoying with her next weekend—in her bed, on the living room rug, here, there, everywhere! The worst is behind you, Jerome, my boy! You know more than a few men who would kill to be in your place."

And he started to dance on the spot, getting hard as he replayed a flood of images of their love-making.

A stabbing pain in his temples stopped him. He'd had too much to drink these past few days. But that wouldn't stop him from knocking back a beer, because his throat was as dry as a desert. He took a long slug, gasped, ran his tongue over his lips, and the stabbing pain went away.

He found himself standing at the half-open door to a small room Normande used as an office. He'd not been in it, because she rarely used it when he was there, and then only to send or receive emails. Out of discretion, and curbing his curiosity, he'd kept away.

Suddenly he thought he understood the mysterious change of feeling his lover had towards him.

Up until now, as a matter of tactics, he'd almost entirely avoided talking "business" or trying, with nonchalance, to draw information out of her that might be useful to his employers—about whom, of course, he cared nothing.

Politics had always interested him, but he rarely raised the subject and she almost never did. He'd been saving his personal enquiries for later, once he felt he'd gained her trust categorically. Despite everything, he was obliged from time to time to throw a few tidbits to Sicotte and his wife, if only to keep his job. But the impatience Francine Desjarlais had communicated so unpleasantly that Monday morning had only pushed him into doing nothing. Perhaps as a consequence, Normande believed that, despite his employment in one of the biggest lobbyist firms in Montreal, he was with her simply for the pleasure of her company. Cupid had done his job.

"Charlie would tell me to be careful," he thought, sidling up to the door and glancing into the office. "This all seems a little too easy. She gives me a key to her place and a 'So long, my love, see you next week!' Who knows what's actually going on in the head of my beautiful Normande! Maybe I'm being tested and there's a surveillance camera on me right now."

The idea was so unnerving that he returned to the bedroom and got dressed. Back in the living room, he approached the office again. His euphoria had vanished. He hesitated for a second, then, a light shiver running between his shoulders, went into the room. Unlike the rest of the apartment, it was plainly furnished. But for an elegant pedestal table placed in front of the window, on which stood a porcelain vase filled with dried flowers, practicality reigned. On a large melamine desk were the usual computer, telephone, notepads, and pen holders; the drawers contained note paper, office supplies, a cheap makeup kit—but also a small brown stuffed spaniel, its left ear hanging half off. A childhood memento? Good luck charm? On the left side of the room was a metal filing cabinet, locked. Hanging above the cabinet was a large photograph of the cabinet standing around Premier Labrèche, who was seated in a chair looking inscrutable, the ministers putting on airs of benevolent respectability appropriate to their station. The face of Normande, who was standing immediately behind Labrèche, was striking to Jerome because of its caustic severity; this was not the woman he had come to know in the past few weeks.

The only other thing in the room was a cupboard to his right. He tried to open it, without success.

"Well, that's that," he mumbled, leaving the room somewhat disappointed. "Until next week!"

After carefully poking about the rest of the apartment, he had to admit the obvious: this wasn't the night when he would get his hands on whatever was the *thing* that, according to rumour, had seen Normande rise through the party's rank and file from a simple MLA to parliamentary assistant, then party fundraiser, and finally to cabinet minister — all in less than two years! And that was just the beginning. If the *thing* was so instrumental to her career, then no doubt it was locked up in a safety deposit box or some kind of safe. And yet hadn't Normande told him a few weeks ago that her protection against possible dismissal was right here, in this apartment?

"Here . . . and elsewhere," she'd said. Jerome wandered through the rooms, and left around nine o'clock. He could have been in a better mood.

AFTER THE SUNDAY, events proceeded at an inexorable pace. Jerome never heard a word about his prowling through the apartment as, obviously, the minister had not had a surveillance system installed.

During the week that followed, he finally gave in to Charlie's insistent advice that he call Eugenie. After chatting about this and that for a few minutes, doing their best to conceal their *malaise*, they agreed to meet at her place later that night. Jerome found her nervous and her complexion pale, but still in possession of the fine, distinguished beauty that had won him over during their first encounter in Varadero. After hesitating, uncomfortably clearing his throat and tugging at his shirt sleeves innumerable times, he described his situation with as much candour as prudence allowed. After all, he'd not abandoned his scheming and needed to continue his relationship with Minister Juneau. Eugenie was attentive and unforthcoming, and when he finished she asked him, with tears in her eyes, if he really loved her.

He took her hands, and immediately she pulled them away.

"You're the only woman I've ever loved," said Jerome, his voice breaking. "My confiding in you, isn't that proof enough, Eugenie?"

"You love me in a really strange way, then," she answered, exasperated. "I don't know how long I can go on living like this."

"I'm a weird guy, I know," he said so quietly he might have been talking to himself.

"You can say that again. Unfortunately, I like weird guys... And not just me... There's a little girl sleeping in her bedroom back there who talks about you almost every day..."

He stared at her mutely, clenching his jaws with all his strength in order to hold back the powerful and unfamiliar emotion welling up inside of him. Then suddenly an evil thought entered his mind, like a jet of hot sand, and buried the emotion. "Come on, Eugenie," he said to himself, "you're not going to hit me with that little-girl-who-needs-a-father bit, are you?" Immediately, he was ashamed of the thought. He shook his head.

"How is she?" he asked.

"She's okay" was all Eugenie said.

Jerome kept silent for a moment, lost in thought. He was in complete disarray.

"I *must* succeed in this, Eugenie," he said with desperate emphasis. "It's the only way I can regain my sense of myself. Do you understand that?"

"While I lose my own," she replied, her smile acrimonious.

"Listen, Eugenie, give me just a bit more time. If I haven't succeeded in, what, two months, I'll quit working for Sicotte, I'll give the whole thing up."

AS IT TURNED out, he needn't have asked. Ten days later, Sicotte called him into his office and told him he could no longer keep him on the payroll. His wife had flown to Cuba the night before, and Fradette was coming back to Montreal to his old job.

"Can I ask why you're showing me the door, Severin?" Jerome asked, red and barely able to contain himself.

"Insufficient results, my boy," replied the lawyer, with a curious bonhomie. "In this job, we're used to things happening faster, you see. You're a bit too . . . how shall I put it . . . *intellectual*."

His averted eyes suggested that he was keeping the truth to himself.

Jerome gave a sardonic laugh.

"I waited until Francine was gone before giving you the news," Sicotte went on, "and especially before giving you this."

From somewhere he produced a bulky manila envelope.

"Let's call it your severance pay . . . In hundred-dollar bills. Francine wouldn't have agreed to it, but it's the right thing to do . . . It's also a gift for your discretion . . . present and future . . ." He looked at Jerome in a peculiar manner.

"On that, too, I insist," he said.

Under the circumstances, Jerome showed a stoic front and managed to keep his feelings about his new ex-employers to himself. What he wanted was to leap over the Boulle desk behind which the lobbyist's fat stomach was inflating, and to flip it over, scream insults at him, maybe more. But that sort of vengeance was too easy for his liking—and full of complications.

He stood up abruptly, took the envelope (refusing it would have aroused suspicion), and, in answer to a question from the lawyer intended to make his firing as painless as possible, he obliged Sicotte and told him what he knew of Felix, whom he saw now and then and who hadn't shown the slightest desire to visit his parents since the day he'd moved out of the family home.

Ten minutes later, he'd collected his personal effects and left the house on Caledonia Road for good but knowing full well that Sicotte and his wife would be hearing from him. But he also knew that by ambushing them, he'd be putting himself in danger. Hadn't he been their employee—not to say their accomplice—for the better part of a year? The most dignified role he could ever hope to play in this story was that of the repentant. But he was a long way from knowing if he would be given the part!

At home, he opened the envelope: it contained fifty thousand dollars.

"I can't touch this money," he muttered. "It makes me sick."

He contemplated with disgust the bundles of bills spread out on his kitchen table, at the same time feeling a sort of pride in the disgust they inspired in him.

"Can I deposit it in a trust fund?" it occurred to him. "Doing so would improve my credibility as a witness, wouldn't it?"

He picked up the telephone, having decided to ask his lawyer, Maître Asselin, for advice.

"Ah so! It's you, is it?" said the lawyer in a diffident voice. "I was just about to call you. How are you, Monsieur Lupien?"

"Fine, I guess."

"What do you know, my efforts in that moose story of yours are beginning to bear fruit. The other party is starting to waver. Monsieur Pimparé's lawyer was in touch with me yesterday and proposed an out-of-court settlement. That augurs well!"

"How much is he offering?"

"Eh . . . it's a bit too early to say. We both have to feel out the other's terrain, you understand . . . That's why I wanted to call you. But I believe we can go after something in the neighbourhood of seventy to eighty-five thousand dollars . . . I think so, yes."

"My antlers are worth twice that, maybe three times."

Maître Asselin coughed, cleared his throat, and then spoke solemnly, the words placed one after another and carefully delivered.

"Monsieur Lupien, the antlers have been sold and that money has been spent, at least in part. How much does Monsieur Pimparé have left? I can't tell you. If you absolutely insist, I can follow certain procedures and Monsieur Pimparé's lawyer will do the same. But all that will cost a lot of money, and it will be you who pays for it. You will also end up paying indirectly for the guide's lawyer, because I understand Monsieur Pimparé himself is in no position to do so. If these things drag out, shouldn't you be worried that you'll be handing over a large part of the money your rack of antlers gets you in lawyer's fees? Obviously, by speaking to you like this, I'm not pursuing my own financial interest but rather my professional code of ethics. I feel obliged to draw your attention to this aspect of the case, as a friend."

Jerome listened and rubbed his chin more and more frenetically.

"All right," he said brusquely, "go for the settlement. Try to squeeze as much out of him as you can. But I'm actually calling about a different matter."

And he talked about his idea of depositing the money Sicotte had given him in a trust fund. "Can a lawyer set something like that up?"

"Yes, we can do that easily enough. Who will be the beneficiary of this money?"

"Er... I don't know. It's money that's been given to me, but I don't want it."

"Why didn't you just refuse to take it, then?"

"I couldn't."

"Monsieur Lupien," said the lawyer, his impatience beginning to show, "may I ask who gave you this sum of money?"

"My former employer."

"Your *former* employer, you say. You are not still working for him..."

"No."

"And what does this employer do for a living, if I may ask."

"He's a . . . a lobbyist . . . an influence peddler, as he likes to call himself."

"Is he someone you . . . respect?"

"No."

"Did you quit, or is he the one who terminated your employment?"

"A bit of both."

"And, when you left, he gave you a certain sum of money . . ."

"Fifty thousand dollars."

" . . . which you don't want, but which you couldn't refuse. Is that it?"

"That's it."

"Would I be wrong in supposing that the money is of . . . er . . . a dubious provenance?"

"You would not be wrong. And I want nothing to do with it. Which is why I want to deposit it in a trust fund, so that I can't touch it and no one else can touch it either."

"Monsieur Lupien," continued the lawyer, bemused, "bad luck seems to have placed some very strange people in your path . . . Unfortunately, I can't be of service to you in this matter. A trust fund must benefit a person or a legal entity, such as a corporation. Do you understand? And even if you have such a beneficiary in mind, I can't become involved with this dubious money. It would make me an accomplice. I'm sorry."

"So what do I do?" exclaimed Jerome, in a panic.

"I really don't know . . . This money must not be found in your possession, that's the thing. Deposit it in a bank and don't touch it. That's the only advice I can give you. Now, I must ask you to excuse me, I have much work to do."

THREE MORE WEEKS went by. The middle of December was approaching, and with it the cruise in the Bahamas aboard the *Fortune*, a three-hundred-tonne yacht belonging to the wealthy construction-company owner Rodolfo Vagra, known in certain circles as Rodolfo the Hammer because of his tendency to come down hard on anyone who got in his way.

"He doesn't have a good reputation, this Mister Vagra," Jerome had said the day Normande mentioned his name.

"Do you know anybody rich with a good reputation?" replied the minister, cynically.

As the weeks passed, Jerome had learned different aspects of her character, some of which were harsh. When she was worried about something, it was best not to speak to her, for fear of invoking a nasty response. On the other hand, she was a veritable workhorse, with an active, methodical, and clear mind; she had no time for toadies and lackeys, the yes-men, and appreciated those who stood up to her (within reason, of course). And she could, on occasion, exhibit remarkable generosity.

She was unable to contain her joy when Jerome told her he was no longer working for Severin Sicotte.

"Don't worry, I'll find you something, my love. There are always positions coming vacant in politicians' offices, either in Montreal or Quebec City . . . not to mention, of course, the civil service. Naturally, in your case, you'd have to pass exams, but you'd do so easily and if there were any difficulties, don't you worry, I'd take care of them."

Jerome's smile was a little contemptuous.

"I don't mean to offend, but I'd rather find my own way to earn my daily bread. I've done fine up till now, you see."

"Well, well, well, what have we here? Look at this little baby who wants to choose all the goodies for himself! You want to be independent? You won't go very far in life, my dear."

"I haven't done too badly so far, have I, my beautiful minister?"

And he started to cover her with such naughty kisses that she broke out laughing and pushed him away.

The scene was taking place in Montreal, on a Saturday night, in Normande's condo. They'd watched the movie *Titanic*, which Jerome had already seen twice a few years before, but his lover wanted to see it again — for a fourth time — because, she said, she loved its "grand passions."

"I don't want to become your gigolo," Jerome said, leaning over to take his glass of red wine. "It's a matter of pride."

"Do you think I need to pay for gigolos?"

She looked at him with amusement, but steel needles formed in her eyes.

"Hmm...If it were me, I'd pay anything to make sure no one touched my sweet minister of love."

She kissed his cheek. "Well said, my love...But how would you like to back up those pretty words with a little action?"

And, with an impish smile, she pointed in the direction of the bedroom.

Jerome nodded enthusiastically and followed, wondering about the truth of a crude remark Sicotte had made about Normande a few months back, saying that the only thing about her more unbridled than her ass was her ambition.

They made love for the third time that day, then, after briefly discussing the Bahaman cruise, due to leave New

York on the twenty-seventh of December and promising to be, she assured him, *ex-tra-or-di-nary*, Jerome fell into a deep sleep. He needed his strength restored, because some carnal recidivism was likely to take place at four in the morning. Normande didn't get to bed for another hour, as she'd needed to tend to an urgent email to her press secretary that she'd forgotten to send earlier.

The next day, Sunday, was decisive for Jerome. Around ten in the morning, half undressed, he was in the dining room setting out brunch (a relatively easy task as Madame's caterer had prepared everything in advance) when a humming Normande appeared in a flimsy chiffon negligée with a pink fringe. She surveyed the table approvingly and, finding the aroma of a cinnamon bun just out of the oven irresistible, broke a piece off with her fingers and put it in her mouth, emitting little groans of pleasure.

"Give me ten minutes, will you, my dear? Time for me to get dressed and put on some makeup before we sit down? It's a question of class, you see: I'm not a pleb anymore."

Jerome's heart was pounding in his chest. He replied with a nod, not daring to say a thing lest his voice betray the emotion grabbing him by the throat.

Earlier that day, from the far end of the kitchen, he'd noticed the minister take a clutch of keys from the handbag she'd left on a chair in the living room, then head to her study. Craning his neck, he'd watched as she unlocked the cupboard he'd been unable to inspect a few weeks before, run her hand over the shelves piled high with documents, and take out a folder. After that, she'd closed the door and spoken at length to someone named Raymond over the telephone. He could hear only snatches. The call ended, and patently happy with the results of the discussion, she'd returned to the living room and put the keys back in her purse.

In a flash, everything fell into place in Jerome's mind.

He had ten minutes to get into her handbag, find the right key, unlock the cupboard, and return the keys to her bag. If by chance Normande noticed the cupboard was unlocked, she'd think she herself had forgotten to lock it. And if she didn't notice, all Jerome had to do was to come up with some pretext for staying in the apartment upon her departure to Quebec City, and then go over the documents he'd wanted to examine for so long. Maybe he wouldn't find anything of interest but he'd be crazy to pass up such a golden opportunity.

It took him two and a half minutes to carry out his plan.

The day went by without Normande returning to the study. Jerome was having a hard time hiding his restlessness.

Halfway through the afternoon she said, "Will you please tell me what's got into you?"

They were sitting on the sofa, watching a ball game on television. It was a sport she was passionate about but that plunged Jerome into boredom verging on despair.

"I've been watching you for half an hour now," she said, a little irritated. "You can't seem to stop fidgeting, you poor thing...Do you want to watch the game by yourself or what?"

"Too much coffee," he mumbled, eyes fixed on the screen. "It happens sometimes, sorry."

He managed to be still for several minutes, but then, at the end of his rope, he turned to his companion; transfixed, she had just cried out in joy and clapped her hands after a fabulous catch by Paul Gillmate, rising star of the Connaught Suburbans.

"Would it bother you if I went for a walk? I've got a bad case of ants in the pants, I'm afraid."

She looked at him in astonishment, then pointed to a window, thin rivulets of rainwater running down the squared panes. Montreal was a brooding mid-afternoon autumn grey; a light but nasty drizzle was falling.

"Doesn't matter," he said, "I need some air. And my windbreaker has a hood."

She was about to say something in reply when the ringing of her cell phone stopped her. He hastened out of the room, afraid that she might head to the study so that she could discuss *confidential matters* privately . . . But as he was putting on his windbreaker, he heard her joyfully exclaim, "Ghislaine! What a lovely surprise! How are you?"

He silently blessed this Ghislaine, whoever she was: obviously a friend or relative. Without her realizing it, she had helped him in his plan—at least he hoped so.

Leaving the building, he hesitated a second. The rain was ice-cold and coming down in sheets. He'd be soaked to the skin after two blocks. All the better: he'd have an excuse to remain in the apartment after she left, so he could dry his clothes. With his head bent against the downpour beating on the glistening pavement, he headed quickly towards rue de la Commune, where the wind coming up from the river was blowing hard. He hadn't lied to his lover: he really did need air, a lot of it, fresh air like this that would soothe his mind, be invigorating, help him make the right decisions.

The weak light of a café appeared farther down the street to his left. He quickened his pace, opened the door, and found himself in a room deserted but for an old man with a mass of curly hair that was unbelievably black, talking to the owner, a glass of Armagnac in front of him. After glancing at the menu, Jerome ordered a hot rum toddy. He was shivering from head to toe. He took out his cell phone.

"Charlie?" he said, his voice low. "Boy, am I glad I caught you! I may need your services tonight... Yes, tonight... Excellent, pal. Can Martine hear you? She's not there? Good, so much the better... No, I can't tell you any more at the moment, first of all I have to make sure that... Yes, I'm at Juneau's now, or close to it... You have a migraine? Since this morning... Shit... Look, Charlie, I'm sorry but I'm really counting on you, old friend, because I might find... If you let me down now, Charlie, the whole thing could go south... That's right, I'll call you back a bit later... Take care of yourself. Goodbye, and thanks in advance, eh?"

He sipped his toddy, plunged in the mechanics of his plan and listening absent-mindedly to the monologue of the curly-headed old man who was now recounting how his career as a maker of violins had ended because of horrible cheap imports. The toddy's warmth spread through his chest like the foliage of a tropical plant. It was making him feel better and restoring his optimism.

A short time passed. Outside, the rain had turned into a storm. It pounded on the pavement in steady blasts and gusted against the trembling glass of the window in thick sheets.

"A true late-autumn hurricane," said the old man, raising his glass as though proposing a toast to misfortune.

The owner, bent over a sink, was rinsing dishes.

"We never have hurricanes at this time of year," she said.

Her customer smiled and adopted a sanctimonious air. "There's always a first time, Madame."

I have to go, Jerome thought suddenly. What's Normande going to think?

He went to the counter, paid his bill, and tugged at the zipper on his windbreaker.

"You should wait until this lets up a bit," the owner advised. She was in her fifties and overweight. She spoke gently and maternally.

"No choice."

"Each to his own destiny," declared the former luthier gravely. He was already in his cups, and ordered another Armagnac.

Jerome left and was soaked to the skin again in no time.

"Well, there's my excuse for staying in the apartment," he told himself, teeth chattering. He moved with difficulty, blinded by the water and disoriented in the liquid magma shot through with thunder and flashes of diffused light. "Unless this bad weather makes her decide to stay in Montreal," he suddenly thought.

The possibility stopped him in his tracks. He was at a corner; a passing car splashed him thoroughly.

"Well? Did your walk do you any good?" Normande asked him sarcastically. She was laughing as he stood dripping onto the carpet. He took off his clothes one by one and dropped them to the floor.

"I stopped at a café to wait for the storm to pass, but it didn't pass."

"Ah. Well, I have to go now whether it passes or not. Affairs of state before all, as they say. My driver should be here any minute. I asked him to come early because of the rain. I'll have something to eat in the limo. I expect you'll eat something here, while your clothes are in the dryer?"

Jerome nodded. "If that's okay with you."

He tried to pass her, but she grabbed him by the hair so forcefully that it made him wince.

"Why were you gone so long in this weather? I was worried about you."

He freed himself and stared at her angrily. "Madame Minister is taking control, I see," he managed to say, trying to sound bemused even as a thousand questions were bouncing in his head like popcorn. Did she suspect something? Was he being followed? Was the apartment under electronic surveillance?

How strangely she was acting—like an inquisitor. What did she know?

"You didn't answer my question."

"I told you," he said, trying to mask his unease with bad temper. "I needed some air, I was suffocating. And when I saw you talking to ... Ghislaine ..."

"We talked for at most five minutes."

"How was I to know how long it would take? Okay, okay, I'm sorry. If I knew—"

The bell chimed its four rising notes. Normande put on her coat and picked up her suitcase, waiting by the door, then put her hand on Jerome's cheek.

"Have a good week," he said, giving her a hug.

"Sure" was all she said.

The door closed behind her. Jerome remained where he was; hesitant, transfixed, jumping at the slightest sound. Should he go ahead with his plan—or leave once and for all? He decided to take a long, hot shower. A few minutes later, able to see things differently, he concluded his lover's strange behaviour was that of a strong loving woman used to being obeyed. As for the rest, the cupboard door would decide the matter: if she had locked it, he would go home and not come back. But if she hadn't ...

He got out of the shower, dried himself, put on a robe, and went into the study.

The cupboard was unlocked.

Hands behind his back, he perused the six shelves in the cupboard at length. Everything appeared to be meticulously arranged. He didn't bother with the top two. Reams of paper were piled on, and sitting on the other was a forbidding set of *The Criminal Code, Annotated and Appended*. Had she studied law? On the next two shelves, pressed tightly together, was a large number of file folders stuffed with documents and held upright by metal dividers; just the thought of going through them made him feel dizzy. The next shelf down contained two cardboard boxes of books, on top of which, strangely enough, someone had placed a queen's costume, or perhaps that of a Good Fairy.

The second-last shelf drew his attention. He had to kneel down to examine it. On the left, two piles of cassette tapes, most of them in their cases but some exposed to the open air; they dated to the early eighties, before the appearance of compact discs, when tapes were the *sine qua non* of audio technology. Charlie surely still possessed a cassette player that would let him hear what was on them, but he doubted they would contain anything of interest. The compact discs and recordable DVDs arranged beside them looked more promising.

Still on his knees, he scrutinized the cases, trying to decipher their labels and careful to touch them as little as possible; after a while, his legs ached and he decided to go find a cushion. He stood up and, wobbling slightly, thought he would call Charlie instead.

Which is when he heard the New Wave ringtone of his cell.

"That'll be him," he murmured. He raced through the living room, then the dining room, trying to figure out where the ringing was coming from. "Shit! My cell's in the flood!" he realized. He hurried to the vestibule, where his windbreaker was lying in a pool of water, and retrieved his soaking cell phone.

"Jerome? It's me," said Normande. "Where are you?"

White noise drowned out her words, as if she were calling from a distant country over primitive phone lines. The storm must have been even heavier on Highway 40.

"Still here," he said. "At your place."

"I wasn't sure, so I called." She paused for a moment, then said, "I'm sorry for earlier, my love. I didn't know where you'd gone and I was worried. You understand, don't you?"

He listened, holding his breath, a wave of shame paralyzing his thinking. What a business! Here he was searching her study for information that, leaked to the public, might do her career terrible harm—and she calls as the repentant lover!

"Are you angry with me?" she asked.

He could barely make out her words through the storm and the bad connection, which was getting weaker every moment and distorting her voice.

"No, no, not at all, I assure you. It's forgotten...*forgotten!*" he repeated louder.

"Okay, I've got to go." Her distant voice was drowned in static. "I can hardly hear you. Good..."

The line went dead.

He took a few steps and dropped onto a chair, tears in his eyes, arms hanging at his sides, seized by a self-loathing such as he'd never known before.

"I'm fed up with lying! I'm fed up with hiding!" he shouted suddenly. "I'm done with it, goddamn it! I'm ashamed of myself! Ashamed! I'm sick to death of it!"

He stopped and looked fearfully about himself. Luckily,

the condo building was well insulated; they never heard their neighbours.

"Right. Let's get to work," he muttered after a moment, seized suddenly by fierce determination. "What must be done must be done."

He picked up his cell phone again, dried it against his robe, and punched in Charlie's number. Charlie answered quickly. His migraine was going away, he said, but he was questioning the wisdom of his friend's plan. He thought it risky, with little chance of success.

"There's no risk, Charlie. It's a simple matter of making copies of fifty or sixty CDs and DVDs, then putting them back where I got them. Before touching anything I'll take a photo of the material, so I can put them back exactly as they were before."

"So why do I have to be there?" asked Charlie. "Bring them here, I'll make the copies at my place."

How could he resist such good sense?

At twenty minutes past midnight, Jerome parked his car near his friend's apartment. The rain had ended half an hour earlier, but the drive had been long and tricky. Large tree branches had come down and blocked streets everywhere. Some sections of the city were without power. On the radio it was announced that around eleven that night a body had been discovered in Longueuil, on Chambly Road, crushed by a fallen tree in the backyard of a betting shop. What was the fellow doing there, at that hour and in that storm?

Jerome didn't need to ring. Charlie opened the door as soon as he arrived, looking pale and drawn, a finger to his lips. Martine had come in a little earlier and gone to bed. He took the shopping bags his friend was carrying and brought them into the cubbyhole he used as a workshop.

"Does Martine know I'm here?"

"Yes, but she doesn't know why."

Three hours later all of the discs had been copied except for one, and for good reason: it was enclosed in a metal case fitted with a lock, and Jerome had not been able to find a key. The extraordinary precaution greatly intrigued them.

"I'll bet the jackpot is on that disc," said Jerome, his expression keen despite the exhaustion overwhelming him.

"Well," said Charlie, "good luck with it — and good luck to me, too," he added, swallowing two more tablets of acetaminophen.

A small creaking sound made them turn around. Martine, in a dressing gown and bare feet, her hair in disarray, was watching them from the doorway.

"How's it going, your espionage?" she asked. "I'm cold in bed by myself, Charlie," she added plaintively, with a long yawn.

THE NEXT MORNING at nine, Jerome was at a locksmith's shop on Papineau. He set the DVD case on the counter.

"Lost the key," he said. "Can you cut me a new one?"

Twenty minutes later he was out of the shop and on his way back to Charlie's apartment to make a copy of the DVD. Municipal workers were scattered about the city, cleaning up debris left by the storm. The copy was made but he had no time to look at it as he was in such a hurry to return the originals. Charlie, using methyl alcohol, had wiped the discs clean of fingerprints and Jerome did the same for the metal case. It wouldn't prevent suspicion from landing on Jerome, if it came to that, but why make it easy for them?

It was almost noon before everything was back in the cupboard. His sleepless night had done him in. Before leaving

Normande's apartment, he decided to sit for a moment in the living room. When the phone rang at two o'clock, he jumped. But he was careful not to answer it.

THE CONTENTS OF the locked DVD case told him his instincts were correct. Here was the bomb that gave Normande such control over Premier Labrèche. The rumours, for once, weren't far from the truth. Still, his discovery astonished him. He felt like a detective who, on the trail of a thief, instead catches a rapist.

The DVD had been used to record a meeting for seventy-nine minutes and eighteen seconds. There was no date, but the evidence suggested it was recent, taking place in what looked like a suite in a big hotel. The private meeting included Premier Labrèche, three cabinet ministers, and three of his closest colleagues: MLAs Jocelyn Lavoie and the veteran Jeffrey Dupire; his cabinet chief, Maxime Davis; the Minister of Municipal Affairs, Jennifer Désy-Pommier; Jean-Marc Levalet, Minister of Federal-Provincial Relations; and his Minister of Culture, Normande Juneau.

It began with a few friendly words from the premier addressed to Normande, whose idea it had been to hold the meeting behind closed doors and who'd gone to so much trouble to organize it. The mood was informal. They were celebrating the happy end to what had been a difficult session in the Assembly. Premier Labrèche sat squarely in his chair, legs crossed at the knee, enthroned at the centre of his colleagues, his corpulence elegant and his blond beard perfectly trimmed. He was following the conversation burgeoning around him with a measured smile, from time to time tossing in a word or two. His subordinates sat around, chatting happily, glasses in hand, or passing bottles of wine or spirits and plates of hors d'oeuvres. Whenever the premier spoke in his calm, careful, articulate way — his, the serious, melodious voice of a *monsieur distingué* — the room fell silent and everyone listened to their Master's Voice.

Most of the recording was of little interest, filled as it was with banalities or remarks that were meaningless out of context. But three short passages made Jerome understand immediately why Normande kept the disc under lock and key.

The first passage came near the beginning, just after Jean-Philippe Labrèche thanked his Minister of Culture.

PREMIER LABRÈCHE: I first want to emphasize the exceptional contribution to our party's finances made by Madame Juneau. The sum now exceeds $300,000, an amount never before raised by a Minister of Culture!

Normande nods, smiling.

JENNIFER DÉSY-POMMIER, *teasing, but with a hint of malice*: The minister of the poor...

Some laughter.

JEAN-MARC LEVALET, *adding*: Or of poor beggars of grants?

PREMIER LABÈCHE, *frowning*: Now, now, a little decorum here, if you don't mind, ladies and gentlemen.

JEAN-MARC LEVALET: This museum project must have played a part, no?

NORMANDE JUNEAU: It goes without saying.

MAXIME DAVIS: We're offering a gold mine to these businessmen, so it's only right that they open their wallets in return. But you need to know how to convince them—and sometimes how to lead them by the nose. (*Slightly sarcastic.*) And that's not always easy, is it, Jean-Marc?

The second extract took place at twenty-eight minutes thirty-two seconds and lasted barely a minute. Jennifer Désy-Pommier, the Minister of Municipal Affairs, was criticizing the Leader of the Opposition, whose attacks against her had made headlines a few weeks earlier.

JENNIFER DÉSY-POMMIER, *in a bitter, caustic voice*: When they're the Opposition, they see racketeering everywhere, but once they get into power themselves, pouf, it doesn't exist! What racketeering? Oh, no! Suddenly they're little angels, little pink and white angels who fly around saying their Hail Marys. (*Laughter.*) But once we're the ones in control, listen to them and you'd think we had the power to... to...

PREMIER LABRÈCHE, *smiling*: ...to change human nature.

JENNIFER DÉSY-POMMIER: Exactly...as if that were possible!

MAXIME DAVIS, *ironically*: It's in all the political science textbooks.

JEAN-MARC LEVALET: Never read them. Too caught up in my work...

PREMIER LABRÈCHE: You should, Jean-Marc. They're very amusing. The tension between theory and practice sometimes has outcomes that are...poetical.

JEAN-MARC LEVALET: I never read poetry, either. It bores me.

NORMANDE JUNEAU, *teasing*: But Jean-Marc, your "rose garden" speech last week in the Jonquière arena was a huge success!

General laughter.

JEAN-MARC LEVALET, *playing along*: One swallow does not a summer make, Normande.

PREMIER LABRÈCHE: Don't worry about it, Jean-Marc, in ten days everything will be forgotten. As I've said before, think of the electorate as a bunch of not very gifted ten-year-olds. Their powers of memory and judgement are weak...Anyone who doesn't understand that will make a very poor politician...Do you remember what Trudeau said in Quebec during the referendum? *"Your No will be a Yes!"* And it worked. It was great art...

Approving nods around the room.

The third passage appeared forty minutes later, and

showed the disinhibiting effects alcohol can have even on experienced drinkers well aware of the hazards of excessive consumption.

Of six bottles of Petrus, only one remained—and it was half empty. And half a decanter of cognac had also evaporated.

A lively debate concerning the language question had broken out between Jean-Marc Levalet and the MLA Jocelyn Lavoie, a thirty-seven-year-old former journalist. Hot-tempered and sanguine, she was a woman whose high spirits and extraordinary capacity for work made people overlook the asperity of her character. The discussion centred on the working language of civil servants in Quebec: the nationalist camp insisted they adhere to the French-language charter just like everyone else; the opposing camp were perfectly happy with the status quo, which allowed people to work in English. Lavoie vigorously defended the application of the Charter of the French Language; Levalet, who was getting drunk and running out of arguments, suggested that maybe his opponent "wasn't a true Canadian." Coming from his mouth, the remark sounded like an insult.

PREMIER LABRÈCHE: Hello, people! Is there someone from the Opposition in here?

The conversation stops; uneasiness floats in the air.

JEAN-MARC LEVALET, *confused*: I tell it as I see it.

PREMIER LABRÈCHE: Yes, you do, just as if you were addressing a member of the Opposition . . . These arguments get us nowhere. In fact, they hurt us.

JOCELYN LAVOIE, *surprised*: You think?

PREMIER LABRÈCHE: Absolutely. (*His face, that of a bon vivant who likes his cognac, is flushed and slightly swollen; his look is evasive and wavering; he continues with a subtly disdainful smile.*) My God, how much time and energy we have wasted... on a lost cause.

JOCELYN LAVOIE, *even more surprised*: Lost?

PREMIER LABRÈCHE: I've been thinking about this accursed language question for a long time, my friend. Until now, no one has had the courage to adopt the only realistic plan in this unfortunate portfolio. (*He stops, empties his glass of cognac, and hands it to Jeffrey Dupire for a fifth refill.*) Through much effort, many battles, and great sacrifices, our people have more or less succeeded in living in French for more than four hundred years, even though we amount to no more than a nutshell floating on the English sea. Well, good for us. Thunderous applause from me! But, for all sorts of reasons, this gamble has become untenable today — and I would go even further: for humane reasons, we have to put an end to this senseless — this ruinous — adventure... Don't look at me like that, my dear Lavoie. We cannot afford to sacrifice another generation to an *idea*, for crying out loud! (*He thanks Jeffrey Dupire with a smile and accepts his glass, takes a drink, and slowly surveys the attentive group.*) I see only one possible plan, but it will require cleverness, patience...

A short silence. Eyes half-closed, he breathes in the vapours of his cognac.

JOCELYN LAVOIE, *cautiously*: Would it be indiscreet of me to ask what plan you're thinking of?

PREMIER LABRÈCHE, *with a Cheshire-cat smile*: Yes.

Burst of laughter all around. Jean-Marc Levalet, laughing harder that the others, gives Lavoie a poke.

PREMIER LABRÈCHE, *serious again*: I won't beat about the bush, my friends; the only way out of this impasse without breaking pots is ... to amend the Charter of the French Language and give Montreal bilingual status. Yes. Surprised? Think about it for a minute. On the one hand, we would only be recognizing a reality that already exists. On the other, we'd be able to count on the unconditional support of all the non-francophones, immigrants and whatever, who are soon going to be in the majority in Montreal and whose dream is to speak English. That's if they aren't speaking it already. Business people, obviously, would kiss our hands. Have you heard our friend Rozon? It's what he's been trumpeting all along! (*Sighs*) In time, we would end up winning the support of most of the citizens of Montreal.

A profound silence reigns in the room; Jean-Marc Levalet is smiling so broadly he looks a bit foolish.

PREMIER LABRÈCHE: The beauty of the thing is once

Montreal is made officially bilingual, it would only take a generation, give or take, for the city to be anglophone in practice. And then, after another generation — maybe even faster than that — the whole province would follow suit. Without dissent, without a revolution. Simply through the momentum of events. Finally, we would be normal. (*He lifts his glass to his lips and, before tipping it, adds:*) The people of Quebec don't dare admit it, but deep down inside, it's what they want, for themselves and for their children: to adapt to the new world order — and have a better life.

Short silence.

JEAN-MARC LEVALET, *bootlicking, as usual*: Well, effectively, that's what I've always thought, how about that.

PREMIER LABRÈCHE, *ironically*: That doesn't surprise me, Jean-Marc. We always end up thinking the same thing.

Some laughter.

JENNIFER DÉSY-POMMIER, *mellifluously, under the disapproving gaze of cabinet leader Davis*: Do you have a bill in mind?

PREMIER LABRÈCHE: We're doing the groundwork, Madame Minister. Everything comes to those who wait.

AT SIX O'CLOCK, Jerome knocked on Charlie's door looking worried, fretful, full of doubts but also bursting with pride: he wanted Charlie to look at the disc immediately. But first they were obliged to eat, because Martine had made crêpes, and crêpes, as everyone knew, don't keep. Never, to the amateur spy, had a meal seemed so interminable. He'd barely swallowed his last mouthful before he dragged Charlie into his workshop. With a grave demeanour, the technician watched the video from the start without saying a word, then replayed the three passages that had caught his friend's attention.

"With your permission," he said, "I'll make some extra copies of this."

"So, do you think..."

"This is dynamite, Jerome. No wonder your minister kept it locked up. There's enough here to blow the government sky high!"

"I doubt Juneau would ever make use of it, though," declared Martine. "She'd go up with the rest of them."

The two men turned in surprise: without a sound, she had opened the door and been a part of the second screening.

Jerome pointed a threatening finger at her.

"You don't tell anyone about this, right?"

"Who do you take me for? You think I'm soft in the head? It makes me sick to have to listen to them, our *elected leaders*—especially the Great Leader himself, with his pompous airs—as they line their pockets with our tax money...And they're going to decide what language my children are going to speak!"

A stray lock of hair dangling over one eye as she spoke imbued her words with even more vehemence.

"Oh, I didn't know you were a mom," Charlie joked. "How many children?"

She stuck out her tongue at him, then turned to Jerome. "Do you really think she'd use that video? It would be like putting a gun to her own head."

"Normande Juneau is no idiot. She'd show what she wanted when she wanted. Most of all, she can use it as a form of blackmail."

There was silence.

"So, Mr. Double Agent," said Martine, "what are you going to do?"

"First, make some copies," Charlie interrupted. "And then you, Jerome, first thing tomorrow morning, you're going to rent a safety deposit box. And hurry."

"Yes, but after that?" Martine insisted.

"*Calma, calma, signorina,*" said Jerome, waving his hands. "Before we play, we must tune our instruments. If not, we'll play so badly the room will empty."

But it wasn't long before panic gripped him. He felt like a man who'd gone out to hunt partridge and stumbled into a grizzly bear. He'd wanted to sink Sicotte and his wife, and by doing so make an honest man of himself (and reap the rewards of that), but now the whole affair was of a different magnitude altogether. One false step and the opportunity before him could be transformed into disaster.

The discussion began. It was wrought and punctuated with abrupt remarks and nervous laughter. Jerome discovered a Martine he hadn't known, a go-getter, a battler, mordant and perfectly at ease with the unforeseen adventure he'd set in motion. She quickly convinced Charlie that the file should be sent to *Enquête*, a prestigious investigative journalism program on the public broadcaster's channel that had exposed a great many scandals. Jerome, unsettled, hesitated.

"That would be unnecessarily humiliating for a lot of

people. Imagine how far Quebec City will go to cover it up..."

"Come on, Jerome," said Charlie angrily, "there've been other scandals. What do you take them for, Easter chicks?"

"No, of course not, but..."

"What are you proposing, then?" asked Charlie, on edge.

Jerome sighed, scratched his head, tugged on his shirt sleeve. "Let's open a bottle of wine. That'll relax us a bit, no?"

It was nearly nine o'clock when Jerome left his friend's apartment and headed to the Mont-Royal métro station. He felt too nervous to take his car. The night was cool, the air a little bracing. Not many other people were about, and his footsteps echoed strangely on the sidewalk. The smell of frying meat and a few bursts of laughter coming through the door of a restaurant reminded him life was taking its course and other people around him were having a good time.

Fifteen minutes later, he came out of the Place-des-Arts station onto rue Bleury and headed towards the offices of *Le Devoir*. He'd decided to offer the newspaper the first shot. After that, there was nothing to stop him from tossing the radioactive brick to someone else.

A deserted lobby with a gleaming floor. The elevator seemed to have vanished somewhere into the fourth dimension; he remembered his first meeting with Normande Juneau at the Ministry of Culture. If she'd known then, the poor woman... She was going to hate him so much!

The elevator door opened abruptly with a plaintive squeak. He entered the empty lift, pressed a button and, while the contraption rattled and shook, checked once more that the disc was in the inside pocket of his windbreaker. A few moments later, he was standing before a woman busily sorting through her desk drawers.

"Monsieur Descôteaux just left," she said when he asked to speak to the editorial director. "He'll be in tomorrow morning. But you need to make an appointment, sir."

She said it with minimal courtesy, as though she were exhausted by her long day and a headache was settling in.

"Thank you, ma'am. I'll call tomorrow."

He went back to rue Marie-Anne, retrieved his car and drove home. His resolve was starting to ebb. Everything seemed mundane, now, drained of any significance. What was he doing, getting involved in this? The earth turned, waves were breaking upon the shore, the sun would rise over here and set over there, and humanity was pretty much as it always had been: ugly, all things considered. A terrible lethargy was coming over him, pulling at his eyelids, blurring his vision, diminishing his concentration. He felt like running a red light, maybe going the wrong way down a one-way street, running over a dog, knocking down a pedestrian... To sleep: that was all he wanted, to sleep to his heart's content and send all else packing. There were always plenty of fools around to defend causes lost before they even got off the ground.

It took him a good quarter of an hour to find a parking space. He was walking along the sidewalk, at his wits' end, feeling like giving something a good kick, when he saw Felix sitting on the steps leading up to his apartment. "Oh no," he thought, "not him, not tonight! What the hell does he want?"

The young man saw him, jumped to his feet, and rushed to meet him, hand outstretched, a smile on his lips.

"Man, it's hard to quit smoking, Jerome!" he said by way of preamble. "I've been waiting here for half an hour, and I haven't been able to think of anything but having a smoke! How are you?"

"I'm tired," Jerome replied, looking down. "What's up?"

"Nothing much...Um...I've come at a bad time, I see... We'll get together another time...I just felt like shooting the shit, that's all..."

He seemed so disappointed that Jerome made an effort to smile. "Sorry, Felix, I've had a hell of a day...But come on up for a minute, have a beer. I've got some Mort Subite in the fridge."

His companion, too well raised to accept an invitation he knew was being extended simply out of politeness, shook his head.

"Another time," he said. "Life is long." After a quick hand-shake, he started to walk away, then turned. "Oh, I almost forgot...I called the old man earlier tonight. He definitely wants to speak to you, if you can wrap your mind around it."

Jerome looked at him sternly. "I don't work for him any-more, Felix. I can't imagine what we'd have to talk about. Did he send you here?"

"You think so!" sneered Felix. "I don't have anything to do with his schemes. I'm just passing on a message, that's all."

Under the light of the street lamp behind him, his face seemed open and honest.

"See you later," he called, crossing the street. "At my place, this time. You still haven't come around. It's not bad, you know."

JEROME WOKE UP at dawn after one of the worst nights of his life. Stringing together the brief moments he'd been able to sleep, would they have added up to two hours? Not even.

Felix's message had not stopped running through his head, giving rise to all sorts of speculation. Had they already brought out the heavy artillery? Was Felix, without knowing it, being exploited by his father? Was the telephone about to sound the death knell to his life's only heroic undertaking? And yet, how could it? Hadn't he taken every possible and imaginable precaution?

Waxen-faced, his hands shaking, he took the landline off the hook and turned off his cell phone. If anyone wanted to get hold of him, they'd have to come to his apartment, but he wouldn't be there. This morning, without even bothering to shave and brush his teeth, he'd go have breakfast in a restaurant near the offices of *Le Devoir* — he remembered having seen one across the street — and wait for the editor to come to work.

BERNARD DESCÔTEAUX WAS listening. Fortuitously, he and Jerome had arrived at *Le Devoir* at the same time. Drawing on his feverish energy, he managed — under the disapproving eye of the receptionist who'd told him to leave a message on the editorial director's voicemail — to convince the man to see him right away.

"But only for a minute. I'm expecting someone."

Sitting before him, disc in hand, Jerome summoned up all his rhetorical skills. "Please, *sir*, you really must watch this DVD right away — or at least have it watched by one of your journalists. Michel David, for example. You have no idea, Monsieur Descôteaux, how important this is!"

"That, my friend, is what I must decide," replied the editor with paternal patience. "You say it's about a secret meeting between the premier and three of his cabinet ministers, and that it was filmed without their knowledge? Why was that?"

How could a man who was so calm and poised be

running such a feisty newspaper! Jerome waved the disc he was holding at the end of his outstretched arm.

"Not just ministers, Monsieur Descôteaux. His house leader and two MLAs were also there, I think. I can't say for sure. They propose . . . if only you knew what they . . . I'll show you the three important sections. After two minutes you'll thank me, I assure you."

"But how did you procure this document, my dear man? Do you work in politics?"

"God forbid, but I have connections with someone who does . . . It's a bit of a delicate matter and hard to explain in a few words, Monsieur Descôteaux, the whole . . . First look at the disc, please, and afterwards I'll gladly . . . Won't you?"

The editor observed the young man, whose face was drawn and haggard, his hair dishevelled, and who seemed to be speaking rationally but looked like he was under extra-ordinary pressure. That, or he was in withdrawal or having some kind of psychotic episode. What don't we see these days, my goodness!

The telephone rang. He picked up.

"Very well, thank you. In a minute."

He looked at Jerome pensively and then, placing a palm on his desk as if to push himself up, he hesitated. A journalist's career, he reflected, was a constant struggle against lost time.

A moment passed.

"Come with me," he said finally.

He pushed his office door open, crossed the newsroom, already in an uproar, and stopped at the desk of a young woman with long blond hair and large black horn-rimmed glasses, hunched over the keyboard of her computer. She looked like an intern or something of that nature.

"This gentleman demands that we take a look at a document, Madeleine. Can you give it a look? He'll indicate the passages he thinks are important."

A WHOLE DAY went by without his hearing from the newspaper. Jerome didn't dare telephone. In the last twenty-four hours he'd eaten virtually nothing and hardly slept. Returning from the *dépanneur* he'd visited to buy a paper — not a word about the story! — a dizzy spell came over him and he had to sit down on the outside staircase for a few minutes: the chilly air eventually brought him back to his senses.

After examining the segments in question, the intern, looking agitated, had come to find him and asked in a tentative, convent school girl's voice (she couldn't have been older than in her mid-twenties), "Where did you get this, sir?"

Jerome, smiling, had placed a finger on his lips and winked at her. "Professional secret."

So she went to Descôteaux's office and knocked on the door. After a minute, the editor opened it and they had a brief confabulation after which he pointed to Jerome and retreated into his office.

"Monsieur Descôteaux asked me to get your coordinates," said the young woman. "He'll look at the DVD this afternoon and be in touch with you when he can."

Now Jerome was at his kitchen table having a café au lait to help him digest an Emmenthal cheese sandwich, which was sitting in his stomach like a lead weight. He looked at his watch for the hundredth time since he'd got out of bed. A delay is essentially immaterial, he told himself in a moment of gloomy metaphysical understanding; it can go on indefinitely, even end up becoming eternity, and still just be a delay.

His cell phone rang. It was on the table beside his copy of *Le Devoir*. He checked the screen.

"Charlie. Damn it! I should have called him."

They talked for a few minutes. Jerome told him about recent events, which didn't take long because almost nothing had happened.

"I've been confined to barracks since yesterday, Charlie, waiting. What else can I do? I can't respond to unknown callers, and really have to be careful not to speak to Normande, of course, if she ever calls ... Oh, and I forgot: there's Sicotte, my old boss, who desperately wants to speak to me, it seems. I heard that from his son the day before yesterday ... But no, really, don't worry, I'll be avoiding him at all costs. If that asshole thinks he's going to corner me ... Once bitten, twice shy! I'm going to arrange it so that I'm here as little as possible, just in case he comes looking for me. You never know. Anyway, I'm going out as it is. Don't try to call me, I'll be at the movies."

HE WAS ENTERING the Quartier Latin cinema when the cell phone in his jacket pocket started chattering like a parakeet: it was Bernard Descôteaux.

"I'd like to see you as soon as possible, Monsieur Lupien. Are you free right now?"

The absence of the usual salutations and the editor's urgent tone, almost guttural, told him the fire was being stoked. Or something like that.

"I'll be right there, sir."

Fifteen minutes later a taxi dropped him off at 2050 rue de Bleury. This time, all smiles, the receptionist welcomed him like an old regular.

"Please be so kind as to take a seat, sir. I'll tell him you're here."

The editor appeared promptly, clearly excited, cheeks flushed, and signalled for Jerome to follow him. Two other people were already in his office: a woman in her early fifties, with a cheerful face, her gaze sprightly and piercing, whom the editor introduced as the editor-in-chief; and a sporty looking man, partly bald, whose smile displayed his very white teeth. He was introduced as the director of information. Jerome's nervousness prevented him from remembering their names.

"Monsieur Lupien," said Descôteaux, lacing his fingers together and leaning his elbows on his desk, "my colleagues and I have just watched your document. Thank you, first of all, for the confidence you are showing in us and our newspaper, and in our..."

"Truly astonishing," interjected the director of information.

"...but you must understand that before we are able to use any of this material, ethics oblige us to ask you how you came by it."

Since the previous night, Jerome had taken the time to consider that question and had decided to opt for caution. He started to answer, but saliva welled in his throat and, choking, he needed a moment to regain his voice.

"You protect your sources," he said, "and I protect mine."

The effect of his answer was mixed.

"Rest assured, Monsieur Lupien," said the editor-in-chief, her voice trailing and very pleasant, "we have no intention of divulging your sources. *Le Devoir* has never done that. But still we must know who they are. You see, it's one of the rules of journalism: we have to know what we're talking about, don't we, especially when it's a matter of this gravity?"

Her colleague placed a reassuring hand on Jerome's arm.

"Do you understand the impact these revelations would have if we were to make them public?" he added.

"Absolutely, sir," Jerome replied, feeling more confident. "That's why I came to *Le Devoir.*"

There was a moment's silence. Bernard Descôteaux cleared his throat.

"Does anyone want a coffee?"

"Good idea," said the director of information with conviction.

Jerome followed suit: he was beginning to feel important.

"I'll pass," said the editor-in-chief. "It'd be my fourth this afternoon, a bit too much."

And while Descôteaux phoned for coffee, she leaned towards Jerome and quietly told him about precedents for what he was doing, nodding often and with many smiles. A young man soon came in with a tray, which he set down on the editorial director's desk. Jerome poured cream into his coffee, but hesitated over the sugar he'd add only if what he'd been served wasn't up to much. He took a tentative sniff and put in a teaspoon of sugar.

He could feel everyone staring at him.

"My source," he declared in a slightly arrogant tone, "is myself."

And with a candour that verged on the self-aggrandizing, he told them everything.

They didn't interrupt once. After twenty minutes, he stopped, his story done, and asked for a glass of water. His throat was as dry as chalk.

"That confirms certain information already in our possession," stated the editor-in-chief, with a satisfied smile.

VERY EARLY NEXT morning, an earthquake of magnitude 6, 7, or 8 (depending on who was feeling it) rocked the province of Quebec. The headline on page one of *Le Devoir* read:

LABRÈCHE'S PLAN TO ANGLICIZE QUEBEC

On page three, the columnist Michel David reacted in his trademark deadpan but scathing style. His column began as follows:

IN VINO VERITAS

Alcohol makes us say and do many stupid things, and it isn't always a good idea to believe everything a person who has been hitting the bottle says. But it is no less true that alcohol can make a person lose his or her inhibitions and, under the influence, many let slip words that would be better left unsaid. *In vino veritas*, as the Romans used to say. The adage is one Premier Labrèche is no doubt miserably contemplating this morning, embroiled as he is in one of the most embarrassing situations of his career — and one, it seems, that is only going to get worse...

At 6:30 in the morning, Minister Juneau's driver dropped her off at the Price Building, in Quebec City, where the premier's official residence is housed. When she came out twenty minutes later, her coat collar pulled up to her ears, she looked utterly distraught and quickly climbed into her limousine and was whisked away. At eight o'clock, a council of war was held in a room adjacent to the premier's office; the meeting lasted a stormy forty minutes, after which a laconic communiqué was drawn up, announcing that an official statement would be released by the government at the appropriate time.

The headline of *Le Devoir* stupefied Jerome. He'd expected the angle of corruption to take precedence, the kind of story that touched on concrete things that anyone could grasp. Would the revenge he wanted elude him? Sicotte, his wife, and all the others who were participating in a degenerate system and shamelessly vampirizing the province: were they going to get away with it?

At a quarter past eight, he had Bernard Descôteaux on the phone.

"It's just that you have given us so much material, Monsieur Lupien," explained the editorial director in a friendly voice. "Read us again tomorrow, and the next day, and you'll see... We chose to divulge the facts in order of their importance... and the issue of the French language in Quebec strikes us as primary. But don't worry, my dear Jerome, we're not going to sit on a single bit of the information you so courageously trusted us with. In any case, you surely have other copies of your DVD; feel free to use them any way you like."

"There, you see!" exclaimed Charlie when Jerome called to report his conversation with Descôteaux. "I was right! And now, if I were you, I'd give the disc to someone on the *Enquête* team. They're the best people to squeeze all the juice out of it."

Which is what Jerome did. Everything went swimmingly. The headline of *Le Devoir* had paved the way: thirty-two minutes later, he was sharing the DVD with Alain Gravel, the *Enquête* reporter. The spectacle of sleaze-bags in action was clearly shown on the screen.

He looked quite stunned.

"I've seen a lot of dirt in my career," murmured Gravel after he'd viewed the disc, "but never anything like this. PACC—the Permanent Anti-Corruption Committee—will surely be trying to get hold of you, my friend. My advice would be to go down to see them. They'll appreciate it. Thanks for trusting me with this. I'm going to meet right now with my team."

Without even stopping for a bite to eat (it's easy to fast when you've lost your appetite), Jerome went straight to the PACC offices, located on a floor of the Télé-Canada Building on rue Fullum. He was there by one o'clock and received by Detective Sergeant Nicolas Leblanc, who listened to Jerome with undivided attention. He was a mid-sized man, seemingly frail, with a demeanour both crafty and childlike that made anyone talking to him entirely uncertain of which leg to stand on. After watching the DVD, Leblanc's attitude towards Jerome was like that of a prodigal son's father welcoming his repentant offspring back into the fold.

"We've been on their trail," he said. "Many thanks for this, my friend: you've made our job a lot easier."

The next day, *Le Devoir* continued its assault.

STUNNING REVELATIONS EXPOSE NEST OF CORRUPTION

There was not one word from the government. A veteran journalist nastily compared the government's silence to that of the former premier Maurice Duplessis during the notorious natural gas scandal of 1958—another exposé by *Le Devoir*. For several weeks, the old lion had withdrawn into his den to lick his wounds, even suspending his daily press conferences, something he'd never done before. The seasoned hand ended his column with the line, "Let's hope we don't have to wait so long this time."

On the morning of the first scoop, Jerome's landline rang so unrelentingly that he sought Charlie's hospitality until things calmed down. Normande Juneau, Severin Sicotte, and a number of their "associates" were desperately trying to get hold of him. Finally, Sicotte dispatched Fradette — hastily summoned from Cuba — to keep a watch on avenue Decelles. Unfortunately, he arrived a half-hour after his former colleague had left his apartment.

Finally, on December 17, Premier Labrèche summoned a press conference in order to "respond to calumnies of which he, three of his cabinet ministers and several of his political colleagues had been the target." As was his habit, he showed up looking elegant, with a cool demeanour and in complete command, even going so far as to avail himself of a little irony. He said, "Half-baked proposals put forward at a private meeting in which the sacred bottle is abused — and I take personal responsibility for that — cannot be taken as representing any government's official position. No one but the most brazen opportunists and lovers of calumny would dare to suggest otherwise." And then he went on to profess his love for "our national language, our precious collective patrimony," the defence and promotion of which he had always considered — to borrow the somewhat over-utilized expression of his predecessor — his "sacred duty."

Journalists smiled.

However, despite all his efforts, the tectonic plates continued to shift. On December 19, Minister Juneau, always a clever tactician, resigned her post in protest against the government's "cultural treason," declaring that she would continue to sit in the legislature as an independent. She was placing herself entirely in the hands of the court in order to help shed light on this deplorable matter, explaining that she had been forced to participate in a fundraising system of which she had always disapproved. Her argument wasn't about to fool anyone but, she hoped, would put her in a better position to defend herself.

The same day, three other members of the National Assembly followed her lead. The Labrèche government was now in a minority. A vote of nonconfidence passed, and an early election was called.

That same day, PACC conducted eighteen dawn raids in Montreal and Quebec City, three of them on parliament, where they managed to pull the plug on a shredding machine that had been working overtime.

Severin Sicotte and Francine Desjarlais were apprehended at home and their passports confiscated. They were preparing to fly to Freetown, the capital of Sierra Leone — a country renowned for its pineapples, gold mines, and the lax attitude of its tax collectors.

Freddy Pettoza was placed under house arrest in his office on boulevard Crémazie where, his cleaning lady being away sick, he was busily culling his personal files. He howled and raged but, worried that he might lose his voice, calmed down and demanded the presence of his lawyer.

Two of the raids had unfortunate consequences.

Joseph-Aimé Joyal, Severin Sicotte's venerable mentor, torn roughly from sleep, became completely confused and collapsed on the ground in front of the two police officers sent to have a morning chat with him. When he came to, his face was a haggard but sublime mask, and he began repeating the words "mess tin" over and over again and in a variety of tones throughout the entirety of his interview, to the great annoyance of his investigators. He was examined by a neurologist, a psychologist, and a psychiatrist, without result. The psychologist, an imaginative and conscientious woman, asked if the old man had ever served in the military, a "mess tin," as everyone knows, being part of a soldier's equipment.

"No," replied his sister. She thought for a moment, then added: "But when he was young I remember he was in the Boy Scouts . . . They take mess tins on their camping trips, don't they?"

"Well, that's it, then," conjectured the psychologist, looking wise, "he must harbour a strong desire to return to a childhood state of innocence."

Her conjecture impressed no one.

The other raid was tragic. Roland Dozois, known as Bled Man, sitting on the edge of his bed with his pyjamas half unbuttoned and a cigarette in his mouth, swore vehemently at the officer who'd had the temerity to awaken him ("It's a violation of my privacy, you little fucker! This is gonna cost you, you can bet on that!"), while his wife sobbed in the bathroom. Suddenly, in the midst of a fit of rage, he fell to the floor, and the Bled Man became the Dead Man. Whatever secrets he carried went with him to the grave.

Premier Labrèche was unable to avoid the bother of a trial, of course, though a verdict would inevitably take years. And his elevated position on the social ladder, as well as the eminence of his defence lawyers, would no doubt guarantee his immunity or the equivalent.

A month later, voters brought the Leader of the Opposition, Aline Letarte, to power, the first woman in the history of Quebec to hold the office of premier. Great rejoicing was heard pretty well everywhere.

The day the scandal broke, Jerome called Eugenie, and their conversation lasted three and a half hours. Charlie wanted to notify the *Guinness Book of World Records*, but he was assured that love could be a lot more loquacious than that. As for the rest, well, that night love produced far more delectable effects; when Jerome presented himself to his former lover, she became his girlfriend again.

Still, Jerome was a little frustrated at having received no recognition for having initiated such cataclysmic events. Who else was able to boast of having single-handedly brought down a government? Especially when the most rotten are often the toughest of the lot.

There was much conjecture about just who was responsible for the fall from grace of, in the words of some pundits, "the valiant servants of the nation." A few names circulated, but no proof appeared. The eminent host of a Quebec City talk radio station, an inveterate loudmouth, challenged the individual, man or a woman, to come into his studio and duke it out with him; calling whoever it was a leftist turd, a union toady, a sewer rat, a guttersnipe, a psychotic separatist, and other epithets of that nature. Jerome decided to retain his anonymity.

He had already recovered much of his self-respect. But after such a turbulent and motley year, he still needed to work on regaining the trust of Eugenie, if it were even possible for their relationship to become whole again. Four months later, she became pregnant—and nine months after that, Jerome, who'd already been through a vigorous course in parenthood with Andrée-Anne, became the papa of a boy named Jacob.

It was around that time that *Le Devoir* took him on as a

journalist, a career into which he threw himself with passion. One day he came face to face with Normande Juneau in the provincial courthouse; she pretended not to recognize him and continued on her way.

As for Jean-Philippe Labrèche, he ended up moving to Bermuda, where the climate suited him and he had taken the precaution of depositing certain sums in a tax-sheltered account; his oldest son owned a fashionable nightclub there and greatly profited from his father's wise counsel. People generally thought the former premier had abandoned politics, but they were wrong. He kept a close eye on the political scene in Quebec. From time to time, a new blunder on the part of his adversary brought a great smile to his lips.

"Courageous Aline is paving the way for my comeback," he said to himself, gently rubbing his hands. "How kind of her."

And he raised his cognac glass to her health.

One evening, while Jerome was leaning over the changing table, nostrils twitching, Eugenie came to the door with the telephone in her hand. Felix, whom he hadn't seen for an eternity, had called to say he'd been accepted by the Faculty of Law at the Université de Montréal.

"How are your dear parents?" asked Jerome.

"No idea," answered Felix indifferently.

They talked for a while. He was in good spirits, Felix, and the two friends were delighted to be back in touch. "Let's get together for a bite sometime next week," Jerome proposed.

"Yes, good idea."

There was a smile in his voice. They were about to continue their conversation, but little Jacob's high-pitched howls obliged them to end it.

THAT NIGHT, A few minutes after sunset, a red moon slowly rose in a sky filled with clouds that soon hid it completely. But then suddenly it reappeared in a clearing, shining with a bizarre lustre that gave its features such a sinister, malevolent expression that people on the sidewalks raised their heads and watched in silence, overcome with an uneasy sense of foreboding.

Longueuil, April 6, 2016.

ACKNOWLEDGEMENTS

For their generous help and valuable advice, I wish to thank Marie-Noëlle Gagnon, Diane Martin, Isabelle Pauzé, Sara Tétreault, Anouk Noël, Jean Dorion, and Viviane and the indefatigable Michel Gay. I also thank my editors at Éditions Québec Amérique, Caroline Fortin and Jacques Fortin, for their patience, Wayne Grady for his conscientious translation, and Maria Golikova, Noah Richler, Alysia Shewchuk, and the rest of the team at Arachnide.

—Y.B.